REINVENTING THE ROSE

REINVENTING THE ROSE

Kenneth J. Harvey

DUNDURN
TORONTO

Editor: Michael Carroll
Designer: Carmen Giraudy
Cover Design: Kenneth J. Harvey
Printer: Marquis

Library and Archives Canada Cataloguing in Publication

Harvey, Kenneth J. (Kenneth Joseph)
    Reinventing the rose / Kenneth J. Harvey.

Issued also in an electronic format.
ISBN 978-1-55488-921-1

   I. Title.

PS8565.A6785R45 2011   C813'.54   C2010-907296-0

1   2   3   4   5   15   14   13   12   11

We acknowledge the support of the **Canada Council for the Arts** and the **Ontario Arts Council** for our publishing program. We also acknowledge the financial support of the **Government of Canada** through the **Canada Book Fund** and **Livres Canada Books,** and the **Government of Ontario** through the **Ontario Book Publishing Tax Credit** and the **Ontario Media Development Corporation.**

Care has been taken to trace the ownership of copyright material used in this book. The author and the publisher welcome any information enabling them to rectify any references or credits in subsequent editions.

J. Kirk Howard, President

Prnted and bound in Canada.
www.dundurn.com

Dundurn
3 Church Street, Suite 500
Toronto, Ontario, Canada
M5E 1M2

Gazelle Book Services Limited
White Cross Mills
High Town, Lancaster, England
LA1 4XS

Dundurn
2250 Military Road
Tonawanda, NY
U.S.A. 14150

For Monique

Art is a human product, a human secretion.

— Emile Zola

~ Part I ~

Conception

Chapter One

Anna: February 16, One Night in a Bed

The surface of the water mattress wavers as Kevin's weight leaves the bed.

Anna lies there, her heart rate barely elevated. She senses her body afloat, warm water sloshing beneath her, the movement seeming to carry her off when she closes her eyes. Yet as the undulations slow, she finds herself stilled, contemplating the senselessness of the sex act, the feeling of remove so oppressive it threatens to obliterate her.

Opening her eyes, she sees through the bedroom doorway. Light flashes on in the bathroom, then slowly withdraws and is smothered as Kevin shuts the door.

Anna's eyes shift to the candle flame on the bedside table. A fly circles the flicker, its slow drone wavering in a pattern of spirals until it settles on the wall. Strange to see a fly this time of year, considering the coldness outside. It should be in hibernation, or whatever it is called: dormancy, Anna thinks the word might be.

Watching the winged black dot, she feels peculiarly isolated.

The fly lives a life nothing like hers. It is designed for other purposes, alien and preposterous.

A sensation between a tingle and a flutter spans out from Anna's centre. Her eyes explore the ceiling while she wonders on the impression. It is new to her, and especially unusual, for she has been going through a period of unfeeling, of emotional numbness toward people and observations, a pervasive inner blankness that is a by-product of deep indecision.

Kevin's voice sounds from within the bathroom, the muddle of his words kept purposefully low as though spoken in conspiracy.

Then the murmur stops, and Anna hears him gargle for so long that she almost smiles. He spits and rinses out the sink. She imagines him checking to make certain he hasn't left a mess and everything has been cleaned up to his satisfaction.

The bathroom door opens, spilling light onto the scene.

Kevin returns to the bedroom and searches for his shirt. His actions are clipped. He already has his pants on and is always quick to dress once out of bed. "I have to go."

"The hospital?"

"Yes," he says shortly, finding his shirt on the back of a wicker chair. "St. Claire's called in the bathroom."

"Paging Dr. Prowse," Anna mutters as the fly lifts off, buzzing while it drifts near the right side of her face, then toward the door and out into the hallway. "The miracle of cellphones." She takes notice of the cactus on the night table beside the candle that has been instrumental in setting the tone for supposed romance. When was the last time I watered it? she thinks. Three or four days ago? She watered the other two plants in the living room at the same time. Yet if she guesses three or four days, she knows that a better approximation would be ten or twelve. The days a blur to her. Despite her neglect, the cactus's bristly red bulbs appear healthy and succulent, about to burst with life.

Where the pot meets the plate beneath it, a tangle of delicate white roots is evident, edging out of the confining space where they once thrived in dirt.

The sight of these roots burdens Anna, a weight pressing in on her chest.

Why must I be responsible?

The plants were all gifts from Kevin, and she is not a plant person. Every sprouting thing she has ever owned has wound up in the garbage, its leaves, stalks, and soil desert dry. Why not just give them all away to a more responsible caregiver? Drop the drooping bundles off on the doorstep of an SPCA for greenery.

She turns her attention to Kevin's back, the way the muscles and tendons tense and relax in the limited light as he pulls on his shirt. It should be a sentimental sight, a mood her mind might have lingered in months ago, but now it is flatly reduced to physiology.

Anna doesn't bother asking how long he might be, for she expects the usual reply: No idea. What she feels like saying is: Don't come back. You're killing everything I feel. Or is she wrongly blaming him for a condition that is solely hers: a private muteness generated by her loss of creativity?

As Anna's mind drifts and her focus slips, the slopes of Kevin's back bring to mind the painting of a rose she has been struggling with for the past two weeks. This new project is far removed from her last show: ragged splashes of bodies and distorted faces juxtaposed with the butchered hinds, quarters, and limbs of animals.

The new works are detailed studies of the merging overlay of petals. Pedestrian, she realizes. Done to death, her mind keeps accusing. Nauseatingly eloquent and crowd-pleasing. But there was some way she had been trying to create it in an odd, detached manner.

The hues of Kevin's skin meld with intention, and she pictures the folds of the petals as flesh-hued.

Anna finds herself halted by these two images forming a distinct idea that clarifies her heart to the point of blunt epiphany, and stops her lungs so that she must force herself to breathe.

"I'll see you later," Kevin says, rising from the chair where he has been tying his shoes. He bends to kiss her, his eyes aimed elsewhere.

The small movements of her head and body, as though shifting to accept or reject the kiss, have generated another watery sway beneath her body. There is nothing and everything between these two bodies that lean together and briefly meet by the lips.

"Okay," she manages, watching him move from the bedroom, his wavy black hair blacker in the shadows, his average-sized body shrinking as he strides along the hallway. Grabbing his coat from the couch, he slips his arms into it, then pulls on his leather gloves, presses each space between his fingers to secure the fit.

Not another word from Kevin as he heads out the door. Not a look back. No kiss directed her way. Open the door. Shut the door. The reverberation of his boots are felt in Anna's bed as Kevin travels down the stairs to the front door of the old divided Victorian house on Lemarchant Road.

Anna flicks her long brown hair away from her shoulder to scratch her skin. She checks her fingernails to discover they are much longer than she imagined, at a troublesome length that cries out for trimming. Unpolished nails. She recalls painting them as a child: red, white, black … Lip gloss, mascara, and eyeshadow stuffed into her pockets on her way to catching the school bus.

The candle flame flickers, the air prompted by the movement of her hand, swaying shadows along the walls. She studies the flame, attempting to define and segregate the waver of colours, the merging yellow and orange that makes the delineation of tones a near impossibility.

A hint of gaseous blue toward the charred wick.

She ponders the physical qualities of the flame, how it burns in thin air, its tip flickering higher, alive, eating up oxygen, yet contained, until it touches, and ignites, conveying its destructive blush.

The flame brings to mind a sculpture by Constantin Brancusi that Anna once saw at the Museum of Modern Art in New York. When she first laid eyes on the slim five-foot-high piece of sculpted marble, she thought it was meant to represent a flame because of its gentle bend, pointed tip, and the way the light caught the varied streaks in the rock. However, upon closer examination, she learned that the piece was intended to depict the spirit of a bird in flight.

Kevin's muffled cough reaches her as he passes on the sidewalk beneath her window. She listens for the mechanical catch of a car engine being engaged, but doesn't hear one. He must be walking. St. Claire's is only a few minutes away.

Anna wonders about the call. A woman gone into labour? An emergency of other sorts? Kevin's gowned body standing between the woman's legs, masked face tilted forward, gloved hands at ready, soon to probe.

Those unsteady moments following sex glaze Anna's eyes. She doesn't know which she feels: muddled joy or sorrow and abandonment.

As the fly re-enters the room, drawn by the candle flame, Anna speculates if this new idea, inspired by the texture of Kevin's bare upper torso, is enough to raise the rose concept above the commonplace.

Mustering the strength to rise, she pushes herself from the bed, catching sounds of the fly banging against the windowpane, frantic to escape. She pulls on her robe, pressing the material between her legs to sop up the spillage. When she does so, her hair hangs down the front of her face. She reaches for a band on the dresser, gathers her hair, and secures it behind her head.

Anna then opens the window to let the fly out into darkness. Soundlessly, it glides off in a slow curve.

A mistake, she thinks. Where will it go? How will it survive in the cold?

She leans forward into the frosty night air to search for Kevin.

There is no one on the snowy street. Not a car. Not a person, only the stillness of shrouded objects that inspires restless wonder in her while the flesh-hued rose gains prominence in her mind.

The Embryo: Hour 10, Day 1, Week 1

Over three million of Kevin's two hundred and fifty million sperm, propelled by contractions, complete the ten-hour journey up the vaginal canal, through the cervix, and into the fallopian tube to track and surround Anna's egg.

The egg, the largest cell in the human body, is the size of a period in a book.

One of the more aggressive of the sperm begins burrowing through the outer membrane to penetrate the ovum.

From the possible combinations of the couple's chromosomes merging, seventeen trillion different types of embryos might be formed.

The head of the sperm secretes an enzyme that slowly eats through the egg's protective layer. Twelve hours later the sperm enters the ovum and releases its contents. A single set of forty-six chromosomes is created, locking in the genetic coding as a new cell is formed.

Seventeen trillion possible combinations have been narrowed down to one.

The embryo will be a girl with blue eyes and blond hair. Her skin will be fair. She will be of average height. A dimple will dent her left cheek when she smiles. She will have Cupid lips and a widow's peak hairline. Freckles will dot her nose and shoulders. She will be able to roll her tongue into a tube-like shape. Her earlobes will hang freely and won't be attached. She will be left-handed. The middle segments of her fingers will be hairless, while her pinkies will lean instinctively toward her ring fingers. She will be able to bend her thumbs backward to a ninety-degree angle. When her arms are folded, her left arm will rest on top of her right. Her second toes will be longer than her big toes. Her blood type will be O positive.

Anna: February 17, in the Studio

Every fifth day Anna buys a new red rose from Mr. Oliver's shop beneath her downtown studio on Duckworth Street. Mr. Oliver has been a great support since Anna met him at her last show, even going so far as to offer her free rent on an old storage space he professed never to use. He is patient while Anna takes her time selecting the flower. He offers one rose, then another, smiling and nodding, anxious to point out the distinct characteristics of that specific option.

"Look," he says. "The richness of the red. Much superior to the others."

Anna studies the softly geometric layering of its petals, unable to detect a difference in colour.

"Look," he insists, guiding his fingers down the length of the rose. "The thin perfection of the stem."

"You always know exactly what I want."

"Excellent choice." He proudly hands the rose to her, understanding that she prefers it unwrapped. "I used to paint a little, too."

"You should have stuck with it," Anna encourages him while cautiously accepting the rose, mindful of the thorns. "Never too late."

"I had no talent for it," Mr. Oliver admits. "But you are great." He eyes her purse when she begins searching for her wallet. "No, no charge," he says as he does on each of her visits. "My contribution to art."

The rose in Anna's studio must be replaced as it achieves fuller bloom, for the likeness no longer matches the image she is determined to duplicate. She has thought of spraying the rose in liquid silicone to freeze it in a state of exactness, yet the idea of suspended animation troubles her.

The sealing in of decomposition.

Before climbing the narrow stairs to the top floor of the

old merchant building, Anna bangs the snow from her boots and switches on the light in the stairwell. A single bulb hanging from an overhead cord flickers to life, spilling yellow light in the enclosure.

She takes the creaking stairs to the second storey and, while fitting her key into the lock, notices a puff of grey scurrying along the baseboards to disappear beneath her door. Despite her startle, she is charmed by the idea of the mouse entering her studio and living among her paintings, perhaps even nesting there.

Anna turns the key to enter. The wide-open space stretching before her offers the impression of limitless possibility and innovation. She takes it all in: the high ceilings, the sounds of her steps over the stained wooden floor, the rows of long, multi-paned windows, the smell of paint, canvas, and musty plaster walls coupled with the intermingled scents of flowers drifting up through the floorboards from the shop below.

Red canvases are positioned around the studio, flush against one another or tilted on dissimilar angles meant to catch the altering gradients of light. In addition to the rose canvases, there are other paintings of nests she previously worked on. Nests layered with feathers, carved out of wood, or forged from steel and bolted together.

Anna studies the rose in her hand, holding its vividness in mind while surveying its likeness on her easel.

She guides the rose in front of the canvas for comparison.

The translation flat. Dispassionate.

Why is she not capable of the same intensity of emotion that painters like Mark Rothko felt? Rothko would weep while painting his colour-saturated canvases and believed that those who wept while looking at his paintings were sharing the same religious experience.

Sick with herself, she shakes her head, casting a glance at the red roses lying in a row on one of her workbenches, their colours deepened by age. Lined off at the back of the table, her collection of bird nests ascends from smallest to largest, and at the foot of the rose stems, weighty volumes featuring the works of artists are open as though in instruction.

Her mind flashes on a rose she received from Brandon Crocker before her junior high graduation. The petals were slightly redder than his face, which glowed with embarrassment as he thrust the flower toward her. Brandon was such an outgoing boy, a popular, tough fellow who excelled in most situations, yet the presence of that rose in his hand distressed him.

Scanning her paintings, she questions not if she might be insanely masochistic — she already admitted this to herself years ago and harbours the inexplicable guilt and shame that personifies her affliction — but how *deeply* she must hate herself for having chosen to tackle this subject matter.

How deeply whatever governs the world must hate her.

Shouldn't she abandon the rose paintings and return to the series of nests?

She watches her palette of dried paints.

There is no winning at this game, for whatever she creates couldn't possibly match what Fantin-Latour, Dubourg, di Lorenzo, or Rossetti have already done to venerate the rose.

Far from inspiring her, studying works by these masters never fails to diminish her own work and slaughter her spirit, making her feel as though she has absolutely no right to lift a brush to canvas.

A fraud. A pretender. A poseur.

The rose series will be a crashing failure. It will never sell.

In fact, she imagines potential buyers scoffing when her new show opens in July at the Maher Gallery, the faces of patrons casting bemused glances at one another to determine if the show might be some sort of surprise gag.

And why shouldn't they be cruel about it? If she attended such a show, wouldn't she be set on mocking the artist, too?

Or perhaps the rose paintings might be a phenomenal success. An inoffensive symbol of adoration loved by all. Every single painting snapped up by a gaggle of rich old ladies in floral heat.

Last week David Maher, the gallery owner, came to her with a corporate commission for a scenic painting of the colourful row houses built near the downtown harbour. Row houses, once considered slummy, are now the height of architectural fashion and are owned by the upwardly mobile. Canvases featuring these yuppie havens are available for viewing on countless office walls, and for sale in every craft shop in every nook and cranny around the island. This new symbol of a historic and playful St. John's has almost replaced the rugged, toothless fisherman standing in his fishing dory as the quintessential image of Newfoundland.

A gust of wind rattles a loose pane in one of the studio's multi-paned windows. The sound prompts a memory of the old fisherman's house in Bareneed that Anna is thinking of buying. She recalls tapping a few of the panes in the hundred-year-old house to find them loose, the putty slack or worn away, the glass warped by age.

Beyond the windowpanes, there was a breathtaking view of a cove in Conception Bay, a view that reminded her of the one she once had from her bedroom in Torbay. Enclosed by high cliffs, the Atlantic Ocean had stretched out to the dividing line connecting sky to water.

Behind the Bareneed house, there was an old barn almost identical to the one on her land at home. Her plan was to convert the barn into a studio when the funds became available.

Anna loved the house. Kevin appreciated the idea of a country home but balked at the prospect of an hour drive into St. John's every day. And what about being on call? And what about eating out at a decent restaurant?

"My colon can only handle so much fish and chips with gravy," he said. A summer house, he suggested. A cottage. That would be the sensible way of looking at it. "And during the off-season we can even come out on weekends to keep up our good-humoured repartee with the colourful, cross-eyed baymen."

But Anna pictured winter in that house. The boughs of

the evergreens laden with snow. The grounds thickly blanketed in white. Animal tracks in the snow that she might learn to identify and maybe even follow into the woods where she would chance upon some wild creature stilled by her presence, watching her in fear and wonder while it hunkered near the secret hole to its burrow.

Each of them with their senses burning bright, dazzled by the presence of the other.

Anna steps nearer the canvas and studies the deep, sumptuous red.

She is trying not to think of Kevin, but he is there now with the memory of the Bareneed house, his sensible words shadowing her path.

When they first met eight months ago, the idea of Kevin being a gynecologist was intriguing, if not a touch exciting, a man who might know the intimate details of a woman's body, the childhood game of playing doctor turned real, yet in the passing weeks she has come to regard his vocation with skepticism.

Why would a man choose to work in such a field, placing himself in that position with so many women?

The more Anna thinks about it, the more it becomes unfathomably perverse. If a man is adamant about being a gynecologist in this day and age, then his training should include him lying naked on a table with his feet up in stirrups. While in that position, a random assortment of female doctors and female medical students should enter through a mystery door connected to God knows where and, without uttering a word to him, take turns poking at his testicles. The doctors and students should then pass speculative comments back and forth and give him a few more solid pokes before leaving.

Anna is distracted by that tingling flutter she experienced last night in bed and finds herself striding across the studio to the calendar beside the table displaying her dried roses, nests, and books.

She studies the dates in February while becoming aware of a drone above her. The sound grows louder, emanating from one of the eaves of the studio's high ceiling beams.

Gazing up, she watches a wasp zip out from the recess. She remains still while the sentinel circles around her, trying to determine if she might be a threat. It makes a few wide, uneven passes and, seemingly pacified, returns to the eave.

She suspects the wasps were made insensible by winter slumber, for there appeared to have been no activity over the past few months.

Anna waits, her eyes fixed on the eave.

When she was a child, she discovered a wasp's nest attached to the back eave of her home in Torbay. She wasted no time pointing it out to her mother, a thoughtful and sensitive woman, who was uncharacteristically alarmed and immediately telephoned someone to remove the hazard.

A man in a baseball cap and dirty overalls arrived in a pickup truck that night. Lingering near, Anna watched the man crouch and use his stained hands to tie a rag on a long stick trimmed from a tree branch, then splash gasoline onto it from a canister.

"They're all in at night," the man said, staring at the nest while standing straight. "Sleeping." Flicking his Zippo lighter, he lowered it to the rag. It caught fire with a poof — a contained, feathery explosion. The stick was then raised, making the man's face glow a menacing orange. "You think you should be watching this?" he asked, grinning, yet gave no time for an answer. He hoisted the torch high until it reached the entry hole of the nest, which ignited in a burst of flames.

The nest blazed, and wasps' wings flashed on fire, creating a magical display of illuminated dots in the darkened air before the bodies dropped to the ground.

The man then used the garden hose to spatter out the fire.

The next morning Anna went out to stare up at the charred eave. The nest was no longer attached. She found it in the grass. A once-dangerous object with the peril removed. Regardless, she was careful when she slowly squatted to see that inside the nest there was a multitude of tiny holes. Motionless, glistening larvae were nestled in several of the cave-like recesses.

This childhood memory prevented her from buying a tin of insect killer with a funnel-like sprayer that shot poisonous foam to smother the nest of any winged, stinging creature. She discovered the nest months ago but left it alone to see if any harm would come of it. The wasps didn't bother her.

The drone gradually dies down to a quiet buzz. Regardless, she continues staring. No storm of wasps bursting out to cloud around her head, to pierce her flesh with tiny holes.

She shifts her attention to the calendar, counts backward and then forward, fourteen days since her last period. She checks the rafter. No sign of activity, but the low-level hum persists.

Anna needn't have consulted the calendar to determine that she was ovulating, having experienced that rigorous desire to have sex no matter what.

She stopped taking her birth control pills, not expecting Kevin to be interested, for he was otherwise preoccupied and rarely visited her in the past two weeks. Regardless, she let him fuck her because that was all it was.

A meaningless fuck.

Anna lay there in that bed, with Kevin on top of her, and allowed him.

Not a word of protest. Why?

Did she try to get pregnant as a desperate means of regaining Kevin's affections, or did she want the complete opposite: to rid her life of Kevin by creating another life that would sever their relationship entirely? Run to that house in the country? Run to her burrow and hide with a new baby in her arms.

Two weeks before her period. Fertile as hell.

Did something go off in her mind following her thirtieth birthday back in April? Babies suddenly popping up everywhere like round-headed, sweet-smelling gnomes.

She glances around her studio, attuned to the throbbing silence.

The drone of the nest has settled.

She should make an appointment with her doctor to get the morning-after pill. Or ask Kevin. He must have samples.

What would Kevin think of the possible pregnancy? He might want her to have the baby. He might insist. And what would become of her paintings then? Her time consumed by the constant demands of an infant. Her career shut down.

She takes an appreciative look around her studio, the desire to create flickering through her. She removes her coat to ready herself for work.

Lifting a brush from her taboret and testing the soft bristles against her palm, she decides she won't give this up for anything.

She will visit her doctor tomorrow and take the morning-after pill to ensure her life remains entirely her own.

The Embryo: Hour 36, Day 2, Week 1

The rounded edges of Anna's embryo begin to dip inward toward the centre until they gradually shape two separate spheres and divide fully into two cells contained within a membrane.

The exact genetic combination has reproduced itself in both cells and will continue to do so in each subsequent cell division.

It will take a further twenty-four hours before a second division forms four cells. ·

With each successive splitting, the cells become smaller as the embryo passes slowly along its four-day journey through the fallopian tube, all the while dividing rapidly into a cluster of cells that resembles a microscopic raspberry.

Glands in Anna's uterus have already begun to enlarge in response to the ovum's fertilization.

Once reaching Anna's uterus, the embryo will attempt to attach.

Anna: February 18, the Doctor

When Anna visits her doctor's office first thing in the morning, she finds the waiting room crowded. All appointments for the day have been filled. The receptionist draws a finger down her book and offers the only available slot: 2:30 p.m. the next day.

That's cutting it close, Anna thinks. The delay makes her feel anxious, even mildly paranoid. As she drives home, she has the sense that something unknown and parasitic is taking shape. Her mind flits over a number of possibilities, other doctors, even a visit to Kevin's clinic at the Health Sciences Complex.

Shadowy images of back-alley abortions distort her thoughts. Why she pictures these archaic procedures is a mystery to her. But a man's vengeful face, lit by torch, is what dominates the scene. His hands are filthy and he is bent over a woman who writhes in agony, dying from multiple punctures that drain the life from between her legs.

Nearly missing a red light, she slams on the brakes and glances in the rearview mirror, then at the car in the lane opposite her. A baby, strapped into a car seat in the back, laughs wildly while watching her, and shoves its saliva-glistening fingers into its mouth.

Arriving home, Anna hurries into the spare bedroom she has converted into an office. She puts her cellphone on the desk and sits at her computer to research information on the morning-after pill. Reading through the sites, she is relieved to confirm what she believed to be truth, that the pill is effective in the prevention of pregnancy as long as it is taken within seventy-two hours of unprotected sex.

While clicking through sites about contraception, she comes across information detailing a baby's development. She merely glances at the chart, not wanting to be lured toward deeper feeling. Regardless, she catches herself wondering how the baby might look, if it is a boy or a girl, but all she sees in her mind is a sexless creature, alien in feature, like the technical drawings or photographs displayed in high school biology classes.

She shuts down the browser windows and checks her email. A few notes from acquaintances or admirers in other parts of the country. A request for an interview for an online arts magazine.

Her cellphone rings.

Kevin's number illuminated on the screen. She watches it ring, deciding that it would be wise to avoid him for a few days. In Kevin's presence, Anna would find it difficult not to mention the possible pregnancy. She isn't good at hiding things from people. To get Kevin involved now would only further complicate the issue. The decision must be entirely hers.

That night she forgoes the burger and fries she has been craving and decides to prepare a small, healthy meal. A spinach salad with strips of chicken and honey mustard dressing.

After arranging the leaves on her plate, she slices away at the remains of a roasted chicken until the carcass shows bone everywhere. She lays the unused meat on a plate covered with wax paper and stores it in the refrigerator.

The carcass sits on the counter, not entirely clean, bits of ragged red meat left clinging near the bones.

She studies the carcass for a while, turns the plate to analyze the figure at an assortment of angles, before picking it up in both hands, carrying it to the garbage bin, and dumping it in.

The sight of the decimated rib cage down in the hollow spurs ideas.

Roses growing up through an indistinguishable carcass in a field.

It reminds her of finding the skeletons of kittens in the family barn when she was a child. How tiny and fragile they were. Stilled like that. Set side by side. Bits of fur fluff gently blowing around when she moved.

Anna checks her fingernails. Small pieces of chicken flesh lodged under them. She brings her hands to her nostrils and sniffs. Disgusted by the odour, she heads to the bathroom for the clippers in the cabinet. She cuts each nail, collecting the trimmings in a small pile on the rim of the sink. When she is done, she brushes the clippings into her palm and sweeps them into the toilet, flushes it.

She looks at herself in the bathroom mirror, toying with the idea of having her hair cut boyishly short. Her eyes traces over her features, the slight movement beneath her throat, her chest rising and settling in breath.

Her stomach grumbles, and she remembers her chicken salad.

On her way out of the bathroom, her cell starts ringing again. She ducks into the spare room to check it. Kevin's number. She has guessed at his reaction to the news, playing out both scenarios: genuine joy or cloaked disappointment. For some reason, watching his illuminated number, she feels vaguely afraid of him and is relieved when the phone falls silent.

The next day, in the doctor's waiting room, Anna surveys the coffee table stacked with reading material. On top of the pile nearest her, there is a pregnancy magazine. In fact, there are several copies of the same issue, as though some dim-witted or inebriated stork has dropped an entire bundle in the office by mistake.

Anna refuses to pick up the magazine, even though she has involuntarily leaned to reach for it. Merely touching it might admit to her predisposition for motherhood. Despite her aversion, her eyes keep returning to the photograph of the smiling mother on the cover. The woman is pretty in a natural way, with a mild disposition and long, flowing blond hair. She is dressed in a pastel-blue-and-yellow smock and is posed in a field of tall grass flecked with purple wildflowers. It is a sunny day, with a clear blue sky overhead.

Envisioning the woman's body with her own face on it, Anna scans downward to the belly, a monstrous mosquito bite, a mommy tumour, and the spell is broken. Anna wonders why these covers never feature a tattooed, chip-toothed pregnant woman in leather with one fist raised in the air while she shouts a rebel call from the seat of her zooming Harley.

A woman with a fussing baby in her arms takes the seat across from Anna. The woman is agitated while she shifts to unzip her jacket and move the baby from one knee to the other. The woman doesn't look anything like the female on the cover of the mommy magazine.

Anna smiles cordially. The woman makes a sound of exasperation as though a smile in return is an impossibility.

Anna can't tell if the baby is a boy or girl because it is dressed in yellow, the non-specific-sex colour of choice given by friends and relatives at chatty, life-affirming celebrations before the baby's birth.

She notices the soft blond hair on the baby's head and stares at the chubby face. The wholesomeness of the sight endows her lips with a smile.

Anna wonders about being a baby. Not a single memory of ever being so small.

The mother sighs and gives Anna a fretting smile. "They're a handful," the woman professes.

The baby bunches its tiny fingers into fists and laughs at Anna, prompting a flash of bright emotion that compels her to lean forward in her seat and make tender goo-goo baby sounds.

She decides that the baby must be a girl.

For convenience sake the pharmacy is located in the same building as the doctor's office.

Standing in line, waiting to have her prescription filled, Anna considers the variety of cases that her doctor must see throughout the day. Every sort of pain, sore, and misfortune. How does she deal with it? Why isn't she constantly in tears?

Anna has heard all sorts of stories from Kevin about women who have lost babies. Some women manage to cope with the loss, while others are afflicted by the tragedy for the remainder of their lives.

She wonders what sort of woman she might be.

Glancing at the small white paper in her hand, she studies the indecipherable name of the drug. She hands the script over to the pharmacist and provides her pertinent information. While doing so, she feels something drop from her back pocket to slap the floor. Turning, she sees an elderly man squatting beside a rack of headache pills to retrieve the pregnancy magazine.

"Here you go," he says, groaning while rising and inclining the publication toward her.

"Thank you." Hooking a length of hair behind her ear, she offers a pleasant nod.

The man's eyes are on her belly. "Good luck," he says, giving her a smile of support.

Anna thinks, the natural order of the world, and smiles in return, feeling that she might actually be cheating the man out of some sort of old-fashioned conviction.

While leaving the doctor's waiting area, she pocketed the magazine for her work. The faces and poses of pregnant women printed on the glossy pages might be of use in a collage.

Artwork featuring pregnant women, while only a notch or two above the artistic gag level of a red rose, could make a comment of sorts if intermingled with the presence of void. But what might characterize the void? The potential energy of the life erased.

Where would that energy then go?

Those with motherly leanings might find the pregnancy paintings attractive, while the more hardened childless might view them with unadulterated cynicism.

When Anna faces the pharmacist, she notices his eyes on the magazine in her hands. "From the doctor's office," she confesses, hoping he doesn't think she tried to shoplift the magazine from their rack.

The pharmacist nods with mannered friendliness. "About ten minutes," he says. "We'll have it ready for you."

Chapter Two

The Embryo: Day 6, Week 1

Entering Anna's uterus, the embryo secretes an enzyme that erodes the mucous membrane lining of her womb, preparing it for implantation.

In anticipation her uterus is swollen with new blood capillaries that will allow the circulation between Anna and her embryo to begin the moment it attaches.

Anna: February 21, a House by the Sea

The drive to Bareneed takes a little over an hour, heading west from St. John's along the Trans-Canada Highway.

The landscape glides by, small patches of barrens exposed here and there in the smoothly textured blanket of snow that extends for miles in all directions. Huge, ragged boulders dot the landscape, while groves of black spruce run in uneven lines far back from the highway.

Driving through this terrain reminds Anna of some sort of desolate moonscape.

It has snowed without wind the previous night, and the snow is gleaming beneath a sun so radiant that Anna must wear sunglasses to avoid constant squinting. A beautiful day, perfect for driving, for the mildness of the temperature has left the asphalt entirely dry and bone-white from the accumulation of road salt. As her car dips into a long, shallow valley, sunlight glints off the cars heading east in the opposite two lanes.

Two days ago Anna decided that Kevin should be informed. Even though there was no tangible proof that she was pregnant, she felt compelled to introduce the idea if only to gauge his reaction. That night, over dinner at Zapata's, she sipped her glass of red wine in awkward silence until Kevin asked what was on her mind.

"I think I might be pregnant," she said matter-of-factly.

Kevin's expression remained evenly regulated. He gave a taut little nod and ate another forkful of beef chimichanga, his jawline tightening while he chewed. He looked away at a couple entering the restaurant and settling at their table, then returned his attention to neatly slicing off another bite-sized portion of food.

The numbness of his reaction almost brought Anna to tears. She gulped a healthy mouthful of wine. "I mean, there's no real reason to believe it's for certain, but it is a possibility."

"I don't see how it could be a possibility, Anna."

"Why's that?"

"The birth control pill is effective in ninety-nine out of one hundred instances." He paused to give her eyes brief consideration, unable to linger there for more than a second. "Unless, of course, you're the one percent."

"Right." Anna licked her lips and moved the chicken avocado salad around on her plate. "The lucky one percent." With the edge of her fork, she broke up pieces of the taco shell base, wondering about nourishment. The shell was starting to turn soggy. "I've often felt like the one percent."

When she first started taking the pill, she always swallowed it in Kevin's presence. He was so adamant about her not getting pregnant that he was certain to remind her every day.

Anna couldn't bring her eyes to meet his, as though she had been caught, had deceived him in some way. "I could take the morning-after pill."

"Yes, of course. If you forgot to take your birth control pill, then that would be the prudent thing to do."

The briskness of his agreement disheartened Anna, for it appeared to betray some lack of faith in her or in them as a unified idea.

Kevin cast his eyes at the table, thinking through the problem. "Why are you telling me this now? At supper?"

"What do you mean?"

"You're talking about the other night?"

"Yes."

"When was that?"

"I don't know."

Kevin sniffed and wiped his nose with the cloth napkin, a sign he was growing troubled. "Wednesday?"

"I think."

"That's three days ago. How could you possibly suspect being pregnant?"

She couldn't come up with an answer, except for the one she told herself: I just know.

"And if it was three days ago, it's almost too late for the morning-after pill, unless you take it tonight."

Anna shrugged, feeling like a defiant schoolgirl.

Kevin shook his head in disapproval while sipping his water. "What about our trip to Italy?"

Anna had no idea what the two had to do with each other.

After a stretch of well-mannered silence, as the plates were collected and dessert politely ordered, Kevin said with a sigh, "We're only in our early thirties. Mid-thirties is the time to have children. I've seen every side of it. You should be more careful."

Anna bristled at his comment about the perfect time to have children. She searched his tactless male face and wondered what exactly he had to do with it. Who was *he* to tell her anything? Did he feel absolutely nothing for the possibility of the life within her that she was beginning to grow strangely protective toward?

Tossing down her fork before she was done with her deep-fried ice cream, she stood, collected her coat from the rack by the door, and went outside to wait for him, her arms folded against the cold. She imagined him inside calmly paying the bill and then visiting the bathroom to scrub his hands.

Arriving home, she left his car without giving him the slightest speck of attention and went into her bedroom to lie down with her thoughts.

Her mind considered Kevin's reaction, sifted through each of his sentences and words, trying to discern hidden meaning, a veiled softness on his part, the vaguest glimpse of approval, but there was absolutely nothing.

Occasionally, her head gave a little shake, her eyes going to the box containing the morning-after pill on the bed beside her.

Emotion welled up in her, and she felt the hotness in her nostrils before tears wet her eyes. She swiped them away, almost furiously.

Her cell started ringing from out in the living room. Kevin, no doubt, dutifully there to remind her the seventy-two hours were just about up.

Thinking of that evening now only renews Anna's annoyance and blinds her to the luminous majesty of the landscape. The scene shaped by light.

Picturing Kevin indifferently seated before her in the restaurant, she almost misses the exit and has to swerve to make the ramp, rising to a higher road and starting the twenty-minute run down the rolling pastures of Shearstown Line that will deliver her to the house in Bareneed.

~ ❦ ~

The front door is locked.

Mr. King, the real estate agent, isn't scheduled to arrive for another fifteen minutes.

Anna makes her way through the ankle-deep snow at the side of the house, glancing at the kitchen window on her way to the barn. She can't wait to get in there and have another look around. The lace curtains shield her view, yet she senses movement and pauses to peer in, cupping her hands against the glass to scan the unoccupied room. It must have been her shadow shifting against the pane.

Words from her mother in Anna's head: "Always such an active imagination." This place reminds her so much of her mother. She takes a few steps back, admiring the navy blue clapboard and the cream-coloured corner boards and window highlights. Her mother would have loved this place.

She continues on, checking the line of trees to the left of the red barn, the branches of a huge dogberry tree widely splayed in the foreground. She hasn't explored the woods yet and looks forward to the pleasure of familiarizing herself with the land. *Her* land, she hopes.

Reaching the slatted barn door with a white heart painted eye level at its centre, she sees that the door hangs unevenly and must be forced open. She checks the hinges to discover the top one is rusty and broken.

As she enters the barn, her breath collects in the air, momentarily clouding her vision. The space is deserted and feels hollow, yet peaceful and calming.

A low bank of snow has blown in under the two large doors to her left. The wide wooden floor slats are nicked and darkened from wear.

Anna checks the back row of stalls where horses or cows were once kept. At the thought of these animals she catches the scent of manure and hide, her ears detecting a faint rustle, a snort through nostrils as a heavy head turns to see who she might be.

She looks overhead to the loft, aware of the lump in her coat pocket, the package containing the morning-after pill she neglected to take. Why is she still carrying it with her? As a memento of a decision made more out of defiance than practicality?

If she is to end the suspected pregnancy, she no longer has the convenience of simply taking a pill. A glass of water and the inherently effortless act of swallowing must be replaced by an invasive surgical procedure in a clinic. An indecency that will be witnessed.

Trying to distance herself from these unwelcome thoughts, she heads for the two-by-four ladder and reaches up to grip a rung. She raises one foot to apply weight on the first slat, testing its construction. It seems solid, so she climbs to the loft.

Nearing the top, as her eyes draw level with the floor, she expects to face some remnants of life laid out before her, perhaps the kitten skeletons from her childhood. But the floor is clear, save for patches of rotten hay.

She leans to climb off the top slat, cautiously positions one foot, then the other, onto the floor. Straightening, she watches her boots take their time turning until she is facing the lip of the loft and the drop. She stares down over the edge and rubs her cold hands on her coat.

The magnetic sensation of an elevated perspective tugs at her core. The space around her throbs with the energy of vacated lives, creating the inexplicable feeling, somehow linked to heightened clarity, that she is definitely pregnant.

The floorboards, worn dark from the presence of animals, are an absorbing study. She notes the warm gradations of browns and blacks.

The barn brings back childhood memories of exploring new spaces, of being excited, of being frightened, of becoming aware.

The awakened sensations are so fundamentally sweet and endearing that tears brim in her eyes. She takes a deep breath, holds the air in her lungs, then exhales. The simultaneous trickle of tears down her cheeks feels ennobling.

The Embryo: Day 6, Week 1

Anna's embryo implants in her womb, its tiny feeler-like tendrils growing into her uterus lining, allowing nutrients to be fed from her body into the embryo.

A voice calls from beyond the barn.

Anna wipes at her eyes and remains where she is until Mr. King enters in a long dark grey coat. His hands are bare and pink. He isn't wearing a hat, although he gives the impression of being that sort of man. Above a high forehead his grey-peppered hair is clipped short.

At once he looks directly at her, as though knowing where she would be. "Children love it up there," he says.

"I guess I'm just a kid, after all." She brings her arms out by her sides and lets them drop.

"Can I tell you a secret?"

"Sure."

"I still have my teddy bear from when I was a boy, so join the club. It's nice up there, hey?"

"Yes." Overwhelmed, she almost starts crying again.

"You ever coming down?"

"I don't think so. I love it in here."

Mr. King glances around. "What's not to love? It's the way things used to be."

Anna takes the ladder slowly, gauging the placement of her boots, the wary grip and release of her hands on the rungs.

"Careful, Anna," Mr. King warns, standing at the base with one hand raised.

She smiles confidently at him when her feet safely reach the bottom.

"You're early or I'm late," he offers.

"I'm early, I think."

"Better than being late," he says, amused, while checking her eyes with a gentle expression.

Inside the house, Anna stands in the chilly kitchen, admiring the lace curtains she stared in through fifteen minutes ago. In front of the window two wooden chairs painted red, a peculiar choice of colour for an outport house, are positioned around a narrow table with a thick top and tapered legs. The oven is ancient, yet in perfect repair. Iron covered in yellow enamel, a bun warmer compartment above the stove. A metal bin filled with splits of wood beside it. A new white refrigerator jutting out like a sore thumb in the corner.

Anna wanders across the hallway into the living room. She crosses the planked flooring, skimming her hand over the carved wooden back of a chaise longue, while her eyes browse the matching wingback armchairs and oak wainscoting around the walls.

The air in the room is colder than in the kitchen, the house unheated.

She turns to face the window nearest the chaise longue, struck by a framed black-and-white photograph of an old baby carriage on the wall. The word *pram* comes to mind. The black carriage is elaborately made, with ornate metal frame, large spoked wheels, and satiny white frills along the bonnet. It is photographed in profile, as an object. No person stands near it.

After giving the print some consideration, she settles on a view of the front yard through the window. The narrow main road borders the property, sloping on a slow incline as it winds around a tree-lined bend toward the ocean. Across the road there is a brook and a thick grove of spruce and pine trees.

She focuses on the trees, discerning flickers of movement obscured by limbs: a small child, its red coat flashing through the gaps in the spruce. She watches and waits, spots another child in a white snowsuit trailing behind. Perhaps the neighbour's children at play, exploring the woods.

Anna glances at the sideboard with its deep drawers. Atop it porcelain figurines and a glass dish with what appears to be a clump of hard candy inside have been arranged by a hand unknown to her.

All of the rooms are filled with antiques, the owners seeming to have no idea of the worth of things. Anna touches the top of the sideboard, recalling Mr. King's words: "Contents included." She won't mention another word about the furniture, the deal she believes she is getting, the steal.

"I thought of taking some of the furniture myself."

Startled, Anna turns to see Mr. King enter the living room. Guilt flushes through her as though she has been caught in the act of masterminding a heist.

"But I'm too honest for my own good." Mr. King has an agreeable nature and a pleasant face that smiles easily. The way he speaks to her is the way she imagines a father might share wisdom with a daughter.

"That's not a bad thing," she says.

"The previous owner was an elderly woman. Her children live in Toronto. I probably told you that already, Anna. They just want to get rid of the place. That's all."

"Why?"

"It's not their life here." He gazes at the window, his attention snagged by something outside.

"Where's the woman now?"

"She's passed on," Mr. King plainly states without regarding her, his breath barely misting in the frigid air. He remains in profile, his eyes moving fluidly as though following an object here and there. "Finches," he says in consideration, "having a feast of the dogberries in your trees. It's their last winter resource."

Anna watches the birds hopping from one limb to another, pecking at the red berries. She counts seven, then three more hiding behind the others.

"There are raspberries and wild rose bushes behind the barn in the summer. The septic must drain down there."

Anna wonders about the septic. Pipes under the earth. What drains down there?

"Everything else is just white now," says Mr. King. "Dead or asleep. The leaves all gone. But those berries hang on for a purpose, to keep the birds alive, I guess."

"I never knew that before."

"Why don't the dogberries just fall off like the blueberries or raspberries?"

Anna shakes her head contemplatively.

"Look at those birds eating."

On Anna's way back to St. John's, the sky turns grey and ponderous. Fat flakes of snow dot her windshield. She glances at the speedometer, slowing her speed to fifty miles per hour.

The offer she has submitted on the Bareneed property has filled her with excitement. She tries not to worry that she might have acted rashly.

What will Kevin have to say?

Was it a mistake? she wonders, not fully trusting her judgment lately. Yet her doubts aren't so great as to waylay her enthusiasm.

A house in the country, near the sea.

Mr. King indicated he would call the owners with her offer

and get back to her in a few hours. The mainlanders were anxious to sell, so he was hopeful.

The snow falling on the highway melts at once, darkening the asphalt.

The sky looms overhead, churning from grey to charcoal with bands of black.

Anna senses the car growing colder. She flicks up the heat and turns down the radio to better concentrate on her driving.

The ring of her cell draws her eyes to the passenger seat where she laid the phone for easy access. Reaching for it, she checks the screen: Mr. King, unknown number. She flips it open, concerned she shouldn't be driving and talking. Does that apply to the highway, or only the city?

"Hello?"

"Anna?"

"Yes."

"Good news."

"They accepted?"

"Yes. I'm happy to say they have."

"Really?" She laughs joyfully, triumphantly.

"Congratulations."

"Thank you. That's great. Wow!" She checks the rearview mirror, then the speedometer, realizing that her burst of excitement has given her a lead foot. She eases off the accelerator and returns her eyes to the highway to witness a blob of white hopping into her path.

"The house is yours."

The rabbit continues bounding around in her lane, patterning an awkward zigzag that is dangerously confusing.

Anna swerves the car to avoid it, losing hold of her cellphone.

The asphalt is slipperier than expected, glazed in a layer of black ice.

The car slides for the gravel shoulder, drifting out of control, taking her body with it.

Dread clutches Anna's heart and stomach, forcing an involuntary whelp of fear. Terrified, she grips the wheel, pulling it as though to hold back the car. Her knee jerks and stiffens, jamming her foot on the brakes.

Snatching a look at the rearview mirror, she makes out a vehicle through the misted back window. Its front end is directly behind her, almost on top of her bumper, sliding, too, on an angle. The voice of her driving instructor in her head: Pump the brakes.

She releases her foot.

Her car quickly sways and quivers, her front tires returning to the asphalt while the back tires kick up a spray of gravel.

She rechecks the mirror.

The vehicle almost touching hers.

She tests the accelerator, her tires spinning.

Sliding sideways, the rear of her car swings toward the bank.

She slams on the brakes as the vehicle behind her slips by in the passing lane, almost grazing her fender.

Her car spins in slow circles before the ground disappears beneath her rear tires, the undercarriage walloping the bank and grinding noisily as it drags along.

The car tilts backward.

Anna makes a sharp sound as she reclines.

The hood rising up, grey clouds billowing before her.

The chassis flips sideways, smacks the earth, and rolls twice through a blast of disorienting, metal-buckling noise before snapping a splay of limbs from a tree and soundly pounding its trunk.

Chapter Three

Anna: February 24, the Hospital

An impressionistic scene shaped by one disconnected glimpse after another. Anna's eyes fidget, unaligned with her brain. A blur of fragmented geometric planes falls together. A wall connected to a ceiling or a floor. Splashes of wavering intermingled colours protrude from a flat surface, uniting into soft and flexible forms. Flowers. The portrayal of light creates the illusion of depth with seemingly tangible textures. The planes become a square. A box. A room. Blunt sounds in Anna's shallow ears. Noises smothered in a hollow in her head. She focuses on linear perspective. Precision achieved through tracing details, and objects clarify, appear more solid and dimensional, giving rise to too much life.

A woman in white appears in the room, a smiling nurse on a maternity ward, treading on noiseless shoes to deliver a newborn.

Anna checks the nurse's hands, how they dangle at her sides.

A human body, vulnerable and imperfect.

"Well, hello," the nurse says cheerfully. "I thought I heard something. You're awake." She tugs at a curtain on a rod, sliding it out of her way.

If not a baby in the woman's arms, then a baby that has been abandoned elsewhere.

"Baby," Anna says, stirring beneath the bed covers as though in want of retrieval.

"It's okay," the nurse reassures her, wrapping a wide black band around Anna's arm. "I'm just going to take your blood pressure."

Anna's capacity for communication is cocooned, jumbled, pressing on her chest, constricting her throat muscles.

"Do you know where you are?"

Anna sighs heavily. Swallows with effort. It is some sort of trick, this place.

Pressure is being pumped into her arm. It pulses to fill her head, making her eyes shut.

"Can you tell me your name?"

She thinks she might know and says it.

"Good."

"And where are you, Anna?"

"Hospital."

"Very good. You've been out for days."

Days.

Anna ponders the meaning of the word while a man in a white coat enters the room, his steps in beat with the pressure that throbs in her skull.

Anna recognizes the man's face. The doctor. The gynecologist.

She was seeing him for some reason. And she is happy to see him now until she unexpectedly remembers.

"She knows who she is," the nurse says.

"Anna," says Kevin, smiling, his hands hidden in the front pockets of his coat. "Nice to see you awake."

The pressure in Anna's body slowly releases, and the nurse speaks a series of numbers to the newly hesitant physician.

"Good," says Kevin, regarding the nurse as though to glean more information that might aid in his assessment of the situation.

The nurse edges a thermometer near Anna's lips. "Open, please."

She opens her mouth, feels the plastic sheath slip uncomfortably beneath her tongue.

A machine chirps briskly three times.

"Good," says the nurse, removing the device. "Perfect."

"Not now," Anna blurts out.

"What?" asks Kevin.

"Don't …"

"It's all right, Anna." Kevin settles on the edge of the bed, too close to her, without her consent. His hand rests on her belly. Long fingers scrubbed clean. Fingernails expertly trimmed. "We're looking after you."

The muscles in Anna's thighs tighten. Her eyes on that hand. His hand. It will move soon. She holds her legs rigid so they can't be forced apart.

The steel in Anna's car was so badly twisted that the jaws of life were required to pry open the buckled metal and make a hole big enough for her to pass through.

She lost a great deal of blood through a gash in her leg.

"Twenty-four stitches," Kevin said, his eyebrows rising. "Impressive."

If they hadn't arrived on the scene in time, she would have bled to death.

Her arms and chest are bruised, and she is stabbed with pain when she breathes too deeply.

According to Kevin, she has suffered no permanent damage other than minor trauma to the neck, which might degenerate into arthritis in middle age. He has used his pull in the hospital to secure a private room for her.

Lying in the hospital bed, Anna worries about the baby. It is in this place that they are taken or born. Did the accident exact internal damage? She has managed to check herself for blood but found none on her fingers. No cramping, either.

Kevin has made no mention of it.

Anna stares out the large windowpane, reviewing the clutter of low buildings and houses that slant down to the harbour. She takes notice of the colours, as though from a dazzling palette, blending them together in her mind, warming to the hues she feels most deeply.

She recollects the house in Bareneed, sitting vacant on a patch of land in the cup of a valley surrounded by hills.

Her hands on the steering wheel on the drive back to the city.

No definite memories of the accident.

Does she still own the house?

She shuts her eyes, trying to locate the pain in her leg, but it has been vanquished by narcotics.

Her thoughts lack urgency.

She fades off to sleep and wakes to remember her situation.

A sound has awoken her.

A knock on the door.

Anna turns her head on the pillow to say, "Come in."

Mr. King enters with what looks like a potted green cactus in his gloved hands. He raises it for her to see. "I thought you might feel like this," he says.

Anna chuckles, the bruises lighting up with pain.

"I'm sorry, Anna. I didn't mean to make you laugh."

"Yes, you did." Her eyes regard the ledge with the flowers. "I was just thinking about you."

"In your misery?"

Again she chuckles, and bites down on her lip. "Please don't make me laugh. Please."

Mr. King sets the cactus on the shelf and smells the flowers arranged in vases. "These greenhouse ones don't give off much of a scent. The wild ones are the most fragrant." He fingers one of the cards, as though trying to read the words written there. "I'm not what you would call a master spy. I forgot my reading glasses."

"Is the house okay?"

Mr. King turns, his expression expectant. "I was behind you when it happened."

Anna wonders what he means.

"I was on my way to the city to look up a deed. I was the one who slid past you on my crazy carpet."

"You were there?"

"I saw you go off the road. My heart tried stopping you. Tried to stop the sliding. You know that feeling?"

"Yes, it's awful."

"Some things you just can't stop."

"I was worried about the house."

"It's fine. Don't worry." He approaches her bed, resting his hands on the white metal footboard. "How's everything? You can't be that bad or they wouldn't have let me in to see you suffer."

"I hope to survive."

"No doubt, although you'll never be the same again. Trauma does that. Might be a good or bad thing. It's a hard call."

Anna considers his words. Do they make her feel better or worse?

"I said I was a friend. I hope that's okay." He takes off his gloves and stuffs them into his pocket, then inclines his hand to the empty chair in the corner.

"Yes, please, sit."

"Thank you." Mr. King shifts the chair a few feet nearer the bed, settles in, then straightens his overcoat across his knees. "I fed the animals for you, by the way."

Anna's brow furrows.

"In the barn."

Her bewilderment evaporates, and she smiles with understanding. "You called me, right? Or was that a dream? I can't tell much of anything. What's real in here."

"Yes, just before the accident. We were still connected, remember? I heard the crash."

Anna tilts her head at the fierce oddness of his comment.

Mr. King studies her face, then regards a painting on the wall: children at play in the snow. A sentimental rendering without adults.

"What did it sound like?"

"Chaos in a blender."

Anna winces with pain. "You're terrible."

"I'm sorry."

"Did I sound ..."

"Distressed?" His eyes return to her. His head leans back a touch, and he frowns in concentration. "After the impact, you were mumbling something I couldn't make out. You were talking to someone, but there was no one else in the car, right?"

Anna swallows. "No."

"All I could make out was: 'Please, baby, please, please.' You kept repeating that as though pleading with a child."

Anna's skin prickles, and her breathing grows hot in her nostrils.

"And then there was singing. After I spun to a standstill, I heard a slow staticky singsong coming from my phone. It took a few seconds to collect myself."

"Singsong?"

"As though hushing a baby to sleep."

Anna shuts her heavy eyelids.

When she opens them again, a man in green hospital scrubs is entering the room. He carries a plastic food tray in both hands.

"Hello," he says, trying his best to be quiet. He sets the tray on the table, gives Anna a considerate smile, and leaves.

"Thanks," she says, but the man is already gone. The distinct odour of hospital food reaches her. What might be steaming under the lids?

After a stretch of silence, Mr. King says, "I lowered your offer, by the way."

"What?" With her eyes newly opened, Anna feels dizzy to the point of nausea. She has forgotten about Mr. King's presence.

"Pain and suffering. I told the sellers you were almost killed coming to view their house. Things might get complicated, particularly where injury is involved. They were shivering in their boots. And they accepted. Between you and me, they don't need the money. It's nothing more to them than getting rid of a nuisance."

"Thanks." Anna checks the cactus, the thorns set there between the flowers. Her eyes shift back to Mr. King. Little by little, she recollects what he said about being behind her, and she recalls what the doctor told her about loss of blood. "You saved my life."

"It was nothing, really. I just didn't want a ghost living in that house. Nothing worse for resale value."

Two ghosts, thinks Anna, imagining the haunting.

The Embryo: Day 9, Week 2

Anna's embryo continues to destroy her uterine lining, creating blood pools and stimulating the growth of new capillaries. This allows the placenta to begin forming. The cells of the placenta invade the capillaries, glands, and connective tissue of Anna's uterus wall, burrowing their way deeper.

Spaces form in the placenta cells that fill with maternal blood and glandular fluid.

As a protective measure, a plug forms to cover the defect in the uterus's ruptured tissue caused by the implantation.

Anna's embryo is one one-thousandth of an inch in diameter, as thin as a strand of human hair.

Anna: February 26, Kevin's Decision

Anna stands at the nurse's station, waiting to be discharged.

"You're good to go," says one of the nurses while flipping through a thick stack of papers clipped to a chart. "Do you have a ride?"

"Dr. Prowse wants to see her downstairs," interjects another nurse seated at a desk. She distractedly points her pen at Anna without looking up. "You know where his offices are?"

Anna nods.

The nurse tells her, anyway. "First floor in the Women's Health wing."

Anna rides the elevator down, wondering why Kevin didn't make the time to come up to collect her. Her overnight bag seems heavy on her shoulder. She feels frail, out of it, yet her mind is hyper-alert.

The elevator stops, and an old woman in a wheelchair is rolled on by a male nurse. The woman has a head full of wild grey hair. She stares at her lap as though to keep everything to herself.

On the first floor Anna passes through rows of silent people seated at the blood collection lab before crossing a wide corridor and entering Kevin's clinic. She makes her presence known to the receptionist, expecting a short visit.

All of this sudden movement has made her light-headed. She takes the nearest seat to regain herself and thinks about the prescription for painkillers in her overnight bag. She will need to get that filled.

Thirty-five minutes later her name is called out.

The receptionist knows who she is and gives her a special smile before leading her into one of the examination rooms.

"Thank you," she tells the receptionist while settling in a seat beside the desk and putting down her bag.

"Sorry for the wait. It's crazy here today."

"Not your fault."

The door quietly closes.

Anna studies the charts and diagrams on the walls. Embryos captured in immutable stages of development.

If she is going to have a period, it should start in about four days, although her schedule might have been thrown off due to stress from the accident.

Favouring her left leg, she stands to get a closer look at the dates beneath each stage. The pain isn't so bad since the stitches were removed, although the scar becomes itchier by the moment.

Her fingers press against the initial fish-like illustration, and her mind drifts off to Bareneed, the smaller bedroom at the front of the house that might be decorated as a nursery. It has a view of the ocean, which seems essential to the growth of a baby.

Refocusing on the chart, she sits and glances at the examination table, her interest caught by the stirrups. She imagines her feet elevated. Kevin standing between her naked legs, watching down, his hands at ready.

The door opens.

Anna turns her head to see Kevin enter with a file in his hand.

"Hi," he says, shutting the door. He kisses her on the cheek, places the file on the desk, and sits in his chair. His manner toward her is as blasé as ever, as though her injury and the thought of losing her meant nothing. Just another injured person brought in to be treated.

"Hi," she says, miffed at being made to wait so long. Shouldn't her trauma have brought them closer together? Made her presence more precious to him?

"How are you feeling?" His air is casual, yet brisk, as though he has asked the question merely out of obligation and wishes to get on with more pressing matters. There are other patients waiting.

"Okay, I guess."

Kevin's eyes shift to the file folder. Some of the papers have angled out, so he taps them back in with his fingertips. "I have your results here." He folds his arms across his chest and sniffs, leans back in his chair. It is a pose that suggests confrontation and superiority.

"Results?"

"From your blood work."

Anna squints at the folder. "Is something wrong?" Her stomach sinks with alarming expectation, for Kevin's manner implies that he is about to offer undesirable news. She thinks back to her mother's opinion about hospitals: "Once they get you in here, you never get out. You become theirs."

Kevin hesitates. "Wrong? I don't know, really. If you mean pregnant as 'wrong,' then yes. That's a certainty."

"What?"

"You're pregnant." His lips tighten with an unsightly smile.

"Really!" She grins.

"Yes, and against all the odds." Kevin unfolds his arms. "Considering the amount of blood you lost."

"I guess I'm lucky."

He clears his throat and licks his lips. "The one percent again," he says with a trace of sarcasm. Shifting in his chair, he attempts another smile, but the sentiment is hopeless.

An inconvenience, Anna thinks. That's the expression he wears.

There is no hug from him. No hug from her.

She looks away.

The scene feels dismal.

Anna remains in her chair and waits.

She checks the carpet, noticing a stain near the desk leg. What sort of stain?

She glances at Kevin's fingers as they tap the folder.

Test results.

Pregnant. She wants to be happy. She *is* happy, despite Kevin's proclivity for being a jackass.

My baby, she tells herself, not yours.

Kevin stares expectantly at her. "I guess congratulations are —"

"Shut up, Kevin."

Again she takes notice of the file.

There is something about Kevin extracting blood from her for a pregnancy test that doesn't sit well. It reeks of underhandedness and violation.

At this thought her mood wilts further.

"Is that something you do regularly?" she asks, gesturing to the file.

"What's that?"

"Give pregnancy tests to all your female patients."

Kevin regards her with occupational interest. "It was important to know at the time. There might have been bleeding. I was concerned for your health. And you're not my patient."

"Oh."

"I find myself in this highly uncomfortable position. It would be unethical for me to be treating you at all, considering our relationship. So I'm seeing you as a friend, in that capacity." His fingertips fidget with her file folder, squaring it up with the edge of his desk.

"In your office with my blood work in a file. Friends don't generally order blood work on each other. Correct me if I'm wrong."

"Well, there were extenuating circumstances."

"Extenuating. Yeah, that's good. You know all the right words."

"I'm assuming this pregnancy happened between us?" Raising his hands, Kevin meshes his fingers behind his head. Casual questions from an expert.

Anna pins him with a stare. He is smothering every bit of her joy. Heat rises in her cheeks. She thinks she will smack him in the face and leave. This side of Kevin she finds repulsive. In fact, she feels nausea stir in her stomach, wavering her thoughts.

"I wasn't sleeping with anyone else. I don't do that."

"I'm sorry, Anna, but this is all wrong, in many sorts of ways."

His hands come out from behind his head. Leaning forward, he pats her hand.

Anna pulls away. "Don't touch me."

"Shhh, please." His eyes go to the door, and he lowers his voice. "I can't have the burden of this for the rest of my life."

"Burden?" If Kevin wants her to lower her voice, he is certainly going about it the wrong way. "Look … you don't have anything to do with it."

"Will you sign papers saying so?"

"Papers?"

"Yes, papers."

"No, I won't sign papers. What're you talking about?"

"It's all fine now, but in the future, you'll still be there with a baby, a child, a fatherless child. Maybe getting bitter. So you've decided to have the baby then?"

"Yes … I don't know. I just found out, Kevin." One hand moves to her belly. Aware of Kevin's eyes on her hand, she shifts it to the armrest. "I won't come after you, if that's what you mean. What sort of person do you think I am?"

"You're a good person, Anna, but people change."

"Yes, and you have. Instantly, as a matter of fact." She stands, grabs her overnight bag, and turns for the door. The sudden movement causes her pause. A rush of dizziness as the space around her sparkles white.

"You can't walk away from this."

"Walk away?" She shuts her eyes, the words muddled. "Walk away." She draws a deep breath, waiting for her eyes to fully regain sight and her ears to hear clearly. Then she faces him, her voice softer. "How is it possible for me to walk away, Kevin?"

"If you have doubts about letting the pregnancy continue to full term, then it has to be dealt with. The sooner the better."

"I'll deal with it. I'm dealing with it."

"Well, I'll be dealing with it, too." He eyes the door, lowers his voice again. "I'm in this as much as you. Me, myself. I'll deal with it."

"Oh, really, how? How do you expect to do that exactly?"

"That's all I have to say. I can't have —"

"What? You're going to kidnap me. Strap me down." Her eyes jerk toward the examination table, her finger stabbing at it. "You butcher."

Kevin frowns, obviously hurt. He stares at her, shakes his head in disappointment, then looks away.

Anna regrets having called him a butcher. How did they ever get along? Why? Why him? Why this heartless man whom she met in an art gallery. A man who said to her: "Your work displays a mystical sensitivity and sympathy for the human condition."

She turns for the door and leaves the office.

Passing through the waiting area, she scans each female face. Some of the women are visibly pregnant. What might be in each of their minds? It is hard to tell from searching their faces. Are they happy? Are they miserable? What choices have they made for themselves?

Kevin in his little room. Business as usual.

I'm pregnant, she thinks cheerfully, despite everything. Yes, pregnant. New life. A new start.

She continues walking.

A baby inside her.

Taking a corner in the wide corridor, she feels a strain in her leg and slows while a woman on crutches weaves around her. She glances at the people in passing, her mind reaching out for friends and family members with whom to share the news. She thinks of Heather, her best friend from the Nova Scotia College of Art and Design in Halifax, and then, of course, David at the gallery, but they have never been that close. She has few friends. The price to pay for being a loner all her life.

Heather Lambe. A pretty, petite, introverted girl with an adorable lisp. Hit by a car while crossing the street. A year after graduating. The most skilled artist in the class, Anna always believed.

A few months following Heather's accident, Anna flew to

Halifax for a visit. She expected to see Heather in a hospital bed; from what she had heard the trauma was severe. But Anna was given a street address when she spoke with Mr. Lambe on the telephone. It was the address for Heather's home.

Mr. Lambe greeted Anna at the door and, after a bit of polite small talk about her flight and the weather, led Anna down the wallpapered hallway to a bedroom where the curtains were drawn.

"She doesn't like the light."

Anna wondered why.

"I'll leave you two alone."

The room appeared to have been decorated by a teenager, from a time before Heather left for college.

Anna studied the unresponsive figure in the bed.

Heather's shadowed face was turned to the wall, her eyes staring, lips twitching while they sucked on her thumb.

Anna was stricken by grief. "Hi."

No response.

"Heather?" A step closer to the bed. It was a struggle to pretend that things were the same, for they were not. What she wanted most was to ask Heather a question and receive a response, to learn how her friend was feeling about this situation.

"She knows you're here."

Startled, Anna turned to see the dark outline of Mr. Lambe in the doorway.

"I'm sorry. She knows you're here. I can see by her face."

Anna checked Heather's face. It looked the same. The eyes passive. The lips sucking.

"It's very subtle." A patient tenderness in his voice. "You get to know every slight movement and gesture. And you just hope for life, that's all."

Heather still alive now, still in that bed, her father looking after her for almost ten years.

She imagines Heather's eyes fixed on her bedroom wall, her body and mind no longer hers. A pitiful existence. If there was anything left of her, what was it? What part of her was still her own?

What would be the point of telling Heather that Anna was pregnant? It would be a cruel thing to do. Anna soon to be a mother. Heather never to be one.

Anna wishes her mother were still alive. Why did she have to die before this? A puny figure in a bed on the palliative ward. Those final days of groaning discomfort. Her mother's eyes like an animal's while she rasped incoherently at Anna.

I'm pregnant, Mom. Tears welling in her eyes.

Anna wanders through the main doors, out into the winter sunshine, the air so crisp against her skin it spurs her to jaunt to the waiting taxi. Climbing in, she pulls shut the door and makes a shivering noise as a shudder rocks her bones.

"Cold, hey?"

"Yeah." Looking down, she swipes at her eyes and sniffs.

"Where to?"

She has to think for a moment to come up with her address, while watching ahead through the windshield: a view of pavement, people crossing over, cars dropping off patients and visitors.

Being inside a vehicle again unsettles her.

"Eighty-four LeMarchant Road."

Satisfied, the cabbie pulls down the transmission stick.

What might her mother think of the pregnancy? A woman who supported Anna's pursuit of individuality and creativity. A husbandless woman incapable of conceiving a child, and yet a woman who raised Anna as her own.

As the taxi rolls off, Anna digs her fingers into the seat and leans to check the windshield.

The asphalt appears dry.

Settling back, she pictures the look on her mother's face when she opened the front door all those years ago.

The ringing of the doorbell and no one there.

A prank.

It had been winter, her mother explained. "One of those clear, crisp nights with an almost sacred stillness."

About to shut the door against the cold, her mother glanced down.

A baby left on the doorstep, bundled up in a garbage bag.

The Embryo: Day 13, Week 2

A stalk appears that will elongate into a section of the umbilical cord. It attaches Anna's embryo to the budding placenta.

Cells assemble in a narrow line on the surface of the two-layered embryo to create a final third layer. The line is called the primitive streak.

The embryo now has the basis for all physical attributes. Specialized cells will continue to divide to build each feature. Once an individual feature has been fully formed, the cells responsible stop dividing through a process known as programmed cell death.

The ectoderm, the outer cell layer, will grow into fair skin, blond hair, blue eye lenses, the lining of the internal and external ear, nose, sinuses, anus, mouth and lips, tooth enamel, pituitary and mammary glands.

The mesoderm, the middle cell layer, will form muscles, bones, lymphatic tissue, spleen, blood cells, lungs, reproductive and excretory systems.

And, finally, the endoderm, the inner cell layer, will develop into the urethra, bladder and digestive tract, tonsils and tongue, and the lining of the lungs.

Chapter Four

Anna: March 3, the Paint Shop

Four days after her confrontation with Kevin, long days and nights filled with Kevin's steady calls and his appearance on the doorstep of her apartment and studio to knock repeatedly, Anna contacts Mr. King and asks if it might be possible to take possession of the house ahead of schedule.

"I can't get any work done here," she admits to him. "I can't concentrate."

"Leave it to me," he says.

Anna provides the name of her lawyer. "I've been trying to get hold of him," she says, "but he doesn't return my calls."

"Telephone Evasion 1001. I hear it's the easiest course in law school. When the prof asks a question, you say nothing and full marks are given."

"That's very good." Anna chuckles. "You always make me laugh."

"Thank you, Anna."

There are enough funds in her bank account to pay off the full price of the Bareneed property. Money left over from the sale of the family house after her mother's move to Glenbrook Lodge when Anna could no longer adequately care for the woman. Her mother spent eight months in the nursing home until she was moved to a palliative ward where she passed away four years ago.

Anna let a good portion of the contents go with the house but couldn't bear to part with a great many boxes of photos and mementoes, and pieces of furniture that had travelled with her mother when she moved to Newfoundland from Ontario. All of it was still sitting in a storage facility on the outskirts of St. John's.

She glances around her apartment, wondering how much packing would be involved should she decide to move to Bareneed. If she intends to return to Bareneed soon, she will require transportation. Anna has been putting off dealing with her car. The thought of talking to an insurance agent makes her tired and agitated, but it is something that must be done. She forces herself to make the call and is told that because she has a replacement clause on her policy she can visit the dealership and pick up a new vehicle. Simple as that.

At the dealership the thin and lively salesman instructs her to review the cars out on the lot and make her selection. She is the given the keys to a new platinum grey VW and signs paperwork transferring the insurance cheque to the dealership.

A fresh start. That is how it feels when she leaves the lot, sitting in all that new car smell.

Back at her apartment, she busies herself with preparations for her trip. She packs a bag with clothes and toiletries, feeling relieved at the prospect of getting away. She stays in that night, hoping to hear from the real estate agent, but he doesn't call. Kevin, on the other hand, continues phoning all night until Anna must shut off her phone or lose her mind. She lies on the couch, watching television and worrying about the baby.

The next morning Anna finds a lumpy white envelope in her mailbox. Two keys along with a note: "Waiting for lawyers is like plunking your life down in limbo. Enjoy your peaceful expansion. Your friend, the Jaws of Life."

A new car. A new house.

Outside, feeling refreshed, she tosses the bag onto the back seat of the car and thinks to bring along her painting case and a few blank canvases to make up for lost time. She has been imagining how peaceful it would be to work out there.

Again her memories drift to her mother. Since suspecting that she is pregnant, Anna finds her mother gaining prominence in her mind. "Why can't you paint out here?" her mother asked when Anna insisted that she move to St. John's. "If you're an artist, then you can paint anywhere, can't you?"

In her early twenties, Anna felt smothered by the monotony of rural life in Torbay. Her mother must have sensed Anna's desperation, for she added: "I don't know anything about art. I'm just being selfish, because I don't want to lose you, that's all. You do what you need to, darling. Don't mind me."

Turning to re-enter her apartment, she leans out of the path of a large copper-haired dog. It pulls against its leash, its neck straining while it draws a young girl along. The girl has a thick scarf wrapped around her throat and advances in fits and starts as though doing a peculiar sort of dance under the command of the dog.

Anna goes back inside to collect some surplus paint supplies, makes two more trips up and down to load the car, then drops by her studio to pick up a few of her partially completed rose paintings.

With a carful of essentials she heads to a high-end paint shop in Churchill Square.

Manoeuvring between two pyramids of paint cans, she fingers the Bareneed key in her pocket, admiring the feel of her freedom. The paint swatch rack is just up ahead, alongside a pegboard display of paintbrushes and rollers. Anna skims the sequences of colours featured in rows. Despite the generous selection, the tints aren't close enough to what she holds in mind. She checks deeper in the store and finds a specialty line that approaches the desired richness of tones.

When the paints are shaken and the lids are lifted for her scrutiny, Anna asks the stout, curly-haired woman behind the counter to add tint in specific increments.

"Sure thing." The salesperson is patient, eager to please, waving the dryer back and forth until the wet paint matures to its true colour.

"How's that?" the woman asks, laying down the sample beside the other three.

"Perfect."

"You certainly know your tints. You work in the paint business?"

"Sort of." Satisfied, Anna loads the seven cans into her trunk, lowering her head against a sudden burst of rain as she makes her way to the car. The air is almost humid, which is peculiar for this time of year. The last she heard on the radio, the temperature was expected to drop and heavy snow was in the forecast.

Her final stop before heading out to the highway is the grocery store. Pushing her cart up and down the aisles, she finds the labels on the shelves so saturated with colours that they pain her eyes. Her attention lingers on the rows of soup cans. Andy Warhol's domain. Supermarkets and satirical sterility. Disassociation via overblown stupor. The stuff of pop art. The bright overhead lights cast not a single shadow, lending the space a dimensionless, cartoon-like quality that disquiets her senses.

Recalling the forecast for snow, she finds herself stocking up on canned goods. The tins rattle the cart when she tosses them in. Items she hasn't eaten since she was a child. Beans, spaghetti, corned beef hash, and fruit cocktail.

Rather than fearing the prospect of being snowed in, she relishes the idea of it.

She remembers seeing wooden splits and logs neatly stacked in one corner of the barn. They might be used in the kitchen stove, and in the woodstove in the living room. She wonders if she has enough firewood to do her the winter.

Some of the food items remind her of Kevin: the things he preferred to eat, the expensive bottles of pickled mussels and pickled artichoke hearts she used to buy for him. She imagines him eating, and her agitation grows, her mind replaying the words from their conversation in his office.

She takes a turn down another aisle. Purples, pinks, blues, and reds in a long row. Bottles of baby food. Padded bags of diapers. Cardboard cartons of formula. She studies a blond baby featured on a package of diapers. On its hand and knees, it has its head turned toward her, smiling adorably. Boy or girl? She can't tell.

Distracted, she slowly rolls ahead, almost colliding with an excessively thin woman with a baby seat in the hollow of her cart.

"Sorry," Anna says, steering out of the woman's way.

The woman pays her no mind, for she is too focused on worriedly surveying the shelves. She mutters to herself as though repeating words on a list.

Food and baby items are piled around the baby seat.

As the woman's cart advances, Anna turns for a view of the baby, only to find the seat empty. She checks the woman's tired, dark eyes.

Where is your baby?

Lips thinning tightly with a smile of discovery, the woman reaches for a bottle of mashed carrots. She holds it in one hand while gingerly cupping her other palm over it. She keeps it nestled there and draws a slow, hissing breath in through her barely parted lips.

Carefully bringing her hands closer to her face, she peeks into the narrowing space between her palms.

Anna tries not to watch, but the woman's actions are oddly compelling.

The woman stares into her cupped palms, her eyes blinking in dismay, her hands catching a tremble. At once she makes a sound of fright, her shoulders jerking in spasm, and the baby bottle drops from her hands. The glass bursts open like a tiny bomb against the tile floor, the mashed carrots splattering out.

"There," says the woman, bug-eyed and pointing down. "Inside things."

The Embryo: Day 17, Week 3

At one-twentieth of an inch Anna's embryo is pear-shaped and as big as a mustard seed.

Centred down the surface, a blunt, concave line, known as the neural groove, begins to lengthen, creeping along to lay the foundation for the nervous system, one of the first organs to appear.

Blood cells continue growing one atop another until, running out of space, they begin to spread, forging inner channels.

Anna: March 5, in Peace

Two days later there is a knock on the door. Anna tries opening the knob without touching too much of its surface, for her hands are speckled with red.

Mr. King stands there with a wrapped flower in his hand. Snow lightly falls in fat feathery flakes that settle on the shoulders of his dark grey overcoat. "Congratulations," he says, inclining the package toward her.

Anna wonders how he knows about the baby. She tries to hide her bewilderment by saying, "Thank you," and carefully accepting the flower.

A moment later, with a blush already rising to her cheeks, she realizes his congratulations were in regard to the new house. "Thank you," she says again, glancing down into the open hollow of the package. A red rose. "You're always bringing me flowers."

"I suppose it shouldn't have been red," he says shyly, averting his eyes. "But that's all they had."

"No, thank you. That's really nice. Come in, please."

Mr. King taps his boots against the front of the house, then steps up across the threshold. "How are you feeling?"

"Fine. Thanks. A little stiff, but I'm managing."

"We're getting some snow."

"Yes, it's nice." Anna checks her loose-fitting work blouse. "I'm covered in paint."

"Me, too," he admits, rubbing his hand over his balding head. "Fortunately, the colour matches my skin." His attention is caught by the scarlet on the hallway walls. "You're going deep and rich in here." Bending, he begins unlacing his boots.

"Yes." She peers over her shoulder, her fingers exploring the wrap on the flower, trying to determine how it might be unfastened. "I don't know if the colour is luscious or just plain tacky. I'm losing any shred of sensibility I ever had." She faces Mr. King again. "Leave your boots on, please. That's okay. The floors are all wood. You can't make a mess."

Mr. King reties his laces and follows Anna, his eyes lingering on the fresh paint. "Whatever you hang here will really stand out. It's a warm, comforting colour, isn't it?"

"I think so. Careful of the walls. Your coat, I mean." She finds the staples in the wrapping and eases the join apart, cautious not to prick her fingers.

"This old thing? It doesn't matter. I've had it since before the dinosaurs."

In the kitchen Anna scrubs the paint from her hands and dries them in a tea towel. She checks her fingernails. A few dots of red on her thumbnail that she picks away.

The crackle of wood burning in the stove draws Mr. King's attention. "Nice warm fire."

Anna gazes at the stove. "I'm very happy with myself."

"You're a good firewoman, it seems."

"Yes. I'll have bones in my hair in no time." She stretches on tiptoe to take down a weighty vase from the cupboard. The vase came with the house and is made of bevelled glass with impressions of roses etched into it.

"Let me get that."

"Thanks. I got it."

"Careful."

Anna senses Mr. King standing behind her, watching her set down the vase, pick up the scissors, then snip a length off the rose stem. Along the cut line a milky fluid leaks onto her finger. She brings it to her nose and sniffs it, wipes it between her fingers until it is absorbed by her skin.

After assembling the fern and baby's breath in the vase, she slides the rose into the centre. "There," she says, smiling gratefully at Mr. King.

"To my mind, there's still nothing that can beat the rose. It's corny, right?"

While Anna feels comfortable in Mr. King's company, the sudden appearance of another person in the room highlights how she has been alone with herself for the past two days. She has been so occupied with painting the house that she hasn't noticed her solitude. But now her visitor's presence has drawn attention to her every action.

"You want some coffee?" she asks, the sound of her own voice making her even more self-conscious.

"I'll have tea if you have it." Mr. King pulls off his gloves and places them on the table. Glancing out the lace curtains, he sits on the chair nearest him, shifting his eyes to the flower that Anna positions on the table.

"I do have tea," she says. "I never could stand the taste of coffee."

"Great." Mr. King nods mannerly. "I'll have a cup then if that's okay."

"Yes, of course. Earl Grey?"

"Sure." He returns his eyes to the flower, fingers the rim of the vase. "I was always fond of a rose. It might be strange to admit, for a man, I mean, but I buy them every so often for myself. I'm not ashamed of it or anything. The woman at the florist must think I'm a real lady's man."

"Why would you be ashamed? That's nice." She fills the electric kettle in the sink and plugs it into the outlet above the counter.

"Sometimes, if I have a rose in the house, I know it's there, over my shoulder where I always put it on top of the piano. I just turn off the TV, and I go over and stand next to it and have a good look. And I can't help but steal a smell, of course. Who can resist, right? I can get lost doing that. Sentimental, I suppose. My daughter used to love a rose."

Anna is touched by his confession and has trouble gathering words. Should she ask about his daughter?

"But now it's just corny."

"No, it's not."

He scrunches up his face as if he has made a fool out of himself.

"Would you like a piece of cake?"

"I like cake. It has lots of sugar in it, I hope. And tons of lard. Not one of those fat-free, sugar-free cardboard cutouts for people pretending to live a happy, healthy life."

Anna grins. "No, it's the real thing all right, with a gazillion real calories. I don't know about lard, though." The electric kettle begins to make noise. She looks at it. "How's the real estate business out here?"

"I sold a few more properties. These old houses are popular. But I don't know if people understand what they want with them, what they're really about."

"How so?" She opens the glass door on the cupboard and

takes down two china cups and saucers, waits for Mr. King's reply, but he doesn't give one, his eyes on the rose.

"You prefer this place to the city?" he asks.

Anna searches around the room, pulling together enough feeling for an answer. "Yes. I grew up in the country."

"Stealing light from Heaven."

Anna smiles, despite not fully understanding the intention behind his statement.

"That's what my mother used to say about the city. They're just stealing light from Heaven."

Anna nods and pays attention to the kettle as it begins to boil.

"That's why you can't see the stars in there. All those lights switched on. You know, you've got to switch them off sometimes and drink in a little sweet darkness. The stars will give you all the light you need. They do. That's what they're there for."

"You sound like a poet, not a real estate agent."

"How's a real estate agent supposed to sound?"

"I don't know." The kettle clicks off, and Anna tends to making tea, pouring water into each cup. "Like you, I guess. I didn't mean anything …" At once colour seeps from the tea bags, swirling in the clear, steaming water.

She carries the two cups to the table, sets them down, and sits.

Mr. King raises his hand to take the spoon she offers and moves the bag around in his cup. "Don't worry. I'm not offended. It was just a question with no spite in it."

Anna lifts her cup, the warm, lemony scent wafting up to her. "Oh, I forgot the cake." She goes to the refrigerator, removes the carrot cake, and cuts a slice for her guest. "Is that too big?"

"Cake's never too big for my mouth."

She slides the piece onto a plate and hands it over with a fork. "It's supposed to be good for you. The whole carrot idea, but the icing is loaded with sugar."

"Looks delicious and nutritious." Mr. King shows his teeth to the cake. "I'm not afraid to eat you, little cake." He digs right in, hurrying a forkful to his lips, as though he has never seen a piece of cake in his life. After a few chews, he pauses to shut his eyes and moan with enjoyment.

This pleases Anna.

"Mm-mm. That icing is nice. Lemon zest, right?"

"Yes."

You're not having any?"

"No."

"Watching your figure?"

Anna chuckles. "No."

Mr. King fits another big forkful into his mouth. He studies her face while chewing, his eyes taking their time, contemplating each feature. Then he sips his tea. "Have you been working?"

"Painting?"

"Yes, painting paintings. Not just walls."

"I've been busy with the house. Painting the house." She finds this amusing, as though she might be claiming responsibility for the house's existence on another plane. A work of art monumental in scale. A life-size installation.

"It's the same thing, isn't it? When you step back from it and have a look."

"Three-dimensional, I guess."

"We're always inventing our own lives. People tend to forget that."

Anna watches him eat, feeling warmed by his words.

He licks the fork, sucking on the tines to get the icing off. "You can't see all the rooms at once, but if you step back, away from the house, you can get an idea. One of the things I like about the country is you can see your house from all these different angles. See where it sits on the land. See what's protecting it. You're in the cup of a valley here. The hills and the trees shield everything from the cruelty of the wind."

"Interesting."

"In the city you can't see your house because everything's so near." Mr. King shoves another forkful into his mouth and chews until he swallows. Pausing before sipping his tea, he raises his eyebrows. "This is tasty, isn't it?"

"Good to warm you up."

"Yes, that's true." He drinks his tea and checks the window. "More snow. You know, each flake is a prism of all the colours in the world." He carefully lifts his cup, studies the bottom. "Fine china," he says, setting the cup on its saucer. "You throw a hell of a tea party, young miss."

Anna laughs openly with an innocence of spirit. "You know, I haven't had this much fun just talking since I was a teenager. I have to admit."

"I'm glad. Does that mean we get to do each other's hair later?"

"Well." She glances at his balding head and purses her lips in consideration. "Hmm."

"I might take a while with yours. It's nice and long." He pats the top of his own head. "But you definitely don't have much work ahead of you on this baby."

That night Anna opens the front door to stand in the doorway, valuing the quiet and darkness. The snow has stopped falling and the air smells fresh. Mr. King has been gone for several hours. Anna has finished the hallway while reflecting on their conversation. What Mr. King said about a prism in each snow-flake has stuck in her mind.

Anna stares skyward and considers her baby, wondering about its face. The deep blue sky is cluttered with distinct patterns of stars.

Far off there is the sound of a dog baying. Water trickles in the brook across the road, flowing against rocks and frozen grass, wearing its way between brittle sheets of ice and clumps of snow. It runs downhill toward a culvert beneath the road where it drops over a cliff to cascade into the ocean, a body of water surrounding the landmass as though the island itself is afloat.

Anna remains in the open doorway, despite the cold, and marvels at the grove of sheltering trees across the road, their black ragged outline set against a sky lit by deep unfathomable blue. Beyond them, a rolling white field that might be crossed under moonlight. She gives thought to buying a snowmobile. It would be nice to go for a ride at night the way she used to do in Torbay. Park the snowmobile in a field, pull off her helmet, and lie back on the seat to stare up at the sky. Drink in all that beauty.

She looks west. Two hundred feet away the closest house sits in darkness atop a long, sloping driveway.

Watching that way, Anna is mystified to see a tiny light flicker in an upstairs room. A small shadow, holding what appears to be a candle, crosses into the window and remains obediently still.

The Embryo: Day 18, Week 3

A fold, meant to form the head of Anna's embryo, thickens and rises on either side of the neural groove.

Muscle cells continue to multiply, nudging into one another, pressing until fusing to form the root of two heart tubes.

There is the sound of humming, seemingly mechanical in nature. It takes her a few moments to identify what it might be. The vibration of steel shimmying against wood. Her cellphone on the kitchen table.

The shadow remains in the neighbour's window.

Distracted, Anna sighs, goes back inside, and shuts the door, the memory of that shadow trailing after her.

When she picks up her phone, she sees Kevin's name and number on the screen. She can't help but feel sorry for him. Is he regretting his behaviour? No doubt he is alone at home. Anna knows that he has no life, other than his work. Why not give him another chance? News of her pregnancy must have been hard on him, too. She lets the phone ring one more time before pressing the talk button.

"Hello."

"Anna?"

"Yes."

"Where are you?"

"Vacationing. Why?"

"I was trying to contact you. You're not at your place."

To this she gives no reply. She sits at the table and slips her fingernail along a groove in the wooden top. Then she lifts back the lace curtain to stare at the side yard filled with blue-hued snow. She checks the window in the neighbour's house, the flicker still there, but the silhouette gone.

"Are you with someone?" The tone in which he poses this question makes him seem desperate and heartbroken.

"No," she admits right away to save him the hurt. She doesn't want him thinking that she is with another man. She isn't capable of such cruelty.

"I have those tickets to Italy. Only ten days away."

"I won't be going, Kevin." This is difficult for her to say, for a small part of her has been clinging to the hope of reconciliation if only to make the trip possible. She has been looking forward to the trip since Kevin gave it to her as a Christmas present a couple of months ago. It would have been a welcome and refreshing change. Kevin had even printed out a detailed day-by-day itinerary for their visits to the museums and galleries in Rome. The National Gallery of Modern Art had been included along with the Capitoline Museums, which has paintings by two of her favourite Old Masters, Rubens and Caravaggio, in its collections.

"Come on, Anna. We can work this out."

"How's that?"

"Have you done anything?"

"About what?"

"The pregnancy."

"That's none of your business, Kevin." She lets the lace curtain fall back. The neighbour's window remains evident as a small lit square.

"Yes, in fact, it is my business." He snorts a laugh.

Anna wonders why, then finally understands the joke. But it is not funny. It is pathetic.

"If you want me to help, I can. Speaking of business."

Anna shakes her head. She makes a sound, a shallow push in her throat. Repulsion. "I have to go." Standing from her chair, she looks around the kitchen, feeling vaguely spooked. She peeks out the curtain, that lone light still burning.

"You're out in that house, aren't you?"

"What house?" She straightens, checks the kitchen doorway.

"Bareneed."

"No."

"Did you buy it after? I know you're there. Where else —"

"Goodbye, Kevin." Anna shuts her phone.

She is alone, after all. Her eyes return to the neighbour's house. She fingers back the curtain.

The faint, wavering gleam drifts from one window to the next as though someone might be carrying a candle from room to room. The light fades away, then glows in a downstairs window before vanishing.

From the black woods behind her barn a small shadow bounds across the white into her field of vision. It appears to be a dog with a bushy tail and long snout. The dog is in profile, facing the road, watching into the dark grove across the brook. It hunkers down, slowly stalking something.

Anna assumes it is hungry. She would like to feed it, coax it into the house. Offer it a warm spot where it might curl up beside the stove. She notices her cell growing warm in her hand and sets it on the table while speculating on what she might have in the fridge.

Studying the animal with greater scrutiny, Anna is astonished to realize it is a fox. Her fingers go up to the windowpane.

The fox, catching sight of movement, stops and turns its head in her direction.

Anna presses her palm against the cold glass. At once the fox sits, facing her like a statue. Then it swiftly tilts back its head to watch the top storey of the house as though something of deeper concern has captured its interest.

Chapter Five

Anna: March 10, the Claim

Anna sweeps the bottom floor of the barn, preparing to calculate the space for her work area. She considers building her studio in the loft but wonders if there is enough room up there. If she has a large window installed at the back, she will have a spectacular overview of the woods and ocean.

After she sketches out her plan, she will need to contact a carpenter.

She has been busy with the house for the past five days. The rooms are almost entirely painted except for the nursery. She can't settle on a colour. She feels that the baby is a girl, but it could just as easily be a boy. She thinks of pouring together the paint left over from all the other rooms to see what sort of colour might be created from the mix.

There have been no more signs of wildlife other than the faint scamperings of mice in the attic. No more trembles of light in the neighbour's house. She has checked numerous times each night. The mystery of that flicker has distanced itself from her, lingering as a low murmur in her mind, kept at bay by the immediacy of dearer preoccupations.

Pausing, she leans the broom against the wall to search through an old tea crate. The crate has words of its origins stamped on its sides. It is filled not with tea but with porcelain doorknobs and liniment bottles fashioned out of blue and green glass.

Anna wonders about Mr. King. He seems the sort who might like one of the bottles as a memento.

A sound outside the barn catches her attention. She faces it and listens. A car approaching, the hum of its engine carrying across the land surrounding her house before being absorbed by the trees.

The vehicle slows, then appears to come to a standstill, the engine idling in a steady pitch. The driver must have stopped to admire the house or seek directions.

A car door shuts, and a short while later someone knocks on her front door.

Who might it be? Her eyes go to the old single-barrel shotgun leaning in the corner, barely recognizable in the shadows. Earlier that morning, while cleaning, she discovered it there, having missed it on her previous inspections of the barn. The sight of it intrigues her, as she has never held an authentic shotgun before.

Stepping to the doorway, Anna sees a jet-black SUV in her driveway, pulled in behind her car. A man in a long tweed coat and matching hat appears at the side of the house. He stands there, flatly watching her. A leather satchel with front flap and buckles hangs from his right hand.

Without advancing, the man matter-of-factly says, "Anna Wells?" The two words, spoken as a question, sound foreboding in the still air.

"Yes," she barely manages, troubled by the formality of the man's tone. She takes a step down into the mild air.

Water drips from the eaves of the house and barn as snow melts from the roofs.

The man walks toward her while opening his briefcase and rummaging through it, his eyes shaded by the brim of his hat. Before reaching Anna, the man speaks his name, extracts a collection of papers, and holds them at ready. The expression on his pale face is removed, seemingly unaffected by thought or action. He is there for one purpose: to hand Anna the papers.

"What's this?" she asks, receiving the document in both hands and scanning the first page in confusion. It bears the insignia of the Supreme Court of Newfoundland, which alarms her.

The man gives no reply, his eyes briefly searching hers before he tips his hat, turns, and walks to his idling vehicle.

Anna reads the word "Plaintiff," followed by "Kevin Prowse." Beneath his name she glimpses hers after the word "Defendant."

She looks up to see the man climbing into the black SUV. He leaves the door open and sits behind the windshield, staring through.

Confused by the papers, she regards them again.

In legal wording something is mentioned about inception. Creation. Gestation. Biological father.

She reads with progressing astonishment, her eyes straining, her mind suffering to make sense of it.

Anna glances at the house, the square two-storey shape of it, then checks the deserted road.

The SUV gone.

Is that why Kevin called, to pinpoint her location, so this summons might be promptly served?

She flips the pages over.

On the very last line of page three, the words: "Seeking retrieval of property."

The Embryo: Day 23, Week 4

Approximately three-quarters of the way toward the head of Anna's embryo, the cells that will shape the eyes cluster together and appear as two wide circles.

The embryo's heart tube has been slowly bending into an arc. It wriggles and twists, adopting an S-shape. The change in form prompts a cardiac muscle contraction. A single heartbeat.

Anna is on her hands and knees scrubbing the kitchen floor. She tries not to think of the summons that sits on the table, yet its glaring whiteness burns in her peripheral vision. She has already read through the pages several times. An insulting and ridiculous document.

She only has so many days to respond to the summons. She fumes at the idea of having to hire a lawyer, tell the lawyer that she is pregnant, pay a lawyer to defend her.

Defend her!

While light fades outside the kitchen window, her agitation is intensified by hunger. She continues scrubbing the floor, remembering how her mother, when engaged in her Saturday morning cleaning rituals, used to sop sweat from her brow with the back of her arm.

Sweat drips down the bridge of her nose. Annoyed, she swipes it away.

There is a crash in the yard that reverberates in the floorboards and gives her pause. Having already ventured out to investigate an earlier noise of similar magnitude, she is confident it is chunks of snow and ice sliding from the roof to belt the ground.

She scrubs the floor harder, her actions blunt to her mind. Scrub and think about nothing. Her arm begins to pain. She stops to catch her breath, rises on her knees, and tosses the brush into the bucket of water. A mirror image of her mother doing the very same thing. Why didn't Anna ever offer to help? Why didn't she give over more of herself to chores? Her mother never complained, never harped on her to help out, only encouraged her to have time to herself and be creative.

Pushing herself to her feet, she ignores the summons, goes to the switch, and flicks on the overhead light. She had no idea it was so dark.

The cupboards contain nothing but tinned goods. Corned beef for supper. She uses the flat key to unwind the metal and scrapes the meat from the can into a cast-iron skillet.

With the black iron prong she lifts a damper at the back of the stove, then pokes in a few splits of wood. The embers burn red, igniting the splits. She slides the damper back on.

When the meat begins to sizzle, she stirs it with a fork, the scent of salty fat rising to her. She is starving to the point of being faint. She hasn't eaten lunch. Her hunger is so concentrated that it graduates to the next level: nausea. At first she assumes the feeling will dissipate. But saliva pools on her tongue, and she hurries to the bathroom, off the living room, to throw herself over the toilet.

She retches once, her eyes watering while she groans.

Another heave, and she vomits, the minimal contents of her stomach plunking into the water.

She wipes at her eyes, trying not to gag. Spitting, she holds her hair out of her face and retches with greater strain, the tendons in her neck pulling taut.

On the third retch she hears a sound, a word that mimics "Mommy."

It repeats itself when she leans over the toilet again, her ears flooded with pressure while she throws up: "Maawwmmee."

Sweat beads on her forehead and dampens her scalp. She wonders if she has a fever, if she is sick, and stands to check herself in the mirror above the sink.

A white face watching back at her.

What has she heard?

A voice crying out from within? Impossible.

She needs to lie down.

In the living room she reclines on the chaise longue, her eyes fixed on the dim ceiling, her head wavering with sickness and stress. Call Kevin, she tells herself. Call him and shout at him: "You are making me sick with your heartless crap." Demand that he withdraw the summons.

The room grows chilly, fills up with dusk. No fire in the woodstove.

Resting her arm over her eyes, she hopes that her nausea will pass. She pictures Kevin's face, curses him, devises elaborate plans on how to get even until, exhausted, she falls asleep.

Anna's eyes open to darkness.

Roused by the sound of scratching, she stills her breath to listen.

The scratching, which appears to be coming from under the house, prompts her to turn on her side and study the indistinct floor. The sound grows more insistent, louder, powered by greater urgency until it approaches the splintering vigour of clawing and chewing.

Compelled to sit up, Anna is conscious of the flimsy woollen slippers on her feet.

It is pitch-black outside the living room windows. She can barely make out where she is in the room.

More sounds, this time from upstairs, the scurrying of little paws, slowing their pace, growing larger, more measured, rhythmic, amplified in her ears.

A hiss like a whisper, "Mmmmmawwwwwmmmmeeeee," startling her to her feet.

The sound of her heartbeat thumping in her chest. Had that actually been the noise? Not scurrying feet at all, but the beating of her heart growing louder?

She begins to tremble, feels unreal in her own body. She breathes deeply, holds the breath, then exhales, trying to ward off the panic attack.

Will dramatic fluctuations in her heart rate affect the baby?

She stumbles forward, the sweat on her body chilling while she blindly reaches for the nearest lamp, her eyes on the dark mystery of the floor, trying to make out bolting shadows. Finding the lamp, she pulls the switch chain, then hurries to illuminate the two remaining floor lamps.

No sign of mice or rats in the living room.

Is something in the house, on top of the house, under the house? She watches the ceiling. Who should she call? Mr. King? What about the police?

She lingers in front of the chaise longue as though to shield her body while she stares expectantly at the living room doorway.

It is noticeably cold in the house. The temperature must have dropped. She can see her breath in the bright room. She needs to put in a fire.

Her ears strain to detect indications of movement.

Nothing. Silence.

Then a scuttling sound in the floorboards, followed by a boom directly beneath her feet as though something has struck from underneath.

Recoiling, she races from the room, down the hallway, where she throws open the front door.

It is gently snowing outside.

She checks over her shoulder. The empty hallway. The red on the walls deeper than she remembers. The paint still maturing.

The stairs leading to the second storey are in darkness, the light at the top burnt out.

She listens for hints of a presence, turns to face the outdoors, but shoots a look back over her shoulder at those stairs. What might be coming down from the second storey? What could it be? Should she just get in her car and drive away?

Anna tries to be rational, not frightened or defeated by the inexplicable. The boom in the floorboards must have been snow falling from the roof. Like before. But it is cold now. The snow wouldn't be melting. It must be the house settling. And mice. Big mice. Why should she be afraid of mice? No doubt they are more afraid of her. She is bigger than them. Much bigger.

Either face whatever it is or leave. She only has two choices. And she won't run away like a panicky child.

Leaving the front door open for the purpose of a brisk escape, she turns and slowly ascends two steps while searching overhead, her neck straining to glean a view beyond the upstairs railing. Once she reaches the top of the stairs, she will make a dash for the light switch in the master bedroom directly to her right.

A rush of cool air behind her back as something darts by her ankles, racing up the stairs.

Anna screams, clutches at the banister with both hands to prevent herself from falling backward.

The shadow curves into the master bedroom, the room where Anna has been sleeping. The space occupied by a matching cream-coloured vanity and dresser, its drawers stained by the smell of mothballs, a wickedly enticing and intoxicating odour she relishes from her childhood. A white chenille spread atop a soft bed with carved headboard and footboard.

From the bedroom there comes a squealing, then scrambling, thrashing sounds of a struggle.

Shrieking.

Anna takes a hesitant step down.

More horrifying squeaking in the ruckus.

She rocks back and forth, summoning the courage before bolting up the rest of the stairs, entering the bedroom, and slapping her hand at the light switch.

The commotion is coming from beneath the bed, something hidden under there, jolting around.

How is she going to get it out? She needs a broom to smack at it, to protect herself.

The red fox dashes from under the edge of the chenille bedspread with three mice clamped in its jaws. One of the mice squirms to get free, its stick-like legs kicking. The other two hang limply.

Anna juts back against the dresser while the fox hurries by her without giving any notice.

She follows it from the room, sees it trot down the stairs and out the opened front door. She braces her hand against the wall to steady herself, her heartbeat pounding in the back of her throat. A gust of cold air races up to meet her.

Moving to descend the stairs, she nudges a frame on the wall with her hand, an elaborate needlepoint pattern she has yet to notice fully. Straightening the frame, she studies the pattern, trying to discern its message. She leans for a better look.

A list of nearly invisible words: "Mary Anna Margaret Helen Elizabeth Ruth Florence Ethel Emma Marie Clara Bertha Minnie Bessie Alice Lillian Edna Grace Annie Mabel Ida Rose Hazel Gertrude Martha Pearl Frances Myrtle Edith Nellie Katherine Ella Eva Laura Elsie Louise Esther Catherine Agnes Carrie Lillie Mildred Gladys Irene Julia Hattie Cora Lena Josephine Mattie Jennie Jessie Maude Alma Mae Blanche Dorothy Ada Lucy Lula Mamie Fannie Stella Ruby Dora Maggie Nora Rosa Beatrice Ellen Sadie Marion Willie Effie May Beulah Pauline Nettie Susie Della Marguerite Vera Daisy Lydia Virginia Olive Kathryn Evelyn Sallie Lizzie Lottie Emily Georgia Flora Nancy Katie Lucille Leona ..."

And beside that frame, another needlepoint comprised of precise script: "John William James George Charles Joseph Frank Robert Edward Henry Harry Thomas Walter Arthur Fred Albert Clarence Willie Roy Louis Earl Paul Carl Ernest Samuel Richard Raymond Joe David Charlie Harold Ralph Howard Andrew Herbert Elmer Oscar Jesse Alfred Will Daniel Sam Leo Jack Lawrence Francis Benjamin Lee Eugene Herman Peter Frederick Floyd Michael Ray Lewis Claude Clyde Edwin Tom Martin Leonard Ben Chester Edgar Jim Harvey Russell Clifford Lester Luther Homer Jacob Leroy Otto Guy Lloyd Anthony Jessie Hugh Ed Bernard Theodore Stanley Eddie Patrick Philip Leon Archie Leslie Oliver Allen Alexander Dewey Ira Everett Norman Horace Victor Cecil ..."

Chapter Six

The Embryo: Day 23, Week 4

Cellular growth accelerates in Anna's embryo, forcing it to stretch and the yolk sac to expand.

On each side of the central neural tube, twelve pairs of square, chip-like segments are arranged that will eventually become skeletal muscle, vertebrae, and the layer of skin beneath the epidermis that cushions the body from stress and strain.

The tubal heart continues to beat, thrusting fluids via miniscule networks throughout the body.

Anna's embryo is an eighth of an inch long. The size of a ladybug.

Anna: March 12, the Man in the Pickup

Anna leaves the house with a list of needs in mind: mousetraps, newspapers, milk, chocolate bars, candy ... She climbs into her car, engages the engine, and blasts the heat, watching the frozen windshield slowly clear tiny, then larger misshapen spots.

Anna has burned up all the napkins, paper towels, and any

scraps of paper that were left in the house. She needs more paper to ignite a fire in the woodstove, which keeps extinguishing itself at night.

In a few minutes, warmth floods around her.

She switches the heat down a notch while watching the house and contemplating the serenity of the previous day. Nothing like the unsettling day before with the delivery of the summons, morning sickness, and the exploits of the fox and mice at night.

Yesterday was not only peaceful but productive, as well. She found a drawbar and hammer in an old wooden tool chest in a cupboard under the stairs and tore out the three stalls in the barn to maximize floor space. The demolition job occupied most of the day.

At night, with the help of a wooden step ladder, she finished painting the lace-coloured mouldings in the hallway.

No calls from Kevin. A part of her hoped for a connection, if only for the sake of setting things right and alleviating hardship.

Anna navigates the seemingly endless road out of Bareneed, glancing at the occasional ancient house nestled amid dense black spruce. All of the houses appear deserted and ill-maintained, roofs sagging, paint blistering off, or clapboards worn grey, barns leaned over by rot. She wonders why her house is the only one in such exemplary condition.

At the head of the Bareneed road she takes a right on to Shearstown Line for the fifteen-minute ride to Bay Roberts. She follows the winding stretch of pavement that inclines toward snow-laden spruce and fir trees, dips into valleys that skirt the ocean until she reaches a set of traffic lights at the base of a steep hill, and comes to a stop.

Ahead of her a boy and a girl slap at each other in the back seat of a blue car. It is a game of some sort, for they are laughing as the rate of their slapping accelerates. The girl catches sight of Anna and turns to wave. The boy makes a mockery of the waving, aping the sentiment while twisting up his face in a scary way.

The car pulls ahead, moving through the intersection.

Beyond the lights there is a newly constructed animal hospital, with an auto parts outlet across the street.

Anna drives on, passing a two-lane gas station, a franchised electronics store, and an American car dealership with a large quantity of new model pickup trucks lined off on the lot.

Bay Roberts has everything that most medium-sized North American towns have: a strip mall with a grocery store at one end, a big-box pharmacy, a once privately owned hardware store bought out by a chain, and the usual fast-food outlets with signs pledging maximum grease for minimal dollars.

Over one shop Anna studies a sign featuring a graphic of a chainsaw. The image is well done, as though painted by a professional. She imagines cutting her own wood. She likes the idea of learning how to do that, of living a rugged life of self-sufficiency and passing on those basic survival skills to her child.

Up ahead, another grocery store and a local flower shop with a fancy, countrified sign lacking the polish of the chainsaw one.

She pulls into the second gas station, climbs out, and fits the nozzle into her tank. The coat she wears is too light for the chilliness of the day. Her bare hands begin to ache from the cold.

A large, stocky man in a puffy black jacket fills his pickup ahead of her. He gives her a few glances, his face showing nothing, his eyes going to her breasts, which suddenly feel highly sensitive beneath her clothes.

Anna pumps in twenty dollars, replaces the nozzle, and heads inside to settle up and buy a stack of newspapers.

"Lots of reading ahead of you," says the young girl at the cash when Anna sets the pile of newspapers on the counter. A silver ring is looped through the corner of the girl's bottom lip, and her raggedly clipped hair is coal-black.

"They're for the fire."

"Oh." The girl looks off to her side. "I've got a bunch of yesterdays there." She points to the floor, then scratches the side of her nose with a single fingernail. "If you want them. We just strip off the date."

"Thanks, that'd be great."

The girl bends and, with a groan, hoists the stack of leftover newspapers onto the counter.

Anna returns the ones from today to the rack. While doing so she notices a cooler filled with milk and juice across the wide, fluorescent-lit store and heads for it, reaching for the fat-free milk, but then realizing she should be drinking whole milk now. She collects a red carton, a container of orange juice, and a dozen eggs, holding them in the crook of her arm.

Next to the eggs there are packages of thickly sliced bologna, a treat she hasn't eaten in years. The smell of it browning in the pan fills her nostrils. Her mother used to cook it for her with a fried egg, sizzling in oil until the edges turned crisp. Lots of salt sprinkled on. Toast smeared into the running yolk.

Anna grabs the bologna before she has a chance to change her mind, then searches for mousetraps. In an aisle of general kitchen needs, she spots a two-pack. Such a simple device. It hasn't changed in years, probably not since its invention. She slides a package off the metal display prong and carries everything to the counter.

She has to wait her turn in line while a large, broad man ahead of her pays for a cup of coffee from one of the specialty java machines, then buys a number of lottery tickets.

"You had gas, right?" the girl asks, her eyes going to Anna's left cheek. She tilts her chin. "You've got something there."

"What?"

"Paint, I think." She leans across the counter and gently picks it away, checks the tip of her thumb where the cream-coloured dot rests. "See."

"Thanks. I've been painting."

"Yeah." The girl chuckles, brushing her thumb on her pants. "You had gas?"

"Yes," Anna says, and states the amount.

The girl rings in the gas and groceries but neglects to charge Anna for the papers, which she slides into a plastic bag. The girl then places the groceries in another bag, arranging the items with care.

"That's not too heavy, is it?" she asks.

"No, it's fine. Thanks."

"Okay." The girl smiles at her. "It's cold, hey?"

"Yes. It sure is."

"Should warm up soon."

"I hope so. Thanks, again." Anna carries the two bags to her car; they are indeed heavy. She loads them into the back seat, her thoughts lingering on the girl behind the counter, her young face and authentic kindness. Good people in the world, offering friendly dialogue with no ulterior motive in mind.

Approaching the flower shop, Anna considers stopping to buy herself a rose. The one that Mr. King brought along as a house-warming gift is blackening at the edges. In fact, the rose shouldn't be for her, but for the baby. The idea of buying a rose for the baby appeals to her. Would the baby know what Anna is doing? She wonders about its size, how it might be developing. The natural course of its growth. Day by day. Subsequently, the summons comes to mind, renewing her anger.

Distracted, she passes the flower shop, thinking she should call Bill Reid, the lawyer who handled the house purchase. She has been putting it off, even though she knows it is inevitable. Unless she plans on representing herself in court. The thought of having to explain her situation to the lawyer infuriates her. After all, her pregnancy is nobody's business.

A salt truck is stopped in front of Anna at the traffic lights, its blue light flashing.

She will have to enter a courtroom, sit before a bunch of strangers while her lawyer defends Anna's right to have a baby. Outrageous. Insidious. What lawyer in his right mind would initiate such a claim in this day and age?

Anna follows the truck up Shearstown Line, keeping back a distance from the spray of salt and sand, grateful that the roads will be safe ahead of her. The yellow truck has a long side mirror outside the driver's side. Anna can see the driver's face and upper torso in reflection. The man's eyes keep glancing there, watching her.

What is he looking at? she wants to know.

The Embryo: Day 25, Week 4

Neural crest cells emerge in Anna's embryo, generating the basis for the contours of the skull and face.

The forebrain closes over, enfolding the cells that will one day trigger thought.

In the beating tubal heart, valve flaps, in their infancy, begin to rise as low ridges.

In no time she is back on the road to Bareneed. She passes the neighbour's weather-beaten house, the one in which she saw the candlelight. When was that? She counts backward to the day she first arrived. Has it been seven days already? A week. She finds it hard to believe.

The plough has been by and left enough of a snow barrier to hamper entry into her driveway. She thinks of making a run for it; she should be able to force her way in if she can pick up enough speed.

She stomps the gas pedal and spins the steering wheel, hearing and feeling the snow scrape against her undercarriage while the car bounces. It is a dreadful sound that reminds her of her accident.

She makes the mistake of stopping.

At once she puts the car in reverse, checks over her shoulder, and gives the engine gas.

The tires spin.

"Great."

She tries forward. The tires squeal.

Making a sound of exasperation, she quickly shifts from reverse to forward and back again, attempting to rock the car, believing that if she acts quickly it will not be too late to free the vehicle.

But the car won't budge. A heavy piece of metal going nowhere.

Anna keeps spinning the tires, expecting to gain traction.

After a while, she remembers the shovel next to the door and leaves the car idling to collect it.

The car is halfway out in the road. Maybe if she scoops out snow beneath the undercarriage she will be able to loosen it up. She checks in both directions, hoping no one will come along to see the mess she has made of it.

Stepping up the driveway, she notices fresh prints in the snow leading to her front door. The tracks were made by boots. Big boots.

Anna recalls Kevin's shoe size: eight and a half. These prints are much larger.

She follows the trail until at her door the prints rise onto the step. Prints facing in, and then portions of other prints facing out.

Whoever it was must have gone inside.

The doorknob turns when she tries it. She didn't lock it. Why would she bother in the country?

She cautiously eases the door open a quarter of the way.

Pausing, she holds her breath, listening. Not a sound.

She reaches for the shovel by the door, silently steps into the house. With delicately measured actions she shuts the door behind her.

The interior has a strong smell of paint. She wonders if the fumes might be poisoning her brain.

Something in her wants to call out "Hello?"

Finally, she does.

No reply is given in return, no words or shuffle of movement. Anna follows the bits of snow dented with sole patterns. The trail leads to the kitchen. On her way there her head tilts while her eyes strain for a view into the room. Automatically, her hand raises the shovel and holds it at a threatening angle. She is expecting a man to be standing there.

Or a man jumping out of a hiding space.

Not Kevin, but perhaps someone sent by him. Would he risk the damage to his reputation? Or does damage to his reputation concern him in the slightest? After all, he sent those court documents. What sort of harm will the court action do to his practice? Were those papers actually filed in a courthouse, or merely fabricated as a tactic to scare her into submission? The man in the tweed coat, a hired actor?

She has no idea what Kevin is really like, what he is capable of. In a matter of mere days, he has become a stranger to her.

The kitchen is empty.

The boot tracks lead to the refrigerator.

Anna notices the summons on the table, its position slightly shifted.

The wilted, black-edged rose has been replaced by a fresh one now as though someone might have been reading her thoughts when she passed the flower shop. It must have been Mr. King, delivering another rose and then helping himself to some carrot cake. No doubt country people go into one another's homes all the time.

Anna leans the shovel against the wall and reaches for the refrigerator door.

Inside the refrigerator, on the top shelf, there is a clear plastic bag. Although the plastic is partially misted, the foot-long object that rests within is visible, the skin brown as though rotted, the four tiny limbs covered in traces of blood, the narrow purplish torso with faint indications of veins ...

The strangling weight in Anna's chest compromises her breathing. In reaction her heartbeat ups its tempo. Her stomach stirs at the hideous sight. If it is human, it is the product of deformity.

Yet her rational mind works to cleans up the mess, assuring her that it must be some sort of animal, skinned.

A clunk beside her.

She spins to face the window. The rose tipped over. A spill of water across the tabletop, inching toward the summons. Did she do that when she came in, accidentally nudge the vase with the shovel handle? She watches the seep reach the document, bank up against the paper, rising to spill over it and smear the printed words.

A knock sounds on her door.

Flinching in near spasm, she makes a tight involuntary sound and clings onto the refrigerator door.

She waits.

The knock comes again.

She shuts the fridge and hurries to the kitchen window to bend across the table, stretching to see up the driveway, but the angle doesn't afford her a clear view.

The knocking again, louder, the wooden door shimmying, its window rattling.

Anna steps to the kitchen doorway and tries peeking down the hallway.

Outside there is a man in profile. He is wearing a baseball cap and has a few days' growth of beard. He turns to face the door, spotting Anna.

In reflex she juts back but catches herself and impels her body forward as though on her way to greet the visitor in the first place.

She opens the door to see a pickup truck, with a plough, idling in the road in front of her yard. Five feet to the right of the man a little red-haired girl in a pink snowsuit, pink mittens, and matching pink woollen cap lies on the snow, sweeping her arms and legs back and forth.

"Hi," says the man without smiling. "I thought you might need a little help."

The man has a steel hook on a winch of wire rope attached to the front of his truck. He lifts the hook, pulls out a length of thick wire while stepping backward. Reaching the rear of Anna's car, he kneels, his upper torso twisting to lean under her car. There is the noise of metal being poked against metal until the man stands and looks at Anna while brushing off his gloves and pants.

There is a rugged quality to the man, coupled with a clean, mannered intelligence that contradicts, in an attractive way, this rough look, as though he doesn't do this sort of thing for a living. He is simply playing the part, trying to fit in.

"Put it in neutral," he tells her.

"Sure." Anna climbs into her car and shifts into neutral. Then she watches in the rearview mirror for further instruction.

The little girl is in the pickup, standing on the passenger seat and leaning forward with her hands on the dash. She seems to be a shy girl, for she hasn't said a word to Anna.

The man works the transmission stick, checks over his shoulder, resets his attention forward, and turns the steering wheel. The truck slowly backs away.

There is a gentle jolt as the wire goes taut, then a tug that gets smoother. Snow scrapes against the undercarriage, while the car moves as though being dragged. At the sound of scraping, Anna automatically hits the brakes, realizing at once that it was the wrong thing to do. She removes her foot immediately, worried that she might have snapped the wire rope, if that was possible, or damaged her bumper. The scraping continues until the car is clear of the driveway.

With her four tires back on the road, she feels relieved to be mobile. Free again. She checks the rearview mirror to see the man climbing out of his truck. He bends behind her vehicle, roots around, then straightens with the hook in hand.

Anna raises her hand as though to wave thanks, but the man has already turned, so she pulls ahead, clear of her driveway, parks farther up the road, and gets out, hoping that he will now clear the snow with his rig.

The blade on the pickup lowers and scrapes the asphalt.

As the truck enters her driveway, she can see into its bed, the feathered bodies of big white birds tied together in groups. The sight brings to mind what was left in her fridge. Not a bird, but something wild. She suspects a rabbit. Did this man leave it for her? Is he from the house up the road?

The man reverses and curves the wheels, thrusts ahead, reverses again. He continues the pattern until there are patches of crushed stone embedded in the snow that has been pushed into a pile deep in her driveway.

The little red-haired girl turns in her seat to keep her eyes on Anna. Waving from the back window, she paws hair from her face, then sucks on her mitten.

Anna waves back.

After four passes, the pickup has cleared the driveway.

The man toots his horn and swerves backward, his truck rocking slightly when it stops.

Anna watches the pickup roll ahead, approaching her. She raises her hand and calls out, "Thanks," hoping the man will stop, so she has a chance to offer some sort of payment, but the man merely nods in reply.

The little girl watches Anna through the windshield, then drops to her knees and scrambles to turn around, staring intently out the rear window.

Buckle up, Anna thinks, wanting to mouth the words and make the motion for securely strapping herself in.

The pickup shrinks in the distance until disappearing around a curve in the road with snow-laden evergreens on both sides.

Anna climbs into her car.

While backing up she wonders if the man was just passing by. If he was from the house next door, wouldn't he have returned there? She pulls into her driveway, delighted by the lack of obstruction.

Along the path to her house she checks for boot prints. The design of the man's tread is different from the first set.

She passes the snow angel and gives it some attention, enchanted by the exactness of the impression.

The Embryo: Day 25, Week 4

The pairs of symmetrical, chip-like vertebrae have grown from twelve to twenty.

Anna's embryo is curved in a fetal arc. It has a tail and a stalk connected to the expanding placenta.

Its head is discernible as a smooth, elongated forehead curving in toward the bumps of two featureless eyes with thickened lens plates connected to the forebrain via optic stalks.

Beneath the eyes there is the bump of a nose and the simple line of a mouth.

The blood vessels in the central nervous system, the most mature component of Anna's embryo, begin to connect.

Chapter Seven

Anna: March 12, the Lost Little Girl

Seated on the chaise longue, watching the fire through the wood-stove's glass door, Anna thinks of Kandinsky, the father of abstract art, and how he claimed to be able to see colours when he heard music. He believed that strong drumbeats created the impression of red, yet the colour also had an enlivening effect on the heart.

Red: the pulse of fire, the crackle of bloodbeat.

While normally she would be entranced by the flames, her mind discerning shifting forms in the waver to gain some sort of inspiration, she now only sees the thing called "fire." A sight with no secret value.

The summons looms in her mind. She has delayed the call to her lawyer, holding out hope that Kevin might contact her, after coming to his senses, and apologize.

The torment of a legal fiasco will be costly in many ways. She can't afford it, not after putting all of her savings into the house. Would it be so bad to call Kevin and try to reason with him? Why can't she enjoy time in her new home without the threat of legal action hovering over her? All she wants to do is be alone and paint.

Kevin can't be serious with this claim. The thought of it continues to baffle her. What judge would ever allow it into his or her courtroom?

Maybe she should countersue.

The situation calls to mind a famous case from years ago where a man petitioned the courts to stop a woman from having an abortion, but she has no memory of instances where the tables were turned.

Her lawyer's number must be stored somewhere in her cellphone. She could call to check on the progress of the deed transfer and mention the summons at the same time.

Whatever happens with the baby, whatever her final choice might be, the lawyer will be aware of it once she initiates contact on this matter.

She mutters a breath of incredulity.

Leaning forward, she picks up her cell from the coffee table, opens it, and scrolls through the numbers.

No recent call from Kevin.

She presses his number. This is it. She will plead with him if necessary. Beg to get the claim dropped. But before the line has a chance to connect, she jabs the end button and curses while scrolling down to her lawyer's number.

If she makes even this one call to her lawyer, she will be billed for it.

This feels like a custody battle, yet it is anything but. She knows it will cost thousands of dollars, maybe even tens of thousands of dollars, to deal with this nuisance should it ever go to court. And the media will be all over the proceedings. It is just the sort of story they thrive on. The thought of media attention brings her paintings to mind. No doubt the publicity would increase sales. She would have no problem selling her work and maybe even be offered a book deal. Plenty of notice focused on her art.

Pitiful thoughts, she chastises herself.

Or will she have to sell the house to pay for cleaning up this mess?

She glances at the window, taking in the view of trees across the street. Two crows drift through the sky. One of them settles on a high branch, while the other veers off.

No one out here to bother her.

The cell in her hand. She checks the time: 4:24 p.m.

Rising from the chaise longue, she presses the number for her lawyer while walking to the kitchen. She can't believe she is actually doing it.

The receptionist requests Anna's name.

Anna states it, paces back into the living room, and waits, the sense of faceless formality tensing the muscles in her shoulders.

The line is picked up.

"Bill Reid," says the lawyer, his tone hasty, made so by years of dealing with trite details.

"Hi, this is Anna Wells."

"Hello, Anna."

"How are things with the deed transfer?" she asks.

"Just about finalized. I was going to call you to come in and sign the papers. When we're done with that, we'll transfer the money."

"Great. When should I do that?" She fingers a bronze statuette of a moose on the sideboard, absent-mindedly adjusting its position, then paces back into the kitchen.

"Whenever's convenient. How about tomorrow?"

"Well, I'm out at the house now." She stares at the lace curtains and touches her lips.

"In Bareneed?"

"Yes."

"Having another look? Too late to change your mind now." He laughs tautly.

"No, actually, I'm painting." She glances at the kitchen walls, a cinnamon brown rolled over blah-beige. The paint toward the ceiling trim is evenly stroked on. No mess. The lines distinct. A trained, steady hand good for something at least.

"They gave you the keys?"

"Yes."

"Hmm."

Anna doesn't want to have an argument over whether or not she should have taken possession before the deal was legally complete, so she quickly moves on. The meter ticking. "There's something else I wanted to mention."

"What's that? If you're in that house, it might —"

"No, something entirely different."

"Oh?"

"I received a summons from Kevin."

"Kevin, your ..."

"Boyfriend. Yes."

"Dr. Kevin Prowse?"

"Yes."

"Not about the house?"

"No."

"What's it about then?"

Anna watches the floor, notices her suede winter boots that she forgot to take off after coming in, the black hide stained with water marks. Not the sort of boots meant to be worn in deep snow. Boots for show.

How to put it? She decides to speak plainly. "I'm pregnant, and he's seeking return of property."

"Return of what property?"

"I don't know. His part of the baby." She chokes up on the last word, rolls her eyes in frustration, and shakes her head.

"Return of property?"

"That's what the summons says."

"It's worded that way in the summons?"

"Yes."

There is silence at the other end, then a faint sound like a huff. "When's the court date?"

Anna searches the document, flips a page, finds it, and reads, "March 28."

"So soon. How'd they manage that?"

"I don't know," Anna says helplessly, realizing the lawyer's question was rhetorical.

"Well, I guess time is an issue. That could be argued. I wonder what judge gave him that date. I'll work on a postponement if you like."

"Postponement? Can this really go ahead? It's nuts!"

"You're having the baby?"

"Yes … I think."

"Okay, and Kevin's the father?"

"Yes."

"I'll contact his lawyer, I know who represents him, and I'll find out what this is all about. Maybe we can come to some agreement, avoid court."

"This is ridiculous, right? Have you ever heard of anything like it?"

"The property claim angle threw me for a loop there. But unfortunately I can see where it's coming from. There was a buzz going around legal circles a while ago when two claims involving vials of semen in fertility clinics were dealt with as property issues. Another case involving frozen embryos. That sort of thing."

"Are you saying this will actually go to court? Are you kidding me?"

"These fertility cases have opened a can of worms in property law that hasn't been adequately sorted out yet. It's going to take a while."

"But this isn't sperm. It's not property."

"It doesn't sound like it'll stand up, as the property is inside you, so to speak, possession being nine-tenths of the law, but I need to see the summons. Do you have a fax there?"

"No." For some reason she turns to look at the refrigerator. Perhaps because it is one of the few machines of modern convenience in the house. She envisions the skinned carcass still inside. She left it on the shelf, not knowing if she should throw it out before hearing from the real estate agent. He must have been the one who put it there, and perhaps he is expecting a meal of it. Anna has never eaten rabbit; she wonders what it tastes like, how it should be cooked.

"Well, bring it in when you come about the house."

"What?"

"The summons. Better yet, I'll get a copy sent over from Kevin's lawyer." He pauses as though taking down notes. "There's a woman here in the firm, Patricia Dicks, who might be better suited for this new situation. She does family law. You've met Patricia, I believe."

Anna sighs, her eyes returning to the water-stained legal document on the kitchen table. "Yes." She recalls a plump, no-nonsense woman with short hair and hard features.

"Should I have her look into this and call you?"

"Sure."

"I'm sorry about all this, Anna."

"Okay. Thank you."

"And congratulations, by the way."

"Thanks very much."

"We'll be in touch soon."

The Embryo: Day 25, Week 4

The rounded edges of the neural tube meet along a join that closes over in Anna's embryo, sealing in the notches of the spinal cord.

Two optic bulges continue to expand, giving root to the retina's blue pigment.

Anna lies in bed, reading by the light of a small shaded lamp on her night table. Before heading out from St. John's to Bareneed nine days ago, she stopped at the big-box bookstore on Kenmount Road to pick up a book on baby development.

According to the book, her baby's heart is beating. The idea surges awe into the inexplicable mix of sensations she has been experiencing since arriving at the house.

The idea of a heartbeat brings baby names to mind. She reaches for a pen on the night table and jots down "Girl" in the outer margin of the page. Then she writes: "Charlotte. Katherine. Emma. Boy: Jacob. Luke. Jordan."

Charlotte is her favourite.

Luke for a boy.

She is using a small calendar card as a bookmark. The days of the months are tiny but not impossible to make out. This is how she keeps track of everything. Otherwise she wouldn't know one day of the week from the next. Her mind has always been distracted, and being self-employed and childless has only helped make her life a blur of uninterrupted minutes.

Anna wonders about the wood out in the barn. How long it will last? She has already put a dent in the stack and suspects she will need to locate more before Newfoundland's late spring arrives.

The man with the pickup comes to mind. He is definitely the sort who would know where to buy firewood. He might even have a chainsaw that he uses to cut wood himself. How to get in contact with him? She could go looking for his pickup. Does he have a wife? His daughter was gorgeous. Adorable. Beautiful red hair.

Anna focuses back on her book. Occasionally, her eyes pull away from the words and diagrams to wander across the freshly painted dusty pink walls. She has plans for painting other markings on the walls, petals and stalks of various shapes and hues. She shifts her attention to the ceiling, the narrow slatted lengths of board.

According to Mr. King, the house is over one hundred years

old, built by a boat builder lost at sea. Its foundation is made of slabs of slate stacked eight inches from the ground. This building method was used so that houses could be moved from one place to another, as was often the case. The structures were rolled along on barrels and pulled by horses toward the water of Conception Bay. Once on shore, the houses were set afloat and towed by boat to another community miles away before being drawn up on a new beach.

Anna lays the book face down on the covers and stands from the bed. She has left her socks on because the floor is chilly. Stepping to the window, she glances at the two mousetraps she has set and positioned along the stretch of baseboard. Blobs of peanut butter on the triggers. She glances at the bottom of her bed, even though she has already checked under there for a suspected nest but found nothing.

At the window she takes in the dark land and sky and is absorbed by the quiet surrounding her.

She watches through the glass, trying to internalize the texture of the sombre ocean, moonlight brushing the deep blue surface with a wide trail of flickering yellow.

The house is so still that even the smallest sounds catch her attention. What she thinks to be a distressing, muted moan from a child reaches her ears.

Suddenly, she is chilled and suspect of her senses.

She faces the open bedroom door.

Not again. Not more torment.

She holds her breath to listen.

A childlike whimper.

Spooked, Anna moves to the threshold to hesitantly search the hallway. Nothing there. She checks the stairway, which inclines toward a view through the window in the front door.

Outside, in the snow, there is some sort of dark bundle with muted pink highlights.

Anna hurries down the stairs and alertly looks out the window, her hand already on the knob.

The little red-haired girl is lying there in the indentation of the snow angel.

An intake of breath as Anna throws open the door and bolts out in her stocking feet.

Bending over the girl, she sees that the child's skin is greenish-white.

"Oh, God." Anna checks around, calls out, "Hello?" No one on her land or in the road. She scoops up the girl and turns with the weight of the small body in her arms. Tilting her cheek near the girl's face to find it cold, she dashes across the threshold and kicks shut the door.

Anna places the child on the floor in front of the woodstove and kneels, leaning to perform mouth-to-mouth.

The girl's lips are blue and freezing, her brittle hair clumped with snow.

Frantically, Anna wonders if her efforts are worthwhile in the case of people with hypothermia. The warm glow from the fire can't mask the deathly pallor of the girl's face.

"Oh, God, please, please." Anna paws hair away from her lips, sits back on her haunches, and presses the girl's chest with her palms. "Wake up." The body moves involuntarily.

It's not working, she tells herself. Not working.

Weakening, Anna moans in despair. Why doesn't the girl's father know where she is? Why isn't he out looking for her? The girl is too small to be wandering on her own. Where is her mother?

Anna should call an ambulance. What is she doing?

She knows nothing about how to save anyone.

Reaching for her cell on the coffee table, she pops it open and jabs 911. With the cell to her ear she rubs the girl's face. "Come on." She bends over the child, pressing her lips against the small, cold lips that seem entirely numb, breathing into her like a balloon.

Anna sobs as the line connects, then dies.

"No!" She checks the phone. The battery is drained. Where is her charger? Upstairs in the bedroom.

She tries calling again, her finger unsteady on the numbers. Nothing.

She tosses down the cell and tilts the girl's head back. The windpipe might be obstructed. The child's lips part to reveal two sets of perfectly formed teeth.

Anna works to breathe life into the girl's lungs. Pausing, she checks the child's chest. No indications of stirring.

Is she dead?

Anna can't take her eyes off the terrifying unrealness of the girl's face, while she presses the child's chest with both hands.

The girl seems bound in her jacket. It must be too tight, constricting her.

Anna flicks up the zipper tab and pulls it, thinking of bolting out into the front yard and flagging down a car. But there is no traffic. Not down here at the end of the road.

Get the charger from upstairs, plug it in, and call.

The orbs of the girl's eyes quiver behind shut lids as the coat opens up.

Anna starts, electrified by hope.

A twitch of movement inside the woolly cocoon of mittens as though something contained within has given a little jump.

Anna gasps, pulls off the mitten. "Yes, yes ..."

Little fingers trembling, the pointer and pinky shorter than the others, smoothed over at the tops and missing fingernails.

Then the girl's lips part.

A few seconds later the sweet release of a single breath.

Anna laughs with joyful relief, invigorated by a barely containable desire to scream out, "Thank you!" She rubs the girl's face, brings the little fingers to her lips while witnessing two eyes slowly open to stare up at her in innocent wonder.

The Embryo: Day 25, Week 4

Floating freely in the amniotic sac implanted in Anna's uterus, the embryo secretes hormones that drift away in wisps and slowly mingle with blood, carrying the signal to shut down Anna's menstrual cycle.

"Hi." Anna raises the girl's head onto her knees, cups her palm to the girl's face. "Are you okay?"

The girl stares at Anna with big eyes, seemingly out of proportion to her head, then slowly shifts her attention to Anna's belly.

Anna laughs with incredible delight while the girl rolls onto her side, lazily sits up, her snowsuit making the fabric's signature sound, and stares at Anna.

"You remember me?"

The girl leans forward, slips her arms around Anna's waist, and holds on.

"It's okay," says Anna, stroking the girl's wet hair. "We'll call your father. He must be worried." She tilts her head to peek at the girl for reaction. "Do you know your number?"

The girl remains silent.

Anna thinks the child might be asleep until she sees her eyes shifting slightly, yet fixed on nothing, her lips parted, her ear pressed flush to Anna's belly as though listening.

"Someone must be looking for you." Anna lifts the girl onto the couch. "We should call them ... Are you okay?"

The girl takes her time, studying each of Anna's features.

"Do you want some hot chocolate?"

Slipping her thumb into her mouth, the girl begins sucking.

"I'll make you some. Stay there. Just rest." Anna hurries to the kitchen but veers away to check the front door. Opening it, she searches out into the night for a vehicle.

Not a sound.

The road is deserted.

"Hello?" she calls in case someone might be searching on foot.

No sweep of a flashlight beam. No shouts of concern.

Anna turns to check the hallway, expecting to see the little girl standing there, wanting out, but the hallway is empty.

She shuts the door and glances into the living room on her way to the kitchen.

The girl hasn't moved. She gazes off into space while sucking her thumb.

Is she in shock?

Anna runs upstairs and collects a quilt from her bed, brings it down, and carefully wraps it around the girl. "Okay?"

The girl shuts her eyes.

Anna waits, watching the girl's chest to make certain she is still breathing.

Satisfied, she goes to the kitchen, takes down a packet of hot chocolate from the cupboard, then grabs a mug with a red heart on its side. She bought the box of hot chocolate at the supermarket in anticipation of warm solace after cold wintry walks.

While the kettle boils, Anna leans for another look into the living room. The girl cocooned in the quilt.

Alive.

Anna has saved her, saved her life.

The girl's parents must have missed her by now. If not, then why? How? Shouldn't they be outside, hands cupped around their mouths, calling out her name?

She brings the hot chocolate to the girl, who accepts the mug, holding it in barely capable hands.

"Careful, it's very hot." Anna sits on the edge of the couch, her eyes on the mug to ensure the girl has a secure grip. "Do you know where you live? Is it the house up the road?" She points in the intended direction.

The girl doesn't respond, as though she is mute.

Did the girl say anything when she was here earlier with her father? Anna has no recollection of a word being uttered.

"Your number." Anna retrieves the cellphone from the floor and shows it to the girl, yet the child gives no sign of recognition nor makes any motion to take hold of it. Anna has no idea of ages, but she guesses the girl to be between four and six. "I bet your father is worried. We should call him. Okay?"

The girl lifts the mug to her lips.

"Hang on. I'll put some water in there to cool it down." Anna motions to take the cup away, but the girl leans back, blows on the liquid, while continuing to stare at Anna.

Anna assumes the child must live close by. Otherwise how would she have made it this far in the cold?

"We should go look for your dad."

The girl slurps the hot chocolate.

"Come on."

Anna takes the mug from the girl, sets it down on the coffee table, and grips her little hand.

The child rises from the couch, her legs wobbly.

"I'll drive and you show me where, okay?"

The girl's attention is caught by the red-and-orange waver of fire through the glass in the woodstove. She keeps her eyes fixed there, her head turning as she tries to slow her step.

Anna coaxes the girl along, pulling on her arm, leading her down the hallway, then pausing to pull on a coat.

"You feeling okay now?"

The girl stares at her boots.

Anna presses her hand to the girl's forehead. It feels normal. "Let's go out." She opens the front door, guides the girl to the car, and buckles her in the passenger seat.

Did the man abandon the girl? It seems impossible. After all, he would know that Anna saw them together. Anna would be a witness.

She heads around to the driver's side.

Perhaps the girl wandered off from her house while the man was sleeping.

Could both the mother and father be so soundly asleep as not to notice their missing child?

Anna starts the car, puts it in reverse, and backs out.

"Do you live up this way?" Anna asks, nodding ahead at the black road.

The girl simply watches through the windshield, her bare hands joined together on her lap.

Anna needs to deliver the child safely to her parents, to be relieved of the responsibility, for she suspects the girl might be sick or damaged and is likely to get worse at any moment.

When she reaches her neighbour's house, Anna turns up the drive, examining each shadowy window while the car makes the long ascent.

There is no sign of a vehicle. No sign of tire tracks, even though the driveway has been cleared.

She parks and gets out.

Approaching the house, with dark trees looming around it, Anna gets the impression that it is unoccupied. Snow has banked up against the bottom of the front door. Regardless, she steps up and knocks, aware of the late hour.

Anna glances back at the passenger seat, the little girl's face barely visible above the dashboard. She knocks on the door again, this time louder and faster, her knuckles hurting in the cold. No one moves through the darkness within to answer.

Back in the car, Anna shuts the door and tries to reason with the girl. "Can you tell me where you live? Just point. That's all you need to do. Can you point for me?"

The girl stares straight ahead, ignoring Anna. She doesn't point.

Anna notices the girl's bare, deformed hands. So brightly pink and full of life now that they almost glow.

Frustrated, she turns the car around in the limited space and coasts down the incline. Taking a right, she watches the deserted Bareneed road stretching far ahead of her and pulls into the driveway of the next dark house.

Chapter Eight

The Embryo: Day 26, Week 4

A series of three ridges resembling fish gills appears on each side of the embryo's neck. These rudimentary crests will form muscles for facial expression and expand into the tongue, upper and lower jawbones, middle ear, and neck bone.

The defining slopes of the face become more pronounced as they stretch and elongate.

The brain and spinal cord are now the largest parts of the embryo.

Valves and dividing walls make the features of the heart more distinct. The heart beats regularly, sixty-five times per minute, thrusting its blood cells out into Anna's blood system.

Anna: March 15, Breakfast

The smell of fried eggs and bologna is turning Anna's stomach. Regardless, she can't pull her eyes away from watching how the little girl eats, the small, malformed fingers holding the bit of remaining toast, the tiny mouth working to take it all in.

Anna's breasts are exceedingly tender this morning. They hurt at the slightest movement, making her want to wrap her arms around them. At any moment she might need to rush to the bathroom to vomit.

The girl makes small noises as she eats. Chewing and breathing. The sound of breath in the hollow of the glass while she drinks her juice and watches the rose in the centre of the table.

The flower has opened completely. Its strong scent fills the room.

Last night, after knocking on the doors of three vacant houses, Anna felt far too removed to drive any farther. The houses seemed empty, their clapboard unusually dry, their structures unsound.

She imagined bringing the girl to the door of a stranger's house and letting the man or woman have a good look at her, trying to decide where the child might belong.

The undertaking began to feel so unseemly that Anna turned the vehicle around. All the while her mind told her to deliver the girl to the nearest police detachment in Bay Roberts. They would know what to do with the lost little girl. They were trained professionals.

Anna didn't want to hand the girl over to strangers.

But wasn't she herself a stranger?

The girl didn't seem to mind being with Anna.

What sort of stranger am I? she asked herself.

Driving back to her house, rounding a slow bend in the road, she was comforted by the sight of distant lights glowing from her windows, the only house lit in that otherwise black valley. Yellow light spilled from her kitchen windows and from her upstairs studio. A light over the front door illuminated dark branches of the dogberry tree in the yard.

Anna made up a bed for the girl in the small bedroom that was meant to be the nursery. She tucked the girl in, those quiet blue eyes remaining fixed on Anna's chest.

With the girl's silky red hair spread out over the pillow, Anna felt an overwhelming urge to peck the child on the cheek but held back, thinking this overly familiar gesture might startle the girl.

The child's eyes then drifted to a stack of books in the corner. Nursery rhymes and slim picture books Anna had bought at the same time as the pregnancy guide.

"Would you like a story?"

The girl scratched her nose and sneezed, the sound reminding Anna of a kitten sneezing, which further endeared the child to her.

Anna selected a book and sat on the edge of the bed. She read a tale of animals adrift at sea, while the girl's eyes grew heavier to the calming rhythm of Anna's words, her lids opening and shutting in slower undulations until fluttering shut for good.

After gently kissing the child on the forehead, Anna went to her own room, checked the mousetraps to find them empty, plugged her cell into the wall outlet, and climbed in under the covers. Sleep came easily.

Presently, the girl finishes off the last of her juice, then stares out the window. She nudges the lace curtain aside and lets her arms rest casually on the sill, her manner implying that the outer world is a mystery to her.

Anna clears away the dishes, occasionally glancing at the girl's back, the curls of her long red hair cascading down. Bent over the garbage, scraping off the bits of congealed yolk and toast crusts, Anna takes extra notice of how the refuse tumbles into the hollow. A repugnantly visceral sensation unnerves her as she places the plate in the sink and runs water over it. Watching what washes away, she retracts within.

The girl will have to be taken to the police. The longer Anna waits the more explaining she will be expected to do. She shouldn't be alone in the house with a child belonging to someone else.

If the police can't find her father, then where will the girl end up?

"I have to take you somewhere," Anna says.

The girl doesn't turn from the window, her eyes carefully checking here and there.

Anna should have rushed the child to the nearby Carbonear hospital. That would have been the appropriate thing to do. She sees this so clearly in hindsight. But she fears hospitals. She might run into Kevin there. From time to time, due to the shortage of gynecologists on the island, Kevin does rounds at Carbonear.

Her nerves are a mess. She thinks it must be her hormones — this niggling inability to make a rational decision.

What is the matter with the little girl? Has she been silenced by some form of trauma, or is she scared of Anna?

The girl slowly turns her head in profile.

There is a knock on the door.

Thank God, Anna thinks, hurrying out to the hallway. It must be the father, standing at the door in desperate, breathless search of his child.

But it isn't the father.

Anna sees in the glass that it is Mr. King, and he is holding another package in his hands. She opens the door.

"I thought it might be time to replace it," he says, leaning the package toward Anna.

From back in the kitchen there is the sound of Anna's cell vibrating.

"Come in." She turns and runs to collect her phone, hoping it might be Kevin with an apology.

The little girl holds the cell in the cup of her hands and leans her head over it. She watches the screen, her eyes shutting to the pulse of each vibration.

"I need that," Anna says, moving her hand near the girl's until the child reluctantly passes over the phone.

Anna checks the illuminated digits. The number for her lawyer's office. "Hello."

"Anna?"

"Yes."

"It's Patricia Dicks. How are you doing?"

"Okay." She hooks a length of hair behind her ear and glances at the kitchen doorway for Mr. King, who smiles and passes into the living room to leave Anna with her conversation.

"That's good. Sorry about this situation. I've had a copy of the summons faxed over from the plaintiff's lawyers. I can't see any grounds here at all. I've already made a call and indicated as much. Also, laid it on pretty heavy about slamming them with any number of countersuits."

"What did they say?"

"Unfortunately, they're not willing to back down. The lawyer's a bit of an asshole. Sorry."

"That's okay." Anna scans the room for the little girl, wondering where she has gone. She leans out the kitchen door, checking down the hallway. The front door is closed.

"We're not going to budge this guy."

"Why's that?" Anna asks. Is the little girl in the living room with Mr. King? She steps that way, but sees Mr. King's back where he sits on the chaise longue. If the little girl is out there, Mr. King would certainly be attempting to converse.

"He's an egotistical imbecile. I've spoken with the judge, another beaut, and of course he's refused to grant an extension, 'considering the time-sensitive nature of the case.' That's the bull he fed me. He's the worst sort of conservative bastard. Infamous for his opposition to lengthening rape sentences. Repulsive. So we need to go for a hearing, at least, on the twenty-eighth."

"What day is it now?" Distracted, Anna returns to the kitchen for the sake of privacy.

"The fifteenth."

"God! Is this for real?"

"I know. It's sick, isn't it? I wouldn't worry too much about it, though. It's a bunch of theatrics. I'd like to know what their real motive is. Publicity or something. It'll take months to get through the process, and then an appeal, if necessary. Public outcry will be pretty resounding. Your baby will be born before any of this is anywhere near being resolved."

Anna mulls over the information while watching out the window at the side yard. She expects to see an animal appear from the grove of evergreens behind the barn, but nothing shows itself. She wonders about the kinds of creatures living in the woods, secreted away in treetops or hidden in burrows. And where is the little girl?

She turns to recheck the kitchen. Nothing. The girl must have gone upstairs to her room.

"What we really need to worry about, though, is the press. They'll see this on the roster and make a beeline for the hearing. So we have to consider damage control. If it's okay with you, I'm going to speak with a colleague of mine in public relations."

"Damage control?" Anna's mind reels at the thought of her private affairs being broadcast across the country.

"Is that okay with you?"

"Yes, if you think so."

"Okay. I'll be in touch. Take care."

When Anna hangs up, she senses her body throbbing with rage. She hears a sound behind her and spins to see Mr. King in the kitchen doorway, trying his best to quietly unwrap the new rose.

"Sorry," she says, looking beyond him for the little girl. "Lawyers!"

"It's okay."

Anna opens her mouth to call out, yet she has no idea of the girl's name.

"What's the matter?" asks Mr. King.

"I don't know. Did you see a little girl going outside?"

"Little girl?"

"Yes."

The real estate agent watches her with interest. He shakes his head. "No. Whose girl is that?"

"I found her outside last night."

"A girl?"

"She was almost frozen."

"Really?" Mr. King searches over his shoulder. "And she's here?"

"Yes."

"What did she look like?"

"Red hair. Blue eyes. Do you know where she's from? I'm assuming it's near, but —"

"How old?" He opens the paper on the flower. The rose beaming a deep, velvety red. He crosses in front of Anna, heading for the table.

"Five or six maybe?"

"I don't think there are any children that age in this area. They're all much younger. You say you found her?"

"Yes, outside the door. Her father ploughed my driveway. A black pickup with a blade on the front."

Mr. King considers this information while drawing the old rose out of the vase.

"He must have left her … I can't believe …"

"I don't know that truck. Most of the houses out here are up for sale. And they need a lot of work." Mr. King slips in the new rose and proudly adjusts the baby's breath. "What should I do with this?" He holds up the wilted rose.

Anna shrugs.

"Do you want to dry the petals? Some people like to hold on to them, press them in a book as a keepsake. Strange practice, really. Collecting perished things."

"No, that's okay. Excuse me." She leaves the kitchen to check the living room. The girl isn't on the couch.

"I guess they preserve them that way," Mr. King continues, raising his voice.

Anna goes to the front door and opens it, leans out to search around. Shutting the door, she heads upstairs to check the nursery, where she finds a lump under the covers. It doesn't move. It remains perfectly still. How might it breathe without being smothered?

Reinventing the Rose

The Embryo: Day 28, Week 4

Arm buds sprout from the torso of Anna's embryo while the lenses in the eyes are brought into being.

Carefully pulling back the bedspread, Anna finds the girl curled into a ball, her eyes closed, napping. Smiling at the uncovered treasure, Anna straightens out the little girl, sets her head on the pillow, positions her limbs at her sides, and arranges the blankets around her. The child doesn't wake. After making certain everything is okay, Anna tiptoes out, quietly shuts the door, and returns downstairs.

"She's upstairs sleeping," Anna tells Mr. King with an apologetic smile. "I don't know what to do with her."

"What should I do with this?' asks the agent again.

"Just throw it in there." Anna points to the garbage, annoyed at the amount of attention Mr. King is giving the dying rose.

"You say she just appeared here? The girl."

"Yes, in the snow last night. Like someone abandoned her." She remembers how the girl fitted into the outline of the snow angel, her arms pointed away from her sides, her legs apart. Did some madman place her there like that?

Mr. King frowns and shakes his head, drops the rose in the garbage next to the refrigerator. "Who would do such a thing?"

"Crazy people."

"People not in their right minds," he mildly suggests. "People making wrong choices."

Anna gives his face stern consideration. A stranger to her. What does she really know about him? "By the way, did you leave a rabbit in my fridge?"

Mr. King chuckles, "A live one?"

"No. It was skinned." Anna folds her arms, feeling out of sorts. The call from the lawyer has shifted her mood, making her question the real estate agent's intentions. Why does he keep coming around? What is he really after?

"Yes, I did. Did you eat it yet?"

"No. I don't know if I can. Did you replace the rose when you were here?"

"Just now?" He tilts his head at the flower, notices the wrapping paper on the table, and crumples it into a ball.

"No, before," she says, raising her voice to an unintentionally hostile pitch.

"I guess I did." Mr. King looks away, a tremor in his lower jaw. He drops the paper ball into the garbage and adds, still without looking at her, "I think I better leave."

Anna watches his profile. The hurt expression. She doesn't offer an apology. Mr. King should go. Anna wants to be alone, to check on the little girl again, to make certain she is protected.

"Are you okay?" Mr. King asks, facing her.

"Yes." She sighs and flicks her hair back over her shoulder. "I'm sorry. Other than being pregnant, I'm fine."

"Really?" His concern is tempered by a smile.

"Yes, really. Without a doubt."

"Well, congratulations." Stepping nearer, he briefly rubs her arms.

"Thank you. The hormones are killing me, though."

"Not literally, I hope."

Anna laughs. "No … or maybe yes."

Mr. King checks his watch. "I better get going. I have a viewing soon. The house just next to yours, in fact."

"Really? I saw a light on over there the other night." Anna follows him to the door to see him out. "Must have been people checking it over."

The real estate agent sweeps his eyes across the walls, then up toward the ceiling trim. "Nice job."

"Thanks."

He opens the door and steps down, his boots scrunching against the snow. Taking his gloves from his pocket, he fits them on, giving them a tug at the wrists so they are snug. "What are you going to do about the girl?"

"I don't know." The chilly air prickles Anna's skin, giving her goosebumps. She wonders when the weather will finally begin to warm up.

"Did you want me to take her to the police? I have a friend there. That way, you won't be involved. You have enough on your mind." He glances at Anna's belly. Gives her a wink. Almost overly friendly now. When he smiles, wrinkles deepen at the corners of his eyes. "I could tell them I found her on the road."

Anna weighs the practicality of this suggestion. With the girl gone, a measure of stress would be eradicated. "That might help."

"Good." He tilts his head back, intently watching the second-storey window, his eyes searching there. "Bring her down."

A shudder runs through Anna. She folds her arms against the cold to drive it off. "Aren't you showing a house soon?" It is becoming increasingly difficult to keep the shiver out of her voice.

"Yes, but I can leave her in the car. Or, better yet, why don't I come back for her later?"

"She should rest for a while."

"Sure. I'll come back then."

"No, that's okay." Anna begins to close the door, wanting to keep the heat in. "I'll take her there myself."

"To me?"

"No, the police station."

"You sure?"

"Yes. I'm sure."

"Okay. Try not to worry too much." Mr. King peers at her

belly. "It's not good for the baby." His brow furrows in consideration. "You don't want anything to happen. There's a big risk of miscarriage early on." On that note of warning, he turns and walks away, his eyes scaling the front of the house for another glimpse of the upstairs window.

Anna shuts the door, rubs her arms for warmth, and jaunts upstairs to check on the little girl.

The call from the lawyer, coupled with the real estate agent's apparent change in temperament, has added freight to her already unsettled thoughts.

Approaching the nursery, Anna discovers the little girl on her knees, facing the wall. Paintings of butterflies and birds surround the girl's head, arcing like a coronet. Her left arm is raised and, with unerring command, applies minute, studied details.

The vivid figures are textured beyond lifelike, conveyed with amazing accuracy and lyricism.

In fact, the little girl appears to be an artist of astonishing ability for her age, or any age, for that matter.

Anna steps nearer, suspecting a trick of the light, yet the practised hand continues stroking, highlighting and shading with eerie meticulousness.

The images are simple and dignified, in the style of neoclassicism. The work of George Stubbs comes to mind. The anatomical precision, the subtle energy and ease with which Stubbs painted horses, lions, giraffes, and monkeys.

Anna gingerly lays a hand on the little artist's shoulder, intrigued by the smooth nubs of the girl's deformed fingers that awkwardly grip the brush.

The girl freezes, as though caught at something she has already been warned against, and remains breathlessly still.

"It's okay," says Anna reassuringly while studying the paintings. "Wow!"

Hesitantly, the little girl turns. Her eyes are shut, not against suspected admonition but in peaceful repose.

"This is amazing," Anna says with pride in her voice.

As though freed from a spell, the little girl breathes and faces the wall again to busy herself with her illustrations.

Chapter Nine

❧

The Embryo: Day 31, Week 5

Three ridges emerge in the embryo's head, giving rise to the midbrain, forebrain, and hindbrain.

The head now constitutes one-third of the embryo's length.

Brain cells appear at a lightning speed of approximately two hundred and fifty thousand per minute.

The kidneys begin developing, while the liver is rapidly producing red blood cells.

If touched near the mouth area, the embryo will quickly draw back its head and twist its body.

The heart's rhythm increases from sixty-five beats per minute to between one hundred and five and one hundred and twenty-one. The average rate for an adult is seventy-two.

Anna's embryo measures a fifth of an inch, the size of a kernel of corn.

Anna: March 20, the Neighbours

Anna has tried to take the girl to the police station, but once inside the car, the girl always undoes her seat belt, climbs out, and returns to the nursery to pick up painting where she left off.

For the past five days Anna has collaborated with the little girl to finish the nursery. The walls are covered in a sweeping panorama of depictions: dragonflies, giraffes, bumblebees, porcupines, crows, swordfish, horses, whales, monkeys … The images are linked in a compelling tapestry. Even the ceiling is crowded with a tribute to all living shapes and sizes that reminds Anna of a fresco in the dome of an ancient temple.

At night, after washing up, the girl settles in the bed beneath it all, her eyes shifting from creation to creation, her lips stirring as though in mute recital.

Anna sits on the edge of the mattress, watching while the child slips off to sleep. "It's done."

In the morning she decides to bring the little girl to the police station. She takes her time serving breakfast, aware that these are their final moments together. The days they have spent in each other's company are precious to her, for despite the girl's muteness, Anna has come to know her through gesture and expression.

Food is neatly arranged on the plate: one fried egg, a slice of bologna, and three wedges of orange.

When she puts the meal on the table, Anna notices splotches of various-coloured paint on the girl's fingers, which now appear perfectly formed.

She pulls up a chair beside the girl, takes hold of her hand, rubs her little fingers, trying not to let emotion overcome her.

The girl pays no attention to Anna. She eats hungrily, scooping up the food as though it is the last meal she will ever be offered.

Leaning back in her chair, Anna already feels an ache of loss.

After breakfast Anna leads the girl to the car. The child stays put this time, staring straight ahead through the windshield. Anna drives off, feeling sentiment well up in her again, for she realizes she has grown terribly attached to the passenger.

"I'll miss you," she says, glancing at the girl's profile. "I will." She touches the girl's hand to find it reassuringly warm.

When she arrives at the police station and parks the car, Anna waits behind the wheel, trying to build up enough courage to look at the girl. Doing so, she sees the little girl's blue eyes fixed on her face.

"Thank you very much for your help with the nursery."

The little girl barely nods. Her eyes search to one side, then the other, as though listening to hear more clearly. She raises one finger to point at the sky.

Anna gazes out the windshield. A huge brown-winged bird with a white head floats above.

Across the street from the station, cars pull over to marvel at the sight of the eagle. Traffic slows. A man gets out with a camera and tilts back his head.

Tears swell in Anna's eyes, and she laughs outright. "It's beautiful."

The girl continues pointing as the eagle drifts away.

Anna strokes the girl's hair. "You're going to be fine," she says, hugging her. "I'd keep you with me, but you're not mine to keep. It wouldn't be right. They'll find your mom." She leans away. "Okay?"

The girl shows no emotion, merely regards the police station.

Anna glances that way, her mind filled with uncertainty. Regardless, she knows she is doing the right thing. She will go in alone to see if there is a woman officer on duty. That sort of transfer might be easier on the child.

"Wait here, okay?"

The girl shifts her eyes to the sky again.

Leaving the car, Anna uses her remote to lock all the doors. The horn gives a veryifying toot.

The girl kneels on the seat, her hands on the dash, trying for a better view of what might be drifting overhead.

Inside the detachment, Anna faces a bulletin board with notices pinned up. A few small posters feature missing children. She scans them, trying to place the girl, but neither of the faces is recognizable. Anna approaches the information window, nervously searching the desks in the open office.

Three officers are present, all male. When one of them glances up to meet her eyes, she says, "I'm new in the area."

The officer smiles. "What can we do for you?"

"I was just … checking in."

The officer's smile widens. "Okay. Do you want some stickers for the phone?"

"Stickers?"

"With our number. Maybe a lollipop, too."

Anna realizes he is joking, but whether he is joking about both the stickers and the lollipop she has no idea.

The officer opens his drawer and pokes around. He removes a few items and comes over to her, laying stickers, pencils, and a key chain on the ledge.

"Thanks," Anna says, silently reading the officer's name tag. Constable Newell. He reminds her of someone. She thinks it might be the man who ploughed her driveway. But there is something different about this man, other than the fact that he is clean-shaven and not sporting a baseball cap.

If he is missing his daughter, he shows no sign of it. Wouldn't that sort of loss be evident in his face, every moment of the day? Anna believes that it would. Then again he might simply be a relative of the man in the pickup.

Anna gives her name. "I'm in Bareneed."

"Nice old houses down there."

"There are." She fidgets on her feet, wondering whether it is okay to tell this man about the little girl. She searches over her shoulder.

The constable is waiting for her to say something more, to state her real reason for entering the building.

Anna is about to reveal that she has a little girl in her car, perhaps the man's daughter, when the officer's radio makes a noise from his desk. Anna watches him go over to answer it, thinking that she should leave.

Too much trouble will rain down on her no matter how she explains the particulars.

She is digging herself deeper and deeper into a situation that is growing exceedingly difficult to rationalize. How will she answer the questions about keeping the girl for so long? The constable will want to know. Why didn't she notify the police at once? She might even be charged with child abduction.

Finally, she blurts it out. "I found a little girl."

Two of the other officers raise their heads from their paperwork to look straight at her.

Constable Newell finishes up his call and returns to the ledge.

"I found a little girl in the snow. She's okay now. She's in my car." Anna points in the direction of her car.

The officer appears both confused and concerned and steps off toward the door adjacent to the ledge, perhaps hoping someone has finally found his missing child.

"She's in my car," Anna repeats for the sake of clarity while anxiously showing him the way.

The officer follows her out.

In the parking lot the girl's head isn't visible. She is too small or has slumped over, fallen asleep during the wait.

But as Anna nears the vehicle, she discovers, with new terror, that the passenger seat is empty. She makes a frantic noise and begins searching around, wanting to call out the girl's name.

"She's gone." Anna turns to Constable Newell, who is facing her directly. One of the other two officers comes out of the detachment door, pulling on his jacket. Another officer appears from the back parking lot.

"Pat, you see a little girl in the back lot?" Constable Newell asks.

The arriving officer stops dead in his tracks and glances around. "No. Why? What's going on?"

Newell checks Anna's face. "What did she look like?"

The other two men regard her, as well.

"Long red hair," Anna says. "You can't miss her."

"Red hair?"

"Yes," she says, waiting for him to be struck by the realization that his own missing daughter has red hair. But he gives nothing away.

"Have a look around the building," Newell tells the other men.

Anna turns to scan the main road beyond the wire fence. She searches the street, then checks the sky for the eagle. Did the girl leave to chase after the bird? Cars steadily go by. The little girl might have climbed in with any one of the drivers, her arm insistently pointed toward the sky.

"Long red hair," Anna says again to Newell.

"Yes, you said."

The two other officers return, shaking their heads. "Nothing there."

"Put out a call."

One of the officers nods and heads for the station.

The other officer stands with his hands on his hips, studying Anna's vehicle.

A flock of birds drifts toward them in the sky. It sways and swirls overhead like the persistent flickering of an image trying to make itself known.

The officers pay no attention, simply waiting for the noise to pass.

"We'll need more information," says Newell.

"Okay."

"Come inside."

Newell leads Anna back into the station, through the door adjacent to the information window, and to his desk.

She takes the spare seat, feeling as though she is in terrible trouble.

The constable listens intently, jotting down notes while Anna describes the girl in exact detail. The officer asks questions in a detached manner, inquiring about dates and times.

As expected, the most worrisome question posed to her is why she didn't bring the girl straight to them.

"I thought she needed protecting."

"Protecting from what exactly?"

"Whoever abandoned her," Anna says, her eyes probing the constable's face for the slightest telltale sign of admission.

The Embryo: Day 33, Week 5

Anna's embryo begins to move inside her watery home.

The esophagus forms, framed by right and left lung sacs, as the intestines continue to lengthen, growing so fast that in a matter of days they will bulge into the umbilical cord.

The upper limbs elongate into cylindrically shaped buds, tapering at the tips that will eventually form hand plates.

Nerve distribution, innervation, begins in the arms.

Pulling into her driveway, Anna watches the barn. She would like to start painting out there right away, but the space requires insulation and wiring for light and heat. The next time she sees Mr. King she will ask for the name of a handyman in the area who charges a reasonable rate. She will also need to apologize for her curt behaviour.

But before Anna can afford to sink money into renovations, she will have to sell a few paintings.

With the little girl gone, she feels strangely guilty, as though a judgment has come down on her. She wonders if the police have found the child yet, or if they have even bothered searching.

According to Constable Newell, there have been no reports of missing children in the area. Regardless, he pledged to check with St. John's and to submit a query to the national computer database of missing children.

In the spare bedroom Anna sets up her easel, paints, a tub of brushes, and one of the flesh-hued rose canvases she brought along from her studio. Conveniently, the bedroom was empty when she moved in, the only unfurnished room in the house, as though the previous owners expected the new occupant to require an area of uncluttered space.

The room has two windows, the first offering a view of the long, tree-shrouded road that leads out of Bareneed, the second, on the back wall, overlooking the facade of the barn.

Within the centre of the flesh-hued rose, Anna imagines re-shaping the innermost petals into the curved walls of a barn. It is an interesting concept, but one that doesn't fully convince her. She lifts the painting down and sets a blank canvas in its place.

The need to start something fresh.

Squeezing out dollops of paint on her palette, she whisks her brush around in the Mason jar and flicks water from the bristles. She blocks in the background with ultramarine blue, then switches brushes and dabs at a blob of iridescent pewter. Leaning forward, she applies paint not in smooth strokes but in expressive and descriptive marks meant to signify scales.

The spontaneity of what courses through her outlines a swimming fish. One fish and then another, and another, head to tail, until there is a massive, silvery school that bleeds over the edges of the canvas.

With her eyes on the gill slits, Anna scratches the bristles around in a blob of Persian rose and applies several wide, curved brushstrokes over a fish head. She highlights those lines with broader, longer strokes of alizarin crimson, then shadows those marks with three strokes of lamp black. Building and blending the colours deeper and richer, she finishes off the figure by accenting the edges and tips with canton rose until a blazing red rosebud has replaced the fish head.

This one will sell, she tells herself, struck by the mystery of what passes through her to guide her hand, the dexterity of feeling required to duplicate reality seeming to have less to do with her and more to do with the playing out of an intuitive process.

While working on each of the rose-shaped fish heads, Anna loses track of time until the energy progressively drains and the exactness of her vision flattens and dulls.

Feeling hungry, she straightens away her paints and brushes and goes downstairs to find her cell. Not a single message. Neither the lawyer nor Kevin has called.

With the little girl gone, Anna feels exposed and forgotten in the house. She would like some company and thinks of Mr. King. He hasn't returned for a visit. Anna considers calling him to apologize. She also feels, as she has for days now, that she should definitely contact Kevin to seek a truce.

She has always been one for reconciliation, just like her mother. She wishes Kevin no ill will. If he doesn't want anything to do with her, that is perfectly fine. She will settle for closure. If she has to sign papers freeing him from paternal obligations, then she will. Anything to get it done with and avoid the humiliation of appearing in court.

What are the fish swimming toward?

The image of a single light bulb comes to mind. Illumination in one room in a house at night. The school flickering in an undulating flash of silver toward the glowing orb.

Where is the girl now? Anna's thoughts shift to Constable Newell. He gave no indication of the child having been with him. No mention of his ploughing her driveway, either. Anna was almost one hundred percent certain that it had been him. Perhaps he wasn't permitted to bring up his personal life when dealing with someone in a professional capacity.

Mr. King mentioned people coming to view the house nearest hers. Were they out on an earlier visit and lost their daughter? The man in the pickup might not have been Constable Newell at all, but a potential buyer, the man sightseeing around the area while his wife had a better look inside the house. This explanation makes perfect sense. Yet wouldn't they have noticed that their daughter wasn't in their truck when leaving Bareneed?

How is it possible for a parent to care so little as to lose a child?

Anna goes out into the hallway and pulls on her coat and gloves. She needs to take a break, to get outside in the fresh air.

Or did the pickup crash on the family's way home, the parents killed, the traumatized child crawling out of the twisted vehicle to wander back numbly to Anna's house. She should have asked Constable Newell about any recent car accidents.

Leaving the house, Anna is chilled by the biting cold and decides to walk instead of drive; the air will clear her mind. What she sees of her surroundings is certain to be singular on foot.

She wanders up the road, searching the trees for movement but spotting nothing. Mightn't the little girl have made her way back here and hid somewhere out of sight in fear of some pursuer?

Before she realizes, Anna is near the neighbour's house. She stops to stare up the long driveway. Fresh tire tracks lead to a car the same make and colour as hers. It rolls to a stop close to the house but remains idling. The driver's door opens and a woman gets out. At once she turns to the back door and opens it, reaching her hand in.

Anna sees pink snow boots appear.

A tingle courses through her.

The police must have found the girl, and the woman has finally retrieved her.

What sort of mother would have taken so long to go looking? Is she an alcoholic or, possibly, suffering from some debilitating illness such as depression?

The girl's mother gently guides the child away from the car door and shuts it.

It seems that the girl isn't the one Anna took care of. This one has long black hair that runs down the back of her snowsuit from the bottom edge of her woollen cap.

The girl stays put, facing the trees. Her posture lends the impression that she is helpless, awaiting instruction or guidance, while the mother leans in the driver's door.

At this distance the girl appears to be the same age as the other little girl.

The mother retrieves an overnight bag from the car. Slipping the strap over her shoulder, she says a few words to the girl and vigilantly turns the child to face the house.

They both stand there, mother and daughter holding hands, made insignificant by the size of the house. A house in shambles. Snow on its rooftop. Cold seeping in through its loose windows. Anna pictures the interior full of mould, paint blistering and hanging in patches from the walls, the steps on the staircase broken or missing planks. A structure made unstable by neglect.

The mother walks ahead, guiding the girl, who moves with a cautionary air as though she might be blind. The daughter is led to the front door by the mother, where they both enter and disappear.

The sound of the closing door booms in Anna's ears. She takes a few steps up the driveway for a better look. The car remains idling, warm inside. She checks the road. If someone should drive by, what would they think of her standing there like a stalker out in the cold?

Anna has a feeling the girl is, in fact, the same one, and the mother has merely dyed the girl's hair to conceal the young one's identity. Has the woman run away from her husband and taken their daughter with her? Wouldn't the police have been alerted? Not if the woman murdered her husband and hid his body in a secret place before fleeing.

In time the front door reopens and the mother appears alone on the threshold. Without pausing she steps out, shuts the door, and with head bowed, hurriedly strides to her car as though not wanting to be witnessed leaving the house. She climbs in behind the steering wheel and waits, watching the front door with a pained expression. What might be her next move? Her head lowers until it rests on the steering wheel.

Anna moves two steps up the driveway, thinking of offering the woman assistance. But then the mother raises her head as though alerted. She turns to reach for the passenger seat, lifts an item in both hands, sets it on her lap, opens the door, and steps out of the car.

The woman carries a vase of red roses to the doorstep and kneels, putting it to rest. After a spell of reflection, she shuts her eyes, waits several moments longer, then stands to return to her car. She shifts the transmission into reverse, backs up, and swerves around.

Racing down the driveway, the mother whips past Anna, ignoring her neighbour completely.

The Embryo: Day 33, Week 5

The nasal plate in Anna's embryo sharpens in feature, becoming clearly recognizable.

A section of the forebrain, meant to be the largest portion of the mature brain, begins to grow. It will coordinate speech, communication, movement, sense of smell, memory, and emotion.

Four major subdivisions of the heart are now clearly defined and fill with blood and plasma.

~ ❦ ~

Mr. King has been by again to refresh the rose.

While the gesture once seemed charming, Anna is beginning to find the man's recurrent, often unseen presence unnatural. She wonders if he will continue to replenish her rose every few days. His persistence is ridiculous, annoying, and even a bit pathetic.

To busy herself, Anna makes supper, her shoulder aching from where she tried to break down the neighbour's door. Her leg, still on the mend from the accident, begins to cause her grief. She must have banged it against the door when plunging ahead.

Working over the stove, her thoughts are elsewhere.

Anna moves the canned meat around in the frying pan, then leaves it to check the kitchen window, her eyes going to the house. She pictures the black-haired girl in there, standing alone, or hiding between the damp, ribbed walls, waiting for a rescuer to lead her out, growing more and more frightened as night begins to close around her.

Losing her appetite, Anna slides the pan off the damper and goes upstairs to resume detailing the fish heads. She works in a fit of energy that approaches frenzy until the room fades to darkness and her eyelids grow heavy.

She switches on a light over her canvas, the colours lurching to life.

She thinks of the red-haired girl, the black-haired girl, and looks at the windowpane, the room in reflection with her in its centre.

Anna stares, transfixed, a woman, a stranger, posed with a paintbrush in her hand, finding it difficult to pull her eyes away from her own oddly detached image.

The tenderness in her breasts and nipples prevents Anna from sleeping. Whenever she rolls over, she is startled by the pain.

Her thoughts are haunted by memories of the woman and little girl entering that ominous dwelling. The mother leaving, driving by Anna without giving her the slightest bit of attention. Anna took down the licence plate number on the small sketch pad she always kept in her pocket, then hurried up to the house to check on the girl.

The door was locked.

She listened for a girl's voice calling out in distress from within, but there was nothing. She knocked loudly, wishing there was a window in the old slatted door she could peer into, wondering desperately what might have become of the little girl.

When no one answered her knocks or shouts, she tried to break down the door, the force of which only caused harm to her shoulder and toppled the glass vase, shattering it against the rock step and leaving jagged slivers pointing skyward.

She kicked the roses around, scattering the red petals that flickered over the snow.

Unable to enter the front door, she rushed around the house, peering at windows, cupping her gloved hands, and staring in to see rooms filled with old floor and mantel clocks, embroidered rugs, and vintage furniture.

No sign of the girl standing or seated anywhere.

At the back of the house she looked in through a smaller window to see a wall beaten out in a porch. A flash of movement between the beams evaded her on closer scrutiny.

Anna took her cell from her pocket and punched in the emergency number but suddenly shut the phone, fearing she might be dragging the police out there for nothing.

Wasn't it possible the little girl was in the car with the mother, had entered from the passenger side without Anna noticing? Hadn't there been some sort of bundle secreted away in the passenger seat when the car had sped past Anna?

Dragging the police out there to search for another abandoned girl would cast a shadow of suspicion over Anna. What would the police think of her then? Would they assume she was some sort of perverse deviant with aspirations to lure little girls into her house?

Lying in bed, Anna wonders where the man, the father, might have been. This train of thought leads to recollections of Kevin. How can he not care about his own baby? Emotion wells up in her, and tears warm her eyes. There were times when they were so wonderfully at ease with each other, moments when their compatibility evoked such vast affection and contentment that Anna would brim with the joyful expectation of having a baby with him.

Rather than bringing them closer, as the pregnancy was intended to do, it has gouged a barren gulf between them.

Is this the absolute end of their relationship? The lawsuit is a horrible bridge burner, the court hearing in eight days. Plenty of time for Kevin to take it all back. He might even be regretting his actions at that very moment. After all, he does have a tender side. It was one of the qualities that endeared him to her and convinced her he would make an excellent father.

Since coming to this house, Anna has rarely felt alone or lonely, but tonight she experiences a throbbing void. She touches her belly, slips her palm back and forth, the motion calming her near to sleep until she has the impression of ever-so-gentle pressure skimming over the entire surface of her skin, as though small hands are exploring her body.

She wakes, staring at the moonlit ceiling, tingling.

Restless, she climbs out of bed, troubled by the biting cold in the house. She grabs her bathrobe from the back of the vanity chair and pulls it on.

From her window Anna watches the sea. It doesn't inspire her, but weighs heavy on her mind, its presence capable of so much destruction. What if the land should tilt and dump all the houses into the water? Anna submerged in it, thrashing around, sinking, her lungs filling up with water.

Drawing the robe closer around her throat, she notices

shadowed movement along the edge of the treeline across the brook. A creature advances with the sleek, fluid actions of a cat. But it is much larger than a cat, its ears tapered to high points, the ends of its thick paws furry.

Anna expects its head to turn and gaze up at her, yet it gives her no notice.

Smoothly angling to the incline of the bank, the lynx leans to drink from the brook. Satisfied, it raises its head and crosses over, striding like liquid silence up onto the road and into her yard before disappearing around the corner of the house.

Anna moves through the hallway into her workroom to search out the side window. Nothing there. She tries the back window.

The lynx passes in front of the barn, heading for the ocean side of the house.

Anna hurriedly returns to her bedroom to check the front window.

The lynx circles the dogberry tree, attentively scouting its branches before continuing on.

Remaining in place, Anna anticipates the lynx's return, but it doesn't make another pass. Where has it gone? Back into the woods? Or is it waiting for her somewhere on the grounds of her house?

Sighing, she brushes her hair back over her shoulders and glances at the two mousetraps, the blobs of peanut butter eaten from each trigger. Not one of them set off. Something too small, too light to snap the traps, has been feeding there.

She returns to her studio to stand in the dark, imagining the lynx prowling beneath her while she watches out the side window.

The black square of her neighbour's house is visible through the trees.

A light appears there, catching Anna's breath.

The light flicks off, flicks on again, continuing in this pattern, beating out a steady rhythm.

An electrical problem, Anna suspects. Faulty wiring.

She hopes the house won't burst into flames.

Chilled, she goes back to bed with her bathrobe on and shuts her eyes while trembling beneath the covers. There is nothing in the neighbour's house. No black-haired girl. Anna has already checked. And, besides, these aren't her problems. She has plenty of her own to occupy her.

Pulling a spare pillow close to her chest, she tries to forget the flickering light and the lynx stalking around her house. What other creatures secretly roam beyond her walls? For all she knows the night-shrouded, moonlit land might be crowded with a procession of the most remarkable, undiscovered animals.

She listens for sounds of movement in the walls.

All is silent.

She takes a series of deep breaths, each slow exhale sinking her deeper into the pull of sleep.

The Embryo: Day 34, Week 5

The slight stub of a tongue protrudes from the back of the oral cavity in Anna's embryo.

On both sides of its head, the smooth swelling of an external ear materializes.

"Anna?"

The voice trembles through sleep; a sound from somewhere removed. The glistening trickle of a creak, or the rustling of dead leaves in the wind, convoluted to mimic her name.

Anna wakes with a start, listening, trying to hone her hearing, her fingers grabbing at the bedsheets.

"Anna?" A tiny, faraway voice.

She throws back the covers and hurries downstairs, expecting to see the red-haired girl lying in the snow.

Instead, there is a small hand pressed against the glass in the door, the lifelines shifting as the palm slides down, smearing the condensation.

A white face rises into view, dark eyes blankly watching straight ahead at Anna's chest. It isn't the little girl with the red hair, but the girl with black hair, standing on tiptoe on Anna's doorstep. Her eyes remain fixed, unmoving, while her lips part to quietly sing out, "Anna?" Her voice is dulled behind the barrier.

Anna yanks open the door. Squatting, she examines the girl's bloodless face, the undersized eyes unknowing. "What's the matter?"

"Anna?"

"Yes," she gasps. "What?"

The girl smiles in a melancholic way, uncovering her crooked teeth, her head tilting languidly as though slowed by water. "I'm lost, Anna."

"No, I know where your house is." Her eyes search beyond the girl, checking the looming blackness of trees across the road. The rustling of limbs as though something might be thrashing around there. The memory of the lynx jolts her heart. A snapping behind her, thin metal against thin wood. She casts a look that way. A trap going off upstairs.

"I'm lost."

"Come in out of the cold." She takes the girl's chilly hand and guides her up over the threshold. "Where did your mom go?"

"I don't know," the girl replies in a confounded tone, her palm out in front of her as though to sense possible obstacles.

"I'll get my coat and bring you home." Fearful of the lynx, she quickly shuts the door and double-checks out the window.

"Anna?"

"How do you know my name?"

"The man from the house."

"Which house?"

"The one who sells houses."

"Stay right there. I'm just getting on my coat and boots." She takes her coat down from the hook by the door.

Upstairs, the trap flicks against the floor, metal rattling off wood, followed by squeaking.

Anna struggles to fit her coat over her bathrobe, hoping the trap will be still, but it continues to flip around. She bends to pull on her boots.

"I have to check upstairs," she tells the girl. "I'll just be a second." She takes the stairs and enters the bedroom, halted by the sight of a mousetrap in the middle of the floor. A mouse caught by one of its back legs and part of its rear body. It raises its head, its minute front paws trying to scamper away. Squeaking louder, it stretches stiff as though to flee as Anna approaches and leans down.

"Where is she, Anna?"

Startled, Anna looks up to see that the black-haired girl has followed her without making a sound. "Who?"

"My mommy?" The girl stares straight ahead, oblivious to the undersized calamity on the floor. "I don't know what she looks like."

Anna regards the mouse. It is alive. Not horribly injured, yet enough of its body is dented by the thin bar to have exacted internal damage. A slow death. It must be in pain. The sight of the mouse's face troubles her. Its black eyes gaze up as it struggles to pull free and squeaks more frantically. Perfectly alive, except for the injury. Its movements as light as a feather.

She lifts the trap.

The mouse dangles, raising its head and front paws as though to right itself.

Anna carries the trap down the stairs, out into the living room.

The mouse opens its mouth and squeaks, the beads of its black eyes glistening while they watch her.

Anna flicks on the light over the back door and goes outside. The snow is brilliantly white beneath the glow. She lays down the trap and carefully lifts the bar from the mouse's dented body.

At once the mouse tries running off but falters to one side. Unable to escape, it squeaks helplessly and stares around, freezing as Anna leans nearer. The mouse's heartbeat is the only movement beneath its grey fur.

"Where's my mommy?"

Aware of something prowling around, out of sight, Anna notices the dark tip of a rock poking up from the snow. A weapon. She quickly pries it loose and crashes it down on the mouse's face.

"Where is she?"

When Anna lifts the rock, a thick drop of blood slowly leaks from the mouse's nostrils. It rounds out so far before stopping. The blood is so deeply red that it is practically black.

The mouse writhes briefly in a life-negating twist before it is utterly still.

The sight of the blood beaming against the snow alerts Anna to the reality of the kill. The immobility of the mouse is final. It is no longer filled with agility and downy lightness but is made heavier by death.

"Anna?"

"We'll find her." Tears rim Anna's eyes. She swallows, overcome by the child's forlorn uncertainty. "Go inside. It's okay." She stands and watches the mouse tremble, flicker, then rise with its crushed face to dart off across the snow.

"How will we find her?"

"I have her licence plate number." The back of the house blurs. She swipes at her eyes. "Don't worry."

"I think she left me, Anna."

More tears flow over Anna's face. "It's okay." She smears the tears away with her palm. "Shhh, please." Crouching, she strokes the child's hair and shuts her eyes to blind herself. "It's okay, sweetie. We'll find her. We will. Let's go."

Making a dash for the car, Anna catches sight of the lynx pawing at snow by the side of the barn. Its ears prick up and its head pivots. In an instant it is bounding for the car.

Anna drags the child along. Breathless, she reaches the car, climbs into the back seat, and lifts the girl over to make room for herself. She slams the car door shut.

"What's the matter, Anna?"

"Nothing."

"Something's after us."

"No, it's okay." Frantically, Anna checks the windows, expecting the slap of paws to thud against glass.

"It wants to hurt me. It has claws, doesn't it?"

Anna's eyes flick from window to window. Sweat rises on her scalp and at the back of her neck as she straps the little girl in, the buckle clicking. She tugs to make certain the belt is secured.

"It has sharp teeth and a mouth that swallows."

"It's okay." Climbing between the two front seats, Anna awkwardly inserts herself behind the wheel. She switches on the headlights. No sign of the lynx in the yard. She peers at the rearview mirror while backing up, catching part of the girl's face in reflection. One of the girl's blind eyes is trained on Anna's seat.

Anna drives up the road, already fearing the mother hasn't returned, her stomach aching with dread. She can't understand what is happening with the little girls. To steady her mind, she glances at the rearview again to make certain the child is actually there.

"Anna?"

"Yes?" She scans around the car for the lynx.

"Would you like to know my name?"

"Yes, I know. I should have asked. I'm sorry." Her hands tighten on the steering wheel. "Please tell me."

The girl says nothing.

Anna shoots a look at the rearview to see the child's head

turned to watch out the window, the landscape drifting by. How does the child sense movement, travelling in a vehicle with no idea where it might be going, unaware of any oncoming calamity?

"Little girl?"

"Yes?" The girl turns her head to face around front.

Anna licks her lips, blinks to make certain she is awake. "You were going to tell me your name."

"I was just thinking."

Anna's eyes flash from the rearview to the dark, empty road that stretches and winds far ahead of her.

Above the road the low sky is black and brooding. A storm coming on, about to smother them with the weight of billions of snowflakes.

"I don't remember, Anna."

Anna scoffs at the silliness of this statement. Again she licks her lips. "You must remember, sweetie. How could you forget your own name?"

Once more the girl faces the window in silent observation, as though sensing the inescapable progression of the vehicle transporting her to places unknown. "You know what, Anna?"

"What?"

"I don't think I have one."

Chapter Ten

The Embryo: Day 36, Week 6

The impression of the mouth appears between the forebrain and jawbone in Anna's embryo.

Specific cells in the embryo's nasal disc begin to self-destruct in sequence, leaving two symmetrical dips. As more and more cells die in a predetermined chain, the dips turn to shallow pools that continue to deepen until, eventually, nostrils are formed.

Anna: March 23, Something Big

Three days later the nameless black-haired girl is still with Anna.

As anticipated, the house was deserted when she tried to deliver the child. Anna was forced to return to her own house with the girl in tow and rush through the front door in fear of the pounce of the prowling lynx.

Her attempt to bring the black-haired girl to the police station proved fruitless, for when Anna left the car to enter the detachment the girl vanished, only to mysteriously reappear later at Anna's house.

Anna gave the licence plate number of the woman's vehicle to the wary Constable Newell, and he assured her he would follow up.

"What about the red-haired girl?" she asked.

The officer avoided her eyes and plainly stated, "No new developments."

Since then she has heard nothing from the police.

Although she has come close to packing up and leaving Bareneed, Anna can't abandon the little girl. And she won't run back to St. John's with the girl in case the mother should return, having changed her mind about the desertion.

Anna suspects that transporting the girl anywhere beyond this place might be viewed as kidnapping.

To keep the girl busy, Anna lends the child some of her older brushes so that she might add markings to the hallway walls. The girl paints words instead of images in elaborate, elegant script while humming along to her brush strokes. "I see the moon, and the moon sees me." The girl stares into the nursery, her hand effortlessly looping letters: "The moon sees the girl I'd like to be."

"That's very good," Anna praises.

The girl smiles, turning her head to show Anna her black eyes, while her arm continues writing: "God bless the moon, and God bless the sea, and God bless the girl I'd like to be."

Anna tries working at her easel, half-heartedly dabbing the brush here and there, but thoughts of the impending court hearing in five days continue to distract her. There has been no update from her lawyer, and no contact from Kevin. She has given up on the idea of calling Kevin, feeling more and more spiteful and agreeing that a court battle might be the way to go so that this sort of offensive action won't be initiated against other women.

Wouldn't Kevin be publicly shamed once this came to light? Every woman on the planet would despise him. In fact, he would probably need to hire a bodyguard. And wouldn't his practice suffer? How could a pregnant woman put herself under his care, knowing he was set on having his girlfriend's pregnancy terminated against her will?

Stepping out of the bedroom studio, Anna is jarred by the sight of a large, uneven seep of red on the wooden floor. The little girl must have spilled an inordinately large quantity of crimson and run off to hide in fear of repercussions.

On the wall, written in red: "A is for Anna who drowned in her tears. B is for Betsy sliced thinly with shears. C is for Cathy sucked up in a storm. D is for Debbie now eaten by worms …"

The letters are sloppy, artlessly smeared over the classic script, as though applied with fingers.

Anna doesn't find anything redeeming about the creation. It is a mess that needs cleaning up. A difficult colour to paint over. The wall will require any number of coats of white primer to prevent the red from bleeding through.

She hurries down the stairway, wondering where the girl might have found a gallon of red paint. At the foot of the stairs she is paused by the brilliance beyond the front door — sunlight intensely radiating off snow. The storm, having hung in the sky without descending, has dissipated, leaving broken and scattered clouds.

Anna enters the kitchen, yet can't find the little girl. Where might she be hiding? In the cupboards with the food? Anna thinks to check there as her cell vibrates on the counter. Anxiously, she picks it up to read the number.

David at the gallery.

"Hello."

"Anna?"

"Yes."

"It's David." His tone is ever-enthusiastic. "How are you, hon?"

"Good. How about you?"

"I'm brilliant like a gemstone, as you know."

Anna smiles with familiarity while noticing a small red

handprint on the edge of the cupboard door. She bends to open it, expecting to see the little girl twisted up in there, her red-stained hands thrust out, waving in panic.

"Anna?"

"Yes." Nothing there except a box of cereal. Then the scurry of something pink, bolting along the back wall until disappearing into a hole so small that Anna can't believe it could fit through. A tiny mouse without fur.

She shuts the cupboard door and straightens.

"You okay?"

"I have mice."

"Yuck."

"Yeah, yuck."

"You should get a cat."

"I should." She imagines allowing the lynx into the house to bound loose on a rampage of extermination.

"You want to borrow Ludwig?" he asks, referring to the gallery mascot, named after Ludwig Knaus, one of David's favourite painters, who specialized in portraits of children. "Although I doubt he's much of a mouser. Pampered, fat old boy."

"No, thanks."

"I have a bit of good news. I've been getting a few calls from the media recently. Newspaper *and* radio."

"Oh?"

"It seems you're Miss Popularity. About time, I might add, because, as you know, I always believed in you. They've been asking for your cell number. I never give it out. Not until I talk to you first. Strict policy of —"

"Any idea what they want?" She opens one of the top cupboards. Cans of fruit, soup, and beans.

"They wouldn't say, Anna. What are you up to? Have you been struck by lightning? Assassinated anyone? Why the sudden interest? I searched the Internet but couldn't find your name in the list of recent lotto winners."

"No idea." Shutting the door, Anna turns and leans on the counter, her eyes scanning the ceiling.

"Should I give them your number?"

"No."

"Okay. That was fast, and a bit hostile, if I might add. Not that I'm offended. I don't offend easily. But is everything okay?"

"Yes, of course."

"That doesn't sound like you."

"It is me." She snorts scornfully, her hand unconsciously skimming over her belly.

"You used to preen for publicity. Have you lost your ego to the spring thaw?"

"Funny, David. Not much of a thaw yet."

"Where are you? I've been by your place. Are you avoiding me?"

"I bought a new house."

"Where? Hang on a sec."

Anna hears him calling off across the gallery, making some sort of witty remark to a possible client. She sighs at the scenario and finger-hooks a strand of hair away from the corner of her mouth.

"Okay. Where?"

"Out of town."

"Really. Hmmm."

"An old place."

"Spooky?"

"Very spooky." A laugh bursts from her so unexpectedly and forcefully that she needs to wipe her lips with her fingers.

There is silence at the other end.

"Okay," says David. "So you've gone all spooky. Is that what you're saying? I don't care if you've lost your mind. In fact, that often works out best for everyone involved. Speaking of which, when can I see some new pieces?"

"I don't know, David. A few weeks maybe."

"Perfect. And how are things?"

"Fine." She wants to tell him about her pregnancy. She wants to share. It seems like a secret that she holds too dearly. Why should there be apprehension about announcing she is going to have a baby? She should be telling everyone, complete strangers on the street. It is cause for jubilant celebration. "How's the gallery?"

"Ugly and depressing. I thought you were going to Italy with the baby doctor on a gallery tour."

"It didn't work out."

"Italy or the doctor?"

"Either."

"Ha. So be it. So no number for the press?"

"No." She adamantly shakes her head. "I'll tell you why soon."

"Fine, mystery lady. Bye-bye. Say hello to the spooks for me. I've got another call."

"See you." Anna shuts her cell.

The media.

David's voice fading.

The quiet of the house settling in around her.

Her picture in the newspaper. On TV. More disruption.

What do I even look like? She touches her face, feels a few pimples high on her forehead. She is hungry. She wants something particular to eat. What is she hungering for? She can't pinpoint it, yet she knows it is exactly what she wants, if only she could bring it to mind.

The furless mouse in the cupboard.

"Hello?" she calls, but there is no answer. "Are you playing hide and seek?"

Movement beyond the kitchen window catches her attention. She approaches the table and leans to move aside the lace curtain, her eyes trailing after a boy, no more than a toddler, completely naked and stumbling across the road. He falls on the edge of her yard, his grimacing mouth open, crying out, yet Anna can't hear a sound through the glass. She bangs on the windowpane to get his attention, her knuckles rapping so soundly that she fears the glass might shatter.

The boy glances back at the road while scrambling to rise and rush deeper into her yard as though in a fit of escape.

Not even boots on his feet.

Anna hurries for the hallway, snatching up her coat on the way out.

A few steps from her door she almost bangs into the man who ploughed her driveway. He jars her to a stop with his opened hands.

Rattled, Anna realizes that the man is, in fact, Constable Newell. The casual clothes can't disguise him.

"What's the matter?" The officer tries steadying Anna, but she pulls away and races around the corner of the house to catch sight of the boy.

She suspects the child has disappeared into the grove behind the barn. Running toward it, she searches for boot tracks but finds instead a trail of paw prints, the size of those that might belong to a lynx.

"Hey!" she calls out. "Be careful!" She tracks the prints to the treeline and stares into the tangle of limbs, leaning to discern the flash of pink skin. "Hey!"

Why is the boy naked? Is he running away from the police officer? And if so, why is he afraid? Did Constable Newell have the boy held prisoner in his pickup truck? She checks over her shoulder. The officer is taking his time crossing her yard, coming directly toward her. What has he done with the red-haired girl? What sort of cover-up?

A snapping of twigs underfoot from the woods compels her to rush in. Ducking to avoid the slap of branches, she shoves them away, their insistent cling trying to snag her body, frustrating every movement.

Twenty feet into the dense growth she pauses to look for a path. There is the smell of spruce needles and rot rising from the earth.

"Hello?" she calls.

Sounds of intrusion behind her.

Anna spins to see the officer forcing his way through the woods.

She must find the boy, shield him. She hurries on with the man gaining on her. Entangling limbs and roots thickly raised above the ground trick her feet. She stumbles with her hands out to protect herself while she finds her legs again.

The trickle of water up ahead.

Out of breath, she pauses, bent forward with her palms pressed into her knees, staring into a brook, noticing the glimmer of a tiny fish flitting near the surface, its scales reflecting light.

"What's going on?" a man's voice asks.

Startled, Anna turns to find the officer directly behind her, his bulk imposing.

He breathes through his nostrils while his eyes search her features before surveying the surrounding woods. "Did you see something? Another child?"

Anna won't tell him about the little boy. Two lost little girls, a lost little boy. She urgently scans the area.

"Nothing," she mutters. "Go away."

"What did you see?"

"What?"

"What were you chasing after?"

She checks the officer's face. "Nothing. A fox, I think."

"A fox?"

"Yes." She searches for a path through the trees. The way she came in. The way out.

What to do about the boy? He will freeze to death. But if he is running from the police officer, then his hiding place mustn't be revealed.

Anna's heartbeat quickens, pulsing in her throat. Her earlobes burn with heat despite the chill.

The officer's brow furrows in consideration. "Are you okay?"

"Yes." She veers around the officer, pushing through the impeding weave of growth that will hopefully lead to her house. When the officer leaves, she will resume her hunt for the little boy.

She glances back to see the man's shadowed form standing still. A blot against all living things. The officer must be gotten rid of. The shotgun in the barn. She should have bought a box of shells to fire shots of warning above his head. Get off my land. You have no right.

Struggling through the trees, she spots a clearing up ahead, her yard, and breathes easier once she is free of the crushing closeness of the forest.

The Embryo: Day 36, Week 6

Blood begins flowing through the newly divided left and right heart streams in Anna's embryo.

The relative width of the torso increases due to the growth of spinal nerve roots, muscular plate, and mesenchymal tissue, which contains branching cells that will multiply and compound until building bone, cartilage, and the circulatory system.

"We haven't heard anything about the missing girls," Constable Newell says while Anna attempts to act hospitable, going about filling the kettle for tea and taking down two mugs.

The officer has invited himself in under the pretense of updating Anna on the investigation. "We're also doing a search for repeat offenders in the area."

"Really?" She feels like a repeat offender, as though his words are meant to single her out. Or maybe he is actually the repeat offender. She drops a tea bag in each of the mugs. Her hand trembles, and she tries calming it. "Do you think they've been abducted?" This would explain the symptoms of trauma in the children.

"I don't know." The officer glances distractedly at the window as though expecting the reappearance of the little boy. "The problem is there haven't been any reports of missing children."

Or you've destroyed those reports, Anna thinks. She looks at him. What can anyone ever learn from the features of a person's face? She thinks of the little boy and wants to ask about the officer's connection to the red-haired girl. After all, the girl was in his truck. She was there. Anna saw the child with her own eyes.

"I checked that licence plate number."

Fussing with the sugar dish and milk jug, she asks, "And?"

"The woman who owns the car swore she didn't have a daughter."

Anna snickers and shakes her head. "And you believed her?" She turns to confront him, arms folded against her chest.

"No. I checked. She has no children."

"How do you know that?"

"I have access to records."

"Access to records? It probably wasn't even her child. It could have been her sister's, a neighbour's ..." Anna's attention is drawn to the ceiling. If the blind black-haired girl is still in the house, Anna hopes she will be quiet, for her own sake.

The officer shows interest in where she is looking.

Anna stifles a shout, "Leave her alone," and turns to the kettle, wondering what might be the most inoffensive way of bringing up the red-haired girl. "What's your daughter doing today?" she asks, trying to sound as nonchalant as possible.

The officer studies the rose in the centre of the table. It is wilted and bent, the red deepened to near black. He shifts his attention to Anna while the kettle boils, his eyes caught by the spout of steam. "Daughter? I don't have a daughter."

Anna smiles uncomfortably. "Really? Well, who was in your truck with you the other day? You left her —"

"In my truck?"

"Yeah, the other day when you ploughed my driveway."

"No one. I don't have a daughter." He sits up straighter in his chair. "Why? Did you see ..."

Anna turns as the kettle clicks off. She grips the handle, restraining herself from flicking the scalding water into his face. She shuts her eyes for a moment. Then she nervously pours the water into the cups. "Yes, I saw her."

"I really don't have any children. Really."

Anna bangs down the kettle, spins around, and throws her arms out at her sides. "So no one has any children. Is that it? God! This is ridiculous."

"What?"

"This is —" Her hands shoot up in frustration. "I don't know what's happening. The girl was in your truck."

"You said she was red-headed, right?"

"Yes. Long red hair." Anna touches her own hair as though in demonstration.

The officer mulls over the information, his eyes shifting and darkening.

"What?"

He shakes his head slightly. "Nothing."

Anna watches through the window in the door, unconvinced of the officer's professed innocence. The pickup backs out of her driveway and straightens in front of her house. There, in the passenger seat, is the red-haired girl, turned to regard Anna.

Anna grabs for the knob, throws open the door, and runs along the driveway in her stocking feet. "Hey!" she screams.

Out in the street, she waves her arms. But the truck is gone before she has a chance to capture the officer's attention.

Hurrying to her car, she pulls open the driver's door and climbs in to chase the pickup. No keys.

"Shit!" She bolts back into the house, fuming at the thought of the officer lying to her. Where are her keys? Why would he lie? How sick is he to have the little girl in his truck while pretending he didn't know her? What sort of twisted game is he playing?

The rattle of her keys. She snatches them from her coat pocket. Is it too late to chase the pickup? She would have to drive super-fast. Too dangerous. She should call the police to alert them that Constable Newell has the red-haired girl. But what if they are in on it with him?

A shiver jolts Anna's shoulders. She shoves the keys away and heads for the kitchen. Pausing in the hallway, she peers at her feet, then behind, the prints her wet socks have left on the floor trailing her in.

Did Constable Newell leave the girl out there while he was visiting with Anna, even warning the child not to come in, to hide on the pickup floor? If so, wouldn't he have tried to conceal the girl when he was driving away, when she was up on the seat, looking directly at Anna?

Anna refuses to believe a single word spoken by the officer. He is responsible. But what about the black-haired girl? What does he have to do with her?

"Hello?" She should look for the little boy. Perhaps he is with the girl.

The girl will bring him back here to safety.

Standing in the hallway, Anna feels a wet peck on the top of her head. She steps back and searches her hair with her fingers while scrutinizing the ceiling.

A dark drop squeezes loose from between the slats.

She checks her fingertips. Red.

The drop plummets to splatter on the floor in front of her feet.

The spill of paint in the upstairs hallway. She should have sopped it up immediately. Either way there will be a wide red stain on the floor. She thought the paint would dry and planned to peel it off in one rubbery, congealed piece.

Get rid of that stain.

What if someone should come across it? What might they think?

Another drop taps the floor.

While she collects an old dish towel from under the sink, she wonders about the little boy in the woods. He reminds her of a piglet. Is that what she actually saw? Someone's piglet let loose from its pen. Is that where it is hiding now? In her barn, where it knows its place?

She makes a noise of disbelief and opens the glass cupboard to take down a large stainless-steel bowl from the second shelf.

When she finishes cleaning the stain, she will look for the black pickup with the plough. Bay Roberts is only so big. She should be able to locate that truck. And when she finds the little red-haired girl with the officer, she will contact the police and tell them about the little boy, who she firmly believes is hiding from Constable Newell.

Once she proves herself right, she will return to St. John's.

She is *not* losing her mind.

A frantic feeling rises in her, trying to push through the top of her skull.

Grappling with the sensation, she runs water into the bowl and tightly shuts off the tap.

Her nerves spark and fire while she wipes away the drops of paint downstairs, then steps upstairs, calling out, "Hello?"

Her eyes linger on the framed lists of embroidered names. The print seeming even smaller than before. What sorts of fingers were capable of sewing such a size?

The stain outside her studio has deepened in colour, the shade and texture implying blame.

On her knees Anna tries soaking up the paint, smearing the red brighter, a compelling saturation that brings to mind a Francis Bacon background she once saw at the Tate in London. Or strips of sky in Edvard Munch's *The Scream*. Her mind disassembles the colour. A touch of titanium white and burnt umber swirled into cadmium red and highlighted with black. Layer upon layer of pigment to create tonal resonance.

She scrubs the red-drenched cloth back and forth, but as expected, the blot is unmanageable. The more she attempts to erase it the worse it troubles her, spreading beyond where it once was contained.

Using both hands, she works harder.

The mark has seeped into the texture of the wood, entering the grain.

Anna checks her hands, stained an intense red that calls attention to the lines in her palms. Startled, she looks up at the wall. Fresh letters frenetically scrawled there: "E is for Emily broken to bits. F is for Frankie scared out of his wits ..."

The barn is dim inside and holds the strong odour of animal hide and manure. The air is comfortable, as the day has turned mild. By the light drifting in from the single front window, Anna can see that the wide floorboards have been washed clean. She checks the shadows in the corners, remembering the shotgun and thinking to bring it into the house.

There is a quick patter across the floor in the overhead loft.

Anna darts a glance that way.

No fleeting shadows.

The lynx up there, Anna fears. No, the patter is too quick for an animal that size. She checks over her shoulder, scans the space between the barn and the house.

"Hello?" She steps in, purposefully heads over to the corner, and picks up the shotgun. It is heavier than expected, the steel solid. Pausing, she listens, holding the weapon for a sense of security, not having any idea how to open it. She searches the top and finds a latch. When she thumbs it aside, the shotgun breaks open. The chamber is empty. She stares into the barrel, then closes it, admiring the persuasive sound of the click.

Nearing the ladder, she inadvertently kicks an object across the floor. The red plastic tube of a shotgun shell, its rusty end spinning to a standstill. She bends and takes it in her hand, inspecting the hollow before slipping it into her coat pocket.

Anna grips the shotgun in one hand, begins climbing the ladder, conscious of the pain in her leg from the accident and, behind her, the throb of vacated space that she rises above.

It is an awkward task to climb.

She must rest to let the pain settle. Her recent dash through the woods must have strained her leg.

Continuing on, she shifts the shotgun to better manage its uneven weight. With her footing soundly placed on the loft floor, she feels more comfortable in taking stock of her surroundings. Strands of hay fall away from a mound that reaches halfway up the wall, uncovering a patch of pink. It might belong to a larger body or be a thing unto itself. A stuffed toy or a sponge ball.

Anna approaches it, sets down the shotgun, and kneels, flinching at the sharp ache in her leg from the pressure. Adjusting her position, she transfers the weight to her other side.

The patch of pink trembles in fits and starts, rustling the hay.

Anna reaches out to caringly press two fingerips to the warm texture. "Are you in there?" she asks, the pulse of pain in her leg fading to a low murmur.

"Yes," says a boy's voice, seemingly from higher up, cloistered around the ceiling.

"Are you the boy who ran into the woods?"

"Yes."

"Why are you hiding?"

"I have to."

"Why?"

"Because it's my birthday," the boy explains with a puff of breath, as though nothing can be more obvious. "I have to hide, so it won't happen again."

"What won't happen?"

"My birthday."

"Where are your clothes? Did someone take them?"

"No. I'm just in my birthday suit."

Anna smiles and tries brushing the hay aside with both hands, but the strands fall back to nullify her attempt. "You have to come out sometime."

"I'm not coming out. Not ever again."

"Okay, then." She plays along, thinking the boy to be a real jokester. "How old are you today on your birthday?"

"The same age I'll always be."

"That's not possible, is it?"

"How can you tell how old I am?"

"By looking at you. By your size."

"What if I'm too small to see?" The form shifts within the hay, and the patch of pink shrinks and varies in tint. "Maybe I'm a dwarf."

Anna chuckles. "Are you really a dwarf?"

"I'm very small."

"I saw you and you weren't so small."

"I keep getting smaller."

"That's not possible. You have to grow. It's what happens."

"Most things never change. They stay the same. Like the way you remember how things end."

"You don't sound like a little boy to me."

"That's because I never was."

Anna takes a right at the lights, veering away from the strip malls, fast-food outlets, and gas stations on the main thoroughfare in Bay Roberts. She keeps an eye on the cars and trucks coming toward her in the opposite lane, hoping to spot a black pickup with a plough.

The road she drives along soon skirts the shoreline. It is the picturesque route through the original community, with older, square fishermen's houses mingled with vinyl-sided suburban bungalows. Here and there a few rustic shops are still in business, their storefronts reminiscent of a time long ago.

A small corner store on the lower level of a house, a cola sign above its door.

Anna recalls a similar shop in Torbay, the converted bottom floor where she used to buy fifty cents' worth of mixed candy from old Mrs. Roach.

On her right she passes an engine repair shop in an orange paint-peeling garage, followed by a white rectangular building with a sign for the Royal Canadian Legion. It blocks her view of the ocean for a moment before the water reappears, the narrow bay framed by land rising to form low hills on both sides.

Farther out, at the head of the bay, the land drops away in ragged cliffs, a plain of steady deep blue stretching toward the horizon.

The Embryo: Day 36, Week 6

Blue retinal pigment materializes in the outer layer of the embryo's optic cup while lens fibres weave together and elongate.

A black pickup in a driveway to Anna's left catches her attention, alerting her to the task at hand. The truck, a huge, gas-guzzling four-door, has silver stripes on its side. It is larger than the one driven by Constable Newell.

Three houses down, two snowmobiles with FOR SALE signs stuck to their wind visors are parked on a lawn.

Anna passes a driveway with a bright yellow pickup, then, across the road, a dock where a cold storage building is built flush to the water. The storage facility reminds her of the barn. There would be fish inside, gutted and frozen to be shipped across the water. Living things raised or caught to be butchered.

No matter how much she pleaded with the boy, Anna couldn't persuade him to come out and show himself.

"I'm warm," he told her, shirking off the blanket she had brought out from the house and placed over the hay. "I'm safe because I've learned to look after myself."

Once she finds the constable and confirms he has the little girl with him, Anna is leaving. She has to verify this one fact for the sake of her sanity. But what about the little boy? She will need to check on him again before nightfall.

She is starving. She glances at the clock on the radio. 5:16 p.m.

Anna makes a left turn, ascending away from the water while studying the occasional pickup. She passes a church with an old graveyard at its side and slows as she comes across another road. Turning right, she checks her mirror, expecting to see a child's face watching her from the back seat.

Who should she contact about the little boy? Social services? They will take him and put him in a house not his own. Is that the best remedy for his situation? Isn't it only a matter of finding someone to care for him, as her mother cared for her?

Anna surveys the driveways while realizing that her ambling pace might be holding up traffic. No one behind her. She takes another turn, entering a street with a brick post office, an electrical supply shop with a lightning bolt on its sign. She passes a hardware store, a fenced lumber yard with an old mill centred in it. A flatbed truck parked there, loading up. This must have been the original street for commerce.

Cruising along at a leisurely pace, she scans the houses and driveways, turning down one side street after another, then retracing her course to make certain she hasn't overlooked a single lane.

While exploring she realizes that the old town is bigger than she believed and starts to doubt her judgment. There are just too many roads and houses. And what if Constable Newell doesn't live in Bay Roberts at all? What if he lives in one of the smaller outlying towns or coves in the area?

Shadows are growing longer in the streets.

She should go back to St. John's now. Forget about Bareneed. Leave it all behind.

But what about the little boy, and the black-haired girl? And what about the red-haired girl abducted by the police officer? At least she should bring them all to her house, feed them, put them to bed together, and tuck them in so they are nice and warm. She could read them a story about the animals singing in a boat at sea until their eyes drift shut in unison.

A burger comes to mind, and a milkshake. The mere thought of a milkshake freshens her outlook, elevates her spirits. Enough searching. She is eating for two now. She should be eating more, not less.

After making her way downhill, she finds herself facing the road that skirts the ocean. Guessing at her location, she takes a right. Her assumption that she is heading back in the direction of food grows unsteady as she recognizes nothing of her surroundings.

Finally, in a fit of relief, she spots the storage facility up ahead. Her stomach grumbles in anticipation. Farther on, she reaches the traffic lights and stops at a red. From there, much to her delight, she can see three fast-food outlets along the main thoroughfare.

When the green light mercifully frees her, Anna races for the first drive-through, pulls in, and orders a cheeseburger and milkshake.

"Cheeseburger with the works and a large milkshake," the voice crackles through the speaker. "Is that it?"

"I need onion rings." Her eyes flit over all the colourful pictures on the panel. Too many choices. She might want fries, too. They look crisp, salty, and delicious. Yes, definitely. "Fries." Before the staticy voice has a chance to review her order again, she blurts out, "And a caramel sundae!"

"Is that everything?"

No, not exactly, she wants to say. It is not nearly everything. How can it possibly be *everything*? Instead she flatly says, "Yes," not wanting her food delayed by a debate over the correct use of the English language.

Pulling out of the drive-through, her paper bag wafting lovely, warm, greasy smells, she digs for a few fries and crams them into her mouth. Cars pass before her as she waits for a break to re-enter the main road. Peering into the bag, she checks for her burger. There it is, wrapped nicely. Golden onion rings. Check. Her sundae, sweetly nestled in its transparent container.

Refocusing on the road while savouring the intoxicating goodness of the salty, fatty mush from another handful of fries, she notices, in the corner of her eye, a black vehicle passing in front of her.

Anna whips her head around to catch sight of the black pickup with the plough. The exact vehicle. Jamming her foot on the gas, she almost nails a white compact that swerves out of her way.

She mustn't lose sight of the pickup. It is there, up ahead, its tail lights flashing on, its right blinker light pulsing as the vehicle slows to turn into a grocery store lot.

"Aha!" Anna watches the pickup pull into a parking space.

She takes a quick corner to enter the lot, almost toppling her food bag. Her hand makes a frantic grab, saving it from spilling over.

Approaching the parked truck, she glues her eyes on the vehicle to see who gets out.

Constable Newell leaves the driver's seat.

Anna passes the truck just as the passenger door opens. She has to crane her neck to see who it is, but she can't determine the person's identity because the vehicle behind her pulls up alongside, blocking her view. Cursing a string of oaths, she quickly circles back and faces the entrance to the grocery store in time to see a red-headed woman following the officer.

"See!" Anna shouts, shoving another handful of fries into her mouth, then slapping the steering wheel. "See, red hair." Newly invigorated, she finds a space and parks, wiping her hands on her jeans. "Mr. Fetish Man with his red-haired obsession." She pokes around in the bag and pulls out her burger, unwraps it, and takes a bite. Chewing, she returns it to the bag and carefully rolls shut the top to seal the heat in.

Inside the grocery store Anna tries to calm herself. The brightness of the overhead lights is offensive and incites her. She feels highly sensitive to the glare. Coming across a deserted cart, she grips the handle with both hands, piling all sorts of fruit into it without even thinking while her eyes search for the couple.

They are not in the fruit and vegetable area, so she moves on.

Three aisles over she spots the officer and the red-haired woman far up the lane. They don't see her, so she circles up the next aisle to come back down the one they are at the head of.

When she takes the turn, she is put into immediate contact with the officer and the woman. Constable Newell sees the expression on her face, and his features darken.

"Hi," says Anna.

"Hi," the officer says in return, his greeting restrained and noncommittal.

Anna pauses while the red-haired woman glances at her, then at the officer.

Newell seems tongue-tied. He checks a row of instant noodles. "You got everything in this aisle?" he asks the woman.

"Yes," she says automatically, her interest in Anna.

Anna wipes her mouth, thinking there might be grease there from the fries or ketchup from the burger. As the constable awkwardly begins to move off, Anna asks, "You haven't got your daughter with you?"

The woman's brow furrows. After giving more attention to Anna's face, she then regards the officer for some sort of clarification.

Anna can't take her eyes off the woman, astonished at how much she resembles the little girl. The woman could be the little girl twenty-five years later. The similarity makes her angry, for

she feels she is being deceived. "Where's your daughter?" she asks.
"The red-haired little girl?"

The woman is bewildered, her lips fidget. "What?"

Anna can hear the woman's breath growing hotter.

"Please," says Constable Newell, raising a palm to her. "Just —"

"You're telling me you don't have a daughter. She looks just
like her." Anna thrusts a finger at the woman.

The woman's face tenses with added confusion. "Who is this?"

"Listen," says Newell, his eyes checking an elderly woman who
has entered the aisle. By the woman's side, a little boy clings to her
grocery cart, trying to steer it. "You need to calm down, please."

"Um-hm," Anna snips.

"What's going on?" asks the woman, noticing all the fruit in
Anna's cart.

"This woman thought she saw me with a little girl."

Anna doesn't like being called "this woman" nor does she
appreciate the tone in which the words were spoken. "He abandoned her near my house. She almost froze to death. But you've
got her again, haven't you?"

"I did no such thing."

"What's going on?" the woman demands, the pitch of her
tone rising, a warning muddled somewhere in it.

"There was a little red-haired girl. He abandoned her."

The woman says the man's name.

Newell shakes his head. "There was no one. Please, keep your
voice down."

Again Anna points at the woman. "She looked just like her.
Exactly."

Newell glares at Anna's finger. She thinks he might grab it,
bend it back, snap it in half. She lowers it.

The officer begins walking off. He says the woman's name,
followed by, "Ignore her. She's crazy. Come on."

The woman watches Anna in dismay and gradually pushes
along her cart of groceries.

"Liars!" Anna shouts.

The elderly woman narrows her shoulders and guardedly glances at Anna. She uses a hand to shield the little boy, who points at Anna and laughs a buck-toothed animal sound.

Anna leaves the fruit-laden cart where it is and storms out of the store.

Back at the Bareneed house, Anna stuffs her clothes and toiletries into her bag on the bed. She refuses to spend another night here. Who knows who might show up? More children? They are not her responsibility. The police officer, wanting to punish her for revealing too much to his girlfriend?

She will leave now, regardless of the dark.

Since her accident, she has had a fear of driving at night, and it has begun snowing lightly. These factors won't prevent her from heading for the highway. She will take her time, drive with vigilance.

The moment she arrives in St. John's, she will file a report with the city police. If there is a conspiracy out here, then an impartial police force might be more likely to uncover it.

Before locking up the house, she will check the barn for the little boy. The temperature is dropping, and the boy must be brought into the warmth. Even if he refuses to go with her, she will take him, drag him out kicking and screaming if need be. She won't have him catching his death in the barn.

Three solid knocks on the front door.

Anna freezes. Constable Newell returning to deal with her as he deems fit, or perhaps to confess the truth.

She doesn't move. She holds her breath, eyes searching for a weapon. The shotgun is downstairs, leaning against a corner in the kitchen.

Three more knocks on the door, and a voice calling, "Anna."

The voice is familiar. Not the police officer's at all.

She leaves the bedroom and warily looks down the stairs where she can see through the door window.

A man stands outside in light cast from the overhead fixture.

A face she knows far too well.

Anna takes her time descending the stairs, wondering how she will deal with this new development. Has he come to apologize, to set things right?

She opens the door with resignation, yet with a trace of hope.

"Hi." Kevin regards her with a practical expression. He doesn't look the slightest bit sorry or happy to see her. In his hand he holds a doctor's black kit bag.

"What do you want?" Anna asks, probing the dark yard where the pale faces of boys and girls unknown to her watch Kevin as though in dreadful fascination.

"We need to talk, Anna," he says.

The bodies begin to shy away in retreat. Step by step they shrink in a degenerative crouch until they are safely out of sight and curled together in the shadows.

The Embryo: Day 37, Week 6

The upper limb buds of Anna's embryo possess the distinct features of shoulders, arms, forearms, and hands.

The lower leg buds round at the tips of their tapered ends, while cells continue duplicating to begin shaping the embryo's feet.

Nerves thread their way through the two primitive legs.

Anna's embryo is one-third of an inch, the size of an average housefly.

~ Part II ~
The Famous Baby

Chapter Eleven

Anna: March 24, the Needle

Anna is awakened by a bar of winter sunlight slanting across her face through the curtain. The brilliance is invasive. She rolls over on her waterbed, trying to sink back to sleep, yet memories of the previous evening forcibly rouse her.

Urgently rising on her elbows, she checks around the room, trying to get her bearings. She is in her St. John's apartment.

Fear prickles through her mind as she scrambles together memories to fill in the void.

Last night in Bareneed, Kevin appeared at her door. A dream or reality? The distinction is tenuous, for she hasn't been long enough awake to divide one from the other.

Kevin was seated at her kitchen table. What was the purpose of his visit?

"We all have choices to make," he said in quiet, reasonable terms, adding remarks about common sense and the incontestable logic of practical decisions.

The words he used were ambiguous, a peculiar sort of jargon that reminded Anna of the bureaucracy-speak she often heard when meeting with government officials about the application requirements for arts funding.

Much of what followed was hazy and disjointed.

Kevin's black kit bag on the table next to the wilted rose. What reason might explain the presence of the bag? A menacing house call that brought her youth to mind.

A child with a fever.

A doctor at the front door. Kevin. Was he in Bareneed or St. John's?

"What's in the bag?" she asked.

"Things you will need," he replied.

Was he referring to supplements that might aid in the healthy development of her baby?

It was the house in Bareneed, for she said, "Look over your shoulder and tell me what you see."

"What do you mean?"

"Tell me what's there."

Checking over his shoulder, Kevin remarked, "Snow. A road. Trees." When he faced her again, he wore the expression of a man wondering if he had passed a pointless test.

Anna was about to bring up the children who were plainly evident when her eyes caught sight of a child lying beneath the wide splay of evergreen boughs, the child's face identical to hers, the staring eyes fixed on the sky.

"What's happening here?"

"What?" Again Kevin turned for a look.

Considering the impending court case, Anna thought it best to delve no further. All she needed was for Kevin to accuse her of being mentally unstable, even though she was beginning to fear this possibility like some creeping, malignant darkness.

What was going on with her mind? Schizophrenia? Diabetes? She had read somewhere that diabetes caused hallucinations. Or was it simply hormones? Hadn't women killed their husbands while suffering from hormonal imbalances? Or could it be the baby somehow fabricating these visions of abnormal children to warn her that her pregnancy was going horribly wrong?

Kevin seated at the kitchen table, expectantly watching her.

"Help me how?" Anna asked, believing he might finally be offering support.

Kevin sighed and frowned, scratching an eyebrow. "How do you want me to help?"

Anna searched his face, hoping the animosity between them might be eased. They were friends, after all. They had been friends before they were lovers.

"I don't know," she said. "How is a father supposed to help?"

Kevin's eyes drifted to his bag. "I have everything that's needed." His voice was contrite when he finally spoke again. "Anna, this is my job."

Blankness.

Her ears gone numb, then her voice barely heard, "Is this how you want to deliver yours?"

Kevin's reply smothered.

Anna made a noise of disgust. "I don't want you here anymore. I don't know what I was thinking to have let you in."

Kevin suddenly on his feet, eyes lingering on his black bag. He began reaching with his right hand, and then his left hand joined the other.

The clasp was popped and the bag opened.

A redness swelled within, growing to climb in a thorny tangle into the air, burgeoning into a flush of bloom.

Roses opening in a multitude of rippling layers.

"Anna." A voice from outside of a room.

Kevin's hands reached in to root among the concealed objects. "Kevin?"

He paused at the sound of his name.

"What are you doing?"

Slowly turning, he held a syringe in his hand, its tip pointed toward the ceiling. "Nothing, Anna … Nothing."

The memory of the needle incites a sting of adrenaline that compels her to climb out of bed. Her feet touch the floor. At once she is light-headed and shuts her eyes to regain herself fully.

Anna should go to the hospital. Or was she already there? Did Mr. King bring her to the hospital? She has a vague memory of being with him in a white room, but was that last night or after the car accident?

A dizzying sensation of rolling in a blur, of landing in the snow beneath the boughs of an evergreen tree.

She takes a deep breath.

Mr. King was at the house, too. When?

She recalls locking the bathroom door to check between her legs for signs of intrusion. She suspected there would have been heavy cramping. Catching a reflection of herself in the mirror, she pulled a clump of snow from a strand of her hair. There was a scab of flesh-toned paint near her temple that she picked away.

Anna was awakened on the chaise longue by Mr. King.

Then she was in the kitchen. She lifted her hands to defend herself. "Don't you dare, Kevin!"

He took a threatening step toward her.

With her eyes fixed on Kevin's ominous stare, Anna blindly reached for the utensil drawer, found the handle, and desperately yanked it open, in need of a weapon. She expected Kevin to lunge for her at any moment.

"The doctor's gone," Mr. King said, kneeling beside her.

"Doctor?" Her thoughts too jumbled to fit together. Squinting, she tried to come up with a reason for a doctor's visit. Was she ill? Did she have a fever?

"He left you to me. I called him."

In the kitchen Anna's hand pawed around the drawer for the carving knife. The shimmering rattle of silverware at her finger-tips. She would drive a blade into Kevin's heart if need be.

Flinching a look at the drawer, she caught sight of the carving knife and firmly grasped it, alerted to the sudden futility of her task by a tiny sting in her left leg. She gasped, watching Kevin's hand in retreat, holding the dripping syringe.

Anna checks her leg now where she is sitting on the edge

of the bed frame. She turns her leg one way, searchingly rubs her hands over her skin. No sign of a needle mark, but the scar on her leg from the accident is pink and pronounced. She leans to run a fingertip over it, sensing the thickened texture of the scar tissue. The tender flesh curls and rises in deformity.

Startled, Anna awakes. She has drifted off.

Her alert eyes, fixed on her bedroom ceiling.

She is still in her waterbed.

Was she dreaming of a memory? Dreaming of waking?

She searches the room. Her apartment in St. John's.

Kevin's face in her mind.

"You better sit down," he said, pulling out a chair.

The knife fell from Anna's hand as her grip slackened. Her head tilted back as though caught by an uncannily swift doze.

She tried steadying herself on legs that felt removed from her.

There was a hand on her arm, someone imploring her, and the repeated sound of banging that seemed to knock her into unconsciousness.

Again she awoke, but this time in a memory.

The presence of a man's face hovering over Anna prompted a whimper from her.

"Anna," said the real estate agent, his expression concerned.

Anna stared, trying to unlock her mind.

"It's okay."

It took some time to regain her senses completely. She was lying on the chaise longue in her Bareneed living room. Her head bluntly throbbed, the discomfort more potent than a common headache. She pushed with her hands to sit up but groaned and weakened, settling down again, her fingers searching her belly as though her stomach was paining her.

"You should never have let him into the house," Mr. King said with feeling, shifting his worried eyes along the living room walls. "Not even in the first place."

"Kevin?" Anna asked, piecing together the words *doctor* and

Kevin. Was it Kevin whom Mr. King was referring to?

The real estate agent studied her eyes, her nose, her lips, then trained his gaze lower, on her belly. "Once you let him in, claims of ownership sprout up like wildflowers."

The Embryo: Day 37, Week 6

The mandible in Anna's embryo becomes visible, set beneath a previously formed upper jaw.

Cells continue to build the skull and face, bridging gaps and conveying definition to the steadily transforming unification of features.

Anna assumes she arrived back at her apartment with the help of Mr. King. She has fragmented recollections of him behind a steering wheel, explaining about the doctor, about snow in the front yard, about pulling her out from under the boughs of a spruce tree.

Which doctor?

She remembers rising from the couch to make her way to the bathroom with the agent at her side for support. Her jeans were wet down one leg. Bits of snow mashed into the fabric.

Why was she outside in the snow? She must have suffered some sort of mental lapse, a convulsion, and fell in the front yard? Or did Kevin drag her there and leave her for dead in the freezing cold?

Rising from the waterbed, she has to sit still through a spell of wooziness. She should call her lawyer right away to inform the woman about Kevin and the needle. No doubt his actions constituted assault. They would have the upper hand in legal matters now.

Was she poisoned in some way? Injected with a drug that tampered with her memory? If she was in the hospital last night, there would be a record of her visit.

Cautiously standing, she glances back at the waterbed, trying to figure out the day of the week. How long has she been sleeping?

On the nightstand the cactus is shrivelled.

Anna notices a plant on the dresser and another on the window-sill. Two new plants that weren't there when she left for Bareneed. They have drooping leaves, their stems wilting brown and their roots unearthed. Did Kevin deliver them while she was away?

Heading for the kitchen, she pulls a garbage bag from the draw-er, flaps it open, and returns to the bedroom to dump the plants in.

She moves around the apartment, pausing here and there to collect Kevin's things: a blue sweater neatly folded over a chair, a how-to book on sailing, a pair of sensible brown slippers. She stuffs everything into the bag and plunks it on her bed.

Why does she feel so out of place here now?

She checks the drawer. Bits of soil left from the plant. Small clumps on the windowsill and night table, as well.

The space is too silent.

She would prefer to be startled by the call of a child's voice, to be enlivened by its vivid, unexpected presence, to help find its way home through whatever calamity might be hurled up before it.

Why did she come back here to this mute place?

The bedroom reminds her of Kevin, the bed where the baby was conceived. The tremendous weight of the warm water fill-ing the sac. The sheets that need changing. Their bodies atop the sloshing mattress. The memory sickens her.

Leaving the room, she passes the bathroom door, which is slightly ajar.

A streak of pink within brings her to a sudden standstill.

Spying through the crack, she carefully presses her fingertips to the door and edges it open, expecting to find a child staring up at her, its filthy hands held up, seeking direction on what to do next.

But the room is unoccupied.

She faces the mirror above the sink. The movement must have been her own reflection.

"Where are you?" she whispers to herself.

She settles on the toilet seat, shuts her eyes, and pees, the trickle in the water reminding her of the brook across the road in Bareneed. She stands and wipes herself, checks the tissue. White.

She is hungry. Famished.

Again she approaches the mirror. Upon closer inspection, her face appears gaunt, betrays signs of being ravenous.

A gnawing at her centre takes precedence over everything.

The baby is draining her, leaching life from her flesh and the marrow of her bones.

She must eat something if she is to be well.

In the kitchen she pulls open the refrigerator door.

A sour odour wafts up to meet her.

The milk.

She eyes the egg carton and flips it open. One egg left fitted in a hollow, its shell so smoothly curved it spurs fascination. She imagines cracking the shell against the rim of a frying pan, its contents spilling out. The yolk always near the centre.

How long before eggs go bad?

She slides open the meat drawer. A package of bacon. Slices of white and brown that turn ragged when pulled away from one another. Fat with splotches of meat carved from a rump. The cool, greasy smell rises to her.

Bread. Toast.

She checks the bag on the counter. A green haze evident through the plastic. She taps it. Mould spores fan out and drift inside like talcum powder.

A pasty waver in her stomach as she stares at the bread. Is it hunger or nausea? She swallows, her stupor broken by the ringing of her cellphone.

Retrieving the phone from her coat pocket on the couch, she checks the number.

Her lawyer.

"Hello?" she says anxiously.

"Anna?"

"Yes?"

"This is Patricia."

"I was just going to call you." She hooks a length of hair behind her ear. Her hair feels greasy. She needs to wash it, to shower, to clean herself up. How long has it been?

"Are you all right?" The lawyer's pressing tone implies she already knows about last night's violation.

"I'm fine now," Anna says. "Kevin came to Bareneed. He tried to kill the baby."

"What?"

"He stuck me with a needle, and I passed out." She stares at her feet. They are cold, the veins and tendons pronounced. "I don't know what happened."

"A needle? He actually injected you?"

"Yes."

"Are you kidding?"

"No." The admission makes Anna tremble. It is cold in the room. She moves to the thermostat on the wall and turns up the dial.

A sound of incredulity from the lawyer. "That's assault, Anna."

"That's what I thought."

"Did you contact the police?"

"I don't know." A memory of Constable Newell seated at her table in Bareneed, asking her questions.

"Are you okay?"

"Yes, I think so." Her trembling increases. She glances back at the kitchen. The refrigerator door left open, light spilling out from the box, staining the air.

"What did he do?"

"I don't know."

"And you passed out?"

"Yes." She goes to the fridge to attend to the door.

"Was anyone else there?"

"No." She wonders when Mr. King arrived, the continuity of events mixed up. She is still hungry, her mouth sticky, as though she might be dehydrated.

"Is the baby okay? Did you go to the hospital?"

Wandering into the living room to get her feet off the hardwood and onto the rug, Anna rubs the butt of her palm into her forehead, straining to remember. "I think the real estate agent took me."

"The real estate agent?"

"Mr. King."

"What did they say?"

"I don't remember." She wraps an arm around herself and takes stock of the living room, her eyes lingering on the painting above the couch. One of her butchery scenes from her last show. "I was so out of it."

"The real estate agent who sold you the house?"

"Yes."

"Was he in the house when Kevin did this?"

"I think he came after." Anna finds herself at the window, drawn by the light. The sky is blue and brilliant. She watches down into the flow in the street.

"This is unbelievable," says the lawyer.

On the sidewalk a woman appears with a child held by the hand. The child is bundled up in snowsuit, scarf, mittens, and a cap that covers its entire face except for its eyes, which are visible through the snipped eyeholes.

"Anna?"

The child is being pulled along by its mother in a scene reminiscent of the crisp realism of an Alex Colville print.

"Anna? Are you there?"

"Yes," she says, distracted, while undulations of warm air rise from the heater beneath the window. "I'm here."

It's hot now, Anna thinks. So cold out there.

"You're not certain if you contacted the police?"

The child trips, yet the mother continues walking, watching ahead, dragging the child on its back over the snow. It is a game or it is cruelty. The child faces the sky, its eyes staring.

"No," she says, feeling vindicated, even strangely fulfilled, by the thought of increased complexity to the situation.

Gazing down from overhead, her presence unknown to passersby on the street, Anna feels guilty, as though she isn't meant to be witnessing these actions.

"Did the hospital do blood work?"

"I said I don't remember."

The moment the child disappears from view a black car pulls up on the same side of the street. The driver leans to shove open the passenger door. He pushes something out. An orange-and-white kitten tumbles onto the sidewalk, freezes, leans back, and darts a terrified look around. The driver shuts the door and drives off.

"If your memory is messed up, it was probably Rohypnol. I've seen this before. And he's a doctor. He has access to any drug he likes. He's a gynecologist, right? Anna, what about ... it might have been something to —"

"To what?" She should go collect that kitten. She makes a motion to do so just as the woman reappears, dragging the child behind her. The woman stops beside the kitten and crouches, rubbing its head, while the child rolls around in the snow, thrashing its limbs back and forth.

The kitten pushes up against the woman, warming to this stranger at once.

"I don't want to scare you, but it might have been something to abort the fetus, to start contractions. You should get blood work done so you know what drug he used. There should be traces."

A drug to abort the fetus.

"Did he do anything to you while you were unconscious?"

Anna thinks: how could I possibly know? Fretting, she runs a hand over the top of her head, her fingers catching on something crusted in her hair.

"Were there any signs?"

The woman lifts the kitten, unzips her coat, and secrets it away in the space above her breasts. Redoing her coat, she curtly calls to the child, who struggles to its feet and follows after her, waddling along and slapping at its mother's back with its mittens.

"Anna?"

She picks at her scalp, easing her fingernail under the edge of a small bump. It comes loose as she pries it away. Pinching it between her fingertip and thumbnail, she pulls it clear to check it. A blot of red. Paint. She flicks it onto the floor and continues scraping at her head.

"Anna?"

"What?"

"Are you sure you're okay?"

"Yes."

"We should get a physical and samples. Swabs. As soon as possible. Did you mention any of this to the people at the hospital?"

Why does the lawyer keep asking the same questions?

"You should contact the police right away. Just in case you didn't last night. Do you have anyone with you now?"

The pressure in Anna's head mounts. The lawyer's words are only making matters worse. She feels a slicing stammer in her brain, then a cramp in her belly. She holds herself still to localize the source.

"Anna? Do you want me to come over? Or you can come here. I'll send a taxi."

Another cramp.

She withdraws from the window, not only confused but frightened now.

"I have to go."

"Okay, you sure?"

"Yes."

"Just a sec."

"What?" Breaking out in a sweat, Anna hurries for the bathroom while gently pressing her fingertips into her abdomen.

"Have you seen the papers?"

"No, why?" Another spasm that snatches a wince from her. Buckling forward, she slaps a hand against the wall beside the bathroom door.

"Anna?"

"What?"

"Are you okay?"

"Yes …"

"They got hold of it."

"Hold of what?" She wants it all to stop: the pain and the uncertainty. Sweat runs down her forehead, collecting in her eyebrows.

"News of the upcoming hearing."

"I have to go." Anna shuts her cell. A sensation of fullness bloats her belly as though she might be starting her period or desperately needs to pee.

Straightening, she rushes into the bathroom and sits on the toilet. The cramping persists. She leans forward. Moaning in distress and denial, she rocks back and forth, then rises to stare into the toilet bowl.

The doctor stands at the foot of the narrow examination table with a chart in his hand. He has short black hair and a dark complexion. Although he speaks perfect English, it is difficult to guess his heritage, for it seems he is of mixed parentage.

Anna lies on the table waiting while the doctor writes a few sentences on the chart. What will he say to her? What news? She wants to know immediately, yet won't interrupt his writing as a gesture of respect. Why is he taking so long? She looks away as pain bears down on her.

The cramps have intensified since the examination. They bring to mind the startling memory of that single drop of blood spreading in the water of the toilet bowl. As though wavering larger, the recollection creates a watery unsteadiness in Anna's head, and she experiences the urge to vomit.

"You're six weeks?" he asks.

"Yes," says Anna, suffering to utter a single word.

"Well, you're still six weeks. Everything is fine."

Despite her discomfort and nausea, she feels thankful. "That's good."

The doctor puts the chart on the metal side table. "I'm fairly certain the cramping was related to the baby growing. You can expect that. A bit of spotting. You're probably experiencing a little cramping now."

"Yes." The way she answers makes her feel like a young girl.

The doctor smiles thoughtfully and pats her hand. "We'll give you something for that."

"Thank you."

"Don't hesitate to come in and see us if you have any worries at all. Okay?"

The doctor's manner is so natural and supportive that it makes Anna feel truly proud of her pregnancy. This stranger offering validation. "Okay."

"That's a pretty famous baby you have there. We need to look after it."

"Yes, thank you." She laughs, and a tear dribbles from the corner of her eye. Embarrassed, she turns her head to face the wall. The tear runs into the hair at her temple.

Famous.

The doctor must have heard of the impending court case.

"I have a clinic in the hospital. Do you have an obstetrician?"

"No." She sighs and looks up at him standing beside her. "Just my family doctor."

"Well, come in and see me if you like."

"Okay." Anna takes a deep, fortifying breath. With her eyes on the doctor, she recalls what her lawyer said about the need for blood work.

The doctor searches her face. "Good. You can —"

"I was wondering what you check blood for?"

"Blood? What blood?"

"The blood they took from me?"

"Standard screening. White cells, red cells, electrolytes. That sort of thing. Everything's fine. Are you worried about something specific?"

"I was injected with a needle."

"Injected?"

Anna wonders how not to implicate Kevin. No doubt the doctor knows him. They work in the same field, in the same hospital. "Pricked, actually. And I wanted to know if there were any drugs in it."

"The needle?"

"Yes ... I was at someone's house, and it was ... in the garbage. I dropped something in there by accident."

"An HIV test should be a priority, and we can do toxicology if you like. Did you feel as if you were drugged?"

"A little."

"Well, I can order tests." The doctor's eyes dip to her arms.

Does he suspect she is a junkie?

"Could you do that while I'm here?"

"I'll order the blood work on my way out."

"Thank you."

"Is your friend a diabetic or a drug user?"

"He's not my friend."

"Okay."

"No, he's not a drug user."

"Good. Hopefully, it's nothing."

"It's the baby."

"Yes, of course. You're concerned."

"Yes."

"I'll have my office call you when the results come back." His eyes remain purposefully fixed on her face. "You can put your legs down now if you like."

Chapter Twelve

The Embryo: Day 38, Week 6

The hindbrain, responsible for heart regulation, breathing, and muscle movement, begins to develop in Anna's embryo.

While the nostrils are still two separate plates, they gradually rotate toward the front of the face as the head widens.

The tube that will convey urine from the kidney to the bladder lengthens as cells multiply.

Mammary gland tissue begins to mature.

Anna's embryo is two-fifths of an inch long, as big as a pine nut.

Anna: March 26, Anna's Lawyer

"It's more private in here," Anna's lawyer opens the door to the boardroom and motions with the file folder for Anna to enter ahead of her.

"Thank you."

The walls are made of intricately carved wood panelling with raised mouldings. A luxurious resonance is given off by the light entering through the blinds. Volumes of books are stacked high on shelves above a large aquarium. Anna assumes, by their gilded edges, that the books are more for show than use. The air smells of old papers and leather as she walks over the plush carpet. The odour makes her aware of how cold her nose has become during her walk from her house, down over Longs Hill to the lawyer's office on Church Hill. The walk was a little treacherous, for there were patches of black ice on the sidewalk that Anna could barely make out. Her unease was compounded by a car that trailed after her. A man in the passenger seat taking photographs.

Anna smells coffee and searches for its source. A machine set up on an antique cart off in the corner. A box of doughnuts next to the urn.

She notices Patricia watching her. The brown pantsuit her lawyer wears does nothing for her appearance. The fabric of the plain, camel-coloured top under the jacket strains against the heft of a large chest. She is slightly shorter than Anna with a face that might be pretty if it weren't so stern, unadorned, and topped by a buzzed haircut.

"Would you like a coffee?"

"No, thank you." As Anna approaches the polished table, her attention is caught by a newspaper laid out there. Her hand comes to rest on the high back of the leather chair nearest her.

The headline at the very top of the page says: COUPLE HEADS TO COURT OVER EMBRYO OWNERSHIP.

The media has been reporting on the story for two days, and there seems to be no sign of the coverage letting up.

Patricia puts the file down, rolls out a chair, and settles in, her attention exclusively on Anna.

The newspaper photograph of Anna is a promotional shot taken from the Maher Gallery's website. It isn't a recent photo. She appears much younger, and her hair is cut in an outdated style. She sits on the edge of a cliff with waves crashing white behind her. David took the photo while complaining about the cold and getting his Italian shoes dirtied by Mother Nature.

The photograph of Kevin is of professional quality. He is more prominent in the space allotted, nearer to the camera lens. Wearing a white lab coat, he is standing in the corridor of a hospital with a stethoscope around his neck. His expression is welcoming, while his posture implies competence.

A flaky, cliff-dwelling artist versus a medical scientist.

"This is making me sicker and sicker," Anna says. "Every time I see it."

"I'm very sorry about all this."

"Thanks, but it's not your fault." Anna settles in her chair, drawing her eyes away from Kevin's smiling face. What sort of monster?

"True. But someone has to offer an apology, and I'm not expecting one from those jerks."

"We haven't even been in court."

"They keep a pretty close eye on upcoming cases."

"Yeah, they're keeping a pretty close eye on me, too." Anna folds the newspaper over to bury the photographs. She doesn't know which one she hates more. Hers or Kevin's. "Two reporters followed me here."

"Where from?"

"Newspaper, I think."

Anna's lawyer tips her eyes to the newspaper. "Fortunately, the editors have actually done some homework on the legalities. They quote one of my old university professors at UNB as saying that this sort of issue can't be tried as a property case. There's an editorial in there that accuses Judge Drodge of trying to send the legal system back to the Middle Ages."

"Then why is it going ahead?"

"Because Kevin's lawyer filed the claim. It has to be heard."

"So I could just drag anyone into court for anything I make up?"

"Yes, unfortunately, if you can find a lawyer to humour you."

Anna shakes her head. "That's funny."

"Sorry. Humour was the wrong word."

Distracted by the smell of coffee, Anna checks the urn. The box of doughnuts. She wonders how full it is, how heavy if lifted.

"Are you sure you wouldn't like a coffee?"

"No, thanks."

"Doughnut?"

"I don't know if I can eat anything."

"You need to eat." Determined, Patricia rises and heads to the cart.

Watching the lawyer, Anna's attention is caught by movement in the aquarium. Two medium-sized red fish with pink undersides float there, while other smaller fish — blue, orange, and electric-green — zip around the miniature fortresses.

The lawyer brings the box of doughnuts to Anna. She scoots her chair nearer, her attitude becoming less formal as she opens the box. "You like the fish?"

"Very colourful. What are the red ones called?"

"Squareback something. I can't remember the full name. They're pretty, huh?"

Anna regards Patricia's face, for the lawyer has spoken in a tone that is sentimental, almost loving. It makes Anna wonder about the lawyer's life outside these offices.

Patricia studies the aquarium with affection, then glances at the file folder. "I think I already mentioned that this particular judge is a dinosaur when it comes to women's rights. He's given out his fair share of slaps on the wrists in abuse cases. He's also a bit of a publicity hound. He revels in it."

Anna checks the arrangement of doughnuts. A tempting selection. She decides on a maple glaze. Reaching in, she licks her lips while lifting out her choice. She takes a nibble. The dough is fresh. They must have been brought in this morning.

The lawyer picks up the newspaper, opens it to the editorial, folds the pages over, and slides it across for Anna to read. "This can't go far. It'll have to be thrown out. Or someone is sure to intervene. I'd say the government is already on the line to Judge Drodge."

"Can they do that?"

"Of course. There'll be so much flak over this that the justice minister himself will be forced to make some sort of statement. I've been in touch with the local women's groups, and they're about to respond."

Taking another bite of her doughnut, Anna reads the editorial. There is a pronounced tone of condemnation, yet a hint of interest in seeing how the case might be resolved, as though it were some sort of intriguing amusement.

"Unfortunately, from what I hear from my PR friends, this is certain to make national headlines, and very quickly. We need to be prepared for that. And if the TV stations get involved, it might become an international concern."

Anna makes a sound as a chill hurtles through her. She takes another bite of the doughnut, pleased to find custard cream at its centre.

"I know," Patricia commiserates. "It must be incredibly frustrating." She tries a reassuring smile and opens the file folder. "We'll do our best to put it to bed quickly so you can get on with your life." The lawyer reads a document, her mouth stirring, silently shaping the words. Done reading, she pins Anna with a look that implies mortal seriousness. "This visit by Kevin."

"Yes?"

Patricia leans back in her chair, pausing, as though to gauge her words. "According to his attorney, Kevin couldn't have been in Bareneed on the night of the alleged assault." She anticipates reaction, surveying Anna's face. "This letter states that he was in the hospital at the time performing an emergency procedure. There are a number of witnesses listed here."

"What kind of procedure?"

"I don't know."

The door to the boardroom opens, and a thin man in a grey suit looks in. His entry seems deliberate, for he gives no sign of being surprised by the women's presence nor sorry for the intrusion.

"Yes?" Patricia says to him.

The man regards Patricia, tilts his head back in a gesture of tentative acknowledgement, then checks Anna. His look is curious. "I thought it was empty," he says while quietly shutting the door.

Patricia's expression remains professional, non-judgmental, yet her lips tighten, betraying her annoyance. She clears her throat. "One of the partners."

Growing uncomfortable, Anna averts her eyes, settles on a view of the aquarium, while she slowly shakes her head in deadening disbelief. The fish submerged in water, floating in place, their colours fading.

"I hope he had a good look," Anna says.

"Sorry. Are you okay? You look a little pale."

"Kevin was there that night."

"I believe you. Maybe it was earlier than you thought."

Anna gives a deep, involuntary sigh, shifts in her chair, and becomes conscious of her breathing. She tries to swallow, straining to do so until her throat muscles finally give way, allowing the swallow.

"Are you sure it was night?" asks Patricia.

"Yes."

"How about a little air?"

What Anna wants is for the lawyer to stop talking. "That lynx," she mutters, flinching at a recollection of the lynx prowling, watching the windows of her house for the faces of children.

"What?"

The room begins to tingle, and she feels as though she might faint. She knows what must be done. Leaning forward in her chair, her head facing the floor, she regards her boots on the burgundy carpet, wondering about the pressure on the baby in this position.

The Embryo: Day 39, Week 6

Central wrist and finger plates form in the hand regions of Anna's embryo.

In Anna's thoughts the lynx continues circling, its speckled grey, brown, and white fur a camouflaged blur against the land.

"I'll get you some water." The lawyer stands and opens the door, asks for an assistant to collect a bottle of water. Her tone is instructive, yet not urgent. Then the lawyer is seated again.

A few moments later a cup is handed to Anna, who senses the breeze of movement against her damp skin.

"Thanks." Her words are muddled as though her ears might be stuffed with cotton. She sips from the cup, feeling the water cool her throat and stomach, aware of the trail of it going down, making her feel more like herself. Slowly, she straightens in her chair and looks at the lawyer. "This happens sometimes."

"You're getting some colour back."

Anna sets the cup on the table. "I don't know what's going on."

"It's all very stressful. And this probably sounds ridiculous, but are you sure you weren't dreaming?"

Anna gives no immediate reply, for she is searching her thoughts to discover if, in fact, it might be a possibility. "I don't know." She is on the verge of telling the lawyer about the lost little children. Constable Newell. The need for an investigation. She wants to share this information with someone, and now seems the ideal time. The lost little children and the lynx. The fox and the mice. The rabbit in the road. The eagle sailing through the sky.

"Are the results back from your blood work?"

"Tomorrow, I think."

"Let's see what they say."

"What difference would it make now?" Anna peeks at the new document. Everyone with a file on her, detailing the specifics of her life.

"My main objective is to spare you the ordeal of having to go into that courtroom in two days. If we have enough evidence, we might be able to persuade them to withdraw the action. You mentioned something about a real estate agent being there."

"Yes." Anna eyes the doughnut she has placed on the table. The impression of her teeth marks along the edge where she has chewed through it. Along a line directly behind the doughnut, the aquarium glows, while fish swim in smears of colours.

"Did he see Kevin?"

"I have no idea."

"Can you contact him?"

"Yes."

"You have his number?"

Anna takes out her cell and scrolls through the stored digits. The real estate agent's number is nowhere to be found. "I don't think I have it."

"Who does he work for?"

"He's on his own, I believe. His sign was on the house. Just a plain sign."

"We handled the house sale, right?"

"Yes." Where is Mr. King's number? He called her right before the accident. It should be in her phone.

"I'll look it up. Do you want me to give him a call?"

"Sure."

The door opens again and a man stands there, this one different from the first. He is burlier, balding, and wears a black suit. He tilts his head in contemplation.

"In conference," Patricia alerts him.

The man nods, wipes a hand across his mouth, and reluctantly shuts the door.

Anna: March 27, the Obstetrician

"Hop up here?" The doctor pats the examination table. "Let's check on that famous baby of yours."

Anna puts her stocking feet in the stirrups. She has come at the prompting of the doctor's office to hear the results of the blood work, yet the obstetrician has insisted on an examination first to make certain the baby is developing along the appropriate timeline.

"Everything feeling okay now?"

"Yes."

"Any more cramping?"

"No, thankfully."

"Good." The obstetrician studies her face while he snaps on latex gloves and applies the lubricant, smearing it around on both hands. "Let's warm it up a bit first."

Anna notices the bulge of his wedding band behind the glove and shifts her gaze to the embryo development chart on the wall above his desk. She flinches as his hands touch her thighs.

"Sorry," says the doctor. "Still cold?"

Anna gives him a brief, conditional nod, her eyes concentrating on the chart, feeling suddenly shy in the company of this man.

"How are you handling all the attention?"

"Not good."

"This business in the paper must be stressful."

Anna senses the pressure of two fingers easing into her. She is not ready. Her shoulders pull back, and her neck stretches as though to draw away. The paper covering crinkles beneath her.

"Sorry. There's a bit of pressure. Right?"

"Yes." The word spoken bluntly, under strain. Her palms press against the black vinyl while her head rises a few inches off the pillow.

"I'll be done in a second." He makes a barely perceptible sound as though he is forcing something.

"Ow! God!" Anna shifts, tries to prevent herself from sliding her bum back, away from his fingers. She turns her head the other way, catching a fleeting glimpse of the doctor's eyes watching her face before she settles on a view of the shut venetian blinds.

"Sorry. Just another second."

There is more pain and pressure, and Anna groans. "Stop," she says involuntarily, her entire body breaking out in a sweat. "Please, please …"

"It's okay."

More pressure.

"What are you doing?" She tilts her head to look at him. His eyes are on his hands where they work between her legs. He slides one warm hand over her pubis to rest on her bare belly and rub there as though to calm her, the gelled latex glove patting her skin.

"Shh. I know. I'm almost done." He twists on an angle and dips his shoulder. "This is going to hurt. I'm sorry."

There is a deep thrust.

Anna's makes a drawn-out, guttural sound. Her hands come up bunched into fists, "Gaawwd!"

"Almost there, just relax, a little bit deeper."

Anna tries closing her legs, but the stirrups secure her feet in place.

The doctor lowers his hand from her belly to push against her thigh. "Please, you have to stay open," he says, using his elbows to pin her legs apart. "You're tightening up too much."

Anna thinks she might faint as another thrust sends pain burning up her spine.

"There," says the doctor, pausing. "How's that?" He stares down between her legs. "I'll wait for a second."

Anna shuts her eyes, her head swimming with nauseating pain.

"Does that feel better?"

Anna shakes her head, her nose growing hot. "No." The word bridging the sentiment to tears.

"I'll take it out in a second once you've relaxed." Slowly, carefully, he draws his hand back.

Anna grunts as though she has been punched in the abdomen.

"I'm out," says the doctor, snorting, strangely invigorated. "Better?" He reaches for the bottle of gel. Aiming from above, he squeezes a stream of it between her legs until the tube discharges a flatulent sound. He gives the tube a shake and squeezes it again. His hand liberally smears the lubricant around. "I need to have one more quick look." His fingers dig into her, swiftly going deep, making a sticky, sucking sound that further sickens Anna.

Tears rise in the corners of her eyes and hotly spill loose.

The doctor clears his throat. He makes a noise of agreement while pushing deeper into her.

"Ow!" She cries at the pain.

"Does it really hurt that much?"

"Yes."

The doctor breathes through his opened mouth while, bit by bit, he draws his arm back, then continues forward. "I need to go just a little deeper. Okay?"

Anna continues sobbing.

"Okay?"

"No, I can't …" She tries writhing away from him, but his hand remains lodged in her.

"You have to help me out here, Anna."

Anna's muscles tighten, and she loses her view of the room, faints away.

The Embryo: Day 40, Week 6

Since conception, Anna's embryo has been generating 2.5 million neurons per minute. At this point the nerves linking the embryo's nose to its brain are created.

When Anna regains consciousness, bile is rising in her throat. She coughs and swallows desperately, while turning her head to the side to avoid choking. The bile burns to such an extent that her throat is raw.

"You were gone for a second."

"What?"

The doctor remains standing between her legs.

She is sweating profusely, and her muscles feel weakened while her perception sparkles a hazy white.

"Ready?"

"I need to —" She swallows, tries to get off the table, but the doctor shoves deeper.

"Stop trying to close your legs."

Cringing, she turns her head, a prisoner to misery. Her clothes feel wet against her skin as her sweat begins to chill.

"Okay." He eases back until he is fully removed.

Anna groans in relief. She wipes her eyes while watching the doctor turn his back to her.

"Done," he says, seemingly cross with her. He removes his gloves and tosses them into the bin. Plucking a few tissues from a box, he lays them bunched together on Anna's belly before sitting at his desk to write in her file.

"Everything's fine," he says, his tone implying he has grown impatient with her.

That was brutal, Anna thinks, feeling a cramp seize hold. She takes the tissues in hand, removes her feet from the stirrups, and slides her legs over the edge of the table.

"Can I go?" she asks, holding the tissue at ready.

"Yes." He takes a quick look at her. "Clean yourself up."

She wipes herself while he briefly watches.

"Careful getting down."

She slides off the table, made aware of the sweat on her backside, the paper sheet sticking to her before releasing. She reaches for her underwear and unsteadily puts it on.

Wasn't there supposed to be a nurse present for that examination? She thinks to mention this to the doctor, the intention burning in her lungs. Does the rule apply to obstetricians or just family doctors? She steps into her jeans, wanting to get out of the room.

The doctor continues writing in her file.

Anna wonders if this man knows Kevin. He must. They are colleagues. How close are they? His examination was far more invasive than his previous one. Was he trying to harm her baby on Kevin's behalf? Another cramp clutches her, and she almost buckles with the stabbing twinge.

"Expect a little cramping," the doctor says in reply to her sound of distress.

Anna straightens by the chair at the side of the doctor's desk. She sniffs, wipes at her nose with the bunch of tissues, won't allow herself to cry anymore.

"Well," says the doctor. Finished writing, he puts down his pen.

Anna glances at what he has been scribbling, the length of text, his words in a slanted, illegible script.

The doctor shuts the file, his impassive eyes turned to her. "Why don't you sit down? It's more comfortable."

"I wanted the results of my blood work."

"Right. You're fine. No need to worry." He reopens her file and shifts the top page aside, lifts another paper. "HIV ...

negative." He picks up another sheet. "Toxicology. Nothing." Another sheet. "Nothing. All clear." He sets the papers down and closes the folder, smiles sympathetically. "Watch out for those needles in the future."

"I won't be anywhere near them."

"Good for you. Come back and see me in a week or so." With a boisterous push he stands from his chair, walks to the door, and opens it, waiting for her to leave. "Or sooner if you like."

Stepping toward him, Anna finds that she can no longer look him in the eyes.

The doctor touches her on the small of her back while she passes before him, another cramp jerking at her insides.

Or sooner if you like.

The words stick in Anna's head as she enters the waiting area.

A patient's full name is called out by the receptionist behind the glass window, summoning another woman to her feet.

Anna drives with her window down. The bracing March air has helped revive her, yet her thoughts remain troubled by the doctor's actions. She feels angry and ashamed, and she thinks she might be bleeding. There is something warm leaking out of her. Gel from the examination, she hopes. She is burning between her legs. If only she could check herself, but she can't stop the car to take down her jeans. What if someone should come along?

Only a few minutes from home.

When she arrives there, she will file a complaint against that doctor. She will get on the Internet and hunt for the name of the person in charge of the hospital, and she will write a message detailing everything that happened. She will copy the message to the health minister.

But what will she say? The examination was severely uncomfortable? Of course, it was. What did you expect? Did the doctor actually do anything wrong? What about the amount of force he used? How could that be measured and described?

More leakage.

While watching the road, she undoes the hasp on her jeans, lowers the zipper to loosen the waist, and slides her hand down there. She shifts her bum on the seat to gain a better position. Pulling her fingers out, she fleetingly checks them to see that the fluid is pinkish. Or is that just the tint of her skin? Eyes on the road, she warns herself, feeling as though she will faint again.

That doctor hurt her. He hurt her on purpose. And he might have harmed her baby.

Her mind calls up a noted image of vengeance. *Judith Slaying Holofernes* by Artemisia Gentileschi, one of the first female painters to gain recognition in the seventeenth century. In the painting a maidservant holds down Holofernes, a bearded tyrant, while Judith grips her victim's hair and slices a large dagger through his throat. Blood gushes in wide strands into the air while the man struggles desperately to survive. A cathartic expression of private rage.

Hang that painting over the examination table in the doctor's office.

As Anna nears her house on LeMarchant Road, her attention is caught by a white SUV, with a logo for a TV network on its door, parked out front.

She has slowed down to pull in but can't stop now.

Passing by, she peeks at the woman standing on her step, talking to a man with a video camera cradled in his arms. The well-known reporter shifts from boot to boot, trying to stay warm.

Troubled by worsening cramps, Anna continues on, eyes straight ahead so as not to be noticed. She expects to hear her name called out, the reporter chasing after her with the video camera aimed in her wake.

She shoots a glance at the rearview mirror to see no one pursuing her.

Running from the press like a criminal.

In art school she used to fantasize about talking to the media, convinced that reporters would flock to the genius and originality of her work, hang on every word she uttered, marvel at her grasp of both the visceral and the eloquent. Yet when no one bothered interviewing her about her first exhibit, followed by an equal indifference to her second show, she faced the reality of true worth, the hiss of her ego deflating while her naïveté and pretentiousness shrank away.

When media interest finally materialized after her fifth show, she was further disillusioned by the mind-numbing repetition of uninspired questions and swore never to do another interview again.

Where will she go now? Her studio.

She is hit by another extended spasm. With a groan of disgust, she squints at the rearview, feeling the need to bend forward to ease the pressure.

The white SUV a parked dot in the distance.

The doctor's face in her mind, his expression while examining her, as though he was wondering how much she would allow, how much she could endure.

What if he was one of those doctors with a history of harming women? A doctor who continued to practise freely because not a single woman ever had the courage to report him.

Was he trying to induce a miscarriage? Was that how he got his kicks? Was Anna having a miscarriage now?

Her hand goes to her belly, rubs it in a circular pattern.

At the lights she takes a right down Longs Hill, fearing an increased sensation of wetness, a flow of blood between her legs.

Growing more worried, she passes her lawyer's office on Church Hill, takes a left on Duckworth. Her studio is only two blocks away. She slows to search the area, which appears clear. She finds a space a few doors up and hurries toward the flower shop, anxious to hide away upstairs, check herself, and be secure.

On her way she thumbs through her keys, finding the appropriate one, and scrapes it into the lock.

"Hello, Anna," calls a man's voice behind her.

Anna peers furtively over her shoulder to see Mr. Oliver out in the cold in his shirt sleeves, holding one arm behind his back.

"Hi." She offers a brief smile, wanting to get inside. She glances up and down the street.

What is Mr. Oliver concealing from her?

"How is everything?" he asks, nodding, his breath misting in the air.

"Okay," Anna says as a delivery truck passes in the street, its tires rolling wetly through the slush.

"This is for you." Mr. Oliver brings his hand out from behind his back. A single red rose. "You haven't been in for a while."

Anna leaves her keys dangling in the lock and jaunts down the steps to accept the offering. "Thanks so much."

"It's nothing." Mr. Oliver nods again, then licks his lips, his cheeks warm with heat despite the chilly air. "The beauty doesn't last. Time for new beauty." Smiling, he points at her. "But you will capture it forever. You have talent. Big talent."

"You're very kind. Thank you." The pain in her abdomen makes her grit her teeth behind her lips. She buries a sound of discomfort.

"Okay, everything's good?"

"Yes."

"The baby's good?" He joins his hands in a gesture of hope.

"Yes." She shifts from one leg to the other, tries to stifle another wince, but the corners of her mouth dip involuntarily.

"Don't let that rotten doctor bastard get to you, okay? That's all I have to say."

Anna briefly touches his arm, her eyes warming with emotion. "Okay, Mr. Oliver. Thank you."

He holds up his fist. "You stick to your guns, young lady."

"I will."

"Good." Mr. Oliver nods, as though it has all been settled, and turns for his shop. "Go make something beautiful."

Anna regards the rose while unlocking the door.

Upstairs she shuts the studio door behind her and checks inside her jeans. To her relief, her underwear shows no signs of blood.

She zips up her jeans and replaces the wilted rose with the new one while scanning her studio. Surrounded by her canvases, she feels a sense of cozy enclosure soothe her nerves until another cramp drives her to a wide, cushioned chair against the wall. She sits and leans forward. "Yuck, yuck, yuck …"

Unable to bear the pain, she stands and moves to the paint-smeared utility sink at the back of her studio. She takes down a bottle of pain pills from the shelf, pops the cap, and shakes two tablets into her palm. She puts them on her tongue, runs water into a glass, and drinks.

The pills go down slowly, straining against her throat muscles.

Anna studies her face in the mirror, thinking of the baby, what it will look like. A likeness of herself? Or a child possessing not a single one of her features?

Crippling forward, she grips the edge of the sink as another cramp almost knocks her over and jams shut her eyes.

She waits, unable to move, sweating.

As the contraction releases, she probes down her pants. A small blood clot on her middle finger.

"Oh, God."

She brings the clot to her eyes, considering what it might contain, expecting to see details.

Upon closer examination it appears to be only blood.

She twists on the tap and rinses her hand, knocking the pill bottle from the edge of the sink.

The pills.

Are pregnant women permitted to take them? She snatches up the bottle to study the fine print, her eyes catching on a warning for pregnant women.

She leans over the sink, jamming her fingers down her throat.

Why didn't I know that?

Gagging, she feels her face flood with pressure, her eyes spill tears. She continues poking at her throat, wiggling her fingers. Retching with greater violence, she writhes against the sink until the pills come up, leaving a pasty, chemical trail in her throat.

She spits them out in the drain.

The Embryo: Day 40, Week 6

The thigh, leg, and foot areas can now be distinguished in the lower limb buds of Anna's embryo.

The taste in her mouth is putrid. She sticks out her tongue. A line of white smeared down the centre.

More water. She glugs down a full glass.

She should go back to the hospital. To emergency. She must be having a miscarriage. But what could they possibly do to help her?

Anna feels a muddled buzz near her hip. The sensation appears physiological in nature, giving rise to panic until she realizes it is her cell vibrating in her coat pocket.

Wiping at her eyes, she removes the phone to check the number.

"Hello?"

"Anna?"

"Yes."

"This is Patricia. Just checking on that blood work. Any news?"

"No, not yet." She sniffs and pinches her nostrils to clear them.

"When can we get those results?"

"It won't be for a few days." She keeps swallowing, trying to wash away the bitter residue of the pills.

"That's too late."

"I'm sorry," she says, secretly apologizing for the lie. She should explain about the doctor's aggressive examination, yet fears what Patricia might think. Was the doctor really doing what was expected of him? Was he genuinely concerned about something he felt that, in his estimation, indicated a problem with her pregnancy? She should have asked him. Will the lawyer think she is paranoid of everyone? Or, more specifically, paranoid of doctors.

"It's not your fault."

She searches her studio, wondering if she should leave.

Another cramp buckles her over and almost brings her to tears. The pain and the fear. She shuts her eyes, holding the edge of the sink while carefully easing down until she is seated on the floor. She rocks gently forward, wanting only to feel well.

"Anna?"

"Yes."

Oh, the pain, she moans to herself, staring at her canvases, the ones of the nests, the ones of the roses.

"You okay?"

"Yes."

"Listen, we can't seem to track down that real estate agent of yours. We never did have a number for him on file."

"I think he lives out around Bareneed." She wants to hang up; her words are growing wet with telltale signs of emotion. She doesn't want to talk anymore. If anything, she wants to paint. There is urgency in her, despite the pain, or perhaps because of it, to transform all of this into something that will hang as a stirring epiphany.

"I tried directory assistance, searched the Internet. Nothing."

Paint. But paint what?

Nests.

Feathers.

Roses.

Petals.

"What's going on with Kevin's lawyer?" Anna takes a deep, fortifying breath. The cramping is easing off. She will stay on the line in case she needs Patricia to rescue her.

"Not much at this point."

Anna continues scrutinizing her paintings, separating the colours, disassembling the images stroke by stroke. They are too weighted by drama. There isn't enough delicate light in them. If only she were more like the Impressionist painters who were so adept at conveying the incalculable subtleties of light.

"Anna?"

Perhaps she should give consideration to changing her palette. The thought that her colours aren't truly hers saddens her. Is it possible that she has been seeing the world all wrong?

"Hello? Anna?"

She has struggled long and hard with her art, through childhood, into adolescence and her teenage years, where she was often ostracized for her sensitivity, treated as an outsider and even shunned in school.

"I think the connection's gone ..."

Feathers with silky underscores of light.

Feathers as petals of a rose, closing in around her.

The pain releasing as though unbuckling, straightening out in a smooth line applied by a steady hand with a palette knife.

"Anna?"

"Sorry. I lost you there."

For years she has endured the clever, self-serving critics who dismissed her as a dabbler incapable of amounting to anything more than a minor talent. Did they have any idea of the harm they were exacting, the turmoil they were causing her?

How to be remarkable? How to be remembered?

"It looks like there's no avoiding court. You don't really need to be there, like I said. I can attend on your behalf. It shouldn't be a problem considering the frivolous nature of the claim."

In her mind Anna pulls together a chart of gradients — the warm and cool colours she has applied on her canvases. Between these primary colours, she squeezes in the names of the colours she has formed by blending one hue with another.

"No, I'll go." Anna hugs her abdomen, leans her head against her knees, the feather petals of a rose rustling closed around her. A nest.

She has succeeded in making a livelihood from work she essentially enjoys, creating a living out of thin air. She hasn't only survived the schoolyard taunts, the critics' derision, but also those savage inner voices that mocked her most.

"Are you sure?"

The nameless black-haired girl.

The red-haired mute.

What were they trying to tell her?

The naked boy in the woods. A smear of huddled pink in a line of stick trees.

Were they some sort of ghastly muses inspiring her to communicate what needed to be said?

All of them here, sheltered with her, in her nest made of red feather petals.

She wants to return to her home in Bareneed. She will be safe in that place; her life belongs in the cup of that valley.

"We should stand up to them."

"Yes, we should, Anna. Shouldn't we?"

"They're not taking anything from me." She raises her head to admire the breadth of her studio. She is more than capable of raising a child on her own, a child who would witness the world in a special way, through Anna's eyes, and continue to see through those eyes long after Anna has perished.

"Good for you."

The media interest will only make her independence a more likely possibility by endowing greater value to her art. A more solid future for her and her baby will be secured.

"How are you feeling?" the lawyer asks.

She wonders if she is seeing with her mother's eyes now, or if, in death, her mother watches through Anna's eyes.

"Good. Better." She straightens where she is sitting on the floor, the cramps weakening, allowing her to rise to her feet. She needs to pee and goes into the small bathroom.

"I'm peeing."

"Not a problem. I've done that once or twice myself."

Emptying her bladder, she then wipes herself and examines the toilet tissue. White. She wipes again. No startling smudge of red. She drops the tissue into the water.

"Everything okay, Anna?" the lawyer inquires in a warm tone. "The baby's all right?"

"Yes." The baby is hers, and only hers. Anna has never felt more certain about being so intrinsically connected to anything. It is the same feeling she experienced when she first began drawing at the age of nine, the uncontainable, chaotic jumble of shape, pattern, and structure that she could barely restrain. It needed to escape her body. Yet only through the instinctive guidance of her touch could it be set in order and find a distinct life of its own.

She flushes the toilet.

"That's a whole lot of sound. Good connection now."

"I won't let them take my baby, Patricia." That doctor, she thinks, or Kevin. No one.

"Good for you, Anna."

She will move to Bareneed where she will live with her baby on land that skirts the sea and is governed by the incredible.

Chapter Thirteen

Anna: March 28, the Hearing

The snow is blowing a gale, limiting visibility. Large, wet flakes melt on Anna's face.

The last storm of the season, Anna assumes, before spring begins to reanimate the earth. The snow won't last in these predominantly mild temperatures of late.

She recalls being out in similar storms as a child, worrying about the swirling possibility of getting lost should she stray too far. Her mother warned her about the little girl caught in a gale so ferocious and disorienting that the child froze to death in her own yard, a mound discovered six feet from her front door once the storm settled.

Coming down the treacherous sidewalk on Church Hill, Anna is able to make out the crowd she has been told to expect. They are gathered in front of the courthouse on Duckworth, on the wide stone steps, turning one way or the other to shield their faces from the gusts of snow.

The court building is made of stone, with copper spires protruding skyward. It is a celebrated piece of architecture, with a long history of meting out punishments, including hangings, which were hosted on its grounds.

"Remember," says the lawyer, her lips near Anna's ear. "Just let me do the talking for you."

As they reach and cross Duckworth, Anna notices a cameraman scanning the street, setting his attention on individual cars as they pass. Another camera is focused on four people holding placards and chanting in a small circle. A few spectators stand off to the sides, curious to see what might happen next.

The lawyer reaches for Anna's bare hand, squeezes it, and lets go.

Anna's fingertips tingle.

They are ten feet from the court when one of the reporters catches sight of them, and the rest of the gathered contingent turns in unison.

The surge of focused energy comes directly at Anna, worse than any blast of weather, battering her and speeding her heart.

The bulk of the crowd stalks toward her, a heave of bodies made magnetic, while others harmlessly linger back.

In no time Anna is at the centre of everything.

The Embryo: Day 41, Week 6

Brainwaves begin travelling through the brain of Anna's embryo, sending electrical signals throughout the body.

Anna's lawyer speaks to the cameras in a level tone that imparts basic information.

Anna catches only an occasional practised word, for she is busy reading the signs and studying the photographs of embryos stuck on sheets of cardboard beneath punchy slogans. She notices a bundled-up little girl holding a woman's hand, only a tiny shadowed patch of the girl's face discernible in her furry hood. A motionless infant in a carrier is strapped to the front of a man's chest. Children brought along as living proof.

When the lawyer is through speaking, she begins edging away from the cameras. She takes hold of Anna's arm to guide her through the bodies that press closer.

The reporters call out Anna's name, vying for comments.

There is a bobbing disunity to their efforts that becomes confusing to ignore. With so many people speaking her name, Anna feels compelled to say something, but she has no idea what. She needs to keep her eyes off them, to watch her boots. Why are they to be ignored, avoided? These people merely doing their jobs.

She follows the lawyer up the stone steps and through the high doors.

Inside, men and women are gathered on either side of the distinguished foyer and down the wide, wooden-walled corridors. They watch her with interest, their expressions varying. Some hold cameras to their faces and back away as she advances.

Flashes go off in brisk succession.

She feels like an oddity.

A fragile-looking, middle-aged woman with a coffee cup in one hand reaches out to touch her arm.

The lawyer bats the woman's hand away and leads Anna toward an opened doorway where a security guard scans them with a wand. Heads turn to regard them from the pew-like seats. The guard nods, and Anna is led to a table at the front of the room.

Kevin is already seated at a table with his attorney. For some reason Anna didn't expect to see him. The reality of his presence beneath these bright fluorescent lights churns in her. She stands next to her lawyer and considers Kevin's profile. He won't look at her as though she no longer exists. It is utterly baffling how they have found themselves here, their intimate moments spent together to be judged by strangers.

Anna sits while her lawyer speaks to her, detailing expectations she has already reviewed a number of times. Anna checks over her shoulder. Stained faces mottled with colour. Bulbous noses and sloppy, slitted eyes leering at her. People leaning near to one another, wide, fat mouths chewing on gossip. Sniggering profanely. The grotesque faces put to canvas by Hieronymous Bosch. The lunatics captured by Goya.

"Order," announces the court clerk. "All rise."

The people start to rise. A wavering bustle of movement.

"Her Majesty's Supreme Court Trial Division for the Province of Newfoundland and Labrador is now in session."

Facing forward, Anna watches the judge in black robes step up to his bench. He moves as though he has entered the room a thousand times; there is nothing the slightest bit unexpected or individual that could be dragged before him. He takes his seat and bows his head for a moment while the people settle back in their places.

"All persons having anything to do thereat may attend and they shall be heard. God save the queen. His Lordship Mr. Justice Drodge presiding."

The judge makes a statement, and Kevin's lawyer stands, summarizing precedents relating to property cases pertinent to the claim before the court.

Listening, the judge blandly looks at Kevin. Then, with equal disinterest, he turns his head to regard Anna. He is baroque, blunt, and forceful, lined by brown shadows. A man with followers seated around a table, preaching reality over idealism. His expression is serious, almost grim, as though disappointment is the only probable outcome. He nods impatiently, signalling for Kevin's attorney to sit.

Anna's lawyer stands. She reads from a paper in hand. Previous actions are noted relating to the current legal proceedings. In a firm tone that occasionally blusters with emotion, she strikes home the point that this case has no place being tried as a property issues claim.

When Anna's lawyer sits, her face betrays upset and a need for approval.

The judge sighs. He wags his head over the papers in front of him as though they are the most ponderous sort of inconvenience. He adjusts his reading glasses and flicks over a page. The words are the same words, again and again, merely put together differently.

There is perfect silence in the courtroom as all present await reaction.

Finally, the judge looks up. This time he doesn't acknowledge Kevin or Anna. Instead he gazes at a space above the gathered spectators, for he will make his pronouncement not to the people but to some higher invisible force that governs the ages. "Grounds are determined to proceed with this action."

A wave of ruckus sweeps through the rows of people seated behind Anna, culminating in a commotion near the door as people hurry to leave.

Anna expects a banging of the gavel, yet the judge makes no gesture to quiet the disturbance. He joins his arms on his desk and regards it all as a lethargic pedestrian might await a break in traffic before ambling forward with no true destination in mind.

When the motion and chatter begin to ebb, the judge pronounces, "The defendant will not leave the province without permission of the court until the court date of ..." The judge nods to the clerk.

"What?" Anna's attorney bolts to her feet. "Objection. My client is hardly a flight risk, Your Honour."

"If I thought she were, Counsel," the judge brusquely interjects, "I would order her locked up."

Anna's thoughts turn frantic. Flight risk? Was the judge referring to her?

Another flourish of mutterings and speculation rumbles through the room.

"Is he for real?" asks a man's voice behind Anna.

A woman's disbelieving chuckle. "Seems to be."

There are further murmurs of protest, and even short bursts of incredulous laughter.

The judge appears deaf to the exclamations.

The lawyer touches Anna's arm, as though to steady herself, and attentively gazes ahead, her profile struck with tension.

The clerk draws his finger down the lines of his calendar. "April 1."

Four days away.

The judge repeats the date and glances at Kevin's attorney, who flips through his notebook and, raising his eyebrows, gives his consent.

The judge then looks at Anna's lawyer, as though in challenge.

"That's a little premature, Your Honour," she says, her cheeks glowing a dusty pink.

The judge studies the clerk, who offers another date.

"No," gripes the judge. He says the name of Anna's lawyer as though it is a question. "Considering the time-sensitive nature of this case, I suggest we stick with the original date."

"Your Honour," protests Anna's lawyer, still on her feet, although leaning slightly on the table as if destabilized.

"Counsel, this issue demands immediate attention. The people in this courtroom, and across this country for that matter, are eager to learn of the outcome. Do you agree?"

"Yes, but —"

"Then let us get it put to bed, the sooner the better. Are you in agreement or not on the date?"

"Counsel requires more preparation time."

The judge's expression is eclipsed by defiance. "There has been a full exchange of all material and documents. Your pretrial briefs show you have had the opportunity to adequately research and prepare your case. This is a simple matter, and I will not abide the theatrics of delays and postponements. I see no point in them. I never have, as you already know, Counsel." Seemingly offended, the judge rises from his chair, towering over the crowd like an omnipotent threat.

"All rise."

The people are compelled to stand at attention, to remain respectfully still, while the judge steps down, his black robes fanning around him as he makes his way from the room and retires to his chambers.

Chapter Fourteen

The Embryo: Day 43, Week 7

While the head of Anna's embryo is still bent toward its chest, jaw and facial muscles begin to form and strengthen.

Primitive germ cells arrive at the genital area, soon to initiate the formation of sexual organs.

Nipples appear on the chest.

The principal muscle in respiration, the diaphragm, forms as a mass of tissue, which gradually pushes the chest cavity away from the abdomen.

Intestines begin to develop within the umbilical cord and will later travel into the abdomen when the embryo's body is large enough to contain them.

Hand regions differentiate further to form distinct fingers and a wrist.

Anna's embryo is a half-inch long, as big as a honeybee.

When Anna sits at the kitchen table, she has to undo the hasp on her jeans. Her T-shirt feels too small around her chest and shoulders. She has started wearing a bra again, for her breasts are so tender they hurt when they shift around. There is uncertainty rooted in her. She has a headache and she feels bloated.

What is the baby doing to her?

One moment she fears that it might be making her sick. The next moment she is astonished to the point of breathless clarity by her ability to carry another life inside her body.

Be more careful, she tells herself, her every action measured.

Is she ready to have a baby? Is the time right in her life as Kevin wondered? What would be so bad about having an abortion? The baby isn't really alive, is it? Not a human being yet. Millions of women have undergone the procedure and moved on unencumbered.

The baby will change her life in all sorts of ways. She will be alone, raising a child by her own hand. She has witnessed single mothers performing their countless tasks, the frustration of having their days consumed, their schedules overtaken by the constant demands of a child. Will she still be able to paint, to find the time?

Slicing a pink grapefruit in half, she glances at the living room window. The drapes pulled closed against the outside world.

She feels like a prisoner, with the media camped on her doorstep.

Holed up in a dark room with her outlaw baby.

In a room boxed in a house built on a street hidden in a city lost in a country locked in a continent, Anna breathes as a bacterial speck on a massive living globe.

And the baby in her, a dot in her womb, constantly growing, soon to stretch her belly until its mass can no longer be contained.

The points along the line, from dot to living baby, are difficult to disentangle in her mind. To consider the growing entity one thing now, and another thing at a later point in time seems deceitful, a trick of double-dealing.

Disposable now, irreplaceable later. The logic of it badgers her.

Then again, what does it matter if someone is alive or not? If she weren't alive, if her birth mother decided to terminate her pregnancy, Anna wouldn't have experienced a single moment of awareness, just as she will be equally unaware when she leaves this earth. Decades of ardour to breathe through a blink of existence.

With all of this attention, she feels the decision is almost out of her hands. What will people think of her if she has an abortion now?

Everyone will know.

She slices the grapefruit in sections, her hand trembling.

"Unfair," she says, on the verge of tears.

If need be, couldn't she just tell them she miscarried? Issue a press release?

The judge's order for Anna to remain in the province, coupled with his expressed desire to have the matter dealt with in an expedient manner, has heightened media interest.

Last night, when Anna returned from the grocery store, the reporters outside her house blinded her with lights while shouting harried, inciting questions that tried to provoke a statement from her. What was there for her to say?

I am a pregnant woman. I am as confused as any person. And I have no answers.

Anna flashes on the courtroom scene. The faces of the spectators. Men and women out for a gawk at her. Any person, in off the street, permitted to sit there and listen in on her fate. The humiliation of it incites anger before hopelessness exhausts her. She will go back to bed, curl into a ball, and sob.

She drops the knife onto the plate and checks the curtained window.

Red and blue lights flashing outside.

She gets to her feet and approaches the window, peeks down.

Two police cars are parked in the road, while four officers direct the media and spectators away from her doorstep to a barricade across the street. A modern scene of social realism.

She notices two children observing her window. One of them turns and tries scraping together snow from the grass, but there isn't enough to fashion a snowball.

For the past two days sleep has come in fits and starts despite the fatigue she constantly feels. During those brief moments of repose, she has dreamt of lengthy scenarios involving the children of Bareneed. She has been searching for them, through darkness and water, concerned about their whereabouts, her belly aglow like a searchlight linking her baby to the lost children.

In one dream her baby whispered, not in words but in swishes of fluid, that the lost children were growing inside her, as well, bobbing around to crowd her hollow insides.

Returning to the table, Anna eats a grapefruit wedge while recalling her conversation with the police officer in the supermarket. The red-haired woman with him. Something changed in the woman's face when Anna brought up the daughter. If the officer is guilty of heinous acts against children, and Anna doesn't report her suspicions, then isn't she an accessory to his crimes?

Yesterday's newspaper sits on the kitchen table. The front-page headline: JUDGE GREEN-LIGHTS EMBRYO PROPERTY CASE, with the subheading JUSTICE MINISTER MUTE ON ISSUE.

Anna already searched through the pages, only to find no mention of the Bareneed children.

Whenever her eyes fall across the headline, her breath turns hot. She imagines women in houses, apartments, and offices reading the headline and shaking their heads, feeling so incensed and powerless that they stare toward their windows, yearning to do away with someone.

Anna snatches up the newspaper, takes it to the trash bin, and throws it away.

After eating two more pieces of grapefruit, she feels her headache ease a bit and notices her cellphone vibrating on the table. She checks the unfamiliar sequence of digits. The cell has been ringing constantly, the media having managed to track down her number.

She carries her plate of grapefruit to the living room, sets it on the coffee table, settles on the couch, and switches on the TV. The national news. Two commentators are engaged in a heated argument. The words EMBRYO PROPERTY CASE. PROWSE VS WELLS appear along the bottom of the screen.

The first commentator, a chubby woman with grey hair and a sincere, business-like expression, asks, "Is it now the policy of this country's justice system to treat pregnant women as common criminals?"

The woman's question is answered by a noted pundit, a young, bald man in a smart suit and thick-framed glasses. "Wouldn't you say that Judge Drodge acted in accordance with the law? Because the property in question is on the person of the defendant."

"Defendant?"

"Yes, defendant."

"On the person of …"

"On the person of the defendant, Ms. Wells. It's not a question of simply seizing the property. You can't order the police to do that." A smirk while the pundit straightens his glasses. "In fact, I'm surprised Judge Drodge didn't hold Ms. Wells and deny bail."

The commentator chuckles crossly. "You can't be serious."

"If Ms. Wells flees," states the pundit in a balanced tone, "then she takes the mutually owned property with her?"

The commentator is bewildered. "This is the sort of brute, male rationale that has seen women repressed for centuries. The next thing we're going to see are court cases claiming *women* as property. Let's go back —"

"That's not the issue here. You're purposefully trying to muddy the waters with the sentimentality of a feminist movement that is archaic and just as repressive as any sort of patriarchy."

"Well, what is the issue?" The commentator folds her arms across her chest. "You tell me."

"The portion of the property that belongs to Dr. Prowse."

"Okay, well, let's agree, for argument's sake, to this ludicrous supposition that Dr. Prowse's sperm is his property. Wouldn't we then assume that the property was given freely to Ms. Wells? That it was hers for the keeping, like a gift. You can't take back a gift."

"Why assume that?" quips the pundit. "Supposing Dr. Prowse was under the impression that Ms. Wells was taking some form of birth control. Therefore the property wasn't meant to be given and kept by the defendant. It was on loan."

"On loan!"

"Yes, out on loan."

The commentator smiles. "Come on. Who really wants their sperm back?"

"I would before it had the chance —"

"But there's always the chance that even if the woman is taking birth control that a pregnancy might occur, so the man is always gambling with the fact that the *property*, if that's what we're calling it now, might, in fact, be retained permanently by the woman."

The news anchor steps in. "We need to take a little station break. Hang around. We'll be back in just a few moments."

Done with her grapefruit, Anna wipes her mouth. She reclines on the couch, settles on her back, and stares at the ceiling. What does any of this have to do with her baby? Those two people, a man and a woman in a television studio talking to each other about realities they know nothing about. They are fools for allowing themselves to be used.

What might her baby think of all of this in the years to come? Anna should record the broadcasts as keepsakes.

She rolls onto her side to watch the television.

The child who survived attempts by its father to have it aborted. What a horrible bit of history to grow into. Did Kevin even think of that? The identity of her child will be known by millions of people. And, eventually, someone, by mistake or with malice, will tell the child what its father tried to do. A sad truth that sparks new longing in Anna to protect her child, to cover its ears and hug it to her belly.

On the screen a colourful commercial plays for a celebrated Southern zoo. Pandas eating, tigers roaming, monkeys screaming, and dolphins jumping through hoops.

The scene shifts to a little boy putting red crayon to white bristol board, spelling out words in wiggly letters: "I almost didn't make it." Then he draws hearts around the phrase.

A woman's voice over the image of the child creating his art: "I decided to have an abortion ... I went to the clinic, but I couldn't do it ... I turned around and went home, where I belonged." The woman's face slowly fades in, replacing the little boy who holds up his sign.

The woman is pretty, like the woman on the cover of the pregnancy magazine in the doctor's office. She stands in a field of grass with flowers in full bloom. "I can't even imagine a life without Jeremy now." The woman kisses the top of her boy's sun-warmed head. "It would have been a terrible, terrible mistake."

According to the report, demonstrations are being organized. A right-to-life spokeswoman gives the time and date and urges people to join them at an abortion clinic in the city where they are staging their appeal.

The pro-choice people have their own protest planned on the steps of the courthouse.

Anna mutes the sound on the television, her mind running through plans of escape. Airplane flights. Road trips. Anywhere away from the asinine philosophies of these people. She rolls onto her back and rubs her eyes with the butts of her palms, pressing hard. Their words are driving her out of her mind.

The house in Bareneed is the obvious choice. A walk in the country would be good medicine. And she would love to work on a painting without interruption, to disappear for an afternoon in artistic endeavour, mentally paled by its dreamlike transience while grappling with the physicality of depiction.

A low, rhythmic drone awakens Anna. She turns her head on the couch to see her cellphone lit up on the coffee table. Reaching, she knocks her plate, then leans higher to grab the cell.

Lying back, she swipes a length of hair out of her face and checks the number, hoping it might be Kevin.

David.

"Hello?"

"Is this the famous artist, Anna Wells?"

Staring at the ceiling, she yawns while answering. "Famous for all the right reasons."

"I see you have plenty of admirers on your doorstep."

"You see, do you?"

"Well, I saw earlier on TV. I noticed that your house needs a bit of paint around the windows. Don't want you living in a slum."

"I'll let the landlord know."

"Good. On to business. You know those three paintings of yours hanging on my walls for well over a hundred years?"

"Yes." She remembers the paintings. The most nightmarishly disturbing of her last series.

"Sold today for three times what I was originally asking."

Anna thinks this over. People buying her name, her circumstance, not her art. A curiosity to show off to their friends. Yet, generally, don't people often buy art simply to own the name? Regardless, it is a strange feeling to have so many sales at once. To be cleaned out like that. She wonders how long it will last. A fleeting fascination.

"It is good news. I don't care what you say, wallowing in your dismal little mood, because I have a nice fat cheque in my hand with your name scrawled on it in my famously illegible handwriting." His tone implies that he has done her a grand favour.

"Again, for all the right reasons."

"Oh, Anna. You're developing the markings of a true artist, so boringly chockablock with cynicism. How predictable."

"Shut up, David." She wouldn't mind picking up the cheque, paying down her credit cards, and shopping for some new clothes. Clothes for a fat person. There is a mommy shop in the mall. She has passed it countless times.

"There's a healthy demand for your work."

"It's really hard to concentrate right now."

"They're looking for more of those cut-ups from your last exhibit, the ones with babies and children. Didn't you have two of those you took back?"

"I destroyed them." She slides one leg up the back of the couch to get more comfortable, her eyes on one of the paintings she professed to have destroyed.

"That's unfortunate. In the present market we could sell for ten times our usual asking price."

The blur of images from the television screen catches in her peripheral vision. She turns to see paintings from her previous exhibit. Strange how they are being broadcast when David just mentioned them.

She switches the cell from one ear to the other.

The paintings appear brutal to her. Fragmented human faces merged with the meat from butchered animals. A few baby heads juxtaposed here and there. The sight of them makes her cringe with shame for her flippant treatment of the subject.

Anna sits up and adjusts the volume to hear what is being said.

"I'll call you back later. Bye."

"Paint faster."

Anna shuts her cell.

When the camera returns to the anchorman, he nods and makes a brief sound of dour concern. "Chilling, and yet sadly foreboding."

"Idiot." Anna switches to a U.S. news channel. A story about a military conflict overseas.

She assumes that the Americans will be picking up her story soon. Just this morning she recognized a logo for an American channel on one of the video cameras outside her door.

Anna turns to another U.S. news channel. A snippet of a painting appears in a box in the upper-right-hand corner of the screen. The flesh-hued rose. Prowse versus Wells.

Anna stands and steps nearer the screen while the newscaster speaks. "A lover's quarrel between a gynecologist and a pregnant artist is on its way to court in Canada. Dr. Kevin Prowse has filed a statement of claim against Anna Wells, demanding that his half of the embryo be returned to him. The highly irregular grounds for the action: return of stolen property."

Stolen property?

The newscaster explains the background on the developing situation, recapping recent court cases involving sperm and frozen embryos while footage of Anna's studio appears. The rose paintings in development. The camera pans the paintings leaning against walls or perched on easels. Anna isn't present in any of the shots.

"What?" Incensed, she turns to the window, hurries to lift back the curtain, and peer into the late-afternoon street. Who is missing from the gathering? Who is in her studio? She rushes to the closet adjacent to the door. While pulling on her coat she decides she needs to pee.

The bathroom seems smaller than she remembers, the floor space limited. On the toilet she wonders if her belly is bigger because of the baby or because she has been eating more. The fit of her clothes is bugging her like crazy.

She knows she shouldn't drive; her agitation would make her a road hazard. She calls a taxi on her cell and changes into a loose sweatshirt and track pants.

Kenneth J. Harvey

The Embryo: Day 43, Week 7

The nubs of ten toes appear simultaneously in Anna's embryo.

Impatiently waiting at the window, Anna examines the faces gazing up at her. She counts them. Fourteen. Cameras are raised. She stays in her place, trying to imagine herself as they see her, a grubby-haired eccentric artist peeking out a narrow slit in the curtains.

When the taxi doesn't arrive promptly, she leaves her apartment, carefully taking the stairs to the lower landing while tightly gripping the handrail so as not to fall.

Shadows shift restlessly behind the frosted glass in the front door. They sense her coming.

Anna opens the door to face the explosion of words. The assault on her senses is startling, as though she has been roused from sleep by chaos. She ducks each question and veers away down the street.

A number of engines are engaged behind her as the media take up her trail in vehicles and on foot. She strides through the slush for her studio. Ignoring their calls, she maintains her brisk pace in hope of catching the intruders in her studio.

A van follows alongside her, camera aimed out the passenger window.

A woman gains on Anna, hurrying up by her side. "How do you feel, Anna, with all this attention focused on you?"

Anna can see the woman's face in the corner of her eye. The woman is struggling to keep up and regulate her breathing. A microphone is leaned near Anna's lips, almost banging her in the cheek.

"Is the baby okay?"

Anna shoves her hands in her coat pockets and studies her boots, careful of her step on the uneven surface. She should slow down, walk more cautiously.

The people are making her angry. Is her rage bothering the baby? Or is her rage emanating from the baby, glowing like a red demon? She thinks of turning on them, of shouting for them to leave her alone, of bursting into tears, but her display would only end up on TV. The property of corporations. She won't sign over her misery.

Making her way down Longs Hill, she regrets not taking her car. She is giving the TV networks too much footage, too much of herself. Or was that her purpose, a sublimated yearning for acclaim?

With thoughts turning more frantic, she finds herself on Duckworth Street and glances each way before crossing the street.

Jaunting up the concrete steps to her studio, she tries the knob. It is unlocked.

She rushes inside, pressing the barrier closed against the bodies wanting to enter. She twists the deadbolt and dashes up over the stairs to find her studio door open. The sight of it knocks her to a standstill.

"Hello?" She enters her space, checking around, her eyes troubled, heart beating fiercely.

Nothing seems to have been disturbed.

How might they have gained access without her consent?

No one has a key except for her and the landlord.

Would Mr. Oliver have let them in? She seriously doubts he would be that underhanded.

Does Kevin have a key? Did Anna give him one, or did he have one cut for safety sake. Bastard! Why is he humiliating her like this?

Anna checks the canvases, leaning one away from another to make certain none of them have been removed or their order tampered with.

She searches for hints of someone in hiding. Who has been in here? What have they done? Violation. She is gripped by the vindicative urge to set the place on fire. Destroy everything.

Pacing across the space, she kicks over a wooden stool. She surveys her paints, fingers the tubes, moves her cupped palm over the tips of her brushes, checks the high ceiling while her cellphone vibrates. She removes her gloves to snatch it from her pocket.

Her lawyer. Perfect timing.

"Hello?"

"Anna?"

"Someone was in my studio." She continues pacing, turning to get a panoramic view of the room. "Here."

"Who?"

"Reporters. On television. Have you seen the American channels?"

"I haven't been watching. What channel?"

"I don't know what channel."

Her lawyer says "Uh-huh" in a slow tone that suggests she is writing. "I'll have someone look into it."

"Look into it how?"

"Make some calls."

"I'm going away. I'm nailing shut my studio door and going away. This is killing me."

"Away where?"

"I don't know."

"You shouldn't try to leave, Anna."

"I don't mean the province." She sweeps her hair back from her forehead, turning on the spot to continue making sure everything is in its place.

"I'd advise you to stay near. It's only two days to court."

Anna's eyes skim her work tables, the dried bits of colours splotched on every surface. The dead roses, the art books, the nests.

This place where she could lose herself in creation. This safe place. This refuge.

"Do you need some company?"

"What?"

"I could come along."

"No. No, that's fine."

"How about a place to stay?"

"I have a place to stay in Bareneed." Her eyes fall on the open door. She strides toward it. What if someone is hiding in the hallway shadows?

"Not a good idea to be out there all alone. We should set you up in a hotel. I could take care of that."

"No, I need to get out of town."

"If money's an issue —"

"No, it's not that." She swings shut the door. But now she feels trapped.

"How long are you going for?"

"I don't know. Just a day."

"Do you really think that's wise?"

"Wise? What's wise about any of this?"

"I know. Sorry. Okay, but make sure I can get in touch. If you want me to come out, just call. I'll be there if you need some company. All right?"

"Yes."

"And, listen, don't feel desperate. This will all work out. Public pressure is coming on strong. I've heard the justice minister is going to make a statement soon. Judge Drodge will be put in his place. I can almost guarantee it."

Anna bunches up her lips and shakes her head, her fury mounting. "I won't run away. That's for sure."

"Good. Women everywhere are rooting for you, Anna. The pro-choice people are on our side, as expected, and bizarrely, the anti-abortionists are in our camp, too. I never thought I'd ever find myself happy to have those guys rooting for me." She gives a disbelieving little laugh.

Anna mulls over the lawyer's words: those guys rooting for me.

"Why?"

"Well ... their politics are a little insane. But in this case we'll tolerate them."

The way the lawyer is talking further sours Anna's mood. The politics of other people's opinions have nothing to do with her baby.

A beep sounds on the line.

"I have another call," Anna says.

The beep sounds again, cutting off parts of her words. She checks the number of the incoming call. David.

"Okay. Contact me if you need anything. I could come to Bareneed. It's not a problem."

"Thanks. Bye." She presses the button. "Hello?"

"Anna?"

"Hello, David."

"Why didn't you tell me about these new rose paintings? Flesh-coloured. Brilliant! My God, the phone hasn't stopped ringing. You're on TV. *American* TV."

Anna's face flushes at the thought of her work being televised before she has deemed it fit. She waves an arm in frustration, makes a fist, wants to punch something. Overcome, she stomps a foot.

"The gallery's site has been barraged by hits. And the phone! Anna! It's the lottery. How many rose paintings do you have?"

"Stop it. I don't know."

"Come on, Anna. Tell your Uncle David."

Her eyes scan the room. "Seven or eight." She thinks of the others in Bareneed in various stages of completion. "Maybe a dozen."

"Fabulous! Let's get them hung."

"I won't do that. I'll burn them first."

David laughs wildly, almost hysterically, like a bird gone mad. "No, don't do that, darling. They're your creations. Your babies. Remember, you used to say that? Are you ready for a show? I think now's the time."

"Now's not the time, David."

"Why? The demand is positively mind-blowing. What could be a better time? Bring me some of those paintings?"

"No."

"We're talking big money, Anna. In the last fifteen minutes I've had calls from five extremely wealthy collectors. I just had a call from Germany! Will you bring me just two? I could have them photographed and get them up for bidding."

"I said no."

"Please, Anna. Three or four."

"Stop begging."

"I like begging."

Anna chuckles despite herself. "I know. You're one of the truly sick ones."

"Excellent. Come by this afternoon?"

"Give it up."

"I'm looking at the Internet. BBC just picked up the story. There's your picture. My feet froze taking that. I almost had to have them amputated. They were green. You owe my frostbitten toes that much at least. You're in their top ten stories. Gotta go. More calls. Talk soon. Bring me those paintings. Don't let me down."

Anna shuts her cell. She steps near one of the tall windows and peeks with trepidation into the street.

Faces staring up at her, their mouths slowly opening to mutely call out her name.

The Embryo: Day 43, Week 7

Teeth buds take shape in Anna's embryo, tiny calcium specks sprouting beneath the gums' surface.

Chapter Fifteen

Anna: March 30, the White-Haired Girl

Anna watches her rearview mirror for indications she is being followed. She has driven down side streets and raced through yellow lights to cut off her pursuers. Pumped on adrenaline, she grows more agitated. Her driving might even be a touch erratic. That is how she feels: jerkily out of control, like being wired on too much caffeine.

Should she have delivered some paintings to David? The ones from her soon-to-be-padlocked studio? A startled and apologetic Mr. Oliver assured her that added security would be forthcoming.

"I saw no one go in there," he said, his palms raised as though in surrender. "What did they take?" His face betrayed signs of anger at the thought of burglary on his premises.

"No, nothing, it's okay," Anna said, trying to convince him that it wasn't his fault. "Don't worry."

"Right away," he said, a threatening look overhead. "Many more locks. You are safe with me."

Would it be so wrong to take advantage of the situation by securing a larger audience for her art? How would her baby feel about it? What would her baby think of her profiting from this perverse publicity? What would her mother think?

Her baby wouldn't approve, she decides, and continues heading west, past the too-familiar fast-food restaurants, car lots, and storage facilities along Kenmount Road.

If reporters are still following her, they might assume she is fleeing. As such they are probably growing eager, capturing shaky video footage of her car on its escape route. Their suspicions that she is running away might be reported as fact, or televised as alleged fact, which amounts to communally suspected guilt.

At the end of Kenmount Road she takes the west-bound ramp that loops up to the highway. Her eyes persistently check the rearview to the point of distraction. She recognizes a van and a SUV far back, the same vehicles from outside her apartment. Will they actually follow her all the way to Bareneed?

Watch the road, she warns herself.

She could lead the media right to those children in Bareneed. Her story might then be transformed into something positive. Wouldn't the media help the children find their parents, or investigate the mystery of who has been abandoning or abducting them?

A few miles out Anna applies the brakes to pull into the lot of the last gas stop before the open highway. She rolls up to a row of pumps, climbs from her car while watching the highway as the van and SUV race by.

The gas nozzle is so cold it pains the bones in her hand. She keeps her eyes fixed on the ascending digits, noticing her breath in the late-afternoon air. She switches hands on the nozzle and shoves her free hand into her pocket to warm her fingers.

A car pulls up in the parallel lane, a large black dog seated in the passenger seat. The woman driver gets out and approaches the pump to make her choices. The dog shifts its head to watch the woman, its coat glistening under the canopy light. Soon, it sets its deep brown eyes on Anna. Its face has a majestic quality that suggests it is a creature with greater capabilities and perceptions than its inferior human master.

It is a gorgeous animal.

Anna smiles at it, wanting to rub her palm over its warm fur. As though in judgment, the dog turns its head away.

Done filling her tank, Anna steps inside, collects a diet cola from the cooler at the back, picks out an apple flip and one of the on-sale chocolate bars, and brings it all to the counter. She glances over her shoulder. People milling around, trying to decide on what will satisfy their needs, then she checks the doorway, expecting the black dog to enter at any moment to meander up beside her, to sit and stare. The blackness of the dog's coat has struck a chord in her. Trying to duplicate the warm sheen, she mixes the colours in her mind, black with the faintest touch of Prussian blue. She considers the areas to highlight, layering the texture stroke by stroke.

"Is that everything?" asks the middle-aged woman behind the counter. She has an all-business attitude, a tight face, perm, and the name EMMA on her pin.

"Yes."

Emma rings in Anna's snack. Flatly reading out the tally, she then begins bagging the items. Her eyes go to Anna's face, and her actions are paused while her attention shifts to a small TV on a ledge behind the counter. She glances at the money in Anna's hand.

"That's okay," says Emma. "It's on me, sweetie."

"What?"

"My treat." The woman grins openly, exposing big teeth and an excess of pink gums.

"You sure?"

"Yes, I'm *very* sure. Put your money away, hon."

"I had gas, too."

"It's all right."

Struck speechless, Anna slips the bills back into her wallet.

Emma directs the holes of the plastic bag toward Anna's fingers and leans to whisper, "You take good care of that baby of yours." Her eyes dip for a secretive glimpse at Anna's belly. "Tell your baby that people are watching out for it." The woman nods, leans nearer, and whispers even lower, "Men are the worst sort of vermin ever put on this earth. They should all be murdered in their sleep."

Anna chuckles uncomfortably. She peeks over her shoulder at a scruffy-looking man in a jean jacket and baseball cap behind her. The man checks her up and down, then fixes his eyes on the display of cigarettes while tapping his bank card on the counter.

Anna smiles in consideration of Emma's generosity and takes the bag. "Thank you very much."

"That's okay. It's a hard thing bringing a life into the world. Always some jackass trying to tell you what to do. Every single day of your life." She shoots a look at the man in the baseball cap. "Stop tapping that damn bank card on the glass. You're gonna break it."

The man raises his eyebrows and glances around as though searching for the true source of the woman's ire.

"Don't let it get you down, okay?"

Anna nods. "I'll try not to."

Emma waves goodbye.

Back out in her car, Anna gazes at the big window. The woman gives her another wave. Anna waves back, feeling charmed by this kind-hearted connection to a stranger.

She pulls away from the pumps and slows at the edge of the lot to wait for a break in traffic. She uses her teeth to tear open the apple flip. Biting into it, she chews the pastry and apple filling into paste.

A gap between cars.

Accelerating, she eyes the dashboard, checking the clock, hoping she can make it to Bareneed before dark. Her attention is caught by two vehicles up ahead, pulled over on the side of the road. The van and the SUV. Whizzing past, Anna sees a woman with an elaborate hairdo talking on a cellphone. The surprised face, following Anna's car, is recognizable from years of television.

~ 🐚 ~

Flashing lights in her rearview convince her that the authorities have been notified. Did the reporter contact the police to add a splash of drama to the scene? A chase captured live on TV?

As the lights grow brighter and the sound of the sirens more pronounced, her heartbeat becomes frantic.

Finally, she is forced to pull over.

A fire truck and a paramedic's cube van zip past.

Relieved that the trouble isn't hers, Anna watches the red lights flash far ahead. She pulls back onto the highway. The blots of blinking lights move at a steady span from her, a stretch of empty asphalt remaining constant between them.

Then the emergency vehicles appear to stop.

Anna studies them holding still, thinking it might be an optical illusion until finally they begin to grow larger.

The vehicles gain more and more prominence in the nearer distance, their lights brightening with warning, becoming lifelike in size as she slows and joins them.

A tangle of torn metal is revealed through a space between the two emergency vehicles. Three cars have collided. What has happened is unknowable because the cars have been tossed and spun. A green minivan has landed with its twisted front wheels on the trunk of an orange compact.

Checking her rearview, Anna pulls over onto the right side of the road, visually calculating the space required to squeeze by on the gravel shoulder. The two media vehicles are fast approaching. It occurs to her that they have been drawn here by the accident, not by her plight.

Barely keeping her tires from slipping over the bank, she warily rolls forward at a snail's pace, tightening her muscles and leaning away from the drop as though to prevent her car from toppling.

A firefighter begins erecting a yellow barrier across the pavement behind her. More flashing lights appear far back toward St. John's.

A few feet and she will be clear of the tight space. She checks her side mirror to make certain it won't be knocked off. Her advance is painful, yet she manages to get ahead of the emergency vehicles where the violence of the crash scene opens up on its own hideous plain of long shadows and anguished lines.

A morbid sight strange to the eyes.

Her hand goes to roll down her window, but she stops herself from making the shock more vivid.

It hurts her heart to watch as the body of a child is lifted from a stain on the pavement. Anna's tires roll over crackling headlight glass. The girl's arms are twisted at seemingly impossible angles. The paramedic must cradle the child's head, which is bloody and missing sections of long blond hair.

Anna gasps in pain, her palm pressing over her mouth, the food in her stomach hardening.

Ten feet away a woman stands in a blood-soaked T-shirt, the fabric shaped tightly to her body as though her flesh is painted red. Her arms hang at her sides. She stares straight into the face of a paramedic who grips her by the shoulders and speaks in a loud voice that Anna can hear through her closed window.

There is another vehicle in the grassy ditch that separates the divided highways. A blue pickup, resting on its roof, billows smoke, its undercarriage of pipes and metal reminding Anna of an industrial basement. Firefighters rush to pull open its doors.

Kenneth J. Harvey

The Embryo: Day 43, Week 7

A sense of smell forms in the brain of Anna's embryo.

The spectacle continues to expand as Anna rolls along — a length of buckled bumper, sprinkles of orange and clear glass, a rumpled plaid jacket — until she discovers a massive brown object lying across the entire road. Inexplicably, it shifts, as though alive and in the clutch of some discordant scream of nature.

A moose, Anna realizes with a start. Peculiar without antlers, as the male is the prominent image captured in photographs.

Anna's front tires approach the animal's back, stilt-like legs that suddenly kick out.

Two wildlife officers in uniforms stand over the moose. One of them, a pale woman with short brown hair, guardedly approaches Anna, who stops her car and rolls down the window, her ears filling up with heightened sounds of pandemonium. Sirens. Shouts of harried instruction. The low, unstable pitch of crying.

"Are they letting people through?" the wildlife officer asks in disbelief, then leans to search down the highway.

"I don't know."

"Keep going." The officer waves an arm, directing Anna ahead just as the cow raises its monstrously large head and groans, struggling to buck up off its side.

Anna's hands flinch on the steering wheel.

"Go on. Keep going." Backing away, the officer continues waving her arm, the gesture weakening while she stares ahead at the spread of the scene.

Anna nudges the accelerator as the moose snorts and fights to rise. Its hide scrapes against the asphalt, yet it can't right herself, as though its legs won't work.

When Anna glimpses the reflection in her side mirror, the hopeless efforts of the moose make her fretful and breathless. Why don't they do something to help it?

The two wildlife officers stand to either side of the animal. The man kneels beside the moose's head and reaches up for the hunting knife extended in the hand of the woman.

With the barricade up, other vehicles haven't been permitted to pass beyond the fatality.

Anna speeds up, her thoughts lingering on the moose, the small broken body being lifted away, the blood-soaked woman, the smoking upside-down truck.

Horrifying memories that knot in her stomach and inspire soul-trembling anxiety.

There have been news reports about the large population of moose on the island, and the government's proposition to cull the animals. Protesters have taken the government to court to prevent the slaughter.

Anna checks the rearview, steadying her hands on the wheel. No other vehicles in sight. An empty strip of highway stretching longer behind her.

In the far distance, a dot of tangled flesh and metal containing the harrowing sprawl of Picasso's *Guernica*. Tormented visions rearing up from it. Bodies in disarray, broken and geometrical.

She rolls along in a state of disquiet, a hurtling body protected by a steel shell, her head playing through flitting images: butchered animal parts intertwined with human limbs. A car airborne against a blue sky. Roses stuffed into gaping mouths. A nest on fire. Her ill mother with eyes like a creature's. Children crawling through black blood. The explosion of snow landing.

The light fades before her.

Shadows lean from the trees, elongated on the highway as though commanding her forward.

With her thoughts lingering elsewhere, suspending time, she almost misses the off ramp for Shearstown Line.

She jerks the steering wheel to make a speedy detour.

In the brooding dusk she follows the road through rolling fields and clusters of vaguely shimmering ponds surrounded by low bush and silhouettes of black evergreens.

She switches on her headlights.

Before the turnoff for Bareneed she pulls into the shallow lot of an old hardware store and waits, trying to remember what has prompted her stop. Something important that she needed.

She reaches into her coat pocket to search for a reminder. The hollow tube of a shotgun shell. She takes it out and holds it up before her eyes in the near-perfect darkness.

A child lifted above a stain, inert and hovering. The outline of the snow angel has vanished.

It is quiet in Anna's front yard: still and peaceful, with each sound amplified in a tone hushed by dusk.

A stain shaped like what?

Fluid creeping away from the centre, lengthening in trails that tap the heart.

In the kitchen she flicks on the light and shivers at the cold, her breath misting. It is colder in the house than outside its walls.

How did she get to St. John's?

It remains a blank mystery that persists in alarming her. She checks the table for a fresh rose, but there is only the old one, bent and black, with a hint of perished red. The real estate agent hasn't been by. She puts the box of shotgun shells on the counter, pulls off her gloves, and takes out her cell, which she has set to silent.

Thirty-seven calls.

She thumbs through the numbers, yet recognizes only one sequence: David's.

Her eyes shift to the box of shells, then to the shotgun in the corner. It is reassuring to know she has protection out here should the media or the deceitful police officer show up to pester here.

How old is the single-barrel shotgun? Will it explode in her arms if she fires it? She has heard of such mishaps and imagines herself with her hands blown off, continuing her career as an applauded oddity painting with her mouth or feet.

The shotgun links to a memory of the crippled moose cow on the highway. Why did they use a knife instead of a gun? To be more involved in the act of relief? To make the decision entirely theirs?

Anna raises the iron poker and slides a front damper off the stove. Cold ash in the hollow. She roots around. Not a single flicker of spark.

She checks the refrigerator for what she might need at the supermarket. Milk, of course, and juice. She can't recall if the supermarket in Bay Roberts has the cranberry juice she likes.

Pulling open the freezer door, she finds the space crammed with frozen meat. The roasts and steaks are packaged on white Styrofoam trays and covered with plastic made opaque by frost. There are no labels on the plastic. The meat within is a deep, bloodless brown.

Anna takes out a steak and studies it, the cut of the bone unfamiliar to her. She suspects it must be moose, a local kill packaged by a neighbourhood butcher, and lays the steak on the counter to thaw for a late supper.

A faint peal of laughter beyond the house. Children fearfully at play in the dark.

Glancing at the window, Anna notices how the rose and shotgun appear aligned from where she stands, both tilted at the exact slight angle.

She twists on the tap to fill the sink, to submerge the steak in cold water to help it thaw, but the faucet gives up nothing. She tries the hot water tap. Not a single drop.

Where is the water?

Frozen in the pipes, she realizes with a chill. Why is it so uncharacteristically cold? March usually brings the thaw with it. Or the glitter of an ice storm that takes down power lines and snaps the limbs off trees.

Out in the living room the woodstove door creaks when she opens it. She crumples up newspapers, creating a rumpled bed before stacking a criss-cross of kindling atop it. Building a fire the way Mr. King patiently taught her on an earlier visit. She lights a match to the edge of paper in three places.

The flames creep to life, the heat gradually warming her face. She holds her hands up to the fire as the kindling crackles and pops embers out onto the steel tray. She lays a birch split at the back of the firebox, then another at the front.

Shutting the door, she continues regarding the flames behind glass. Smoke clouds the interior. She stands to open the flue wider; fire requires oxygen to thrive.

On her way from the living room, she hears the flames blazing, beginning to rage in the stovepipe. The living room will be warm in no time. It will be nice to sit there and bathe in the luscious heat.

She appreciates the quiet in the house, the sense of being alone, coupled with the certainty that she will be able to work without interruption. Switching on lights as she goes, she heads upstairs to check on her paintings, wondering if the cold has harmed them. Outside her studio the red stain on the floor has deepened to black. Its shape captures her imagination, enticing her nearer. The outline of a hand. She kneels and presses her hand to the stain, but the one on the floor is infinitely larger, the fingers long and jagged.

A rustling sound from her studio.

One of the children?

Excitedly, Anna gets to her feet and grips the doorknob, finding the metal warm to the touch.

Who has been painting for her, as though in her hand?

She turns the knob and opens the door a crack, hoping not to disturb the little painter standing at work.

Anna's face is swarmed by heat, pooling out around her while she stares in. A light is already on in there.

No one at her easel.

But the sound again, issuing from the closet.

Stepping in, she finds her studio stiflingly warm. The room must be on the side of the house that catches all the sun.

A scratching at wood followed by the splintering sound of teeth gnawing.

When will her baby have teeth? she wonders. Are they born with teeth? No. Where is her mind? She remembers reading about teething pain. The need for chew toys and salves to rub on aching gums.

Standing in the fostering warmth, she examines the three-canvas sequence of the silver fish with rosebud heads. Someone has added another layer of details that makes the fish appear so remarkably lifelike that she reaches out to touch. Wet. She checks her fingertips to see traces of paint, yet the painting remains unsmudged.

She leaves the room, avoiding the stain on her way to the nursery, for she suspects there might be life hidden away in there. The air grows warm as she nears, the paintings on the walls evident through the opened door, the individual brush strokes that coloured each animal, bird, and insect.

Anna flicks on the overhead light to search the bed. No child tucked away beneath the covers.

She studies the details on the walls. How it is necessary to know the bone count in a dove's foot in order to paint it properly.

She checks the window, for something has commenced thudding against the pane. An egg-sized flash of white with flickering wings. A large moth.

How the knee and ankle in a tiger's leg are higher than expected, the fur made with a mix of raw sienna and light hansa yellow.

Above her the scurrying of tiny footsteps against the slatted ceiling.

The bright chrome yellow in a buttercup butterfly. The greenish veined wings. The concept of symmetry as a means of expressing the relation of parts to one another and to the whole, translating into pulse, echo, and rhythm.

The moth's powdery wings still banging against the transparent barrier, its movements growing louder, more aggressive, rattling the loose pane.

A zebra with one set of stripes mixed from titanium white and payne's grey, the other set, Prussian blue blended with a tiny dab of bone black. The disorienting tension of duality in negative and positive stripes, a mirage of itself, severed halves never to be melded into one.

How could a child so small know these things?

The feathers of a crow not rendered with black paint but with a mix of burnt umber and ultramarine blue. The brush strokes always guided in the direction of growth.

"The living world," whispers a child.

Anna turns expectantly in search of the voice.

The hallway. Empty.

Deep brown words newly scrawled along the wall, letters dipping more and more at their ends, diving toward the stain on the floor: THE LIVING WORLD.

Anna steps out to examine the new mark.

Leaning nearer, she presses a fingertip against the letter L. Not paint at all but a mixture of some sort of syrup and tint. She touches her tongue to the tip of her finger. Sweet and metallic, like molasses. She glances over her shoulder at her open bedroom door across from her studio. Stepping there, she pokes her head in to see her room exactly as she left it except for a suspicious lump beneath the bedcovers.

Hesitating, she holds her breath to see if the lump will budge, while smiling in advance of the possible amusement. She tiptoes to stand at ready by the side of the bed.

"Are you hiding?" she playfully asks. She waits for some sort of response, a smothered giggle or the confined shifting of covered limbs. Her hand reaches for the quilt, gathers up enough material in its grasp and yanks the covers back.

A naked doll with white straw-like hair. One of its eyelids shut, the other open and trained on her.

A missing arm.

Three broken toes.

Chipped lips garishly painted red.

"The living world."

Anna spins to look behind her.

A laughing white-haired girl with a severed arm in her hands. Her fingers worm against the plastic flesh as though testing its composition. With her head at a twisted angle, she takes a rickety step forward, tilting and straightening as though one of her legs is shorter than the other. Her bare feet leave black prints on the floor.

The sight doesn't disturb Anna. In fact, she thought to expect it and is happy to see the little girl.

"Hi."

The little girl continues wildly laughing, drawn to the doll on the bed. She limps faster across the room and hurls herself onto the mattress. Hovering over the doll, she shrieks with delight while stabbing the arm at its belly, trying to fit it back on.

"It goes here," Anna instructs, patiently taking the arm and picking up the doll. She wiggles the arm into the hole until it clicks.

The girl stops laughing and stares menacingly at the doll.

"It's fixed," Anna says.

The little girl shakes her head, snatches the doll away, plucks out the arm, and begins to limp from the room.

"Wait." Anna reaches to touch the girl's hair, her fingers finding their mark.

At once the child's movements are arrested. She tilts her head lethargically, her actions becoming increasingly fluid until she is soothed to absolute stillness. Placated, the child lets her muscles slacken. Her eyes slip shut, and she lowers her head to nuzzle into Anna while making purring sounds.

None of this is frightening, Anna thinks, as she strokes the girl's hair. Why?

In fact, Anna feels comforted with the girl at hand, as though her perceptions aren't failing her at all but are functioning at the heightened level she always wished for. To witness what is there, or more essentially, what is almost there.

When Anna removes her hand from the girl's hair, the child returns to her senses and jerks away, limping from the room in a pattern of hasty clip-clops.

While Anna sleeps she dreams of children laughing. They are competing with another, calling out silly jokes from their individual hive-like tunnels. Pausing to laugh harder, they hold their bellies and throw back their heads, their eyes jammed shut with hilarity.

Anna stands before the wall of tiny compartments, observing the amused children who appear identical to her. They can't stop laughing, so their jokes are never completely expressed, only sequences of words that fail to deliver the punch lines.

The laughter is so intense that it squeaks from the children, turning them red-faced and breathless.

By merely being in their presence, Anna is incited to chuckle.

The laughter is contagious, and she wakes laughing, alone in her room.

There is a smile on her face in the dimness while she shifts to find a more comfortable position.

Pale moonlight spills in through her lace curtains, further calming her sensibility.

The white-haired girl sits illuminated at the foot of the bed, her head bent at a disconcerting angle, her eyes tilted to better make out Anna's questionable existence.

"Shush, shush," the girl says in a lyrical tone ill-fitted to her appearance. "Shush, shush." Her little hand pats the quilt.

The girl's company is consoling, for she appears to be set on looking after Anna.

Lulled by the melodic quality of the voice, Anna begins drifting into slumber and continues laughing with the children.

Half asleep, she senses something crawling beneath the covers beside her, but she can't open her eyes to see. A warm, full-blooded presence sliding up the length of her body until slowly losing its substance as though blending through a barrier.

The Embryo: Day 44, Week 7

The windpipe and vocal cords in Anna's embryo begin to take shape.

Anna: March 31, at Work

In the morning Anna wakes without suffering the slightest spell of anxiety or dislocation. She feels well rested and searches the bed for the white-haired girl but only finds the doll, the butt of its broken arm stuffed into its torn mouth.

Anna is ready to tackle the frozen pipes. If she can't free up the water, then she will gather snow and melt it on the stove like a true pioneer woman. The melted snow could be mixed with her paints. She has read somewhere that this grade of water helps maintain the brilliance of pigment.

Shifting her legs over the edge of the mattress, she steps to the window. Fresh snow on the ground. It must have fallen silently last night while she dreamed of the grinning children. A blanket of white radiating in the sun. She searches for an indication of tracks, but the snow is unblemished.

In the kitchen, hoping to have a cup of tea, she automatically tries the taps. Nothing. She crouches and opens the cupboard door beneath the sink, staring in at the copper pipes.

Her cellphone buzzes from the table, ringing twice before she gets to it and picks it up.

"Mr. King" is displayed on the screen along with "Unknown Number."

Now Anna can ask him about the other night with Kevin. Or should she even ask at all, for she is beginning to suspect the entire episode was some sort of stress-inspired nightmare?

"Hello?"

"Hello, Anna. How's the baby?"

"Which baby?" The little children so near in her thoughts. She catches the scent of fried meat and remembers the moose steak from last night. It wasn't as tough as she was often led to believe. A bit gamey, but similar to cow steak.

Mr. King chuckles. "All of them, I guess. You expecting triplets?"

"Don't know, but they're all out of water."

"I saw you driving by yesterday evening. It's been cold and you haven't been there." He pauses, as though awaiting an explanation. When one isn't offered, he adds, "You've been busy with your other life."

Anna sniggers and brushes hair away from her face. "Yeah, my other life in my other world." She scratches her nose while eyeing the mess in the frying pan. She should have poured some water in there to make cleanup easier.

"Exactly."

"Now I don't have any water here."

"You have pipe problems. The cold."

"Yes." The snow beyond the curtains is glowing so white it

eradicates definition in the yard. Close to the house, something drops from the roof and smashes to tinkling bits on the earth. An icicle, Anna assumes.

"I've seen it happen to that house before. Do you want to know how to cure it?"

"Yes, please."

"At the rear of the house there's a hatch that opens into a crawl space. Your trouble is under there."

"Why?" She tears a piece of bread from a French loaf on the counter and opens the cupboard to take down a jar of peanut butter.

"The pump hose runs through a hole in the floor in the back room and goes into the earth. It's buried beneath the frost line, over to the well."

"So I need to get under the house?" Biting off a bit of bread, she uses her finger to scoop out some peanut butter and adds it to her mouth.

"Yes. I should have warned you about the water. We're not so nature-proofed out here as in the city. That length of pipe in the crawl space is probably frozen. I'll come over."

"No, that's okay … Sorry, I'm chewing … I can do it. How much room in the crawl space?"

"About two feet."

She makes a sound of restrained distress, eats more bread and peanut butter, feeling like a savage while she sucks on her finger.

"That's why they call it a crawl space. I can help. I've been in tighter spaces than that."

"No, I'll be fine."

"You sure?"

"Yes." She doesn't want the real estate agent in the house. She doesn't want anyone around to disturb her peace or to scare the children into hiding. Besides, she prefers to fix the water herself. She is a person just like anyone else, with a brain and hands that can solve problems. "I can handle it." She tears off another section of bread and adds peanut butter.

"Okay, tough lady. You need to put a heated wire on that pipe. I don't know if there's one already wrapped around it. If there's a wire on that pipe, then the wind must be getting in through somewhere. Either way you have to heat that pipe."

"How?"

"There's an old space heater in the back room."

"Where?" At the far end of the counter there is a door that leads into the back room. Anna wipes her hands on a dish towel and opens the door, scanning the articles hung on nails on the wall: a rusty trap with jagged metal teeth, loops of picture wire, a set of snowshoes with leather straps.

"On a shelf by that barred back door."

Anna spots the space heater. It has a wire grille on the front, and a frayed cord dangling to the floor. There is a door behind the shelves with a deadbolt, and three lengths of planking nailed across it.

"Found it."

"Plug that in under the house next to the hose. It's a tight crawl. I'd be happy to do it, even if I can't squirm like I used to. Old bones, you know."

"No, really. Thanks."

"You sure? You need to be extra careful now."

"Yes."

The real estate agent huffs with disapproval. "All right then. I'll call later to see how you're doing. By the way, is your pump on?"

Anna makes her way deeper into the back room, squeezing by the storage boxes to find the red pump bolted to the floor next to the hot water tank. A three-foot piece of wide black hose runs horizontally from the front of the pump before being coupled at a ninety-degree angle. The hose then travels vertically through a hole in the floor.

Anna checks the switch on the small panel box with PUMP written on the wall above it. The switch is over to ON.

"Yes."

"Either you blew a fuse or the pump burned out from trying to draw water when it couldn't. Your troubles might be worse than I thought. Open the panel box."

Anna does as instructed, yanking the door open with all of her fingers. Two breakers in there. One flicked over to OFF. She snaps it back to ON and the pump comes to life, rumbling in the floorboards.

"Uh-oh."

"Is that the pump?"

"Yeah," Anna says anxiously. "The breaker was tripped. Is that good or bad?"

"Look at the needle on the pump gauge."

"Pump gauge?" She squats and finds the needle, which is trembling while pointing at zero. "Okay."

"Is the needle moving up?"

"No."

"How about now?"

She gives it extra attention, expecting the pump to blow up or spew smoke at any moment. "No."

"Okay, shut off your pump, or you'll burn it up."

"Okay." She stands, slams the panel door closed, and whacks off the main switch.

"You've got blockage in the line. I can cart some containers of water to you if need be. I'll call later to see how you're doing."

"Okay, thanks. I'm going to get at it right now. I want water."

"Leave the heater on for a few hours. It'll probably take that long to free up. Be very careful under there."

"Okay, thanks. Bye."

Anna shoves her cell in her jeans pocket, lifts the space heater from the shelf, and hurries into the kitchen where it is warmer. Setting the heater on the counter, she closes the door and goes off to pull on her coat and boots, finding herself out of breath when she bends over and straightens again.

"What am I in for?" she mutters while passing through the

living room. The woodstove fire has remained lit overnight. She must have done a good job banking the logs, although she doesn't recall doing anything differently.

Standing outside at the rear of the house, she stares at the hatch in the wooden skirting. The nip in the air chills her nose and fingertips. There is a simple wooden latch that pivots on a nail to release the small square door.

Anna crouches and turns the latch, glancing at the row of icicles treacherously dangling from the eave, hoping they won't fall on her head and impale her.

The hatch opens a few inches before jamming, its bottom blocked by snow.

Straightening to kick the accumulation away, she yanks on the door with freezing pink fingers until it opens wide enough for her to squat and see in.

Clay darkness beneath a vague impression of the underside of floorboards.

It gives her the creeps.

Before she crawls in there, she will need a flashlight and gloves.

She straightens and takes another wary look at the icicles pointing straight down at her skull from high above. A drop from the melt hits her square in the eye, making her flinch.

Back in the kitchen she rummages in the drawers, noticing tiny brown pellets scattered here and there.

"Great," she mutters, remembering the warning she read in her pregnancy book about diseases that might be contracted from mouse droppings, particularly dangerous for pregnant woman. Now she can't wash her hands.

She finds the flashlight and turns, paused by a scratching against wood overhead.

"Little bastards!" She stares up and listens. A mouse trying to claw its way through. Why do they claw and chew like that? Are they attempting to dig their way out? If so, to go where? She imagines a nest tucked away somewhere. Pink bald mice curled together for warmth. When she was a child, she had two hamsters as pets, and they had a litter, despite the fact that they were named Georgina and Florence.

Leaving the house again, Anna pulls on her gloves while catching sight of a cat sitting on the window ledge of her barn. The creature's fur is predominantly dark brown with faint orange streaks, as though it has muted fire in it. The cat watches her with interest.

She wonders if it is a stray. Its eyes seem gummy, plugged with infection.

The cat jumps down and runs with a broken gait, apparently missing one leg. It darts toward the hatch and disappears inside.

"Great." Anna follows the cat to the hatch and squats, making a sound to coax the animal out. She doesn't want to be attacked by a diseased cat, particularly in a confined space where her escape route is compromised.

She holds the top of the hatch with one gloved hand and kneels, shining the flashlight in. Floor joists two feet above dirt and rocks. No sign of green eyes glowing back at her. The sweep of the light catches a rectangular piece of wood with rusted metal about five feet in on the packed clay. A large trap.

Anna makes a sound of disgust and attempts shining the light deeper into the space, but the beam isn't strong enough to travel that far, the batteries weakening as the shaft skims over darkness.

She leans her head in, trying to realize an angle that will allow her a view of the full length of the house.

The space smells of wet earth.

On her hands and knees, she inches in, raising one hand to shine the light ahead and spotting the black hose about fifteen feet in.

It is difficult to crawl this way, her head so close to the floor beams while she tries to hold the flashlight. She imagines rusty nails poking down and lowers her head.

As she nears the hose, light sparkles on a sheath of ice covering it. Daylight is visible in a few spots along the wooden skirting where, no doubt, the bitter wind has been blowing in. Beneath the ice a black rubber-coated wire is wrapped around the hose. The wire is plugged into an extension cord poked through the hole in the floor. Anna will be able to use it to connect the space heater.

The space heater.

She left it in the house.

The thought of going back to collect it pains her.

Slowly turning, she groans and, raising her eyes, catches sight of something large and grey skittering along a line of rocks. A rat heading away from her. Startled to the point of seizure, she drops the flashlight. Thankfully, the flickering light stabilizes and doesn't go out. She anxiously grasps it up from the earth, her heartbeat accelerating. Gripping the flashlight with both hands, she casts the beam in every direction to make certain she isn't surrounded by a pack of prey.

She mustn't panic. If she makes a dash for the hatch, she will injure herself in the close space.

Anna continues taking stock of her position, becoming more and more aware of being under a house, the weight of two floors above her, the rooms and the furniture and the items in the drawers, cupboards and closets. It is a peculiar sensation to be hidden away down here, with the entirety of a household looming over her.

Drawing a deep breath through her nostrils, she holds herself still, listening. She will take her time leaving. Once back in the house, she will contact someone else to do this for her. A plumber or Mr. King. She should have accepted his offer of help in the first place.

She edges in the direction of the hatch, trying to remain calm.

A gurgling sound from deeper under the house. Mucous in a small throat. Indications of activity in shallow water. Something drowning in fluid.

The rat?

Anna stares toward the depths where the flashlight can't reach.

"It's okay," says a girl's voice, plainly evident in the hollow. Flinching, as though struck, Anna drops the flashlight again. The beam goes out, and her flesh prickles wildly.

She tries to stand and strikes her head on an overhead floor beam, thudding her skull so soundly she sees sparks.

"Baby," the girl says soothingly. "It's okay. Mommy's here."

Anna winces, reaching for her head while shouting, "Hello?" A mild ringing in her ears. She pulls off her gloves to search the ground, trying to locate the flashlight, her fingers coming up against something wet and slimy. What must be a large slug stuck to her fingers. Anna jolts back and lands on her bum, her hands flicking at each other before going out at her sides, sweeping around until finding the flashlight.

She raises it and struggles with the switch, clicking it back and forth.

Nothing.

Practically in tears, she bangs the flashlight against her knee until the beam quivers on.

No presence near her.

She aims the beam into the dark hole.

The light trembles over greys and brown. Vague bits of contours. Clay and rocks from which Anna attempts to discern a form.

The top of her head throbs with pain. She dabs it with her fingertips. Finding it raw, she quickly examines her fingers. No signs of blood.

Another gurgle.

"Shush shush, shush shush." A singsong whisper. "Shush, shush, shhh ..."

"Hello?"

"Don't cry, baby."

The stink of opened earth becomes more pronounced as she inches ahead, not closer to the hatch where she should scramble, where the light of day is barely evident through a slim crack, but closer to the dark hole where her body is drawn by morbid curiosity.

The flashlight beam reaches farther into the darkness, catching sight of bare feet slowly splashing in a dirty puddle. The beam is tipped upward, revealing the white-haired girl, her wide black eyes glistening with reddish clumps while they watch Anna. In each of her arms the girl cradles a premature naked baby.

The babies are sticky. Their limbs jerk in convulsion while they gurgle.

Anna gasps at the sight but won't flee.

She wants to know. She wants to understand why.

The girl hears the sound, her ears pricking up. She shifts her head. "Mommy?"

"What are you doing here?"

"Mommy?" The question sharper, bordering on frantic. "Is that you? Mommy?"

"No."

The flashlight beam flutters over the little girl. The skin on her face is practically transparent, green veins through which fluid pulses, lines of muscles that thicken as they contract, a skull that shifts in dimension as the light wavers.

"It is you." The girl stirs her feet in the dirty water. Smiling dreamily, she adds, "Why don't you ever say it is?"

Anna is trying to be sympathetic, but the sight of the unformed babies in the girl's arms is thoroughly repulsing.

"Why won't you be my mommy? You are."

Anna shakes her head, summoning the courage to remain.

"A mommy would keep us warm. A mommy wouldn't shut out the light."

"Why are you in this house?"

"Under. We are always under. And we are here because we are cold and we are not ..."

"Not what?"

"You are my mommy." In concert with the girl's mounting anger, the limbs of the tiny babies jitter fitfully as though incensed.

"No, I am not."

"You are." The white-haired girl's expression turns savage, her teeth gnashing as her rattling jaw shrieks open. She hurls the babies forward and leaps for Anna.

Anna recoils, bangs her flashlight against the dark earth, knocking the light off. She drops to her hands and knees and scurries for the hole in the hatch, the light glowing outside, yet not entering, nor dissipating the darkness.

The muscles in her legs torment her.

Her knees slam against packed earth and protruding rocks.

She expects hands on her body at any moment, claws and teeth piercing her flesh, tearing and chewing their way into her to find their way out.

She collapses on her belly near the hatch.

Arms desperately grasping ahead, she shoves open the door and writhes through the hole into the white blare of daylight.

~ Part III ~
Court

Chapter Sixteen

Justitia: April 1, Details

"Property," the attorney for the plaintiff reads from a document in hand. Each word of the text was considered, argued over, and rearranged in extended meetings with the attorney's associates until a consensus was reached on the turns of phrase most capable of influence.

The attorney stands in the open space between the defendant's table and the judge's raised platform. This position gives him a sense of command and infinite leisure. He takes professional pleasure in being in the defendant's eye line.

The attorney is wearing a jet-black suit, jet-black shirt, and matching tie, all purchased at an exclusive boutique specifically for this occasion. A tailored, severe appearance was foremost in his mind when he slipped his arms into the sleeves of a selection of designer jackets and perused himself in the mirror, smoothing back his hair to see if the fit was complimentary. What he was hoping for was the look of a seasoned assassin.

While talking the attorney for the plaintiff moves his arms in sweeping gestures meant to corral the people in, to bring them onboard. There is plenty of space to permit him this freedom. The popularity of the litigation has persuaded the clerk responsible for logistics and scheduling to book the proceedings into the main courtroom.

"Property," repeats the attorney for the plaintiff, "as defined by the Webster dictionary ..." He pauses to level his gaze at the crowd, impressing upon them the authoritative weight of his words. "Ownership." He directs his attention to the judge. "Right of possession." He nods with innuendo at the plaintiff. "Enjoyment." A brief yet accusatory stare at the defendant. "Or disposal of anything, especially of *something tangible.*" The attorney ruffles the papers in his hand, making an excessive amount of noise. He raises the papers while addressing the audience. "Something ... tangible."

The attorney for the plaintiff surveys the floor. He takes two pensive steps forward. "Tangible," he says, as though involuntarily, yet in a tone that is considered and measured.

He turns to face the audience, licks his lips, and opens his mouth wide.

Holding the pose, with eyebrows scrunched together, he appears frozen in the process of a silent shout.

Audience members stir uneasily in their seats, having no idea what has provoked the attorney's bizarre display.

With squinting eyes flicking from face to face, the attorney for the plaintiff slowly slides out his tongue, the centre of which is pierced with a transparent ball stud. He sets down the papers and nimbly goes to work seizing the orb between the fingertips of his left hand. The fingers of his right hand slip under his tongue to unscrew the backing, remove it, and let it drop into his open palm. He closes his fist around it. With the stem now unsecured, he attempts plucking the stud from his tongue, but seemingly stuck, it presents him with a difficult time.

He shuts his mouth, pulls a black silk handkerchief from the breast pocket of his suit jacket, flaps it open, and dabs at his watering eyes.

"I've been told this might hurt a little." Chuckling uncomfortably, he pokes the handkerchief away. "I shouldn't have left it in for so long. People kept telling me there was a time for it to come out. " He reopens his mouth, wider than on the previous effort, and gives the stud a tug, then another, yanking until it tears free with a tiny fleshy sound.

Wincing, the attorney leaves his mouth open. Tears spill from his eyes as he inclines his head forward. Blood dribbles from the hole, marking a brilliant trail toward the tip of his tongue. Before the bead can plummet from the end, he shuts his mouth, swallows, gives his eyes another swabbing, and rejoins the fastener to the bottom of the ball stud.

"My girlfriend, or *partner*, if you will, is an embryologist." The attorney for the plaintiff sniffs and wipes at the corners of his eyes. "She gave me this tongue stud as a gift." His injured smile implies melancholic recollection. "Sadly, we broke up a few days ago, and she contacted me, wanting the stud back." The attorney holds the orb at eye level, inquisitively examining its interior. "Inside this tiny sphere there is an embryo." He gives the stud a rousing shake, his eyes shifting as though following something caught in a fantastical swirl. "One night in her lab we created it together in a Petri dish. As it turns out, the embryo is of value to her. She wants it back. I have no objection."

"Objection, Your Honour!" shouts the lawyer for the defendant, springing to her feet. She makes an unflattering face, presses her fingertips against the tabletop, and shakes her head, restraining herself. "Counsel for the plaintiff is giving evidence, which he is not permitted to do."

The judge seems unconvinced, spurring the lawyer for the defendant to add with an expression of bewilderment, "And what does this stomach-turning display have to do with anything?"

"What is the point, Counsel?" the judge inquires, obviously amused by the demonstration, as there is a tight grin on his face that shows off his short, flat teeth.

"The point?" asks the attorney for the plaintiff, glancing around with a look of naïveté as though he were caught by surprise. "My point is simple. I found myself a new tongue stud." He slips the stud in question into his pocket and takes out another, raising it with a comical expression while people in the audience smile and titter.

The new stud is matte black and gives off no gleam.

The attorney for the plaintiff holds up the stud, sticks out his tongue, and tries fitting the stem through the hole, poking and jabbing all over the place as though purposely missing the mark.

After a half-dozen attempts, he approaches the lawyer for the defendant and leans near to her. "Can you give me a hand?"

Pink-cheeked with fluster, the lawyer for the defendant ignores the request. "Your Honour? These theatrics are highly inappropriate and, as you know, a serious breach of etiquette. Please instruct him to stay at his table or find him in contempt of court for unprofessional behaviour."

The judge appears to resent being told what to do. "Counsel for the plaintiff?"

"An aesthetic argument, Your Honour. As the defendant is an artist of some renown, I suspect appreciation on her behalf." To double the impact, he leers at the defendant. "Perhaps I might even make it into one of her paintings, which have suddenly skyrocketed in worth and popularity."

"Objection, Your Honour."

"Aesthetics, Your Honour," the attorney continues, pulling his eyes away from the defendant's temptingly troubled face. "Must we dwell constantly in the realm of verity? I believe the law amounts to more than that."

The judge assesses the lawyer for the defendant, expecting a retort.

"This is a highly irregular and insulting procedure, Your Honour."

Look at her slumped shoulders, the attorney for the plaintiff tells himself while studying his adversary. Look at her unsightly face. The body language of a loser.

"Fair enough," says the attorney for the plaintiff, aloofly shrugging and sighing. "Let us trail one another down the vapid judicial corridor toward tedium." He slips the tongue stud into his pocket, picks up his document, and waves his hand above his head with a flourish of bravado. "If I may, I would like to draw the court's attention to the 2008 semen as property case, Hecht versus Superior Court." With an air of courteousness, the attorney pauses to glance at the lawyer for the defendant, who is shuffling through her papers. "Are we all on the same page, Counsel? Can I lend a hand? No ... Good. Excellent." He returns his attention to his proffered document. "In this case the superior court ruled that a man, the late Percy Kane of Mississauga, is permitted to will his frozen sperm to his girlfriend, Julie Hecht of Oakville, and that his frozen sperm is, in fact, *property*, over which the Ontario Court of Queen's Bench had jurisdiction.

"Earlier in this case, a probate court initially ordered the destruction of the sperm. Hecht sought to have the sperm distributed to her either as a gift or ..." The lawyer's words trail off as a hubbub is heard beyond the courtroom. The interruption is highly irksome, for he was just getting up to stride. Muddled shouts draw his attention to the wooden doors.

The outer commotion nears, becoming louder and disturbingly irregular in pitch, threatening to become inner, while men and women shift in their seats and turn their heads with greater curiosity. A woman's screaming is followed by the clanging of fire alarms throughout the building. A number of people rise to their feet in fright, wondering on their next move.

The security guard reaches for the handles on the courtroom doors just as they burst open. A hairless, gurgling woman spins in a whoosh of flames. Screams coupled with the anxious movements of bodies charge the room with frantic energy. The woman's burning arms flail above her head. She stumbles, reeling into a wall, while her skin melts in a slow liquid stream.

An obese woman shouts from the audience, then another woman cries out before covering her mouth and collapsing. The smell of gasoline wafts in the air, followed by the scent of seared meat.

People in the last row jerk away protectively as the burning woman flounders about, her flesh bubbling and crackling.

The colours are astonishing.

The attorney for the plaintiff removes his cellphone from his suit jacket pocket and raises it to capture a photograph for the book he plans to pen on the case.

Smoke streams from the woman as her flesh hisses and sputters. She thumps into the back wall, bouncing and toppling onto the carpet as the muscles in her legs are consumed. Flames have leaped from the woman to a nearby man, who flicks at himself and is promptly extinguished by others. Another man pulls off his coat and tosses it onto the woman, but the fabric merely ignites and burns.

While bucking with convulsions, the woman makes sticky, puny, guttural noises that issue from deep in her throat as though her tongue might already have been burnt to a pulp.

The attorney for the plaintiff steps around the unruly action to get a better angle. He excuses himself while squeezing through the harried onlookers in hope of capturing another photograph before the commanding majesty of the flames ebbs.

A security guard runs in, a fire extinguisher raised to aim.

"Let her burn!" shouts a man in the audience, hands bunched into fists, horrible eyes stretched wide.

The attorney for the plaintiff snaps the man's picture.

Pulling the extinguisher's trigger, the security guard douses the woman with a jet of white foam.

When the court is reconvened two days later, there is a large black burn on the carpet where the burgundy nylon fibres have melted. A plain table has been positioned over the stain, which delineates the malformed shape of a body.

The interior of the courtroom has been scoured with some sort of chemical cleanser, yet the fresh scent is unable to mask the charcoal smell of smoke and the traces of burnt flesh.

The number of security guards stationed at the courtroom doors has been upped from one to three. They stand side by side, their arms behind their backs, blocking the exit. No further disturbances will be permitted.

The attorney for the plaintiff clears his throat, searches the audience for indications of attentiveness or telltale expressions of menace, and picks up where he left off. "Earlier in this case a probate court initially ordered the destruction of the sperm. Hecht sought to have the sperm distributed to her either as a gift or as an asset of the estate. However, the probate court ordered the sperm destroyed." The attorney raises his eyebrows, lips pursed in speculation. "Destroyed as property.

"In response Hecht filed a petition for peremptory writ to vacate the order and requested an immediate stay. The stay was granted and the destruction order was reversed and remanded." The attorney licks his forefinger, then his thumb. He peers at the audience for reaction while flicking over a page in his document.

His train of thought is compromised, for there have been news reports of fresh protests in the making. Scanning the men and women, he suspects any one of them might be homicidal. Why else would they be present if not drawn here by their sinister aspirations? Who wears the best disguise? His attention is caught by a young woman in a wheelchair parked at the back. The woman's head is slumped to one side. What is she doing here? Are they trying to prove a point by wheeling a vegetable into the courtroom as a prop? An older man standing by the side of the wheelchair leans to wipe spittle from the young woman's lips.

"The lower court determined that Hecht was entitled to *twenty percent* of the sperm as *assets* of the estate. Twenty percent.

The court executed an order that gave Hecht possession of three of the fifteen sperm vials." The attorney for the plaintiff approaches a blackboard to the left of the judge's platform. He raises a stick of chalk from the ledge and draws one vial, then another, until there are thirteen in a row. He then erases three. Studying the board, he checks the audience's faces.

Simple math for simpletons, he tells himself.

"That's thirteen, not fifteen," a man's flat voice calls from the audience.

"What?" The attorney for the plaintiff begins to turn for the board, but his attention alights on a baby being bounced in a woman's lap. The baby, facing the attorney, begins giggling. The pleasure of its appearance is distracted from by the fact that there is something the matter with its eyes. Pressed against the woman's right arm, a girl of seven or eight grins at the lawyer, exposing the hole of her missing front teeth.

The attorney for the plaintiff puts down the chalk and gives his fingers a cursory glance. The white dust smudged on his fingertips with no way of being wiped away. He slips his hand into his empty pant pocket, rubbing his fingers in the lining. Best to ignore the math and move on. He hadn't anticipated the chalk residue. Neither had any of his associates. He makes a mental note of it for future performances.

"Kane's children appealed this order, and the executor of Kane's estate refused to comply with the lower court's order pending the appeal. Hecht then sought a writ of compliance."

The girl with the missing teeth raises her arm and extends it in front of her face. Her index finger points at the attorney, her thumb cocks back. She shuts one eye to aim, her face scrunching up like an old woman's.

"Bang!" shouts the girl.

"In Hecht III," the attorney continues, bluntly ignoring the interruption yet sensing an odd tension in his stomach, "the Court of Appeal for Ontario, in establishing jurisdiction, determined the semen must be *property*, at least under the probate code, because, and here I quote: 'the power of the probate court extends only to the *property* of the decedent.'"

The attorney for the plaintiff peeks at the little girl, who is now up on her knees, hand cupped around her mouth while she eyes the attorney and whispers into her mother's ear.

The mother has her gaze steadily fixed on the back of the defendant's head.

A man in the next row watches the girl's face. He frowns, as though sickened, and moves his lips, muttering something. It appears to be the man who shouted "Let her burn!" Would they have allowed that man back in? How could they have stopped him? On what grounds?

Clear the courthouse, a voice cries in the attorney's head. He imagines the walls splattered in blood. A man with an assault rifle out to clarify a point. Poisonous gas leaking in through the heat vents. A woman with a bomb strapped to her distended belly.

Will any one of them live through the day?

"The court held that Kane retained decision-making authority over the gametes and had an adequate ownership interest in his sperm at his death to amount to a property right under the province's probate law, which defined property as 'anything that may be the subject of ownership and includes both real and personal property and any interest therein.'"

The attorney for the plaintiff sets down his document on the table before his client. He scans the bright courtroom, sensing the sweat glazing his scalp at the edge of his hairline.

The baby in the woman's arms commences crying.

All of these people with what inside them?

The "what" in them that wants to know. What everyone wants to know.

Seven media interviews scheduled for this evening. A book offer from a respected international publishing conglomerate. Calls from potential agents in New York.

"Both real and personal property. Again something *tangible*."
Silence.

"Counsel for the plaintiff rests." He watches his client while he approaches his chair. Sitting, he is conscious of a million eyes trained on the back of his head. The crosshairs of a rifle scope seeking the most critical point of entry.

The stuttering cries of the baby are nettling his nerves.

The judge clears his throat, makes a few notes on the papers before him, and raises his eyes to the lawyer for the defendant. She stands just as the woman with the baby springs to her feet two rows back.

The judge watches the woman hoist the crying baby up over her head.

"If you're going to kill anything," bawls the woman. "Kill this one." She tosses the baby high into the air.

The baby ascends, reaching a seemingly weightless pinnacle, where it momentarily lingers in an untouchable hover, before tumbling toward the front of the courtroom.

The attorney for the plaintiff stretches overhead with both hands, the soft material of the screeching infant's zip-up jammies skimming his fingertips.

All eyes are fixed on the baby as it plummets.

Utter silence, save for the baby's scratchy howls.

The moment the infant's head cracks against the edge of the judge's platform, its cries are silenced and the building quakes on its foundation as though in reverberation.

The trial is moved from the downtown courthouse to an undisclosed location on the outskirts of the city.

The attorney for the plaintiff and the lawyer for the defendant are contacted via cellphone half an hour prior to the court time and given specific instructions on the most expedient route to the new site.

"Fifteen minutes outside St. John's, after Clovelly Stables, there is a road on the right-hand side identified by a street sign as Red Cliff Road," explains an officer of the court. "It is paved for 1.7 miles before it breaks into a dirt road for another 1.2 miles."

The attorney for the plaintiff and the lawyer for the defendant receive the information at the exact same time, as the directions are relayed via conference call.

"Approximately forty-two feet back from the cliff edge there is a war barrack where munitions were once stored during the Second World War. The proceedings will reconvene in that venue."

A gleaming collection of cars is parked in front of the blue tarp that surrounds and conceals the building. A BMW, a Jaguar, and a Hummer are parked beside two black police emergency response vans. The vehicles are dusty toward their bottoms from travelling the dirt road.

Four men in navy blue shirts with patch insignias, grey pants, black bulletproof vests, black fabric neck protectors, steel helmets with face shields, and automatic weapons guard each corner along the periphery of the building. In the woods three sharpshooters are positioned in a triangular formation that surrounds the site.

The outer walls of the dilapidated, one-storey concrete building are evident when passing through the buffer inside the draped tarp. The grilles of the vertical windows are rusty and missing their panes.

Inside the barrack the walls, ceiling, and floor are made of poured concrete. Space heaters have been placed strategically, powered through lengths of extension cords plugged into generators that hum outside. Water trickles down the west wall, emanating from some unknown source.

There is an eye-watering smell of pine disinfectant.

Two more police officers, similarly outfitted to the ones guarding the exterior, are stationed in each of the two corners at the back of the room.

The lawyer for the defendant stands. She is smartly dressed in a dark grey shirt with matching jacket and slacks. She has had her hair trimmed and hennaed the previous evening. The woman in the hair salon had the most delicate touch that almost lulled her to sleep.

Although she hasn't availed herself of the media offers to state her case on global news, nor accepted any other deals, she is biding her time, speculating about the morality of profiting from these proceedings.

A book deal with the earnings donated to one of the local women's shelters might be acceptable, or an endowment to help care for the baby dropped in the courtroom, who, it has been reported, has suffered permanent brain damage.

"Your Honour," she says, "if we are to classify semen and ovum as *property* as my learned friend has taken it into his head to do, we must keep in mind that the plaintiff freely gave this property to my client. At the time of deposit there was no understanding of contract, verbal or otherwise, between these two parties of ever having the plaintiff's property returned to him."

The attorney for the plaintiff rises to his feet. "Yes, but the property was not meant to be retained, Your Honour. There was an unspoken understanding between the two parties that the property would pass into the obscure, not be willfully used to create another property without my client's consent."

"Your Honour, would you please instruct him to remain quiet?"

The judge regards the lawyer for the defendant with a bull-headed expression. His eyes survey the back of the room, the two officers outfitted compellingly and standing in wait.

"No more interruptions," the judge blandly states.

The lawyer for the defendant continues. "Your Honour,

I would like to direct the court's attention to the Planned Parenthood of Ontario versus Lawton decision of the Ontario Court of Justice, August 15, 2005, that states a woman does not require the consent of her husband to obtain a legal abortion. This decision determined that the fetus is the sole property of the wife rather than the couple."

The attorney for the plaintiff springs to his feet. "That ruling was challenged, Your Honour, and is still before the courts."

"Your Honour ..." The lawyer for the defendant throws her arm out toward the source of her interruption. "If he does not stop, I ask that you find him in contempt or have him removed."

"The challenge to that ruling, Your Honour, is pinned on the argument that in the case of divorce the husband would have to pay support for the child ad infinitim, and in event of the husband's death, the fetus would be entitled to a share of his estate. Also, Your Honour, the ruling mentioned by my learned friend conflicts with the McElrea versus Barnes decision of the Supreme Court of Newfoundland and Labrador, Family Division, June 23, 2003, that determined a mother cannot put up children for adoption without the father's consent."

"Your Honour, again, if I may please have my say."

The judge eyes the lawyer for the defendant with a look of barely suppressed vexation. Shifting his head, he nods to the attorney for the plaintiff. "Continue, but I caution you to be brief."

The lawyer for the defendant remains standing, rigid with contained rage. "Your Honour!" She checks over her shoulder. No one present to witness what is happening, except for the two police officers.

"Continue, Counsel."

"So far the half-dozen provincial Supreme Courts that have handed down opinions governing embryos in divorce cases have sided with the individual's right not to be forced into parenthood.

"The first such case, Ring versus Ring as decided by the Alberta Court of Queen's Bench, clarified the status of embryos.

In 2002 Michael and Mary Ring, who hadn't signed a premarital agreement over the ownership of their fertilized embryos, filed for divorce. The lower court declared their embryos 'human beings' and gave them to Mary Ring. Michael Ring appealed, and the Alberta Court of Appeal decided in his favour, stating that the partner who wanted no part in procreation should be given his or her due, an opinion that courts in ensuing cases across the country have adhered to.

"The court also acknowledged that embryos were neither human nor property, but 'occupied an interim category deserving a special respect.' It ordered the embryos destroyed."

"Your Honour!" cries the exasperated lawyer for the defendant. "Your rulings obviously show a reasonable apprehension of bias here, and I respectfully request that you remove yourself from the proceedings —"

"Counsel, your position is noted, but I am fully aware of my rulings and am confident that there is no reasonable apprehension of bias, and I shall not recuse myself. Your remedy is in the court above, at a later date, if you wish."

Justitia: April 4, Examination / Cross-Examination

The lawyer for the defendant stands, refusing to let the judge's obstinacy get the best of her.

"How are you feeling?"

The defendant shakes her head despondently.

"A little overcome, I bet."

The defendant lowers her eyes.

"How is the baby?"

"Objection, Your Honour, the use of the term *baby* is

inappropriate, as the property in question remains, technically, an embryo, which is without definable identity."

"Sustained."

"How is your embryo that will eventually develop into a baby if permitted by this court?"

"Objection."

"Overruled."

"I can only assume it's fine."

"Have you been examined lately?"

"Yes."

"And everything is developing according to plan?"

"Yes, the baby's healthy."

A groan issues from the table where the attorney for the plaintiff shuts his eyes distressfully. "Objection."

"To what exactly?" asks the judge.

"The use of the term *baby*."

"Let's try to stick with the words *embryo* or *property*," the judge cautions the defendant.

The defendant nods.

The lawyer for the defendant steps toward her table and lifts a book. It is a pregnancy guide. "I would like to read from this book, which features a comprehensive outline of fetal development, Your Honour. Both you and counsel for the plaintiff have received copies in my filings."

The judge clears his throat and makes a sour expression.

"At this stage in the development of the property in question …" The lawyer for the defendant pauses, distracted by movement low to the ground, caught in the corner of her eye. A rat scurrying along the base of a wall before disappearing into a ragged hole.

The lawyer for the defendant checks the judge, who is watching her without alarm. She looks to the attorney for the plaintiff. He, too, is nonplussed.

She continues reading. "A network of criss-crossing nerves begins to develop in the scalp of the defendant's embryo. Eyelids begin to grow and may fold. Kidneys produce urine for the first time. The arms have developed fully and are proportional to the embryo while the hands have notches indicating the future divisions in the fingers and thumbs. The heart beats at one hundred beats per minute." The lawyer shuts the book and returns it to her table, allowing a silent spell of time to carry the echo of her words. The lawyer's eyes drift to the smaller officer, a woman, standing at ready in the far corner. The officer has made a sound of discomfort that implies commiseration.

"This procedure that the plaintiff is attempting to force you to undergo, to return an equal portion of the property to him through a process that will see the property in question destroyed, do you have any desire to undergo this procedure?"

"No," says the defendant, her eyes glazing over while she watches the ceiling. Three bare bulbs hang there on unwound coat hangers secured over a rusty lead pipe.

"So it is safe to say that you will be forced to undergo this procedure against your will?"

"Yes."

"Entirely against your will?"

"Yes."

The lawyer steps toward the defendant and touches her client's arm.

The judge watches down on the display. Two women engaged in a show of affection to gain the upper hand.

"No further questions, Your Honour."

The attorney for the plaintiff stands while the lawyer for the defendant takes her seat.

"According to my client, Dr. Prowse, you stopped taking the birth control pill days prior to the encounter that led to the creation of the property in question. Correct?"

"Yes."

"Were you intentionally trying to deceive my client?"

"Objection."

"Overruled."

"Thank you, Your Honour. However, I will rephrase the question. Were you attempting to bring into creation the property in question without the knowledge of my client?"

"No."

"Then why did you stop taking your birth control pills?"

"Usually when two people have intercourse there's always a chance that a pregnancy might occur. He was aware of that."

The attorney for the plaintiff turns his gaze to the lawyer for the defendant and gives a little smile and nod, acknowledging the fine coaching.

"Very good, but you're not answering my question. Why did you stop taking your birth control pills?"

"I don't have an answer."

"Wasn't my client of the understanding that you were taking the birth control pill?"

"I can't speak for him."

"Really. Well, isn't that what you're doing here now? Speaking for him?"

"Objection. Your Honour, Counsel is badgering my client."

"Sustained."

"Sorry. Was my client surprised when you told him about the possible creation of the property in question? I believe it was at a Mexican restaurant when you informed him." The attorney for the plaintiff shuffles through the papers in his hands.

"Yes, it was at a Mexican restaurant."

"And was he surprised?"

"I couldn't really say."

"Did he tell you that he was not interested in retaining the property in question as his own and wished to have no part of the creation in question?"

"Yes."

"Well, then wouldn't it be a natural step to surmise that he was surprised?"

"Objection."

"Sustained."

"In your opinion do you believe that my client was surprised at the news of the creation of the property?"

"Will you stop saying that!" the defendant shouts.

"Saying what?" The attorney for the plaintiff mildly inquires.

"Creation of the property."

The attorney for the plaintiff, understanding that he might soon rouse tears from the defendant, tears that might work against him, desists for a moment and paces to his table where he puts the papers down, takes a breath, and turns.

"From the first time my client was told of … the situation in question, did he express his desire to have no part in it?"

The defendant is reluctant to speak one way or the other.

"Please answer the question," instructs the judge.

The defendant regards the judge. "Yes, he expressed his desire to have no part in this pregnancy. This creation of a living baby that —"

"Thank you. No further questions."

The attorney for the plaintiff looks back at the helmeted police officers. The bigger officer, nearest the makeshift door, points while speaking into a wire microphone running horizontally in front of his lips.

At once the smaller officer raises her rifle and, taking steady aim, follows the trail of another fleeing rat.

The attorney for the plaintiff casts a glance at the front corner to catch the tail end of the vermin wiggling through a hole.

A shot goes off, and the judge bucks on impact, toppling from his chair.

Justitia: April 7, in the Realm of the Incongruous

The lawyer for the defendant sits beside her client in the board-room of her law office on Church Hill. The slatted blinds covering the row of windows have been twisted shut; the room remains dim and cloaked in a secretive hush. Fish float placidly through the aquarium's greenish light.

On the table before the lawyer and her client, a laptop computer is opened and radiant.

Three additional attorneys from the firm stand near the table, gazing at the laptop.

Judge Drodge appears on the screen, surveying the papers on his desk. His head and neck are supported by a steel, vise-like brace, and his left arm rests in a sling. He awkwardly looks up while the shot tightens on his face.

"Decisions on these sorts of issues are always challenging." The judge's mouth barely opens, for the brace is applying pressure on his jaw. "With the changing face of scientific endeavour, where embryos are now, quite often, considered property that falls under the jurisdiction of the court, the court must remain current with these advances and be prepared to adjudicate any issues required in these matters."

The lawyer for the defendant makes an involuntary sound of distress and entwines her hands tightly on the tabletop.

"While the arguments put forth by counsel for both parties were based in precedent, and while courts, generally, have been reluctant to pronounce that an embryo is, in fact, property, there is, in my opinion, unequivocal precedent on hand to give merit to this supposition."

One of the standing attorneys snorts in dissatisfaction and quietly leaves the room.

"The plaintiff in this matter will be responsible under existing law to support this fetus should it be brought into this world. And yet, as we have heard in these proceedings, there have been rulings that state the biological father has no say in whether a child is born or not. Of course, this is disparate reasoning. Regardless, with these issues, we often find ourselves dwelling in the realm of the incongruous." The judge gives a diminutive smile, his cheeks rounding out, while his eyes check to one side, as though to catch a stray bit of non-existent laughter. "Any biologist will inform you, in a very fundamental manner, that creation of an embryo is unachievable without the addition of semen, which triggers cell division and growth."

The lawyer for the defendant shifts in her chair. Her head shakes abruptly while she hotly whispers an oath, her eyes caught by the stream of bubbles in the fish tank. Behind her there are uncomfortable sighs from the remaining attorneys.

The judge pauses, as though sensing these indications of unrest, and enduringly waits for them to be quelled. "It would be trite law to state that an ovum is the property of the woman who produces it. To my mind, that fact would go unchallenged. The ovum is an item, an object, a thing, to which no other person could ever claim rights. So, in the name of parity, equality, and impartiality, why should we ever doubt the equally fair and unchallengeable supposition that it is trite law to state that semen is the property of the man who produces it?

"The creation and subsequent development of an embryo is the result of the property of two individuals merging their properties to create a single new property. Neither party contributes more than the other. The property in question would be non-existent without the input of both parties. Unfortunately, by nature's random and perhaps regrettable choice, the new property comes to be housed within the body of one of the two co-creators. I am hesitant to agree that this property is governed by 'possession is nine-tenths of the law' simply because this property merely resides in an inconvenient location, much like stolen treasure stuffed away behind a barred door where the law still holds jurisdiction."

The lawyer for the defendant worriedly checks her client's face.

"Pertinent cases involving the co-creation of property have been explored in my courtroom. When a party seeks return of their property, or a specific portion of their property, it is the obligation of this court to safeguard the rights of each individual by ensuring the property is given over, or divided in a manner — while not satisfactory to both parties — that is expedient, realistic, unsentimental, just, and equitable." The judge pauses and levels his eyes to stare into the screen. "The court rules in favour of the plaintiff."

The Embryo, Day 53, Week 8

The skeleton of Anna's embryo begins to harden from soft tissue to bone.

At seven-tenths of an inch it is the size of a maraschino cherry.

~ Part IV ~

The Third Accident

Chapter Seventeen

Anna: April 9, the Imposter

Anna fits her eye to the peephole in the hotel room door.

A knock this early in the morning hasn't only roused her, but her nerves, as well. No one is supposed to know where she is being kept.

Her lawyer's distorted face is seen turned in profile as though searching down the corridor.

Anna twists the brass handle, automatically unlocking the mechanisms within.

"What's going on?" she asks.

Anna's lawyer steps into the room and shuts the door behind her. "There's an order coming down to put you under protective custody." Patricia secures the deadbolt and slides the chain on its track.

"What?"

"They're assigning two officers," she says, short of breath. She spins around, and her long black coat falls open, exposing flesh-toned cotton pants and matching pullover that hug every line and curve of her body. "It's just a sickening way of detaining you."

"When are they coming?" Anna's eyes shoot to the door, then explore the room for her suitcase.

"They've told me that it's my obligation to escort you in."

"What?" Anna steps back, bumping into the bed. She notices sweat on the lawyer's face, spots of wet on her pants and top. A smell of mustiness and perfume wafts off her.

"No, no." The lawyer extends her arm, yet maintains a respectful distance. "Don't worry."

"Why are they doing this?"

"It's not *they*. It's *him*. Judge Drodge, in all his idiotic wisdom, decided that your safety is in jeopardy because of those extremists causing trouble." Patricia gestures to the blank TV screen.

Anna's eyes go to the door. "Kevin's the one who should be put under protective custody. He's the bastard getting the death threats."

"Yes, and Judge Drodge, too. They already had a shot at him once, and by a police officer no less." The hint of a smile crosses her lips before it is reined in.

Anna shakes her head, eyes checking the lawyer's face. "I should leave, right? How?"

"I rented a car for you. It's in my name." Patricia fishes through her pockets and removes two keys on a ring attached to a white plastic fob.

Anna watches the keys dangle.

"You should get going."

"Where?' She takes the keys in her fist, studies them as though stunned.

"Out of town. I don't know, Anna. What do you want to do?"

"Go away." She shoves the keys into her pocket and retrieves her suitcase from next to the bathroom door. Lifting it onto the bed, she whizzes the zipper around. Most of her clothes are already packed, for she has been anticipating a quick departure. She need only collect her toiletries.

"You want me to go with you?"

The imploring tone of Patricia's voice makes Anna glance from her suitcase to the lawyer's expression of genuine concern. "That would only get you in trouble."

"I'm already in trouble. I rented the car."

"No, I'm in trouble." Anna places a palm on her belly.

With a pained laugh, the lawyer steps nearer to grip Anna by the shoulder and slips her hand over her client's arm. "Just take care, okay?"

"Okay."

"And keep in touch. The appeal is underway." She gives a little squeeze. "We'll get through this."

"I really hope so because it just keeps getting worse."

The lawyer's lips part. She hesitates, searching Anna's eyes while her tongue lifts as though uncertainly considering her next choice of words.

Anna studies the lawyer's hand on her arm, while Patricia gently rubs back and forth.

"I need to go," Anna says.

Shutting her lips ruefully, the lawyer removes her hand.

Anna notices the lawyer's erect nipples beneath her flesh-coloured pullover. "I have to leave." Distracted, she heads for the bathroom to collect her makeup bag and toothbrush.

"It's a dark green four-door," Patricia calls out. "Right by the elevator on level two."

When Anna comes out of the bathroom, the door, already half closed in the lawyer's wake, continues sweeping forward until it soundly shuts.

Anna tosses her suitcase and overnight bag into the trunk of the rental and slams the lid. A booming echo in the underground parking garage. She climbs into the driver's seat and engages the engine, wondering about the paperwork for the car. What might happen if she is pulled over? She searches behind the sun visor, then in the glovebox. Nothing.

She checks over her shoulder while backing out.

Her own car is parked one level up where she left it two days ago before taking the elevator to the room Patricia booked for her. What will happen to her car? She needs to empty the trunk.

Pulling the transmission shift down to drive, she glances at herself in the rearview mirror. Sunglasses and a black tam. It might be a good idea to cut her hair. She has been threatening to do so for weeks.

The lawyer must have the documentation with the make, model, and plate number of the vehicle. What if they come looking for Patricia? What if they search her office and apartment?

Anna navigates the turn in the concrete chamber and rises. On the next level she slows alongside her own car, lining up the ends of both vehicles. She stops, puts the rental in park, presses the button to pop the trunk, and gets out. Quickly fishing through her keys, she unlocks the trunk of her own car, wraps the shotgun and box of shells in a wine-coloured blanket, and makes the transfer.

The rental's trunk closes, followed by the thudding echo of her own trunk shutting. She glances around, slips back in behind the wheel, and drives off.

There are no vehicles waiting at the exit to the underground parking garage. She feeds the ticket left by Patricia into the slot on the yellow post, and the barricade rises.

Emerging from underground into daylight, she takes a right up the hill. No one appears to be following her. She switches on the radio and listens for the news.

A woman announcer: "... the court decided that Anna Wells be placed under police protection for her own safety. Protests continue to grow outside both ..."

The highway is mostly clear, but as Anna makes her way deeper inland, she is forced to slow for patches of slush. As she glides through these tricky spots, her muscles tighten as though to ward off the potentially terrifying sensation of skating out of control. Two hours outside St. John's she stops at a coffee shop in Clarenville for a tea and toasted cinnamon bagel with cream cheese. News stories on the radio change little on the additional hour-and-a-half drive west to Gander. She has chosen Gander because it is almost two hundred miles from St. John's and is the only other town on the island with a major airport.

Along the drive she ponders the idea of travelling from one place to another, the abrupt feeling of dislocation, of removal. She watches the rugged vastness of the spruce forests all around her while thinking about the peculiarity of how people live in remote coves, towns, or cities spread out everywhere at great distances from one another. Car rides. Plane trips. She likes the idea of driving, of being alone on what might be considered an adventure, yet she would prefer to visit a place entirely unknown to her.

Her last airline flight was years ago. A trip to Halifax to see her friend, Heather. She used to travel much more when she was in her late teens and early twenties. Working two part-time jobs, she would stash away every penny earned. Montreal. England. New York. Spain. She had made plans to go to Japan with Heather after art school, before Heather's accident.

Anna recalls the second day in court when she arrived to notice a wheelchair parked at the back of the room. Not recognizing Heather at first, not only because of the way she was twisted up in the seat, but because Anna's mind wasn't accustomed to placing her friend in St. John's. Heather was supposed to be in Halifax. But then the heart-tugging realization as she saw Mr. Lambe standing by the side of the chair.

Anna left her lawyer's side and went over, crouching down at once. "Hi. What are you doing here?" she asked before lifting her eyes to Heather's father.

"Heather wanted to come," Mr. Lambe said.

"I'm so glad to see you."

Heather continued staring off at the back wall, saliva dripping from her mouth until her father cleaned her lips with a tissue.

"Thank you," Anna said, giving Heather a big hug, not wanting to let go, holding her tightly and stroking her hair, which was thin and silky and smelled of strawberries.

"We should get up there," Anna's lawyer quietly interrupted. "Sorry." She held out her arm, indicating the direction.

"Heather wouldn't have missed it for the world," Mr. Lambe professed as Anna was guided away. "She said she hadn't seen you in such a while."

"Thanks." She couldn't think of anything more to say. She only felt guilty for not visiting again.

Heather's father nodded respectfully, implying that being there was merely the right thing for them to do.

Anna would like to see Heather now. That is where she should go. Halifax. It isn't that far away. An hour-and-a-half plane ride. The idea of being with Heather makes her feel safe. If only they could sit at the Split Crow with a pint and talk about a book or a movie like they used to do. She always enjoyed watching Heather talk. They were so similar in their tastes and sensibilities. If Heather hadn't been damaged by the accident, Anna would have visited more often. She was sure of this. So why not now? What really has changed?

The memory of Heather twisted up in her bed, bent in on herself.

It brings Anna's baby to mind. The way it is curled inside of her. The way she is already protecting it with her body.

But what if she isn't protecting it? What if everything that is happening is a warning not to bring another life into this non-sensical world? She can't seem to shake that premonition.

What if her baby is born sick?

Isn't it possible that through some genetic flaw or mishap at birth her baby will turn out just like Heather? Existing as an infant forever.

Does it matter?

Yes, of course, in the short term.

But in the long term it would mean little, as long as the baby is born alive.

I love it already, she tells herself. I know what I feel is inexplicably profound. I don't care if the world is some sort of botched fantasy. We can live in our own blameless world in Bareneed. No television. No newspapers. Two inseparable figures in a house. Day by day, a mother stilled by awe, watching in giving increments the mesmerizing discovery of growth in each of her child's maturing features.

Arriving in Gander, Anna turns off the highway onto a road running alongside Hotel Gander. She finds it peculiar to be travelling at a slower speed after careening over a strip of asphalt framed by hundreds of miles of wilderness. Anna winds through streets lined with suburban houses until finding a big-box pharmacy chain across from a bank and a coffee shop. Civilization. A town plunked down in the middle of nowhere. She pulls in and parks the rental in the pharmacy lot. She is hungry again. The car clock tells her it is 11:53 a.m.

Will anyone recognize her in this small town? Her sunglasses might help mask her identity. Lucky for her the sun is shining. Otherwise the sunglasses would only work against her desire for anonymity by drawing attention.

Inside the pharmacy she wanders the aisles, picks out a shade of black hair dye, searches for scissors and tanning cream, and places them in her basket. She thinks twice about using the tanning cream, particularly since they are passing through the tail end of winter. Also, if the cream goes wrong, she might end up looking like an orange with a frightful tan. She fits the box back on the shelf and picks up bottled water and a few bags of snack foods.

At the checkout she grows concerned that the cashier might question the fact that she is buying hair dye and scissors at the same time. Wouldn't the cashier be able to guess that Anna is going to cut her hair and dye it? An obvious plan to disguise herself. She separates the scissors from the dye, sticking a bag of pretzels and a bottle of water between them.

Thankfully, the cashier barely pays attention to the items as she rings them in and bags them.

Out in the car Anna backtracks to Hotel Gander, finds a space in the lot, and parks. She leaves her suitcase in the trunk and takes her overnight bag from the back seat.

The old building seems to have undergone a number of renovations that have failed to bring it up to the expected standard. The lobby is small with an entrance to a restaurant off to the right of the registration area.

"Hi," says the young woman behind the desk.

"Hi. Do you have a room?"

"Sure. How many nights?"

"One."

The woman checks her computer, then slides a registration card across the counter.

Anna stares at the form. Name … She writes down Heather's name in place of her own because it is the first one that comes to mind. Best to keep her identity a secret. She gives Halifax as her address and hands the form back to the clerk, who smiles politely.

"I'll just need a credit card," says the woman.

"Really? I don't have one. Don't like them. They rack up so easily. Can I just use cash?"

"Certainly, but we'll need a deposit." The woman dips her eyes to the computer screen, taps a few keys, and states the amount.

"I'll find a bank machine." Anna edges away from the counter, adjusting the strap of her overnight bag against her shoulder.

"We can use a debit card if you like." The woman is trying her best to be helpful.

"No, that's okay. I need some cash, anyway."

In the car Anna sits still and waits for her heartbeat to calm. She is useless at lying.

A man in a long grey coat passes in front of her, watching through the windshield on his way to his car. Continuing on, he takes another look back.

Anna drives around the unfamiliar streets, growing edgy. If the young woman at the hotel becomes suspicious, won't she try to authenticate the information that Anna jotted down on the form? Did the young woman recognize her and just not show it, deciding to check with the manager before determining the proper course of action?

Along the streets the older houses and shops have an antiquated, secluded feel to them that brings to mind images of silence and loneliness. Edward Hopper's melancholic moments played out in stark rooms in a small town.

Anna spots a sign for a cash machine on the front of a bank in a low brick building. Parking, she goes inside and waits in line. One person ahead of her, a woman, talks on her cellphone. Anna can hear both sides of the conversation relating to the brand of canned corn and French fries she is meant to pick up. Fortunately, there are two machines. As people move off, the woman goes to one, Anna to the other. She makes a withdrawal, then returns to her car.

Back at the hotel, she apprehensively circles the lot, searching for a police car. None in sight. She pulls into the parking space she previously occupied.

Maybe she should just go to a bathroom in a mall to dye her hair. Hide in a stall while the dye sets. People would be coming and going. She needs a sink and a mirror to see what she is doing. She needs a private bathroom.

With a self-admonishing shake of her head, she reluctantly goes back inside the hotel.

The young woman at the counter smiles at her. "Hi, again."

"You have a nice town," Anna offers as a distraction.

"Thank you," the woman replies, counting out the money Anna has presented. "It's quiet. Not much happens here."

"That's a good thing."

"I suppose." The young woman hands Anna the key card. "Have a nice stay."

In her hotel room Anna enters the bathroom and locks the door. She lays the pharmacy bag on the counter, takes off her sunglasses, and glances at herself in the mirror. She hasn't slept in days. Her face is marked by lines of deprivation. She can't stand the look of it.

Anna stares into the sink and breathes, sensing the pulse in her chest, and wonders about her baby's heartbeat. Do hers and the baby's ever beat in harmony?

Another hotel room. It seems like she just left the one in St. John's minutes ago. Being shut away in a strange room in a distant town reeks of desperation. She wants to go somewhere away from Newfoundland, but to a place where she will be welcome. Where would that be? Halifax. Since art school, the city has felt like a second home to her, with its harbour and bridges and small-town feel. Heather is there. She can visit Heather, hide away in a bedroom with the curtains already pulled. The thought of being in Halifax brightens her outlook. Hopefully, Anna will be offered a room. A place to stay where no one would ever think of looking. Wouldn't Mr. Lambe protect her until the baby is born? How could he not understand, considering his situation?

Sighing, she opens the box of dye and removes its contents, laying out the bottle, tubes, gloves, and instructions on the counter. Then she takes the scissors, grips a long strand of hair, and raises it to eye level. She studies her face, tracing each of her features as though to store away what might be remembered of herself, and begins cutting.

Anna parks her car in the section of the airport lot reserved for rentals. She shuts off the engine and leaves the keys on the passenger seat.

Where am I going? she asks herself. I have nothing with me. My apartment. My studio. My paintings. Everything of my life left behind. Is that what must be done?

The shotgun in the trunk. What to do about it? Leave it there. Bring it with her. She pictures herself walking into the airport with a shotgun, levelling the barrel at anyone who stands in her way while demanding a plane to some exotic destination. Her and her outlaw baby on the run. A fitting end to her televised circumstance.

She has packed only the bare necessities. Retrieving her suitcase from the trunk, she hoists the overnight bag over her shoulder and heads for the departures' entrance. She wonders about the limit on her credit card. Will the court freeze her credit card and bank account once they learn she has fled? She should have delivered those rose paintings to David, picked up her cheque, and asked for a cash advance. Enough money to get her settled somewhere.

The Embryo: Day 53, Week 8

The nerves in Anna's embryo grow toward its brain where attachment is initiated. The connection allows its muscles to make spontaneous actions. As though suddenly engaged by apparatus, its upper limbs begin to move and bend at the elbows.

~ 🦢 ~

The glass doors slide open.

Anna steps in, pulling her suitcase behind her. The terminal space is static and still. It has a sense of being vacant even with people milling around or waiting in rows of chairs. It feels like limbo.

Wherever she decides to go, she can buy supplies and make more paintings. Wouldn't any gallery buy her work now? She pictures herself delivering her paintings down a dark alley to a messenger meant to smuggle them across a border.

Or would the world even care about her story anymore if she has escaped, if she is no longer in danger?

Years ago she might have purchased a ticket under another name, but now, with the stricter air travel regulations, she must show a photo ID. The idea torments her as she nears the airline counters. She hopes there are people who haven't heard her name.

There is a lineup for the check-in, but no one in the queue for ticket purchases. She steps up to the counter, unsure whether she should remove her sunglasses. They might highlight the fact that she is attempting to hide herself from public scrutiny. Regardless, she leaves them on, not wanting the airline representative to see the troubled expression dredged deep in her eyes.

"I'd like to buy a ticket, please."

"Sure." The woman clicks a few keys on the keyboard. "Where would you like to fly?"

"Where are you flying today?"

The representative gives her a quick look, as the question appears out of the ordinary. "We have a flight to St. John's in fifteen minutes."

"Anything else?"

"Our flight to Toronto leaves in four hours at 6:25."

"Four hours?" She should have checked the departures' board before attempting to buy a ticket. "Does that stop in Halifax?"

"Yes, but no plane change."

"I can get out there, though?"

"Sure. You can buy a Halifax ticket."

Halifax. Four hours.

"What do you have leaving sooner?"

The woman takes extra interest in Anna's face. "Any flight?"

"Yes. I'm not particular."

"We're just boarding an overseas flight to London, England."

"Okay." She can't believe she said okay. But the farther away, the safer her baby will be. "It really doesn't matter where. I just need a vacation." She laughs the tired laugh of the overstressed and fingers her sunglasses tighter to the bridge of her nose.

"Don't we all? So should I book you a ticket?"

"Yes, thanks."

"You have luggage?"

"One bag."

"You packed it yourself?"

"Yes."

"Can you lift it up there, please, and can I see your passport?"

"Sure." Anna sets the suitcase on the scale and opens her purse, frantically digs around.

"And you have one carry-on?"

"Yes." She tucked her passport in her purse days ago just in case. After a bit more rummaging, she finds the document and hands it over, relieved that everything appears to be going smoothly.

"Thanks," says the representative, beginning the ticket-issuing process. She takes a look at the passport and pauses to raise her eyes to Anna's face. "I'm going to need you to remove your sunglasses, please."

Anna tries not to be nervous, yet she feels a tic in the corner of her mouth. She wonders if she is actually smiling or merely trying to coax a smile to her lips.

Slowly, she does as instructed, the woman's face becoming clearer; colours take on their truer hues. The scene becomes immediate, explicit. She finds herself growing tremendously nervous, wretched under the gaze of this woman.

Anna gives her head a little shake, tears warming her eyes. She sucks her bottom lip into her mouth, nibbles on it.

The representative continues studying her features, the same way Anna watched her own face in the hotel's bathroom mirror. What is the woman seeing? What is she expecting?

"That's fine." The woman goes back to clicking her keys. "How will you be paying?"

"Credit card." Anna exhales with joy, almost laughs. She opens her purse and searches for her wallet. She is aware that her actions might be too brisk, almost panicky. She licks her lips, trying to calm herself.

Finding her wallet, she opens it and slips the credit card from its slot. What if the court gets hold of her credit card bill and sees the purchase? They would then be able to track her. She thinks of using her bank card instead, but they could obtain those records, as well.

"Is something the matter?"

"No." Anna hands over the credit card and checks the representative's name pin, which is shaped like wings: Charlotte.

Charlotte accepts it. "Would you like a window seat?"

"Aisle, please," she bursts out with relief, a quick laugh. She swipes a tear from one cheek.

There comes the crackling sound of the boarding pass being printed. Charlotte reaches for it.

Anna has her hand out in anticipation. She is so moved by the woman's kindness that she has to finger another tear from her face.

"Here you go," says Charlotte, giving Anna the pass with a sympathetic smile. "You should hurry through security."

Security, thinks Anna.

"I'll call the gate and tell them you're on your way up. They'll hold the plane."

"Thank you so much."

Charlotte raises a telephone receiver, waiting, while whispering to Anna, "I hope you enjoy your flight. I bumped you up to first-class for a bit of extra room."

Entering the security area, Anna tenses at the sight of men in white shirts and black pants up ahead. They will want to inspect her boarding pass and passport. She counts the travellers ahead of her in the lineup. Twelve. She checks her boarding pass. Will she make it through the line in time to catch her plane? Her body wants to hurry ahead, to skip to the front of the line, while explaining about her departing flight. But that would only single her out even more.

She removes her sunglasses. She has already received a couple of double takes on her way through the terminal, no doubt people recognizing something about her from television or newspapers, the dyed hair not enough to trick them completely.

A few of the travellers in the line keep glancing back at her as she tucks her sunglasses in her bag.

One woman is using a mobile device, pressing the tiny buttons with her thumbs. She might be contacting anyone with that unit.

Closer to Anna, a man holding the hand of a little curly-haired girl is watching the tile while talking on a cellphone.

The little girl stares at Anna.

Anna counts the number of security guards within sight. Seven. Five men and two women. They are wearing skintight latex gloves. Anna twinges at the memories of the doctor performing an internal. She hopes that a woman might take her boarding pass. But if they stop her, if they detain her, she will be violating the court order. Will that mean she will be jailed immediately? She thinks of the shotgun in the trunk.

If she is locked up, then there is no hope for her and the

baby. But if she leaves now before being detained, she might hide somewhere else in the province. Is it the duty of these guards to apprehend her if they suspect she is trying to escape? Are they concerned with matters other than those that threaten the security of air transport?

There are only six air travellers ahead of her now. Too many. How long will they hold the plane? She counts off the waiting people, assigning each one to a guard, trying to determine how they might be dispersed between the male and female guards, one on each side of the opening, checking passes.

According to her calculations, she will be inspected by the man. He is tall and broad-shouldered. Stern-faced with a crew-cut. He scrutinizes the documents and looks at the face, matching identity. He will read her name, and he will know.

Anna hikes the strap of her carry-on up on her shoulder.

"I saw you on TV." A child's voice. The little curly-haired girl.

Anna stares down to see the girl still holding the hand of the man on the cellphone. She presses her lips together and gives her head a futile shake as though to silence the child.

"You're having a baby," says the girl. Laughing, she bunches her shoulders and covers her mouth with both hands. "Daddy?" She pulls at her father's pant leg. "That's the lady from TV."

The man ignores the child, continues talking on his cell.

Faces turn to study Anna.

She glances ahead at the security entrance. The guards haven't heard. They continue going about their business.

Anna wants to bend down to the little girl and ask her to be quiet. Please, she would say, gripping the girl's shoulders. Please, not another word. Slap a hand over the girl's mouth if necessary. When she checks the father, she sees he is now watching her with curiosity.

"What are you going to name your baby?"

Anna swallows and clears her throat. People begin to pass comments back and forth to one another. An old woman watches her and frowns, sighing through her nostrils and seeming vexed with Anna.

The man on the cellphone says, "Okay, I'll check in later," and shuts it.

"Daddy, that's the woman on TV. You were talking about her." The girl points at Anna, then grabs her father's hand, wags it back and forth.

Anna tilts her head as though wanting to shake it in denial.

"Remember, you told Mommy she was wrong."

Anna tries to smile. She swallows and peeks over her shoulder. A number of people standing there, all eyes trained on her. When she faces forward, she sees the man with his cellphone pointed at her, taking a picture.

"Let me see," says the girl, stretching on tiptoe, knowing what her father is doing.

"Passenger Anna Wells please report to gate four," announces a woman's voice over the speaker system. "Your flight is departing."

Frantic, Anna turns and makes her way back toward the end of the line. "Sorry," she says, brushing past people.

At the escalator she dashes down the moving steps while checking over her shoulder. No one in a uniform, but a few people have followed to watch after her.

The little girl, now up in her father's arms, waves both hands at Anna. "Bye!" she calls out.

Straight down, at the base of the escalator, a security guard passes. He is looking ahead, unaware of her presence.

Anna walks to the sliding doors and out into the spring air. Crossing the road, she is almost clipped by a passing taxi. The fright only increases her pace. She finds her car and climbs in. Fortunately, the keys are still on the passenger seat.

Leaving the airport lot, she wonders about the aircraft being held for her, her suitcase being loaded into the belly of the plane.

A SUV with a local TV logo on its side zooms by Anna. She checks in her side mirror to see the vehicle continuing to the airport.

Anna tries setting her mind on where she might go now. Back to St. John's? She can't face the idea of being followed by the media. She checks her rearview mirror: the SUV pulls up in front of the airport terminal. A man leaps out from behind the wheel. Video camera in hand, he runs for the sliding doors.

On the highway twelve miles east of Gander, Anna switches on the radio, pressing buttons from channel to channel until finding a news report. The latest on a possible pandemic. Another channel. Violin music. The next channel. A man reading the news: "... Wells, the Newfoundland artist who, earlier this month lost her fight to keep her embryo in a return of property legal battle, has seen her appeal denied. The three-judge panel of two men and one woman, in what critics are calling a questionably expedited decision, ruled unanimously that precedent must be observed."

Appeal denied for what? Her challenge to being held in protective custody? Or her main case? It can't be her main case. These things take years.

An interview with Anna's lawyer: "We will be petitioning the federal court in Ottawa to intervene in hopes that justice will be adequately served in this matter."

"What's going on?" Anna asks out loud, turning up the volume.

The announcer's voice: "While public outcry continues to mount, critics suggest that any federal intervention would come too late."

Too late.

"Meanwhile, protesters continue to block access to government offices, the courthouse, and abortion clinics, demanding Anna Wells be released from protective custody. Several incidents of violence have been recorded in —"

Anna switches off the radio, unable to bear any more news. She blows out a breath and motions to slap the radio.

"I am not in protective custody!" she shouts. The court must know this by now. They must be looking for her, hunting for her.

She needs to talk to her lawyer. Her cellphone is definitely dead by now. She forgot her charger in St. John's. She should use a pay phone, anyway, so the incoming call can't be traced.

Bareneed? The press has never bothered her there. How would it be possible for them to know about that house? Regardless, the law knows about the house because Kevin knows about it; the original summons was delivered there.

The Bareneed house, her haven, is no longer safe.

She imagines the grove of woods behind her barn. Can she hide there, if only for another week? Would the woods be safe enough? How would she keep warm? What would she use for shelter? A leanto cut out of spruce boughs. What about the barn? Bury herself in a haystack up in the loft.

Another week.

They won't be able to legally perform an abortion in another week. But would that stop them? Two weeks? Three weeks? Does it matter what is legal to the legal system?

She will hide.

If need be, she will have the baby in the woods like an animal.

The Embryo: Day 53, Week 8

The cells committed to shaping the embryo's nose stop dividing as the organ and its cavities are now fully developed.

Anna has been travelling for almost two hours. A green highway sign informs her she is approximately one hour away from

Bareneed. The sun is not too low to obscure her vision, but it is beginning to head for the horizon, brushing the landscape with the restful hues of late day.

She switches the heat to high and directs the force at her feet, which are cold and wet from traipsing into the snowy woods a while back to pee. She turns on the radio to keep up on the latest developments in her life.

The final guitar notes of an unfamiliar song fade away.

The introduction for a special news bulletin is trumpeted before the newscaster opens up with: "Anna Wells, the Newfoundland artist who has been ordered by the court to return embryonic property to her former lover, has allegedly attempted to flee the country. This report from Kirian Gushue, live at the Gander airport.

"According to eyewitnesses in Gander International Airport, Anna Wells was about to board a plane departing for London, England, when she was recognized by fellow travellers and fled the scene. Gregory Payne was waiting in the security lineup when he spotted Ms. Wells."

"She was standing right next to us," says a man's voice, "and my daughter recognized her from television. She had her hair cut and dyed black. Really pale. She was scary-looking, frightened my little girl, the way she was staring at her."

"There are unconfirmed reports that Ms. Wells was planning on seeking asylum in England," states the reporter, "by throwing herself at the mercy of the British government. Andrew Tyler, the British embassy's first secretary in charge of migration with the U.K. Border Agency."

"As this point this department has not received a request for asylum from Ms. Wells."

"Would your department consider such a request?"

"We are open to reviewing any request for asylum. That is the business of this department."

"No doubt," says the reporter in a tone of grim closure, "a distraught woman with the fate of her unborn child at the forefront of her mind. Kirian Gushue at the Gander airport."

"Thank you for that story, Kirian. We'll have more details as they develop. In a related story a man has received a $75,000 online bid for an early painting by Ms. Wells titled *Baby Meat*. The painting features ..."

"Asshole." Anna twists off the radio. She checks her rear-view mirror. A tractor trailer gaining on her. She can't stand those things barrelling right up behind her. Should she speed up or slow down and hope the truck will pass? If she slows down, she fears the rig will plough right through her. She applies a bit of extra pressure to the accelerator and keeps checking the rearview.

The car ahead of her is going too slow. They are almost bumper to bumper.

To her relief, Anna spots the sign for a passing lane up ahead. As her car reaches the widening highway, the rig veers out and roars by her, the wind from its passing nudging her vehicle, while slush noisily splatters her door and windshield.

Anna grimaces and switches on her wipers.

She is concerned that the rented car might soon be identified. Can the media access car rental booking information? And if they can, would they be clever enough to link the rental, in her lawyer's name, to Anna? How many car rental agencies are there in St. John's? Not a great many. No doubt the media are already canvassing the various branches, offering financial incentives to each customer service representative.

Worrying through a long and tangled string of possibilities, Anna eventually stops at a gas station in Clarenville to have something to eat. She is starving. She has exhausted her snacks and needs to use the washroom again.

Before entering the gas station she calms her heartbeat. She is not a criminal. She is not fleeing. Here she is, still in the province. She has committed no crime. A woman who has done nothing wrong. A woman who wants something to eat, just like any one of the travellers who has stopped here for nourishment.

The woman at the airport might have been another Anna Wells. It isn't an uncommon name. But what about the picture taken on the man's cellphone in the security lineup, and the contents of her abandoned suitcase?

No one pays attention to her when she enters the station. Why would they recognize her, although the cellphone picture looms large in her mind. A digital image that could be sent to any number of TV stations in an instant.

Anna passes by the potato chip racks, the snack cake and chocolate bar racks, and heads into the adjoining restaurant. She can't eat any more junk. It will make her vomit. The strong smell of cooked food sets her stomach gurgling. She feels light-headed from hunger and pauses to wait for a spell of dizziness to pass. She grips the back of a nearby chair to steady herself.

The waitress, in an apron-motif uniform, smiles at her and raises a menu from a stack.

"Just one?"

"Yes."

"This way." The waitress leads her to an unoccupied booth between two others.

Anna slides in and accepts the menu with a thank-you. "Can you bring me a cheeseburger right away?" she asks. "I'll look in here for more food."

"Sure." The waitress chuckles. "With fries?"

"Yes, please."

"No problem."

Anna opens the menu. The items listed are illustrated with colour photographs. The pictures make her even hungrier until her stomach rumbles and stings. She scans the tables that crowd the centre of the room. An elderly man and woman quietly nibbling. A young couple with a boy in a baseball cap. A woman feeds a baby in a high chair, carefully spooning food into its mouth. Neither one of them shows any interest in her. They are too focused on their blessed food.

She finds herself almost salivating. Across the way there are three plates on an unoccupied table. Plenty of leftovers there. Enough to scrape together a good-sized meal.

Her food doesn't arrive as quickly as she expected. She turns to watch the waitresses coming through the swinging kitchen doors with a plate in each hand. It is a large place with many people eating.

The noise of chatter and cutlery hitting dishes grows louder.

Anna finds herself becoming agitated. She wants to snatch a plate from the hand of one of the passing waitresses, devour the food before the plate can be wrestled away from her.

A glass of water is delivered, the ice cubes jingling. Anna glances at the glass, then watches the waitress with a "you can't be serious" look in her eyes.

"It won't be long now."

Anna says nothing in reply. She takes the glass and tips it back. The remarkably cold water soothes her burning throat and stomach, but it isn't filling. Ice cubes fall against her teeth. She sets down the glass and promptly looks around for any sign of her food.

After waiting a while longer, she feels her face flush with anger and decides she will leave and grab a submarine sandwich from the cooler and a snack cake on her way out. This is what she should have done in the first place. In and out. No time for lingering, but she wanted a hot meal. A cooked meal. Something comforting. She wanted a cheeseburger more than anything in the world, and some delicious, crispy french fries. If she doesn't get food soon, she will burst into tears. What is the matter with these people?

Ten more seconds. I'll give it ten more seconds. She checks over her shoulder to see the swinging doors held open by her waitress. Inside, past the waitress who speaks with a man wiping his hands on a towel, there is a small TV playing on an elevated shelf above the other workers.

Footage of an airport. A shy little curly-haired girl being interviewed.

The waitress has a plate with a cheeseburger and fries in her hand. The waitress nods toward Anna. It is Anna's plate. It must be.

The man tosses the towel over his shoulder, then snatches the plate from the waitress and turns back into the kitchen.

The waitress watches the man go before regarding Anna so that Anna wants to shout: That's my food! Bring my food here.

Instead she rises from the booth and hurries from the eating area, past the counter. She rushes for the exit without buying any potato chips or chocolate bars or snack cakes. Bolting out the door, she bumps into a woman who is entering, feeling that she has struck something hard and protruding. Anna falters, checks the woman while she steps off. The woman has her hands on her pregnant belly and is glaring at Anna.

"Sorry," she calls out, nearly in tears.

Finding her car, she climbs inside and starts the engine, hunger gnawing at her stomach. She just wants something to eat. Why can't she get something to eat?

There is a knocking at her window, which makes her flinch. She thinks it might be the pregnant woman stepping up to give Anna a piece of her mind.

But it is the face of the waitress staring in with a fretting expression. She holds up a white plastic bag. Inside there are two Styrofoam containers.

Despite the fact that Anna assumes it might be some sort of trap, hunger gets the best of her and she quickly rolls down her window.

"It's good and hot," says the waitress, fidgeting with her hair. "Take it, please."

"Okay," Anna agrees at once, checking behind the waitress toward the main door, then reaching for her purse.

"Don't worry about that." The waitress tosses a thumb in the direction of the restaurant. "Our cook, Jordan, said there was no charge." Her eyes nervously glance at the back seat as though searching for something hidden. "He took the plate from me so he could fill it with more food when he saw you, but you left."

"Thank you." Anna accepts the bag. It is warm in her palms. She glances at the waitress's name tag. "You're very kind, Katherine."

"Not really, just sometimes." Katherine smiles openly, showing teeth stained yellow from nicotine or coffee.

Anna laughs, smelling the food through the containers. Up this close she notices foundation makeup carefully applied around the waitress's left eye. Beneath the makeup, a hint of speckled purple.

"You keep fighting, okay?" says Katherine, giving a thumbs-up and a quick peek at Anna's belly. "Can I touch?"

"Touch?"

"Your belly."

"I ... I guess so." She hesitantly shifts the bag out of the way. Katherine reaches in and gently rubs Anna's belly. The gesture is familiar, soothing. "There, there," she whispers supportively.

Anna hears a cry and notices three seagulls ravaging a garbage can at the edge of the parking lot.

"You promise me you'll keep fighting." Tears spill from Katherine's eyes without warning. "I'm sorry." She wipes them away. "They tell me I shouldn't be like this."

Anna nods resolutely, joining the woman in tears. "I will. I definitely will."

"I gotta get back." Katherine turns her attention toward the gas station. Drawing a breath for courage, she smiles uncertainly at Anna. "I can't have any babies of my own." Her smile fades to sad acceptance, and tears gloss her eyes again. "There was an accident. Well ..." She looks away with mute resignation. "No accident, really."

"I'm sorry." Anna rubs beneath her eyes with the edge of a finger.

"I've got you crying now."

"It's okay. I need it." Anna laughs wetly and tightens her lips. "I'm crying all the time lately. It feels good."

"You ever have doubts?"

"About what?" Anna checks the bag, refocusing on the food. She wants to eat. She sniffs and keeps swallowing in anticipation.

"Having the baby?" Katherine's hand comes up to rest on the window frame.

"I did, but not anymore."

A burly man and a boy pass in front of Anna's windshield, climb in the car beside hers, and pull out toward the exit.

"If you do, you just let me know." Katherine pats Anna on the shoulder. "I'll take that baby for you, okay?"

"Sure."

Katherine shuts her eyes and smears the tears away. "Okay? Just remember. I'm here." She tosses her arm toward the gas station and utters a bewildered laugh. "Always here."

"Yes, okay."

Katherine squeezes Anna's shoulder. "Remember me, okay? And come show me that baby."

The Embryo: Day 53, Week 8

Although the eyes are well developed in Anna's embryo, they still rest on the sides of the head.

Hands begin to incline toward each other across the abdomen.

Feet, too, start leaning to touch each other; the toes are still webbed.

At this point ovaries become distinguishable.

Anna's embryo is three-quarters of an inch, the size of a buttercup flower.

Chapter Eighteen

Anna: April 9, Back to the Sea

As Anna turns off Shearstown Line, the temperature drops. The snow that has been melting in the trees along the road to Bareneed begins to freeze, coating the branches of the evergreens, birches, and maples in a silver glitter. Leaning eastward under the weight of ice, they echo one another in visual rhythm.

A mist floats from the land, illuminated by a low sun trapped behind grey clouds along the horizon.

It is a sight so magically passive to behold that it compels Anna to slow the car, pull over, and put the transmission in park.

Climbing out, she is relieved to feel her feet touch the ground after such a long drive. Her shoulders ache, and the muscles in her right leg are weak from constantly pressing the accelerator.

She finds it warm despite the ice in the trees. Her breath puffs and lingers in the close air that carries not a single sound.

She checks both directions. No sign of a car.

The entire landscape appears as one fragile, crystallized plain, as though each piece of it, each tree limb, each blade of grass, each rock, might be snapped off in bits in her hands.

She remains still, aware of the changing light in the open air, governed by the formation of darkening clouds and the pivot of the masked sun.

It seems like ages ago since early this morning when her lawyer came to see her with the rental car. What she has done in a single day makes her feel disjointed — the distances she has travelled and the situations she has found herself in. Enough drama to fill a small lifetime.

Anna's house can be found near the end of this shimmering road. She should stay in the house and wait, for she will be protected there. She envisions the lost children surrounding her, grasping her hands, guiding her away to the heart of their secret hiding place.

She takes a few steps into the middle of the deserted road. Nothing moves. Not a bird in the sky, not a creature on land. Everything coated in a greyish-blue film of ice.

What should she do with her car? The presence of an abandoned vehicle anywhere near her house will be cause for suspicion. Should she leave it here and walk the rest of the way on foot?

Too long a walk to consider.

She waits in expectation, the light waning. Ashen clouds darkening to black until the deeply shadowed landscape appears faintly lit by some indefinable source. Not the sun, for the sun is now gone, and not the moon, for the moon in nowhere present.

The irreversible linger between light and dark when animals see most clearly.

She climbs back in her car, switches on her headlights, and checks her rearview mirror before pulling out. As she drives deeper into the darkness, the trees emerge as one growth, looming denser, leaning nearer the sides of the pavement to the point of closure.

She will need to disappear.

Her mind speeds ahead, gliding beyond her house, beyond the abandoned church and graveyard at the very end of this road to the cliffs that tower above the ocean.

What will she leave of herself in the car when it tumbles over the edge?

She checks her hands. No rings. No watch on her wrist. She pats her pocket. Her cellphone.

With eyes on the road, she removes her cell, briefly checks the dead screen, and leans to open the glovebox. A quick peek. The box is empty, a small light glowing inside. She slides the phone into the hollow, shuts the door, and straightens in her seat.

This destruction of the rental will leave her lawyer with the cost of the insurance deductible, which Anna will gladly repay. Of course, there will be questions about who was actually driving the car. Not the lawyer. Then who *was* driving the car? They will know when they find the cell. Isn't her lawyer set to make a substantial amount of money from her association with Anna? The cost of the deductible would be insignificant.

All of this over an embryo, a thing of purported insignificance that might easily be disposed of, a non-entity causing such chaos. Isn't that what it is, what she has heard a man on TV call it: "a non-entity"? It isn't even a baby yet, not at all. Then why is she picturing it as a baby? The problem is with her imagination.

As her head fills up with the contrary positions expressed by people on her predicament, Anna loses track of her location and fades until she is jarred back to the physical world by the bang of her car striking something. Slamming on the brakes, she cringes with terror and disgust and jumps out from behind the wheel.

No sign of anything injured near the front wheels. She paces the length of her vehicle. Nothing at the rear. Immediately, she drops to her knees, frantic to know what might be under the chassis.

When she glimpses red hair against the pavement, Anna feels her arms lose their strength. She has to catch herself from falling face first onto the asphalt.

Sinking lower, she leans beneath the shadowed bottom of the car. It is difficult to see, as her body is blocking the light. She lies flat and strains to reach, her fingertips sweeping around, unable to locate their mark.

Anna wriggles her body in deeper until her fingers touch the hair. It is short and warm. In reflex her hand juts back.

Groaning and twisting her legs, she works her body in another ten inches. She stares into the depth while her eyes gradually adjust, bringing the space into definition.

A fox on its side, perfectly still.

It is complicated to manoeuvre, for she feels pinned in the confining space with the heat of the instruments above her, the metal so close to her face and arms, able to burn or tear her flesh.

She places her palm on the fox's body. It is seemingly unharmed, as though it might be sleeping or stunned. She takes hold of one leg, feels the fur shift over the thin bones, and pulls. The body follows after the leg as Anna squirms to get back out from under the constricting threat of the vehicle.

Dragging the fox onto the road, she rises onto her knees. It is almost completely dark, the sky black and low, the landscape an equal envoy of gloom. The car's headlights stretch ahead, offering the only source of light.

Anna lifts the fox in both arms, pulls the rear door handle open with her fingertips, and places the fox on the seat. Under the dome light she examines the body. Not a cut, not a drop of blood.

She touches its snout, her fingers lingering, wanting to raise its lip to check its teeth. The colour of its coat is bewitching. She runs her hand over it, noticing its eyes trembling behind shut lids.

Anna closes the door and climbs in behind the wheel. Continuing on, she glances in the rearview, expecting the fox to rise, while growing larger than life to fully inhabit the space between the seats.

Distracted, she approaches her house, finding her driveway clear. She pulls in, her eyes on the dark windows. Anna was certain she left two lights on, one upstairs in her studio and one downstairs in the hallway. The bulbs must have burned out.

A rustle from the back seat. Anna checks the fox to find it lying on its side.

She sits in the car with the headlights on, glancing around for signs of the lynx.

Again she surveys the upstairs window at the side of the house. If the car is to plummet over a cliff, then her paintings will go that route, as well. It seems a fitting end. Burial at sea. The sumptuous colours washed away, diluted and dispersed into the ocean.

She opens her door to the darkness and steps out. The air is still and immaculate. It holds that sacred clarity her mother once described to her, a night similar to the one when Anna was discovered abandoned on a doorstep.

Those paintings won't be left for others to claim.

Unlocking the front door, she steps inside and tries the light switch. Nothing. She crouches and searches in an alcove, finding the flashlight where she hid it.

She switches it on and aims the beam upstairs. The stairs are clear. She shuts the door behind her and begins her ascent.

In her studio she swipes the flashlight beam around the room, feeling like a burglar in a place unknown to her.

Anna lifts out her paintings of the multitude of fish with rosebud heads, carefully taking them down the stairs and out to the car, sliding them into the floor space in front of the fox. She smiles at the idea of the fish swimming free.

She goes back upstairs and collects other paintings, determined to clear her studio of every canvas.

On her final trip downstairs, while stepping out the front door, she hears a commotion off in the woods, the air alive with the shrieks of fighting cats. Anna rounds the corner of the house. The cries clarify and are coupled with the frenzied sounds of bodies thrashing through the undergrowth.

The clamour appears to be coming from behind the barn.

The panicky cry of a little girl.

Is the lynx attacking the child?

Dropping the final canvas, Anna hurries toward the barn but stumbles in hesitation. She returns to the car, throws open the trunk, unwraps the shotgun from its blanket, and lifts it out. With the flashlight in one hand and the shotgun in the crook of her other arm, she treads along the side of the barn, holding the flashlight, which jitters with her erratic step.

The savage shrieks have died down.

Anna listens for indications of distress from the little girl.

There is no path by the side of the barn. No boot prints, just a plane of untouched snow framed by light and shadow.

Her step slows as the snow grows deeper. Her feet sink in, the holes almost tripping her.

The scent of wild roses fills her nostrils, its rich aroma wafting through the air. Hidden within the scent is another earthier smell. Sewage.

A low, girlish whimper.

Anna is almost at the back corner of the barn. She aims the flashlight ahead and awkwardly holds the shotgun in the other hand. The beam skims over worn, narrow clapboards and a white length of corner board before extending beyond the structure to reveal a scene in bloom: a multitude of raspberry bushes cluttered with fruit, intermingled with wild roses, their pink delicate petals flatly opened.

In the midst of this organic vision, there is the rustling of low movement in the bushes and the sloppy sound of sucking.

Anna takes a step forward to see dots of red smeared in the snow. She aims the flashlight at the crackling movement that nears the edge of the undergrowth.

She expects something to lurch up at any moment. Agitated, she breaks open the shotgun and checks the single chamber. The flat brass circle of a shell.

Anna shuts the weapon and takes aim at what is hidden.

The flashlight beam shivers over the spot where the movement has stilled.

She waits, thinking to flee, yet if she does, whatever is lurking beneath those bushes will undoubtedly bound after her.

There is another rustling before a pale creature straightens from its curl, its misshapen bald head veined with green lines, its great eyes, set beneath a protruding forehead, glinting with light, its webbed fingers raised to its red-spattered mouth.

Bucking with fright, Anna drops the flashlight, both hands going for a sturdier grip on the shotgun. The light blares brilliant against the snow, then dies, yet her brief view of the creature lingers in her mind. Oblivious to Anna's presence, it raised its red fingers to shove raspberries into its mouth, staining its face. Toothless, it gummed the berries as though not knowing how to eat, the fruit falling out of its face to colour the snow.

The dark image of the creature slowly makes its way from the bushes. An indistinct shadow dragging itself forward, groaning in pain like something crippled.

Anna follows it with the shotgun. She clicks back the hammer, her finger tightening on the trigger. If she kills this thing, this injured beast in hiding that she fears might well be the source of her consternation, then all might be made normal again in her house in Bareneed.

She stiffens her grip on the trigger.

"Don't, Anna."

Jerking with a start, Anna spins around, aiming the shotgun at the bulky shadow ten feet away. "Who's that?"

The shadow holds its hands out at its sides.

Beyond the black silhouette, a car idles on the dark road, its headlights stretching ahead.

"Mr. King."

"Stay away."

"It's okay, Anna."

"It is not okay!" she screams, sweeping the shotgun back at the creature that nears her boot and latches on.

Anna shrieks and violently shakes her leg, aiming the weapon down. The creature clings tightly, wraps its arms and legs around her leg, and begins climbing.

Screeching in terror, Anna shoves at the soft flesh with the shotgun barrel, poking and prodding until it drops from her.

She raises the shotgun and aims at where it squirms on its back against the snow.

"Don't."

"Why?" she cries out. "It's in pain."

"No. It's just alive, Anna. That's all."

"It's sick."

"If you kill it, you will suffer the same lack of imagination that put it here."

Anna shakes her head, edging down the path alongside the barn while keeping the shotgun trained on Mr. King. "Why are you always here?"

"I came to check on you."

"Why?"

"Because I care."

"Care! About what? None of this is real. This place. I'm realizing —"

"Of course, it is," Mr. King assures her soothingly. "But only if you have the talent to see it."

Anna rushes off, her boots sinking deep into the snow, pitching her forward. One hand plunges into the snow, the biting cold crystals at her wrist, her fingertips meeting a warm, fleshy surface below. Revolted, she rolls onto her back, then over again, up on her knees, holding tight to the shotgun while struggling to her feet.

Stumbling, she makes her way to her car, throws the shotgun into the opened trunk, then checks to see the shadow making its way alongside the barn. Slamming shut the trunk, she hurries for the driver's door, slides behind the wheel, and switches on the headlights.

Mr. King is revealed, stunned by the lights. He raises an arm to shield his eyes.

No creature behind him. Where is the creature? She checks the rearview mirror.

Anna backs up in a quick arc, smashing into Mr. King's car and busting one of his headlights. She yanks the shift into drive, eyes on her rearview to see Mr. King step from her driveway and out into the road, his hands in the pockets of his long coat, one headlight glowing behind him, burning his shadow blacker.

Mr. King remains still, watching after her car.

Why is she afraid of him? Why is she running?

Anna brakes and comes to a quick stop. She studies the rearview, the red glow of her tail lights, Mr. King standing there without moving, a shadow against a black sky. A blot in the road.

Mr. King would be able to help her, conceal her.

Anna's heart jumps as the shadow springs into movement. How might Mr. King help her? He has a car. She could go with him, ditch the rental miles away, and have him drive her back to Bareneed. That way there would be no evidence.

The real estate agent's figure grows larger, further startling Anna. Increasing his gait, he removes his gloved hands from his pockets.

Anna holds her breath, eyes shifting from the rearview as she turns to look over her shoulder. In that brief moment the agent has advanced much nearer, no more than six feet from the back of the car.

She presses her foot on the accelerator, returns her attention to the windshield while glancing at the rearview. Mr. King's step slows as distance is gained between them. He turns to hurry back to his vehicle, then disappears as Anna navigates the curve in the road.

To Anna's left, black spruces slowly thin out and vanish, the road towering over a charcoal abyss skirted by a silver guardrail. The ocean far below. Dense forest occupies the land to her right, concealing a few abandoned houses. Soon the road will veer sharply right and connect with a dirt road that rises to run beside the old neglected church and graveyard.

Speeding ahead, Anna catches sight of movement in the trees. A mass of blackness lumbering into the road.

She slams on the brakes. The car slides, angling sideways before jerking into a spin.

Pulling her foot off the brake, Anna frantically tries

straightening the wheel, expecting to tumble into a ditch or the ocean, while her body is thrust one way, then the other, by the magnetic pull of rotation.

Slowly, mercifully, the vehicle comes to a stop and the view through the windshield steadies.

She discovers that the car is pointed back toward her house.

A pair of four-legged figures stands in the road, their antlers shaped like tangles of dead tree limbs. The moose face away from Anna, staring into the distance, where a car's headlights are fast approaching.

Anna must turn around in the middle of the road, a tight, anxious negotiation of back and forth in drive and reverse until the task is accomplished. She races away from the moose, follows the road to where it sharply arcs and rises inland. Ascending on a steeper grade, her tires spin on slush, slowing her progression in a spasm of lurches until she succeeds in making it up the hill.

The dirt road between the graveyard and church is clear, not much snow banked up. The car bumps over ruts, tires spinning.

Stuck.

Rubber squeals as she accelerates, but the vehicle goes nowhere. She reverses to get free, then bolts forward, clearing the shallow hole. Checking her window, she sees through the graveyard's wire fencing that a car is on its way up the hill.

How did Mr. King get by the moose?

With her headlight beams stretching before her, Anna speeds along the rutty, snow-patched land and is tossed around behind the wheel. Two hundred feet ahead the earth ends in a black void of fused sky and sea.

Anna has witnessed this sort of action in movies countless times, yet feels she won't be able to jump when the time comes, and if she does manage to leap from the moving vehicle, she might harm herself and the baby.

In anticipation her heartbeat pounds in her chest.

She should stop, drive the car near the edge, and simply push it over. She glances at the shimmying rearview mirror as her car tremors across the uneven ground.

The jitter of headlights in the far distance.

No time for stopping.

If they believe she has committed suicide, then they will leave her alone.

But what about the agent? Will he contact the authorities to try to save her from the wreckage as he has done before?

There is the sound of movement in the back seat.

Eyes on the rearview, Anna eases up on the gas pedal, the end of the road no more than a hundred feet away.

This is stupid. Insane. What might be accomplished? Divers will be out there in the night. Or would the agent contact the authorities at all? If Anna fears Mr. King, then isn't that fear based on him wishing to do her harm? But why? Why harm?

The cliff seventy feet away.

Anna checks the rearview. A blurry waver of lights reaching for her, closer now, illuminating orange hair rising above the canvases in the back seat.

The car pounds into a deep rut, jolting Anna around, her head banging against the roof. Disoriented by the blow, Anna slams on the brakes but hits the accelerator by mistake, the car gliding into a pool of slush with ice at its base.

The car commences spinning.

Scrambling for her door handle, Anna grips it and pulls. The door swings open, the smudge of ground speeding in a whirl beneath her.

A flash of the cliff just ahead. Then woods. Then another car. Orange hair. The sound of a hiss. An animal, or the tires punctured. The cliff again …

She tries jumping, her seat belt strapping her in. She struggles to undo it, but the buckle is stuck in the hole.

The spinning hurts her eyes, nauseating her. Straining to get her bearings, she stares through the windshield, waits for the car to swivel away from the cliff, then slams on the accelerator. The tires gain traction too late, and the car slides before roaring along the very edge of the cliff until it hits uneven ground where the wheels on the passenger side run out of earth.

Anna yanks at her seat belt buckle as the vehicle tips toward the jagged rock facing and begins leaning unstoppably.

The driver's door slams shut.

Screaming, Anna feels the breath being drawn out of her, yet has the presence of mind to roll down her window. She won't drown. When the car smacks the water, she will escape. Her only chance now.

The vehicle arcs into open air, plummeting sideways in a mesmeric pull of descent that locks the breath in Anna's lungs and pins her against the door.

The end, she thinks, bracing herself for impact. Please, save us, please …

The vehicle pounds the surface of the ocean.

Anna's body quakes in an exploding spasm of smear.

The water ebbs and rolls around the exterior of the car in thrusting fits before gravity drags the front end on a forward angle. The car dips, begins to sink faster, on a steeper incline, its rear end tipping toward the black sky.

Water gushes in through the window, filling the interior.

Drawn into the suck of the sea, Anna floats, unaware.

The Embryo: Day 53, Week 8

The left hand of Anna's embryo rises through fluid. Its mouth opens. Its fingers slip in.

Anna's embryo hiccups.

Chapter Nineteen

Anna: April 9, Birthdays

Splashing through a drenching rainstorm. Anna's mother on the doorstep, her voice calling out a name akin to Anna's. A flesh-toned embroidered party dress soiled with cherry icing. A shadowed man not her father. Scissors snipping through a cord. Strapped to a white table, a blind woman sinking in a bottomless gorge. A cat growing taller while trotting down the centre of an icy highway. The collision point of three cars twisted into a metal chair parked in a courtroom.

Anna is uncertain of the position of her head, the location of her feet and arms incalculable, her body a suspended mystery to her.

She wonders if her eyes are open; a fuzzy stream of pink, red-veined spots lingers before her as though light is being filtered through her shut eyelids.

She attempts to move, yet her body feels uniformly weighted and warm.

She tries opening her eyes, but they will not.

Moments later she suspects that her eyes are already open.

The sight before her clarifies, acquiring detail.

A gelatinous swarm of jellyfish drifting by, contracting and pulsing while softly pressing against her.

She begins to discern features within the transparent sacs,

each one in harmonious proportion.

Anna gains the presence of mind to sway her arms.

The motion causes her to rise.

She realizes she is holding her breath, yet experiences no urgency to burst above the surface where oxygen might replenish her lungs. Her shoulder strikes something rigid; her body languidly revolves to face rock, hardened and black with the fossilized imprints of spines and hand bones. She continues rising until she breaks the surface, the fresh sound of surge far off.

The inlet where she finds herself is sheltered from the wind by fingers of rock jutting out. In deeper, the rock has been hollowed by the relentless thrust of waves.

Trying to keep her head above the surface, she is drawn into the cavern by the warm current. The back of the grotto is trimmed by an arc of broken shore, the rough walls composed of gradations of primitive browns. Small figures stand there in wait, or crouch and lean to fish glowing orbs from the water.

Anna believes she is in shock, for she is not feeling the expected intensity. She has no sensation in her face, not an inkling of defining features, only a plane of exact numbness.

Sighting Anna, the children gather excitedly and bend to outstretch their hands.

A child's voice says, "That's a big one."

Others extend words of encouragement: "Come on," "You can do it," "That's it."

So many small hands. What might they accomplish? Yet they manage to take hold of her, and little by little, haul her from the water and onto the earth where she lies on her back.

Gazing up at the children, Anna recognizes two of them. The red-haired girl and the black-haired girl step forward to lean their faces over Anna, take her hands, and drag her to greater safety nearer the rock facing.

The children gather around, enclosing her, the heat from their bodies radiating into hers as they assemble closer, the sounds of their breathing merging as one dull, insistent throb that mounts to echo percussively throughout the cave.

Anna finds herself walking along a rocky shoreline with children leading her by both hands. It is an awkward path, made even more precarious by the darkness and how the children pull anxiously as though in a hurry to show her one of their prized possessions.

She stumbles and tries to keep up. The beach rocks beneath her feet continue to shift, implying the movement of something not only above but beneath the surface.

"She killed it," says one child to the others, who ignore the comment.

Then one small voice pipes up, "It wasn't her fault."

"Killed what?" Anna asks.

"Don't listen to it," the red-haired girl far ahead calls out. "And, besides, she pulled me out and made me alive again."

The night air is warm despite the season. The breeze has completely dried Anna's clothes and hair. She checks her bare feet but can scarcely make them out. In front of her, three children lead the way, balls of lovely pink gleams cupped in each of their palms.

Some of the children vie for positions next to her, while others trail cautiously behind. Their hands, too, are filled with orbs. Incandescent cores slowly bobbing within.

"Your turn is up," one girl informs the girl gripping Anna's left hand.

"No, it's not."

"Here," says the little boy holding Anna's right hand, "you can have this one." He releases his grip, allowing a younger boy to accept it. The boy stares up at Anna with big eyes and sucks on his bottom lip as though spellbound.

"Where are we going?" Anna asks, spurred by the fear that a

search party must be on its way to rescue her. She casts her eyes over the dark sea.

Far across the bay there are pinpoints of light on a finger of land blacker than the water.

How long before they know she isn't in the sunken vehicle? How long before the authorities give up searching for her body and pronounce her dead? Or begin looking on land, scouring the entire area?

"To our hiding place," says the younger boy, nodding.

"Up there," says a girl, pointing to the incline of a cliff that towers above the water.

Anna sees a darker patch against the clay surface. Again she turns her attention to the ocean to search for boats, but the inky expanse remains entirely blank.

The children begin climbing the cliff.

At first it is an almost effortless ascent, since the grade isn't too steep, but soon Anna feels the strain in the muscles and tendons in her calves and thighs. A quarter of the way up she must lean forward to touch the ground, grasp at the rocks and clumps of grass with her hands in order to advance cautiously against the escalating drag of gravity that wants her down, broken on the rocks.

The smaller children rush ahead of her, scampering toward the dark patch, which gains depth and definition as the orbs of light enter there.

It is a relief to reach the lip of the cave and stand on level ground.

The children hurry ahead to the shadowed crevices off to the sides where they carefully lay the luminous balls on the ground. Two children gather around each globe and stare down as though in solemn concentration.

"What are they doing?" Anna asks the blind black-haired girl.

"Giving over their lives," the black-haired girl explains, her sightless eyes staring into the space beside Anna's head. "How else are the new ones to grow? We know what we have to give over. We get smaller and they get bigger." She pauses to listen, focusing on the spiral of breathing to ensure that she is synchronized with the others. "It's because the ones who made them didn't understand that."

"Understand what?" Anna asks.

"The part of themselves they needed to give over. The part that would make them new again. They wanted to keep that because they thought it would mean more life for their own selves."

Anna gazes at the nurslings of light growing stronger in the recesses of the cave.

"But it never means more life, Anna. It just means more want."

Anna stands at the lip of the cave, gazing out, feeling elevated, yet in the midst of black sky and water that swell as one stark chasm. She turns to watch the children in the dimness, their bodies barely visible in the faint glows that spot the hollow.

One by one the children lie down and curl up.

"You should sleep," one of them says.

Anna can't determine the source of the voice, sunk as the bodies are now in the shadowed earth.

"You can't grow unless you sleep, Anna."

Anna isn't the slightest bit tired. She feels mellow yet alert, belonging yet apart, held by the quiet drama of fleeting moments.

The rhythm of the throb slows as slumber takes hold. The cadence is lulling until a low, inharmonious beat makes itself evident.

A small head pokes up from a burrow to listen. "You hear that?" asks the child.

Other heads rise from their earth beds and still themselves as though to authenticate the sound. As the diminutive beat continues, the heads all turn to stare at Anna.

The littlest girl struggles to her feet and limps over, both hands held out before she arrives. She places her palms on Anna's belly, her mouth hanging opening.

"Ooow," croons the girl.

The other children rise and advance in numbers. A small indistinct crowd rustling forward, drawn by the novelty of the echo.

"Let me," says a boy. He puts one hand on Anna's belly and grins up at her. "You're lucky. You have it in there." He turns to call back at the others. "She has it in there. She's protecting it. I told you."

The other children wait their turns, oowing and ahhing with delight as they press their hands to Anna's belly and shudder with excitement as they catch the signature pulse.

Anna is brought awake by the sense of a presence, of her breath running up against another body and returning to her, made warmer.

She opens her eyes to see a child's face, a set of small blue eyes staring directly into hers.

While Anna isn't familiar with the blond-haired child, she senses a tingle of recognition in the girl's diminutive features. The child is lying on her side, her face almost touching Anna's. Despite the child's proximity, Anna isn't startled. In fact, she is made even more serene and reaches out to stroke the girl's hair.

"They almost took you, Anna."

Anna studies the child's plump lips, wanting them to shape more words. "Who?"

"Before you were born. Your mommy. She went to visit a man."

"How do you know?"

"I can see out your eyes, out her eyes."

Anna shuts her eyes, her hand resting in the girl's silken hair.

"Even when you're sleeping, I can follow your dreams."

"What man did she visit?"

"A man like the one you see now. The man who wants to take from you. The one you've returned to without knowing." The girl's hand delves into the front pocket of her pleated jumper, rummages around, and raises a transparent sack of fluid to Anna's eyes. "But your mommy couldn't do it, Anna."

Anna watches the orb in the girl's hand, yellow tinged with red growing luminous. She checks over her shoulder to see the moon hovering in the middle of the cave, its light both crimson and golden.

"You would have been one of us," explains the girl, secreting the ball away. "You would have been an it."

Anna nestles her palm against the girl's cheek.

The child takes time inspecting Anna's face, her close observation conveying spirit. "You're going to name your baby, aren't you?"

"I hope so."

The little girl smiles bashfully. "Lucky."

Anna delights in the girl's expression and feels proud of her for just being herself.

"If I ask you something, will you say yes?"

"I'll try to," Anna pledges.

"I don't know how hard it is to do."

"What is it?"

"Will you give me a name?"

A tiny shake of Anna's head. "You don't have one?"

"No."

"Why?"

The little girl shrugs. "No one ever gave me one. They didn't have time, I guess." She scratches her nose. "Will you, please?"

"Yes." Anna bursts out with a moist laugh. "Of course, I will, sweetie." She rubs the length of the child's cool arm.

The girl rises from her side, sitting up with her legs crossed. She licks her lips in anticipation while watching Anna right herself.

Anna studies the girl's blond hair, her cool blue eyes and cherub lips, her pearly skin with a silky bloom in her cheeks, the sculpted curve of her jawline, the slim, graceful slope of her neck, the slightness of her chest, her skinny legs and feet with long toes. She raises her eyes to inspect the girl's outward appearance, how it exposes her inward character, the name coming into her mind: "Emma."

"Emma?' the girl repeats in surprise. "Really?" She sits straighter, allowing the name to pass fully through her. Nodding in confirmation, she grins at Anna. Then she turns to the others and calls out, "I am Emma. Hello? Did you hear? I have a name. I'm Emma. Pleased to meet you, everyone."

The children stir from sleep. One by one they groggily rise to mutter, "What?"

"Hello, you and you, my name is Emma." She springs to her feet. "Would you like my autograph?"

"How do you know that?" demands one little boy straight from sleep. "How? Tell me."

"Anna told me."

"But she's not your mommy."

Emma stares down at Anna in wonder while the other children continue to climb from their sunken sleeping places. At a distance they have smooth, anonymous faces, yet as they crawl to gather and settle as near as possible around Anna, they gain definition.

The Embryo: Day 53, Week 8

The primary teeth in Anna's embryo are fully grown. They sit in rows beneath the surface, waiting to push through each arc of gums.

Watching the children, Anna recalls her own youth, the disarming simplicity of childhood, of living through each idealized scene, bathed in the strongly contrasting effects of light that capture a tender image without over-romanticizing.

"Will you be my mommy?" asks Emma.

Anna caresses the girl's cheek. "If you like."

"I'd like that very much," Emma answers with a gleeful smile.

"My mommy, too?" pipes up a voice to the side of her.

Anna laughs and looks at the boy. "Yes, of course."

"Name me," says the boy, poking her.

"Me, too?" calls out another girl, crawling across the earth and squeezing in between the other children until she is directly beside Anna. "You be my mommy now."

"Yes, okay."

"What's my name?" asks a girl with a cleft lip, barely old enough to form the words distinctly.

"What name do you like?" asks Anna.

"I don't know any names at all. How many do you know?"

"A lot."

"Wow!" The little girl gives a half-suppressed laugh, which continues to escape her, growing louder until she is snorting.

Anna considers the girl's face, taking into account her gestures and the subtle motions of her body. "You're a Katherine to me."

Katherine giggles and covers her mouth. Then she lowers her hands and asks quickly, "When's my birthday now because I want to have cake?"

"How about December 8?"

"Okay. December 8. That's my birthday, everyone."

The little boy persists. "And who am I? Tell me."

Anna checks him over. "How about ... Jordan?"

The little boy throws up his arms. "Jordan is great. Everybody loves Jordan now."

To each request for a name, Anna answers until the children appear satisfied and sit still as though placated by a stupefying daydream.

All is tranquil and seemingly mollified until the silence is pierced by the cry of a lone baby, the unnerving pitch turning heads to check the shadows where nothing is evident. No blot of light.

No movement.

"Are you all right?" asks a voice.

Another baby joins the first, and then another, their rattling cries fuelled by body-quaking shivers.

"Who gave you the right?" demands the voice.

From the back of the cave more babies begin to wail, the collective pitch growing in force and volume until crescendoing in a warped measure that gradually recedes, only to rise again in a screaming see-saw.

A tiny hand reaches up to rest over Anna's mouth. "Shhhh," the children say. More tiny hands slip in to cover her nose, ears, eyes … "Shhhhh."

Chapter Twenty

The Patient: April 9, Rescue

The wailing in the patient's ears draws her attention to the hollow space around her. It seems that she has fallen backward, for she is lying on her back. The hand on her mouth forms a transparent cup into which she breathes. A mask, she thinks, giving her the sense that she might be disguised.

The wailing rises in pitch, then falls, rises and falls, in a confounding rhythm.

There is a man in a long overcoat crouched near her feet, watching her face with interest. "You're going to be all right."

A confined space in which she glides along at its centre.

"Her name is Anna," he says to a man in white beside him.

The man in white nods and busies himself with preparations.

"Anna?" says the man in the overcoat, patting the blanket that covers her legs. An older man, familiar in his tranquility.

The patient shuts her eyes. Opening them, she looks to the right of the man's head. Two windows through which fluttering blackness sweeps by, interrupted by a pulse of red.

A whiteness shifts beside her. She turns her eyes to see the other man, checking a line of plastic that leads to her arm.

"I had to call them," says the man in the overcoat. The patient knows who he is now. The one who sold her the house. "I'm sorry."

She wonders why he is saying this. Who? She wants to ask, Call who, but she is exhausted, and she closes her eyes.

Is he talking about the children? Where are the children she has just named? Have they been rescued?

"*FrWhht?*" she manages to say in response to a question that might have been posed hours ago. The sounds of her words like leaking mist behind the mask.

The real estate agent appears to have understood. "For having them rescue you."

Although her thoughts waver ambiguously, the patient believes she is being sped toward something entirely the opposite of rescue.

"It's okay," says the agent, making a simple mark on her forehead. "I'm here with you."

The Patient: April 11, Incarceration

The patient's body is a mass of uncomplicated weight against the bed. The moment glistens as an extraordinary thing that bars her thoughts from passing beyond. Although what rests before eyes is fascinating, it is finite. Colours and textures add up to nothing that the patient realizes.

A grey-haired man in a long white coat sits on the edge of her bed. He touches her hand. "Hello," he says. "How's our famous patient doing?"

She sputters in reply, her lips a clot, her mouth a bloated pit filled with nothing.

"Everything's fine, just so you know."

"*Whftt?*"

"With the baby."

This news sets off waves of pleasure, radiating down the patient's spine.

Everything is, she thinks.

Fine.

Where? Her eyes flit around the white room.

The baby?

White curtains masking a large window. A white lily framed on a white wall. The flower's unnerving passivity blurs in her mind.

The doctor watches the patient's face, then inclines his head away as his smile slips into a frown. He stares at the ground, his hands joined and dangling between his legs.

The patient tries focusing on the painting, gradually making out the subtle tonal transitions of what might be Georgia O'Keeffe's work. Her fondness for painting natural forms at close range.

Beneath the lily, a silver wheelchair parked in the corner. How am I? she wants to think or ask.

How.

The doctor regards her face, again, his expression more realistic.

"*HowmI?*" she asks, the words a slurry mess.

The doctor swallows and nods. Again he touches her hand.

She thinks that he squeezes it, dull pressure, barely perceptible.

"You've suffered a number of injuries," he explains.

"*Whhr?*" As much as she tries, she cannot shape words.

The doctor's eyes shift to the top of her head. "Multiple injuries," he says quietly to himself, it seems. "Fortunately, you're able to breathe on your own. That's a good sign." His attention bluntly returns to her face. He sighs deeply and stands. "I'll drop in to see you later, okay?"

The patient urges her throat muscles for a sound that signifies agreement, but nothing happens.

The doctor smiles in consolation, turns, and passes through the door as a woman in white enters in his place. She lays a few items on the side table.

"How are you doing?" the nurse asks, filling a needle from a tiny bottle.

Is that bad for the baby? the patient asks herself. But the question is displaced by a curious interest in the consistency of the woman's eyelashes.

The nurse raises the blanket. She wipes the patient's thigh before poking the sharp tip into her flesh. It digs in without resistance.

"This might make you a bit sleepy," the nurse warns, putting the needle aside. "Do you want the TV on? It might help you sleep."

The patient follows the trail of the woman's stare, unable to nod her approval until the woman steps around to the other side of the bed where she pulls a small television on a metal arm in front of the patient's face.

The nurse switches on the screen, uncoils the earpiece, plugs the jack into the slender hole, and firmly fits the listening device into the patient's ear. The sensation is like something small and alive burrowing into a space in the side of her head.

"Okay, Anna?"

Anna.

Anna watches the images come to life. So much complexity crammed together in a limited space. So much tonal drama, poetic delicacy, and conflict of colour. A meticulous rendering of reality.

She is growing sleepy. She hears these words in her ear. "I don't think any of us has ever witnessed such a spectacle before, Peter, where left- and right-wing protesters join forces to show their solidarity. Both sides condemning the court's decision for entirely different reasons."

Even though Anna can hear the words, she can't see who is speaking. The impressionistic shimmers on the screen are of a massive crowd gathered with flames lit in darkness; tiny dots glowing and flickering in a dreamy, nostalgic way.

"Still no word from the minister of justice, and it's only ten hours and fourteen minutes before Anna Wells, the Newfoundland artist who has gained the love of the nation, will be subjected to what most people in this country consider to be an unconscionable and highly degrading act."

"Who can ever understand the way our legal system works?" muses another voice.

"And, of course, we're now faced with an even more pressing question introduced since Anna's terrible accident. Will she even be capable of looking after the baby? Many people are asking: will she be better off?"

"I've heard that she's named the baby."

"Really, Wendy? Any idea of the name?"

"Hopefully soon. We're in contact with hospital personnel on a moment-by-moment basis to ensure that our viewers receive up-to-the-minute information."

"Millions of people are anxious to know if it's a boy or a girl. It's a very exciting situation."

"Look at that crowd, Peter. Can you believe the outpouring of support?"

"It certainly is a poignant sight."

"People have travelled from right across Canada, from every province, to show their solidarity."

"And from outside the country, as well. Over the past few days we've chatted with visitors from the United States, England, Germany, Sweden, and even Japan!"

All of these words spoken while the patient sleeps.

The Patient: April 11–12, Vigil

The patient's eyes open, her deep, mucousy breath in her nostrils, the sound thicker, more laboured than seems fitting.

Hands are on either side of her head, turning her face to look up. A man is above her. He is wearing a black shirt with a white collar. He picks up a book with a black cover from where it was lying on her chest.

The man's face is sorrowful, lined. The way he watches the patient with his old, soft eyes makes her believe he might care for anyone. She knows this man, but who is he?

"How are you feeling?" he asks. "I hear it's your birthday. Is that right?"

When the patient tries to move, she is aware of her limbs. Dead like an animal struck down. She strains to shift beyond the situation, yet feels groggy, indistinct, and frail. She shuts her eyes to ward off ill sensations.

Nestled within herself. That is how she feels. Safely nestled away inside herself where nothing can make its way to her through her skin.

The man in the black shirt is speaking to her, but his words settle somewhere outside. He might be talking beyond the walls of a house, although near to her. Her ears are almost working, swelling toward the capacity for sound.

"... day to celebrate one life centred in another," says the man, setting off a complicated pattern of expanding circles and spherical dots in the patient's head.

While trying to follow the patterns, Anna falls away, deeper into forgetfulness until the patterns reform and place themselves as objects in a room.

She realizes that her eyes are open again.

The man is standing at the large window with his back to her.

"There are thousands of candles out there in the dark. They go on for miles." He turns halfway to regard the patient. He is wearing black pants and a black shirt with a white collar. He smiles for the idealistic, romantic sake of something and faces the window again. "Thousands of people are here for you, Anna. All that pulsing light. They've each lit a flame."

The patient barely understands what the man is describing.

"There are young people and families. Mothers and fathers and children." The man's stirring words meant to portend drama.

What might this be about? There is something stuck in her ear. While she watches the blank screen near her face, she thinks she might be hearing murmurs through the earpiece. Whispers like the sound of blood rippling through veins. She is frightened now. She wants someone to comfort her, to assure her that she will not die.

The man steps from the window to approach the patient's bed. He watches her with imperishable longing.

She notices the white band at his throat, her eyes stuck there.

"I'm a retired minister," the man explains. "I should have mentioned that, I suppose, but these things rarely come up."

She makes a sound and tries shifting in the bed but can't budge an inch.

"Patricia was here earlier while you were sleeping. She said she's expecting a call from the justice minister."

The patient shuts her eyes.

"There's always hope, Anna."

I want to get up, she thinks, and soon wakes to the clarity of a room. She is alone.

The size of her in the bed, and the bed in the centre of the barren room.

Noise beyond the curtained windows. A disruption that assembles itself into a harmony of resonant chanting.

A plump middle-aged woman in white drifts in beside the patient. "A ton of people out there." She glances at the window, smiles kindly and slips a glass stem into the patient's mouth. "They're all trying to get in."

Please look after me, she says in her mind. Please.

The kind woman removes the glass stem, checks it, puts it aside, then fills a needle. "Did you have your dinner?" Her eyes search the tray. "I heard you had a special dessert for your birthday. Cherry cobbler, right?"

Protect me, the patient groans to herself.

"Are you feeling all right?" The woman pricks the patient with the needle.

Feeling? she wants to ask. Who?

The kind woman smiles again and touches the patient's arm. "It's okay, sweetie. We'll look after you. You're taken care of here. There won't be any pain."

Chanting builds to reverberate against the outer walls, rattling the windowpanes.

Moment by moment, as the medication enters her bloodstream, she struggles to hold on to what might be in her heart.

Do you love me? she wants to know. Really love me?

She thinks she might have spoken as her head lolls to the side.

"What was that, dear?" The kind woman smiles with surprise and glances over her shoulder. "I think she said *love*."

The Embryo: Day 56, Week 8

The head of Anna's embryo is erect and rounded. Its eyes are half open, each retina entirely blue.

The curves and lobes of her ears are completely developed.

The arms are well formed and bend at the elbows. Fingers continue to grow longer. Occasionally, the legs kick out to exercise their muscles. Webbing on the toes dissolves as the cells responsible expire at the appointed time.

The upper lip is perfectly formed.

All digits are separate and distinct. Ten tiny fingers and ten tiny toes.

Anna's embryo is one inch long, the size of a cockroach.

~ Part V ~
The Exhibit

Chapter Twenty-One

Painter with Models

A man enters the room dressed in a freshly laundered white hospital gown from his neck to his knees. A white cloth cap is fitted on his head, and a white mask covers his nose, mouth, and chin. His hands are scrubbed clean inside sterile surgical gloves. The scene is brilliant with light.

The painter is barely able to speak through the lag of narcotics, yet she believes a sound, a word, has escaped her at the sight of the man. The word echoes off to faintly shape the impression of two letters: *N* and *O*.

The man resembles a man she once might have loved, although she can't be certain, considering the way he is disguised. She believes she is here to watch him at work, that he has asked this of her, to bear witness to his ingenuity.

The man takes up position between the painter's open legs where her feet are raised in metal hoops. Two masked women with whiteness leaching from them stand on either side of the man.

There is the sensation of air touching her from the movements of the man checking his instruments. The feeling is refreshing.

The painter shuts her eyes. She is seeing and not seeing at once. She believes she should rise, and she does, freely, easily drifting upward, yet when she comes back to herself, she finds she is in the exact same position, as though fastened to the bed.

"Pull your legs back," a woman's voice says, and a hollow cylinder is raised.

Her muscles are a trick to her, seeming entirely unrelated to her thoughts.

What the painter sees in her mind when her eyelids are shut are the four chambers of her heart shrinking until they form nothing more than a primitive tube.

She tries to lift her head, but it hasn't moved. Her eyes stare toward her belly at the length of the white hospital gown that ends at the space between her legs where the man is engaged in preparation work with one of the masked women.

Trying to open her mouth, the painter believes that the gap between her lips is increasing, but the words she thinks to say lose their urgency. She attempts to lick her lips, while taste buds form on the surface of her embryo's tongue.

"Breathe in and out. Come on, breathe."

What is this? she asks herself.

Something enters her, the chilling rigidity finding no resistance.

"Suction."

There is a whirl of sound as a machine is switched on.

The sedative takes fuller effect so that the room billows and vanishes.

The feeling she experiences is one of fierce pleasure.

She whispers to herself, drifting back to a morning in summer. Feet in sneakers. Hopscotch on the dry asphalt. A shrill peal of laughter.

Early years of stylization and imagery preceding realism.

"We're almost there."

There is a prying sensation that she barely notices. Something done against a body without exact feeling.

She moans, swamped by another wave of euphoria.

Hands in the soft green grass.

She shuts her eyes, or they are open, watching what?

"She's doing a really good job."

A radiance, aglow like the sun, giving off splashes of vivid colours.

"Expect to feel some burning."

And her lips part, her tongue scarcely able to move, stirring thickly, trembling, then jerking as though in mute spasm.

"The worst is over. It's coming. It's time for it to come out."

A journey, a hollow in a rock, a game of burial.

Memories broken into bits.

Two masked women studying a clear container on a white metal table.

A vase, the painter thinks, filling up with roses, roses, roses.

Acknowledgements

The sections detailing the development of Anna's embryo are lifted from embryology texts and rewritten in informal terms for the sake of headache-free comprehension. Extensive research was carried out to ensure scientific veracity. My thanks to Dr. Gary Paterno, who teaches embryology to medical students at Memorial University, for reviewing the text and for educating me.

My appreciation is extended to my lawyer, Bob Buckingham, who agreed to read the manuscript and advise me on the particulars of court proceedings. Unfortunately, as the court proceedings occasionally drift into farce, proper etiquette could not always be respected. My apologies to Mr. Buckingham for staging some of the courtroom scenes and having to ignore portions of his stellar advice.

My special thanks to the various women from across Canada who agreed to read early drafts of the manuscript and add a word or sentence here and there to the text, thus leaving traces of themselves throughout the book.

About the Author

Photograph: Emma Harvey

KENNETH J. HARVEY is an internationally bestselling writer whose books have been published in more than a dozen countries. He is the author of *Blackstrap Hawco*, *Inside*, and *The Town That Forgot How to Breathe*; has won the Rogers Writers' Trust Fiction Prize, the Thomas Raddall Atlantic Fiction Award, the Winterset Award, and Italy's Libro Del Mare; has been nominated for the Books in Canada First Novel Award and the International IMPAC Dublin Literary Award; and has twice been nominated for both the Giller Prize and the Commonwealth Writers' Prize. Harvey sits on the board of directors of the Ottawa International Writers Festival. His website is *www.kennethjharvey.com*. He lives in an outport in Newfoundland.

MORE GREAT FICTION FROM DUNDURN

Providence Island
by Gregor Robinson
978-1-55488-771-2
$21.99

Returning to Ontario's northern lake region to
bury his father, Ray Carrier is taken back to the
woods and swamps that haunted his teenage dreams. He'd been enchanted by the grace and privilege of the Miller family, especially Quentin
Miller, a beautiful girl a bit older than himself. But something happened
near the abandoned railway tracks that must be settled before Ray can
finally achieve peace.

Six Metres of Pavement
by Farzana Doctor
978-1-55488-767-5
$22.99

Ismail Boxwala made the worst mistake of his
life one summer morning twenty years ago: he
forgot his baby daughter in the back seat of his
car. After her tragic death, he struggles to continue living through a
divorce, years of heavy drinking, and sex with strangers. But his story
begins to change after he reluctantly befriends two women, each of
whom make complicated demands on him.

Waiting for Ricky Tantrum
by Jules Lewis
978-1-55488-740-8
$17.99

Jim Myers is a painfully shy kid living in Toronto's Bloorcourt Village. On the first day of junior

high, Jim crosses paths with Charlie Crouse, a brash, mouthy boy full of wild stories about his past and present. Charlie takes Jim under his wing, and as their friendship grows, the realities of looming adulthood seep into their lives with surprising consequences.

Something Remains
by Hassan Ghedi Santur
978-1-55488-465-0
$21.99

Andrew Christiansen, a war photographer turned cab driver, is having a bad year. His mother has just died; his father, on the verge of a nervous break- down, gets arrested; and he's married to a woman he doesn't love. Keeping Andrew sane is his beloved camera, through which he captures the many Torontonians who ride in his taxi. Paral- leling Andrew's plights are the agonies and anxieties of his best friend, Zakhariye, a Somali-born magazine editor wrestling with tragedy and trauma. *Something Remains* probes the various ways humans grieve when the lives they build for themselves fall apart but the joy they discover remains.